BOUND BY PASSION

Taking a deep breath to gather her courage, Johanna waded into the icy, refreshing water of the brook.

"Good afternoon, little wood sprite!" an unfamiliar male voice said.

Startled, she spun around quickly, and just as quickly slipped on the slick stones under her feet. Landing in a most undignified manner, she sat in the water with her clothing clinging to her body and wisps of blond hair plastered to her face. Determined to ignore the stranger, who was watching with amused interest, she tried to rise to her feet only to fall again.

Chuckling, the man extended his hand to her. Time seemed to stop as she looked directly at the handsome stranger and found herself warmed by an inexplicable fire radiating from his touch.

Suddenly the man, a dazed expression on his face, lost his footing. He slid unceremoniously down the bank, pulling Johanna with him.

Her face flushed and alive with humor, she laughed. "You really shouldn't wear such fine clothing for swimming," she giggled.

"And you, my lady, are in no position to tease," he said, his blue eyes glimmering with desire . . .

SATIN CHAINS

MEGAN BLYTHE

ZEBRA BOOKS
KENSINGTON PUBLISHING CORP.

ZEBRA BOOKS

are published by

Kensington Publishing Corp.
475 Park Avenue South
New York, NY 10016

First printing: May, 1988

Printed in the United States of America

Part One — Johanna

Chapter One

April 1566—
Brabant Province, the Netherlands

Doing her best to ignore the shiver that rippled up her spine, Johanna tentatively dipped the toes of one small foot into the brook. "A little cold water won't hurt anybody on a day like this," she assured herself. Taking a deep breath to gather her courage, she plunged both feet into the icy water up to her ankles.

"Good afternoon, little wood sprite!" a strange male voice said.

Startled, Johanna spun around quickly to see who was interrupting her outing; and just as quickly, she felt herself slipping on the slick bottom of the stream. Her scream a high-pitched squeal, she grasped at the air for support in a futile effort to stop her clumsy fall.

Sitting in the icy water with her clothing clinging to her body and wisps of silvery blond hair plastered to her face, she glared at the amused stranger. "Who are you? What are you doing here?" she cried, attempting

7

to crawl to her feet. However, as fate would have it, she was weighted down by her soaked skirts and found herself forced back into the water a second time.

The man could no longer control himself and laughed robustly as he extended a hand to her. "Allow me, mademoiselle."

Angry green eyes shot sparks of fire as they looked into the man's blue gaze, and he felt himself lost in the girl's beauty, causing him to wonder at his luck at finding her in the very spot he had chosen for a rest after riding all morning. He was no longer laughing. In fact, he felt magically transformed by the lovely face, and he had no desire to fight the spell she had cast over him.

"I don't need any help, thank you!" Johanna said, spurning his offer. "Just get away from me! This whole thing is your fault. My mother will be furious!"

"I beg your pardon, little girl," the man chuckled, his self-control returning in light of her childish accusation. "I was only being friendly. 'Twas not I who caused you to fall, but your own clumsiness—and, I might add, your bad temper! You ought to be spanked for your poor manners," he suggested, enjoying the freezing girl's discomfort immensely—not to mention the way the cold water made her prominent nipples seem as if they would burst through the straining muslin of her wet dress in order to be free.

"How dare you speak to me like that? Do you know who I am?" she yelled, her shaking voice shrewish even to her own ears.

"Obviously, you're not the grand lady of the manor," he surmised with a sardonic smile, at last managing to avert his gaze from her bodice.

8

"I'll have you know I'm the daughter of the lord of all this land on which *you* are trespassing," Johanna replied indignantly. "My father is the count of Ledenburg, and he will be very angry with you for being here without an invitation."

"So Count Ledenburg is your father, is he?" the man said with a disbelieving arch of his eyebrows.

Determined to ignore the man and save her last fragment of dignity, Johanna tried to rise to her feet again—and fell again. But still she refused to ask for help. Instead she demanded, "Well, why are you standing there? Get me out of here before I die of exposure!"

Admiring the peasant girl's audacity, the man laughed lustily and extended his hand to her.

For a moment, time seemed to stop. Suddenly, she was no longer aware of the cold water rushing all around her; she was oblivious to the wet clothing clinging revealingly to her body; and the hair that hung past her waist into the swirling water was totally forgotten.

For the first time, she looked directly at the stranger and found herself warmed by an inexplicable fire radiating from his touch. He was taller than average, with broad shoulders tapering to slim hips and long, muscular legs. His strongly curved jawline and slightly crooked mouth gave his near perfect features an aura of masculinity and virility that even the most innocent girl could not fail to see. She couldn't help being fascinated by the unusual color of his hair, which was a mixture of reds and golds that seemed to change color as he moved in the sunlight.

Johanna noticed that the elegant young man wore a

neatly trimmed beard and mustache, and that he dressed in the style of the Spanish authorities, though she could tell by his speech that he was not Spanish. He wore a doublet with sleeves of light striped silk, matching short breeches, and a sleeveless black velvet cassock embroidered in gold. The neat, narrow ruff at his neck matched the lace at his wrists. Obviously, he was a man of means, and Johanna cringed at the thought of what she must look like to him.

Suddenly, the man, who had been just as paralyzed by their physical contact as Johanna had, lost his footing. A stunned expression on his face, he slid unceremoniously down the bank, pulling Johanna back into the water with him.

Her face flushed and alive with humor, it was now her turn to laugh, and she did. "You really shouldn't wear such fine clothing for swimming," she giggled, the iridescent light in her eyes mischievous.

"And you, my *lady,* are in no position to tease," he said, the levity in his tone not disguising the intense desire glimmering in his blue eyes. Without warning, his sinewy arms went around Johanna's small waist, and he gently kissed her open, surprised mouth.

Aware of the warm, firm feel of his chest where her hands were trapped by the embrace, Johanna was lost to all reason as he kissed her again and again, each kiss sending glorious new sensations cascading through her trembling body.

Taking his mouth from hers with obvious reluctance, he gazed hungrily into questioning pools of green. But instead of seeing acquiescence, as her kiss had led him to expect, he saw only astonishment and fear.

Frightened beyond understanding by the reality of

10

the handsome stranger and her own awakening passion, Johanna pushed at him with all her strength. "What are you doing?" she gasped breathlessly, not daring to admit how affected she was by the stranger's kisses. "I don't even know who you are! Let me go!"

She broke away from him and scrambled up the slippery bank to her dry shoes with the agility that had been denied her only moments before. Stumbling as she snatched up her shoes, she righted herself and ran away from the stream as fast as her cumbersome clothing would permit.

"Another time, little wood sprite, another time," the man called after the fleeing figure. Then he assured himself, "Most definitely another time."

Dragging himself from the water, the man knew it was time to turn his thoughts to more serious matters: the business which had brought him to Ledenburg.

However, no matter how he tried, he was unable to stop thinking of the girl's slender body next to his; and the memory was so warming that he forgot the chill running rampantly through his athletic body, caused by the wet clothing hanging heavily from his wide shoulders.

He shook his head in disgust. He didn't have any business allowing a woman to interfere with his thoughts right now. He had too many important things to think of.

With jerky, angry motions meant to put the girl from his mind, the man hung his cloak on the branches of a nearby tree and placed his cassock next to it on a protruding limb. But still he could only think of the wood sprite he had found in the stream, and his thoughts made him ache with need. He'd been on the road for several months and without a woman just as long. Perhaps when his talk with Ledenburg was through he would seek out the girl. She should be easy enough to find. An afternoon or evening of pleasure with her wouldn't complicate anything seriously—and it would certainly help to get his mind back on important matters if he could assuage the ache in his groin.

Closing his eyes for a moment, he allowed himself to envision the girl's young, firm breasts springing free of her clothes. He licked his lips, imagining the sweet taste of them, and his mouth grew dry with desire.

I must stop this ridiculous behavior! During these troubled times, I can't allow myself to dwell on my own personal desires.

But no matter how he chastised himself, he could not stop thinking of the young maid.

Johanna bolted from the forest like the frightened elf the man had likened her to, thinking only of how she could get into her room and into dry clothing before her mother found her. As she rounded the corner at the back of the house, planning to sneak in through the passageway from the kitchen, her hopes were destroyed. For there stood her mother and the cook, Greta, discussing the evening dinner menu. There was no escape.

Looking at her daughter in horror, Katryn van Ledenburg exclaimed, "Child, what has happened to you?"

Johanna's older brother, Frans, came up behind his chagrined sister. "Looks to me like she decided to take a swim. Aren't you a bit old to be behaving this way, Johanna?" he teased, picking up a handful of the girl's wet hair and wringing it out with exaggerated dramatics.

Trapped, Johanna drew herself up to her full height of five feet and started to march past her mother and the cook. "I fell into the creek," she stated matter-of-factly. "Greta, please have Hildie bring some warm water to my room so I may bathe before dinner."

"Young lady, I think I deserve an explanation!" It was her mother speaking in the low, even tone that meant, *Stop where you are, if you know what's good for you.* It was the same voice that could bring Johanna's strong father and older brothers to an abrupt standstill, no matter what they were doing.

Johanna stopped and bravely turned to face Katryn's ire. She opened her mouth to speak in her own defense but was cut off by her mother.

"Never mind, I'm sure it will be some lame excuse. How many times have I talked to you about going out unescorted? And in such clothing! What would people think if they saw you running around like some ruffian of ten, instead of a young lady of position? One who should already be married! I don't know what to do with you, Johanna. I've tried and tried." Now the martyrized whine Johanna hated to hear began to creep into her mother's speech.

"This time you've gone too far. You need a husband to settle you down, and that's all there is to it. Most girls are at least betrothed by the time they reach your age, and many are already nursing babies. And you're still climbing trees and wading barefooted in creeks! You leave me no choice but to speak with your father

13

this very day about accepting Count Hammen's proposal. I'm tired of your childish, unladylike behavior, and I'm going to see you married before the year is out!"

Johanna's teeth were chattering, but she didn't dare interrupt her mother's angry tirade. Of course, the small woman before her didn't mean what she was saying. After all, hadn't she been saying the same thing over and over again during the last year? But Johanna was certain her mother wouldn't *really* force her to marry someone she didn't care about.

On the other hand, what if her mother truly had reached the end of her patience and meant what she was saying?

Just in case, Johanna continued to listen, trying to look as respectful and contrite as she could manage.

"Every suitable man who has come to court you has had something wrong with him! But I'm tired of hearing about their faults, as if you had none of your own. It will take a very special and patient man to put up with you, Johanna, and I think the count of Hammen is that man. You should consider yourself fortunate he has expressed an interest in you. He's a perfect catch. One of the higher nobles, still in his prime at thirty-eight. And very rich! Besides, a girl who insists on behaving like a wild, undisciplined child can't be too particular, can she?

"It's time you tried to do what will please your parents and quit thinking only of yourself and your childish pleasures. Now, go and bathe. And please try to make yourself presentable. Your father is expecting a guest this evening, and I warn you, I won't put up with any of your outlandish behavior! He's the son of an old and dear friend, and I won't have you embarrassing your family."

Turning back to the cook, Katryn added with a mischievous wink, "Did I tell you Dirk Corlear isn't married? He'll be the next count of Leuven, you know! Perhaps . . ."

However, Johanna didn't see the more pleasant expression on her mother's face, for she had taken her dismissal with relief and was already dashing up the back stairs two at a time.

Shivering with cold and anger once she was alone in her room, Johanna kept thinking of her mother's desire to see her married off—as if at eighteen she were already too old and decrepit to find a husband. Getting married shouldn't be the most important thing in the world. What was so terrible about wanting to wait a few more years to marry, or at least marry someone she loved? How could her mother expect her to wed a man like the count of Hammen, with his pockmarked face, bald head and huge nose?

She shook her head and wrinkled her nose in distaste. No one could be rich enough to make the thought of marrying Hammen bearable. An involuntary shudder of revulsion ran through her with the thought of knowing Count Hammen intimately—of having his children!

"Ugh," she groaned out loud. "Mama wouldn't do that to me. Papa wouldn't let her!" But no matter how she assured herself, suddenly she was not certain at all!

She consciously removed the worried frown from her brow as Hildie, a slight girl two years younger than Johanna, came into the room carrying a large bucket of warm water.

The quiet brown-haired girl had been born to Ledenburg's best tenant and had been taken in by Johanna's parents when her own family had died in a plague a few years before. She was personal maid to Johanna, and helped Greta in the kitchen. Though she said very little, she was closer to Johanna's age than anyone else in the household, so Johanna shared all her hopes, dreams and secrets with the unassuming little maid.

"You probably shouldn't do things to upset your mama that way, Miss Johanna," the girl suggested shyly, wanting to spare her mistress any more of Katryn's anger.

"I don't mean to. Every day I promise myself not to fight with her. But she nags at me all the time—'fix your hair, learn to sew, find a husband'—until I can't stand it anymore. Why can't I just be me and get married when I meet the right man? Why is she in such a hurry? I could have frozen to death out there! But did she notice my teeth about to clack out of my head? Or the icicles forming in my hair? No! She just kept on talking and saying all the same things she's said a million times before. It would serve her right if I got the consumption and died this very night! Then who would she have to marry off? No one. That's who!" Johanna threw her arms into the air and stomped dramatically around the room.

"Miss Johanna, you know she loves you more than anything in the world. That's why she's so hard on you. She thinks your papa spoils you and that you won't be able to take care of yourself if anything happens to him. She just wants to see that you're taken care of proper. Everybody needs someone to take care of them. You should be glad you've got a mama to worry about those things for you."

"I know you're right," Johanna said, somewhat abashed. "I don't know what gets into me. I have a terrible temper, but I get so afraid when she starts talking about making me marry someone I don't love. Stay with me always, Hildie. I don't know what I'd do without you to talk to!"

"I'll be here just as long as you need me." The girl smiled comfortingly. "Now we'd better get you into that hot water before you truly do get the consumption."

Dirk had been right about Count Ledenburg's understanding nature and sense of humor. Matthew had laughed heartily when he heard of his visitor's experience with the peasant girl at the creek, and the reason for his casual attire. Actually, Dirk was more comfortable in his loose-fitting shirt and ankle-length drawstring trousers of light wool, and he found himself wishing the garments he was wearing were more proper for a gentleman of his station.

Patting the younger man on the back, Matthew guided Dirk into the library. "Tell me, my boy, how is your father? We were sorry to hear of his ill health!"

"He's doing well, all things considered. Mother and the servants are finding him a most difficult patient, though. He won't stay in bed and refuses the herbs the doctors leave for him."

"That's Rombourt, all right! I've known him since we were children, and it sounds as if he hasn't changed a bit!" Indicating a seat for his young friend, the short, heavy man dropped himself into a nearby chair.

"But tell me, why this urgent meeting?" Matthew asked, his serious expression belying the jovial sound in his voice.

"I'd like to discuss this with you *and* your sons, if it's possible, sir!"

The gravity in Dirk's tone confirmed Matthew's suspicions. Troubled times were ahead, and he knew he and his family were going to be called upon to make a stand that could endanger all their lives. "Of course. I'll send for them." Still attempting to keep his manner light, he left the room to have someone locate his three sons.

As Dirk sat in the upholstered chair, he looked at the huge ceiling-to-floor windows draped in burgundy velvet and tied back with gold chains to allow the last of the fading sunlight into the room. Despite its aura of comfort and intimacy, the room was enormous and had one entire wall covered with shelves of elegantly bound books, while another proudly displayed a huge mantel and fireplace. The furniture was heavy and covered in the same rich velvet that adorned the windows.

He was fascinated by the warmth of the room and thought of the rooms in the tenth-century castle which had been his home since birth. The castle's dark passages and drafty corridors had been a source of many frightening and lonely hours spent as a child—all the more reason why the Ledenburg mansion, obviously built in the last fifty years, with no forbidding walls or moats, instantly called out a silent welcome to Dirk. It was one of the few modern homes he had ever been in, and he made a vow to build himself one like it someday.

It wasn't long before the count had returned to the room, saying, "The boys will be here shortly. Will you drink some brandy in the meantime?"

"Yes, that will be welcome," Dirk answered warmly, needing to shake off the lethargic haze the comfortable home had caused to envelop him. There was no time to think of such things as future homes now. The entire Netherlands was about to be at war if matters were not taken in hand by men such as the Ledenburgs and himself. He had to concentrate all his efforts on that one purpose and nothing else.

Just as Matthew had filled five snifters with the amber liquid, his three sons entered the room. "Ah, here they are! Dirk, I want you to meet my sons. This is Frans, our oldest, and these two fellows are Helst and Hugo."

Frans appeared to be about twenty-five, the same age as Dirk, and he was an exact replica of his father, small of stature with a tendency to heaviness around the middle and the same ruddy complexion and red hair as the older version. Dirk immediately liked the quick smile dominating Frans's face, and he recognized a comrade the instant their eyes met.

However, he wasn't able to make as quick a judgment about Helst and Hugo. Nineteen and blond, the twins lacked the healthy coloring of the other two men and seemed somewhat shy.

"Dirk is the son of my oldest friend, Rombourt, the count of Leuven." Matthew seated himself in one of the cushioned chairs, indicating with a sweep of his hand that the others should do the same. "But don't keep us in suspense any longer, Dirk. What is your urgent news?"

19

"I'll try to be brief," Dirk began. "As I'm sure you know, for several years now the lords of the Netherlands have been excluded from their rightful share in the conduct of our government. With the spread of Protestant ideas and the king's determination not to tolerate any deviation from the Roman Catholic church, on top of the encroachments made on the liberties of all the Netherlands provinces, things have reached a very volatile point. But now, with the rapid spread of Calvinism, dangerous tensions are coming even closer to an explosion."

As Dirk spoke, the other men in the room could sense his passion for his subject. "Despite William of Orange and his argument that it's not feasible to force religious unity, and Count Egmont's personal appeal to the monarch in October, King Philip still refuses to lighten his harsh decrees. So, despite all we've done, the regent remains under orders to see that the ordinances against heretics—namely anyone who doesn't follow the Roman Catholic church—should be inexorably applied.

"Though many of us are still faithful to our Catholic beliefs, we believe there's room in the Low Countries for all religions, and we resent the religious persecution enforced by the king.

"His continued harassment of the Protestants and total disregard of our petitions has resulted in the formation of the League of Nobles, a group of about four hundred lesser nobles who have united to insist on an end to the Inquisition.

"Many of our members are Calvinists, who are desperate and not at all adverse to a violent solution to our country's problems. But we're hoping that our united front can force a relaxation of the edicts without resorting to a total outburst of rebellion."

"What are you suggesting?"

"Hendrik, the count of Brederode, who has worked with the prince of Orange in the past, is leading our delegation with Orange's brother, Louis of Nassau, to see the regent this month. We're going to petition for relaxation of the unfair decrees against Protestants—which brings me to why I'm here. We would like for you and your sons to ride with us when we petition Margaret de Parma. Even though she's the king's sister, we feel we can talk to her and convince her to be more lenient."

The four men had listened attentively until Dirk finished his impassioned statement. Helst was the first to speak when he was through. "What difference does it make to us? We aren't the heretics the king is rounding up. We're true to the Church and always will be."

"Yes, but it's the church we chose for ourselves, not a religion forced on us by a king who sits in Spain working to crush all other religions." Hugo spoke with an emotionalism that surprised his brothers and father.

"How do you feel about this issue, Papa?" Frans asked cautiously.

"I supported Orange when he, Egmont and Hoorne announced they wouldn't attend the king's Council of State so long as Antoine Perronot de Granvelle was left in office. I think they were right when they withdrew from the council in November, when Philip still refused to change the laws. And I don't think it's right for kings or princes to presume to rule over the consciences of their subjects, so I definitely believe in religious freedom.

"However, I find the thought of an out-and-out rebellion repugnant. So I will align myself with your League of Nobles, but only for as long as it takes to petition Margaret. And, I must make it clear, I will not take part in a rebellion against the monarch. I feel we must avoid war, at all costs. Perhaps this league of yours will be the way. As for my sons, they must decide their own consciences," he added, looking from Frans to Helst to Hugo with questioning blue eyes.

"I say we fight for our freedom, both religious and political. How can it be right for King Philip to live in Spain and determine what happens in the Netherlands? Are we not capable of ruling and governing ourselves? I say we are and must prove it to him. I will join you, Corlear!" Frans said adamantly.

Dirk was pleased with the reception he had received from the count and his sons and couldn't conceal a smile of satisfaction. Though not one of the higher nobles like Orange and Egmont, the count of Ledenburg had been friends with the regent for a great many years and was always welcome at her court. He would definitely lend a much needed air of stability to their cause.

Just as the five men were standing to leave the room, the door to the library flew open, and Johanna rushed in. "Papa, Mama says that your guest must be tired after traveling and will probably like to freshen up before . . ." She stopped in the middle of her sentence when her surprised gaze came to rest on Dirk as he stepped out from behind Matthew's blocking frame.

"You!" she shrieked in shock, her face red with renewed anger. "What are you doing here?"

Dirk looked from Johanna to her father, who was

grinning mischievously. "You mean . . . ?" he said to Matthew. The count nodded his head. Dirk turned back to Johanna, his expression amused and surprised. "You really *are* his daughter?"

"Johanna, come in," Matthew invited before she could answer. "I want you to meet our distinguished guest, Dirk Corlear, the son of the count of Leuven. Oh, but I forgot! Unless I'm misreading your shocked expression, you've already met under less formal circumstances, haven't you?" He'd recognized Dirk's "tenant's daughter" by the young man's description. But seeing the look of horror on his daughter's face, he felt guilty for not warning either of them sooner.

Despite his tinge of shame, Matthew was unable to resist teasing the young people further. He winked at Dirk and asked, "Young man, is this the young woman who threw you into our creek this afternoon?" By the time he finished speaking, he was doubled over in glee—to the total chagrin of his daughter.

Although Dirk couldn't bring himself to laugh, a merry twinkle lit his sapphire-colored eyes as he took her hand and kissed it gallantly. "I hope you will forgive me for not believing you this afternoon."

Her face an indignant shade of pink, and with all the aplomb she could muster, Johanna coolly nodded her head and acknowledged Dirk's presence. "Monsieur."

Her attempt at detachment set her father off with new peals of laughter, and she narrowed her eyes threateningly at her brothers, who should have been helping her, instead of joining the cruel teasing at her expense. "Dinner will be set in less than an hour, Papa. If your guest wants to rest, Hildie will take him to his room," she said stiffly, then turned and ran out of the room.

Tears were streaming down Matthew's red face, and he soon began to wheeze from the exertion. "Please forgive me my little joke, Dirk, but you see, she's my only daughter and also my youngest child. I've spoiled her sinfully. Her mother's been telling me for years that someday her wild ways would come back to me if I didn't make her settle down. But what can I say? She's the light of my life, a weakness which has caused me much criticism from my wife, but I can't help myself. Just you wait until you have a daughter of your own. You'll understand."

Chapter Two

Johanna hurled herself across the bed, pounding her fists in frustration, crying out to no one in particular, "How could my own father do that to me?"

As she began to calm slightly, she permitted herself to remember the man from the creek, and she found that the thoughts were really quite pleasant.

So, his name is Dirk and he'll be a count someday. Mama said she doesn't think he has a wife. Now, if someone like Dirk Corlear came to court me, I might be more inclined to think about marriage!

A plan for her own survival suddenly began to form in her mind. *If he would show an interest in me, it might help make Mama forget about the silly idea of forcing me to marry Count Hammen!*

She crossed the room to view herself critically in the mirror. "Well, Johanna," she told her reflection, "if you want him to show an interest in you, you'd better do something to convince him you're not a foolish, bumbling little girl who runs away from every problem.

"Hildie! Come here! I need you right now!"

Hildie came running anxiously from the room across the hall, which she had been readying for the family's guest. "What's the matter, Miss Johanna?"

"Quickly, we have less than an hour to make me into a lady!"

"What are you talking about? You frightened me to death! You shouldn't do that to a person, Miss Johanna. I thought you were hurt."

"Quit babbling, Hildie, and help me out of this old dress! I'm going to give him a chance to see what a lady I can be if I set my mind to it!"

"Who, miss?"

"Who?" Johanna shot a guilty look in the maid's direction. "Why, Papa, of course—and Mama!" *And Dirk Corlear,* she added silently.

When Dirk appeared precisely on time for dinner, everyone was already awaiting his arrival in the grand hall. However, the only face he saw was Johanna's. The wet wood nymph and the red-faced little girl of the afternoon had been replaced by a sight which caused the ache in his loins, begun in the stream that afternoon, to intensify unbearably—an ache that must go unappeased now that he knew the object of his desire was the daughter of an old family friend.

Johanna had donned a long-waisted gown of rich green silk, making her waist seem even tinier than Dirk recalled; he ached to reach for her, despite the edicts of honorable behavior. In fact, he was so engrossed by her loveliness that the low neckline of her bodice, elaborately festooned with shimmering pearls, went unnoticed. And though the wide oversleeves she wore had been painstakingly embroidered with tiny jewels, they might as well have been made of sackcloth. Dirk only saw the glitter in Johanna's sparkling emerald eyes. Nothing else.

He stifled an instinctive gasp when he realized that through the fine lace yoke topping her chemise, he could see the suggestion of the desirable fullness of her breasts being held back by the shapeless bodice encircling her slight figure.

Small and pleated, the ruff at her throat was held in place with a necklace of precious stones and pearls. In her hair, she had woven a network of gold and silk ribbons ornamented with delicate gems. Since the tiny tendrils of hair around her face refused to obey, they had been allowed to fall where they willed, in a soft complement to her glowing face, and Dirk knew he would never behold anything lovelier than Johanna van Ledenburg.

"Shall we go in to dinner, monsieur?" Johanna asked coyly, taking Dirk's arm and leading him into the dining room.

"Husband, I believe our daughter has decided to act her age," Katryn whispered, taking her husband's offered arm. "I hope this behavior will last, but I imagine it isn't likely," she sighed.

"They do make a handsome pair, don't they, Mother?" Matthew beamed.

"But our fussy Miss Johanna will find something wrong with him. Just you wait and see."

"Perhaps not, Katie. If we don't press the situation, and simply let nature take its course, she may find someone who not only pleases her, but us as well!" he mumbled out of the corner of his mouth as they entered the room.

"We'll see." She smiled warmly as her husband

helped her to her seat. "And hope!" she mouthed to the man she had loved for thirty-two years. He gave her arm a loving pat, then took his seat at the head of the long oak table, which had already been heavily laden with food.

Conversation at the dinner table was mostly political and gave Johanna a chance to secretly observe their good-looking guest. Although she definitely had opinions on many of the subjects the men were discussing, it would have been completely unheard of for her to express her views, views she wouldn't have hesitated to voice if the company had been just her family; and since she was determined to stay on her best behavior tonight, for once she kept her ideas to herself. Instead, she allowed her mind to wander to thoughts of Dirk Corlear.

Recalling his lips on hers a few hours before, she experienced a new tightness in the pit of her stomach. She thrilled anew to the memory of his strong body next to hers in the stream, and she wondered again how she could have felt so warm in the cold water—why she felt so warm now.

"Johanna, where are you? You must be sleeping. Monsieur Corlear suggested he would like to see the gardens, and I told him I knew you would be happy to show him through them. The servants have lit the lanterns, so you should be able to see your way around." Katryn gave the young people a sweet smile, her lack of subtlety not going unnoticed by her husband, who sent her a suspicious glance—which she ignored.

Blushing as she recovered from her fantasy, Johanna's answer was breathless. "Oh, yes, it has become rather warm in here." Regaining a bit of her composure, she took Dirk's offered arm and led him outside. "Of course, monsieur, you will not really be able to appreciate all of our beautiful flowers, even in the lantern light, but the fresh air should be pleasant."

As they walked into the night making small talk, a lightness and excitement pervaded Johanna's soul, and she found the new feeling thrilling.

"I do hope you will be able to stay long enough to really enjoy our spring flowers, Monsieur Corlear. They are just starting to make their appearance, and people come from miles around for a glimpse of Mama's gardens. We have fresh flowers all summer long, but my favorites are still the first blossoms of spring," she chatted nervously, wondering what she would say next.

Stopping as they rounded a neatly trimmed hedge, Dirk caught Johanna's chin and tilted her face up to his. "I've already seen the most beautiful flower in your mother's garden, and she's every bit as lovely in the moonlight as in the daylight."

A sigh escaped from Johanna's lips as Dirk reached for a lock of her hair that had worked its way out of the ribbons with which it had been so carefully dressed. Pushing the wayward curl back into place with the backs of his knuckles, he let his hand linger lightly on her hair for a moment.

His lips barely touched her as he brushed her cheek with a feathery kiss, but it rocked Johanna to her toes, and she swooned slightly.

Then slowly, as if he were handling a valuable treasure, rare and fragile, his hands slid down her neck, over her trembling shoulders, and along her arms to her tiny waist.

Johanna was entranced by Dirk's touch, and her hands rose to caress his disquieting face. Exploring with soft fingers, she wanted to memorize his features: the straightness of his slender nose, the blue of his eyes, the fullness of his eyelashes, and the gentle arch of his sand-colored brows. She thrilled to the softness of the neatly trimmed beard curling immaculately along his strong, square jaw; to the hollows of his suntanned cheeks; to the two worried furrows between his eyebrows; and to the wonderful curve of his slightly crooked smile.

Lost in time and unaware of anything but the moment, they stood that way for long minutes.

Drunk with the fragrance of her nearness, Dirk pulled Johanna to him and kissed her lightly. Her mouth tasted delightfully fresh, and he wanted to drink in all of her, never to stop.

Savoring the sweetness of his kiss, Johanna wound her arms around his broad shoulders, drawing herself closer to him to mold her body against his strong frame.

"So sweet, so soft," he whispered through loving lips that traveled over her face to her closed eyelids, along her throbbing temple, and down the sensitive paleness of her neck, kindling the growing flame he had ignited inside her.

The passion in Johanna's newly awakened body was great, and Dirk's exploring hands caused a searing heat to progress through her veins, leaving her limp and breathless, certain she would fall if Dirk released her.

His caress roved tenderly to the curves of her breasts, straining against the confinement of her clothing.

30

Suddenly frightened by her own unbearable desire, Johanna pulled away from him. "Please, we must go inside before someone comes searching for us."

"Don't go, little wood nymph," Dirk pleaded hoarsely.

"Why do you call me that? It makes me sound like a child. I'm not a child. I'm a woman," she insisted, leaning back to watch his face.

"Half woman, half child." He gave a knowing smile. "Are you real? I think not. Surely you're a wonderful dream. And if you are, I pray I never awaken."

"Of course I'm real!" she said, pleased with the effect she seemed to have on him.

"But every time I get close, you disappear. Like a butterfly flitting through the summer sky. If one walks very carefully and stands totally still, maybe he won't frighten it away." Dirk whispered with such expression that Johanna could actually envision the summer butterfly.

"But!" he said suddenly, causing Johanna to take an involuntary jump. "One wrong twitch of a muscle and off she flies! That's it! If you're not a nymph, not a child, and not a dream, then I'm certain you are a butterfly."

Forcing herself to step back from the exciting man, Johanna laughed, "Well, whatever I am, you will have to find out another time. Mama and Papa will be wondering what we could find to discuss for so long a time. Besides, I know Papa will be anxious to hear more of your political talk. Perhaps tomorrow I can show you the rest of the grounds," she suggested—as casually as she could manage with her heart pounding its excitement so loudly in her ears.

"A pleasure I shall anticipate with relish," Dirk returned.

Having regained some of her composure with the harmless flirting, Johanna took Dirk's arm and directed him back into the house, doing her best to appear completely in control of her racing heart.

Although Johanna said all the correct things when she and Dirk rejoined her family, Matthew and Katryn exchanged secret smiles when they noticed the appealing flush to their daughter's fair skin, and the mysterious glow in her eyes.

Johanna's dreams that night were filled with wondrous visions of Dirk and the feelings he had aroused in her. She awoke in the morning to the memory of his kisses and lay in her bed reliving the passionate minutes of their first meeting and the stolen moments in the garden. As the haze of sleep cleared and she became aware that the night had ended, she could still only think of Dirk Corlear.

Realizing a whole new day had begun, she jumped out of bed and ripped off her nightclothes, leaving them on the floor as she made ready for her morning toilette. As usual, Hildie had brought hot water up from the kitchen earlier, and the temperature was now perfect.

However, the splashing of the water on her face brought Johanna fully awake and presented her with worries that had not occurred to her before. "What could he possibly think of her?" she wondered aloud; and as she dressed, she continued to talk to herself, pondering how she should behave when she saw Dirk again. Should she act as if being kissed were an everyday occurrence for her? Or should she pretend it had never happened? No, that wouldn't do. She wasn't good at masking her feelings. Anyway, perhaps she was taking his attentions too seriously.

"No, it won't do for him to think his kisses were my first. Or that they meant anything to me. He already thinks I'm a little girl. Besides, the whole thing probably meant nothing to him!"

Garbed in a simple spring frock of yellow muslin, Johanna dashed down to the kitchen, where she found Greta preparing a huge breakfast in honor of their guest. Hildie had just returned from the yard with more wood for the stove.

Hugging and kissing Greta as Hildie set down her burden, Johanna chattered gaily. "Good morning, you two! Isn't it a lovely day?" Before either of the confused servants could answer, Johanna ran out of the kitchen and back into the house.

"What do you suppose is putting Miss Johanna in such a gay mood?" laughed Greta, waddling over to the fire to stir the aromatic porridge in the huge black pot. "Could it be that she has an eye on that handsome Monsieur Corlear? That'd sure make Miss Katie happy. And he is good-looking, he is. If I were forty years younger, and seventy-five pounds lighter, I'd be tempted to give our girl a bit of competition for that young man."

Entering the large dining hall, Johanna skidded to a stop when she saw her parents, brothers and Dirk Corlear already seated at the table.

"Johanna, where have you been? Can't you walk into a room like everyone else?" her mother scolded, disappointed that her daughter hadn't kept up her ladylike behavior from the evening before.

"I'm sorry I'm late, Mama," she answered dutifully, chagrined that her mother had seen fit to treat her like a child in front of Dirk.

"Well, Mother," Matthew interceded with a broad grin, "she's here now, and I must say my favorite daughter looks especially bright and radiant this morning!"

"Thank you, Papa," Johanna said, blushing under the uncomfortable focus of all the eyes in the room.

Sliding self-consciously into her chair, Johanna again felt the rush of excitement that Dirk's nearness brought, and she wasn't certain she could make it through breakfast without giving her feelings away.

She kept her head down and busied herself with spoon and napkin, paying no attention to the conversation that surrounded her. But even though she refused to meet his gaze, she was pleasantly aware of the penetrating blue eyes that studied her bowed head with mischievous understanding.

When breakfast was finally finished and Hildie came to clear away the dishes, Katryn realized Johanna had barely touched her meal. "Aren't you feeling well, dear? You usually have such a healthy appetite in the morning!" Turning to Dirk, Katryn thoughtlessly added, "She usually eats more than either of the twins. We often wonder where she puts it all!"

Totally humiliated by her mother's words, Johanna pushed her chair back and stood up abruptly. "I feel fine, Mama. I'm just not hungry! May I please be excused?"

Without waiting for her mother's answer, Johanna fled the room full of questioning faces. But once she was outside, she realized how childishly she had behaved. *He'll never find me attractive now. He'll go away and they'll make me marry the count of Hammen.*

Johanna began to run until she came to the stream. But her thoughts immediately returned to the day before in that very spot where her gaze now lingered. She didn't want to think about Dirk Corlear just then, so she continued to run until she came to her favorite tree, the one her father said was several hundred years old. Its spreading branches called out to her, telling her she was welcome and safe beside its sturdy trunk. Accepting the old tree's welcome, she threw herself down on the ground and sobbed.

"Nothing can be that terrible," Dirk said compassionately as he rounded the huge tree several minutes later.

Johanna bolted upright, looking around like a frightened wild thing.

"What do you know about it?" she lashed out, searching frantically for an escape. It was bad enough that he had observed her childish behavior at breakfast. Now to add to her embarrassment, he was seeing her with weepy red eyes, a running nose, and messy hair. Taking a swipe at her nose with the back of her hand, she turned her back on him, hoping he would take the gesture as a chance to leave. "Please go away. I can't talk to you now."

Ignoring her command to leave, Dirk answered her question. "I know you've stolen my heart with your sweet face," he said, walking toward her.

"How could I do that?" she sniffed, still refusing to look at him.

"To tell you the truth, I don't really know," he chuckled, sitting down on the grass beside her and resting his arms on his knees. "I only know you have."

Johanna felt herself falling under Dirk's spell, a spell created by the wonderful words she was hearing, had longed to hear. She turned to face him, thinking she must be dreaming.

Unable to stop himself from touching her any longer, Dirk moved a piece of dried moss from the tangled mass of Johanna's hair, and his other hand went to her wet cheek to gently brush away the tears glistening there. "Don't be frightened, little butterfly. I won't hurt you. I only want to see you smile again."

He leaned toward her and kissed her temple, then her damp eyelids, her cheeks, traveling at last to her open waiting lips. Moving his hands down to her waist, he tenderly lowered her to the grass and covered her vulnerable body with his own.

"Dirk," she sighed.

"Shh, don't talk now," he whispered in her ear, the tickle of his beard on her neck sending flurries of excitement skittering through her.

Forgetting his vow to himself and the consequences if he betrayed those vows, he slowly unbuttoned her bodice, exposing the pale yellow chemise she had donned so quickly that morning. He thrilled to the involuntary shudder he saw pulsate over her, and he lowered his head to kiss her breasts, first one, then the other, through the thin material.

His passion controlling his thoughts now, he gently

pulled the undergarment down over her shoulders, exposing her beautiful young body to his greedy eyes. He gasped unintentionally as the roundness of her inviting breasts sprang free from the confines of her clothing. "Oh, my God," he groaned, bending to circle a rosy bud with his lips and tongue.

Electrifying sparks crackled throughout Johanna's being. Somewhere in the depths of her conscience, she knew she should stop him, should tell him she wasn't supposed to be here with him. Instead, her hands threaded into his golden hair and pulled him hard against her.

Intoxicated with the consummate purity of her beauty and innocence, Dirk knew he must not go any further—had in fact gone further than he had meant to. Her naïveté and untapped love were being offered to him unconditionally, and it would be so easy to take advantage of her inexperience. But only the worst blackguard would betray his father's best friend by seducing his daughter.

"I want you," he said softly, stunned by his lack of control.

"You want *me?*" she asked in astonishment. He hadn't said anything about love, but it didn't matter. All that mattered was that if Dick Corlear wanted her, she wouldn't have to marry Count Hammen!

Then a horrible thought occurred to her. What if Dirk was too late? What if her parents had already sent word to Hammen consenting to a marriage between him and Johanna? No! That was impossible. It would be too cruel a trick of fate.

A shocking idea stormed through her brain. One last way to ensure that she would not be an acceptable bride for Hammen. He wanted a virgin!

"I want you, too!" she said to Dirk, pulling his mouth down to hers to offer her lips as a seal to their agreement. No matter what her parents had arranged, she would make sure Count Hammen wouldn't want her anymore. "I want to belong to you, Dirk." She took a deep breath. "Will you make me yours today? Now?"

The breath caught in Dirk's chest, and he studied Johanna. "Do you know what you're saying?"

Johanna nodded her head and gave him a tremulous smile. "I know what I'm saying."

With a sharp intake of air, he bathed her face with light kisses before he blazed a fiery trail along her neck to resume his worship of her breasts. She groaned helplessly as his lips traveled over the rich fullness, barely touching them, yet leaving none of the silky flesh uncelebrated by his tongue and lips.

Instinctively arching her back, indicating her hunger and need to have him even closer to her, Johanna's head tossed from side to side as she moaned her pleasure aloud.

Slowly and tentatively, Dirk flicked his tongue in and out on the peaks that had grown erect with desire; and as his own passion became more impossible to ignore, he pulled her enlarged nipple further into his searing mouth, while his hands kneaded the smooth mounds of flesh with sensuous purpose.

Johanna cried out loud, and Dirk, thinking he had hurt her, pulled away to look into green eyes filled with love and wonder. "Please don't stop. I never . . ." she whispered.

"I know, I know. Sweet, sweet Johanna," he murmured. "I don't want to hurt you."

Reaching up to pull his head down to her own, Johanna declared in a small voice, saturated with emotion, "Dirk, I—" Her words were cut off by his kiss, hard and urgent on her lips.

His lips coasted lazily along the rim of her ear as his hands resumed their exploration of her body. One hand was cupped behind her neck to make a slight pillow for her head, and with fingers entwined in thick, luxurious silver hair, he raised himself up on one elbow to appreciate more fully the loveliness of her face, eyes closed and lips softly whimpering.

His other hand glided down to the waist of her dress, then to her stomach, where he could feel her body's gentle rising against the pressure of his hand.

Watching her through passion-filled eyes, Dirk moved his hand to the inside of her upper thighs. Through her light dress, he could feel the soft tuft of hair guarding her feminine glory, and again he was pleasantly aware of the spontaneous movement of her lower body rocking unintentionally toward the ever-increasing pressure.

Dirk's hand moved away from his destination and down to lift her skirts up to expose her slim legs to the morning sun, its heat adding luxuriously to the warm passion she was feeling as he claimed every part of her willing body for his own.

With his resumption of the bone-melting rain of kisses on her breasts, Johanna began to kiss his ears and temples, shyly at first. Then, as her confidence built, she put her hands in his thick hair and brought his mouth back to hers with a force that surprised and excited Dirk. He gratefully returned her passionate kiss.

Continuing his worshipful journey down her body, he nestled his face between the two glorious mounds of her breasts, and he knew he could never feel such contentment, such delight, with any other woman.

Listening to Johanna's heart pounding heavily, in rhythm with his own passion, Dirk's hand moved to her legs once more, this time with a determination that could not be deterred. Until that moment, he could have—should have—ceased. But the point of stopping was past, and it was all he could do to delay the inevitable until he knew she was ready to receive him.

Dirk's hand, moving with lustful purpose, raised Johanna's skirt higher, until it was encircling her hips. Levering up on his knees, he gently parted her legs and moved her underthings aside, exposing a blond triangle of soft, curling fur to his ravenous gaze.

After hurriedly removing his own breeches, he positioned his body between her open legs, where he knelt almost reverently before her.

Lying there, so trusting beneath him, Johanna didn't show her fear. Instead, she smiled tremulously and apologized in an embarrassed and uncertain voice, "I don't know what I'm supposed to do."

Returning her smile, he bent to kiss her mouth again, this time with all the fervor and passion he had been trying so unsuccessfully to hold back.

Johanna held him close to her, her arms tight around muscular shoulders, her fingers alternating between gentle caressing and digging ardently into his flesh.

At last, he reached down to touch and adore her virgin opening, and when he found it damp with desire, he could no longer keep himself from knowing the secrets that lurked within her body.

Lowering his body onto hers once more, Dirk

allowed his swollen manhood, which was straining beyond all endurance to be safely ensconced in the warmth of her, to explore the forbidden folds between her slender, naked thighs, bringing her to an unexpected and shuddering response.

When his passion touched the wet, twitching threshold of her femininity, a cry of pleasure escaped from Johanna's lips, and she arched her back with a sudden motion that invited Dirk to begin his penetration of her susceptible purity.

His entrance begun, Dirk made one swift lunge, plunging himself into the untouched depths of her body. As the stab pierced the protective membrane which had defended her chastity for eighteen years, Johanna cried out again—this time in pain.

Wondering how anything that had begun so pleasantly could end so painfully, she forced herself to relax as she waited for it to end. *At least Count Hammen won't want me anymore,* she consoled herself. *That in itself is worth any amount of pain.*

Seeing the shock and disappointment in Johanna's expression, Dirk stopped his movement and kissed the tears trickling from the corners of her eyes. "I'm sorry I couldn't spare you that, but I'll make up for it. I promise. I vow I'll never hurt you again."

Johanna was so touched by the genuine anguish in his tone that her pain seemed to ease abruptly. She placed her hands on his face and looked into his eyes, her love replacing the pained expression of an instant before.

Drawing her legs up so that her knees were bent, instinctively knowing she was telling him she was ready to go on, Johanna moved her hands over Dirk's back and down to his firm buttocks, pressing the lower part of his body to her own rising hips.

Slowly he began to move in and out in a gentle motion. Entwining her legs around his hair-roughened thighs, she matched his movement with her own. With each thrust, he entered deeper into the velvety sheath of her.

Dirk and Johanna were breathing heavily, and each became more conscious of the growing strain in their bodies. At last, the agony of waiting unendurable, Dirk groaned loudly as the fluid of his passion erupted in a flood, filling Johanna and mingling with her own fevered juices. At the same time Dirk's wanting was relieved, Johanna's mounting tension came to blessed completion in a burst of glory which left her body limp with joy.

They lay together for a few minutes, their energies spent, before either had the strength to speak.

"I had no idea it would be so wonderful," she giggled, feeling drunk with her new discovery.

"I want to marry you, Johanna," Dirk said suddenly, the expression on his face stunned as the importance of what he'd just said registered in his mind. It hadn't been in his plans to marry for several years yet, not until things were settled in the Netherlands, anyway. But now that he'd said it, actually said the words out loud, a strange relief washed over him and he found himself liking the idea. "Will you marry me?"

"Oh, yes, Dirk! Yes! Yes! Yes!" she squealed, tears of joy welling in her eyes. She threw her arms around his neck, knowing in her heart she would never marry another—no matter what her parents might have planned. They would understand. They had to!

Chapter Three

At the luncheon table, Johanna's family noticed a new electricity in its youngest member. She chatted gaily about the gardens and the spring weather, and even ventured an opinion or two on the government. Her mother felt certain the change from the shy, self-conscious girl at breakfast must be connected with their young guest at the table, but she didn't know how.

When Johanna hadn't returned to take Dirk on his tour of the Ledenburg estate, Dirk had set out on his own, saying he enjoyed solitary exploring of new places. Obviously they had found each other, because they'd come back together shortly before noon. Johanna's hair and dress had been slightly mussed, but then she always returned from her outings like that— which was a very sensitive point with Katryn. She had no doubt been climbing a tree when Dirk came upon her. She might have even dropped from her hiding place and surprised him, as she had done with her brothers many times in the past. Shaking her head in hopeless frustration at her daughter's wild ways,

Katryn said to Dirk, "Did you see much of our place before you found Johanna?"

"Yes, I did. Very beautiful," he said, looking directly at Johanna, his grin mischievous.

Katryn's excited gaze flew toward Matthew to be sure he was aware of the current running between Johanna and Dirk. Realizing her husband and sons were too busy eating to sense anything unusual, she returned her anxious attention to Dirk. "I hope you were able to see most of our land."

"Oh, I saw more than I ever expected. And I must say I'm impressed with everything I've seen. Johanna is a very good guide. She made me feel most welcome," he answered, smiling obliquely at Johanna.

The remainder of the meal was spent discussing the upcoming trip to Brussels, although Katryn noticed that Dirk looked away from Johanna only when he was forced to answer a question. And her daughter seemed to be equally enchanted with him!

Thrilled with the possibility that Johanna might have at last found a man to her liking—and that he seemed to return the interest—Katryn could barely contain herself. Dirk Corlear would be a perfect husband. He was young enough to keep up with the girl's unbridled energy, yet old enough to control her unpredictable actions. He was extraordinarily handsome—no pockmarks on Dirk Corlear's face! And from a good family! How could Johanna ask for more? How could a family ask for more? *If only he isn't betrothed!* She vowed to speak to Matthew about discussing a contract with Dirk's family.

Katryn was jerked away from her reverie by Dirk's voice, low and serious, speaking to Matthew.

"I'd like to speak with you privately, if I may."

He was very formal, Katryn noticed, and she thought she detected a nervous tremor in his voice. Her excited gaze flew to her daughter, whose smiling face told her nothing. Frustrated, she looked back at her husband and their guest.

"Of course, son. We'll go into the library. If you will excuse us," he said to the others. Patting Dirk on the back, he guided him out of the dining room.

"What are they going to talk about, do you suppose?" Katryn asked Johanna, unable to disguise the excitement in her voice.

"Why, how would I know? I imagine it's more of that old rebellion talk, don't you?" she said, her expression annoyingly innocent. "May I also be excused, Mama?"

"Yes," Katryn replied absently.

Not giving her mother the opportunity to ask any more questions, Johanna ran from the room and upstairs to the safety of her own bedroom.

Wondering how long Dirk and her father would talk, she sat down at her dressing table to examine her reflection in the glass as she vigorously brushed her long hair. Looking back at her she saw the same familiar face she'd washed that morning. But now it was changed.

Instead of the girl's face she had seen that morning, it was a woman's face that beamed at her from the mirror—the face of a woman who had a deep and wonderful secret, the eyes of a woman who was in love, and the smile of a woman who had just discovered her own womanhood. Yes, it was definitely a woman's face staring out of the mirror at Johanna!

As she pondered the wonders of her new knowledge,

Matthew and Dirk sat downstairs in comfortable chairs drinking snifters of brandy. Matthew couldn't help noticing that Dirk was more ill at ease than he had seen him before, and he wondered what he could have on his mind.

"Well, my boy, what is it we need to discuss?"

"Sir," Dirk began, "I know this is quite sudden, but I would like to request your daughter's hand in marriage." His words were delivered in an anxious rush, as if he had to say them quickly before his courage could desert him.

Matthew was stunned and had to think before he replied. "Dirk, I don't know what to say. This comes as quite a shock to me. You know these things are usually arranged between parents."

"Yes, sir, I understand that. But my father's ill health prevents him from attending to things of this nature. And my parents have always wanted me to decide on my own bride, with their approval, of course. I know they will be greatly pleased with my choice." His argument was reasonable, but Matthew had other considerations.

"No doubt, no doubt. Your father and I were like brothers when we were children, and I would welcome you with open arms into our family. But there is another complication even more pressing than *my* approval," he said hesitantly.

My God! It's true. He must have signed the contract with Hammen! Dirk realized, panic swirling through his head. *They'll have to break it. That's all. After today, she's mine. No other shall have her!*

"Sir, you can't be serious about forcing Johanna to marry the count of Hammen. He's more than twice her age, and I understand he has gout. I was hoping I was in time to stop it. You must cancel the contract!" he insisted urgently.

"What are you talking about, boy? There's been no agreement with Hammen. Where did you get that idea?" Matthew asked.

"Johanna told me that just yesterday her mother said you were going to go ahead and make the arrangements. Weren't you?"

Matthew laughed. "No, boy. That's just Katie's way of making the girl behave. I don't know why Johanna decided to take her mother seriously now. Perhaps even she realizes it's time for her to grow up!"

"Then what's the problem? I don't understand. If she's not already betrothed, why do you hesitate to give your consent to our marriage?"

"You may have noticed I've given my daughter her way in too many things, but that's beside the point. The fact is, I would not consider arranging a marriage for Johanna that didn't have her approval. Times are changing, and I believe young people must decide these things for themselves, a point on which my wife strongly disagrees. If Katryn had her way, Johanna would have accepted her first proposal over a year ago!"

Standing up to walk around the room, Matthew continued speaking. "I like the idea of having you for a son-in-law, but we must be careful about the way we introduce the subject to Johanna. She's a very willful girl, and you will have your hands full if she does say yes. Let me talk to her and get her feelings on the idea before I give you my answer. In the meantime, please don't mention your intentions to my wife. You understand, don't you?"

"Yes, sir." Dirk smiled. "But I hope you won't make me wait too long for an answer!"

"No," Matthew laughed. "I'll go and talk to Johanna now. And then if her answer is positive, we'll announce your engagement this very day."

Smiling as the older man left the room, Dirk found it hard to contain his joy, already knowing Johanna's answer. Again he wondered about his good sense. The day before he'd not given marriage a thought, other than that it was something he was going to put off for a few more years. But it was too late now for that kind of thinking. He was about to become an engaged man; and his decision made, he would stand by it with eagerness.

Leaving Dirk to ponder his future, Matthew made his way up the stairs to Johanna's room, where he found her anxiously waiting.

"Johanna, I would like to discuss a matter with you," he said as he entered her room.

"Yes, Papa, what is it?" she asked, her voice high with anticipation.

"Monsieur Corlear has asked for your hand in marriage." Matthew closed his eyes and awaited the expected explosion. When it didn't come, he suspiciously opened first one eye, then the other.

"What did you tell him?" she squealed in delight, nodding her head eagerly.

"Of course I told him I would need to discuss it with you before I made my decision!" he answered, totally puzzled by her response.

"Why didn't you tell him yes, Papa?" Johanna scolded.

"Why didn't I tell him yes? After all we've been

through the last two years interviewing suitors your mother has dragged up from God knows where? No father in his right mind would consider making a decision about your marriage without your approval!"

"Papa, I approve! I approve!" she exclaimed. "Please tell him yes! Yes! Yes!"

"Are you sure, daughter? You would live at Leuven. Are you ready for that? It's on the other side of Brussels, and you know what a long, tedious trip it is to visit the city. It would be even farther."

Was he trying to talk her out of it? No, of course not! What father would deny his only daughter such an advantageous marriage? And to the man of her own choice? In that instant, Matthew realized that letting go was going to be more difficult than he had ever imagined.

"Oh, Papa, I'm sure! I was sure the first time I saw him! I just couldn't let myself believe he would actually want me too!"

"Not want you? Any man would be honored to have such a beauty as his bride. Dirk Corlear is the fortunate one to have won your love so easily!"

"Let's go tell Mama! You haven't told her, have you?"

Matthew shook his head, not only in answer to her question, but at the curious outcome of events.

Johanna went on chattering, oblivious to her father's stunned expression. "Oh, good! I want to be there when she learns she's finally going to be able to quit worrying about her stubborn, old maid daughter. Let's go find her right away!" Tugging at Matthew's sleeve, she pulled her bewildered father after her.

When Matthew, still in a state of shock, told his wife

of the upcoming nuptials, Katryn let out a loud cry that exclaimed her joy to all within hearing range.

Katryn announced the glorious news to everyone: Helst, Hugo, Frans, Greta and Hildie; and Johanna was being hugged jubilantly by the servants and gaily danced around the room by her brothers when Matthew suddenly remembered Dirk. "I left him sitting in the library waiting for my answer!" His words of dismay were scarcely noticed as he made a frantic dash out of the room.

The next few days were a flurry of activity and commotion. Not only were the men readying themselves for their trip to Brussels to see the regent, but there were priests to talk to, banns to be posted, letters to be written to Dirk's parents, a dowry to be agreed upon, and a wedding date to be set. They were all of one mind, agreeing that the wedding would be late summer, since Dirk and Johanna insisted on an immediate ceremony. Fortunately, the priests were able to shorten the waiting time by backdating the banns twelve months, and an August wedding was settled on.

Although the days were filled with activity, Johanna and Dirk found stolen moments to spend alone, walking in the gardens and making their own plans for after the wedding. He told her of his home in northern Brabant and promised he would build her a modern home, not unlike her parents' house. And she enumerated the many children they would have and tried to imagine how soon she would be able to give Dirk his first son. They talked of everything, and nothing; and before the week was out, each knew the other's innermost thoughts and dreams.

Then, of course, there were the nights. After everyone in the house had gone to sleep, Dirk would silently steal into Johanna's room across the hall, where they would spend precious time demonstrating the extent of their newfound love. Each morning it grew more difficult for Dirk to leave her, needing to slip out of her room before the rest of the household began to rouse.

As the week drew to a close, Dirk's mind was forced to return to the original purpose of his visit, the delegation to Brussels. Nobles from all over the Netherlands—Artois, Hainaut, Luxembourg, Gelderland, Holland, Friesland and all the other provinces—were converging on Brussels under the leadership of Hendrik, the count of Brederode, and Louis, the prince of Nassau, carrying a petition to the regent demanding the relaxation of the edicts against the Calvinists and other Protestants.

So, leaving Johanna with his promise to return as quickly as possible, he set out for Brussels with Matthew and his sons, just one week after he had first found her in the stream.

Hendrik, the count of Brederode, rode southward toward Brussels, discouraged by how little he had been able to accomplish since joining the compromise with the great nobles two years previously. True, they had successfully obtained the removal of Antoine Perrenot de Granvelle from his position as chief counselor to the regent, Margaret de Parma. But that hadn't been enough.

Though the government had given way to their demands that time, the high nobles had been unable to run the affairs of the country and found themselves in disagreement on absolutely everything.

Disgruntled with the way the higher nobility couldn't take control of their own government, and angered by the monarch's infringement on traditional noble privileges, Brederode had become the leader of another group of lesser nobles in December of the previous year.

Since it had become obvious the notable aristocrats would not accomplish the loosening of the laws against non-Catholics, the initiative had been taken from them by Brederode's group, and the delegation to Brussels had been organized.

Some four hundred influential men were expected to be in Brussels to sign the petition to the regent. And if his young friend Dirk Corlear had been successful in obtaining the support of the regent's old friend Matthew, count of Ledenburg, Hendrik felt they stood a chance of being successful with their appeal.

As his procession neared Brussels, Brederode was joined by others—some on horseback, some in carriages, and some on foot, but all there to support the fight for the Netherlands.

Seeing his mentor for the first time in several weeks, Dirk was painfully surprised to see how Hendrik had aged and how tired he looked. The hours and sleepless nights spent organizing the delegation and preparing the petition had obviously taken their toll on the vibrant man who was only ten years older than Dirk. It saddened Dirk greatly to realize how much of himself the other man had found it necessary to sacrifice to their cause.

"Dirk, my friend," Hendrik called out over the confusion of the gathering men and horses. "I've been watching for you. It's good to see you again."

"We've just arrived, and I sought you out immediately," Dirk shouted over the cacophony of sounds coming from the large number of men.

"'We?'" Hendrik asked with raised eyebrows as he neared Dirk. "Does that mean you were able to convince Ledenburg to come?" he asked with a hopeful smile.

"Not only the count," Dirk said proudly, "but his three sons are here, too. I know Matthew will be a great asset when we speak to Margaret. She's turned to him for advice in the past, and she trusts him."

Patting Dirk on the shoulders, Hendrik bellowed, "Good work, my loyal friend! I knew I could depend on you." Then he added sentimentally, "You can never fully understand how it takes the weight off my mind to know you're standing beside me in this endeavor." Then, with his usual vigor, he declared cheerfully, "Now! Let's go renew my acquaintance with the count and his sons!"

"Matthew!" the rugged Brederode called out. "It's been too long since we've talked. I'm looking forward to visiting with you before we see the regent tomorrow!"

"It's good to see you, Hendrik," Matthew answered, immediately invigorated by the dynamic man's energy. "I understand Louis of Nassau will be joining us, also."

"Yes. We're fortunate to have him with us. If only his brother would align himself with our cause!" Brederode shook his head sadly as he thought of how they could use the prince of Orange's aid.

"Perhaps in time William will see fit to join you," Matthew consoled. "I hear he has strong leanings in this direction and that he stays informed through his close ties with Louis."

"I know he feels great sympathy for our desire to have a united Netherlands with freedom of religion, but he's still a Catholic, as you are, and he hesitates to take part in anything which might go against the Church." Then Brederode added confidentially, "However, I do feel that sooner or later he'll be forced to join us when he sees this is the only way for the noblemen of our country to regain our rightful position and power in the Netherlands."

"I agree with him that we must do everything to avoid armed action," Matthew said with determination. "Hopefully, we can accomplish something of value here that will leave the Calvinists and Protestants other recourse besides declaring war against the monarch!"

"I certainly hope so, Matthew," Hendrik said, but he shook his head doubtfully. "Unfortunately, religion's not our only problem. The people are being taxed so highly since Philip became king, and they don't like the idea that our country is supporting Spanish wars and acquisitions in other parts of the world, especially when our own people are going hungry." The anger rose in Hendrik's voice. "Philip even wants to control our commerce and agriculture, as well as our religion! He wants to leave no control in the hands of the Dutchmen!"

"Yes, I know, Hendrik," Matthew said, dismayed to see how concerned Brederode really was. "It was different when his father was emperor. Charles was born here and spoke our language. He loved the Low

Countries as his homeland. But Philip is a total foreigner, and you can't blame the citizens for resenting having a man who doesn't even speak our language dictate their lives. But I still can hope we're able to avoid bloodshed—no matter how hopeless things may seem."

The encampment where the delegation spent the night took on the air of a celebration. Men wandered from tent to tent, seeing old friends and meeting new ones. The excitement grew as they realized that Dutchmen—Catholics, Calvinists, Protestants, wealthy, poor, from the north, south, east and west—had come together for one purpose, and the single-mindedness of their goal drew them close in a feeling of brotherhood and comradeship.

In the morning, after a night of little rest, the delegates began, one by one, to sign the parchment containing the requests Brederode, Nassau and Ledenburg would be taking to the governess that day. It was a momentous occasion, the culmination of months of work, and Hendrik was forced to look away self-consciously to wipe the tears forming in his eyes.

Watching the gesture from a distance, Dirk was moved by the strong man's emotion and vowed to support him, no matter how long the fight went on or where it might lead him. He prayed the delegation would be a success, but he sensed that any progress made this day would be short-lived. He was greatly depressed to think there would be fighting all over his beloved Netherlands before the year was out, but he knew deep within his heart that it would come to pass.

Following Nassau and Brederode into the audience

with Margaret de Parma, Matthew smiled warmly to see his friend, the regent, once more.

Stepping forward to meet him, Margaret clutched Matthew's hands with a tenderness one reserves for the oldest and dearest of acquaintances. "Matthew, I was surprised to find you were with this delegation. I hate to think you and I have any differences that can't be worked out amicably. You know I've always counted on you as one of my most loyal supporters!" There was a desperate sound to her high-pitched voice.

"That I am, Your Excellency," Matthew said, smiling broadly. "None of that has changed. I remain one of your most ardent followers. But I felt I had to come. Despite my personal loyalty and friendship to you, I believe it's wrong for the government to designate what religion a man must practice, and that it must be stopped at once. I'm certain that by easing up on the ordinances against non-Catholics, you'll be protecting the unity of the Netherlands. To continue with these oppressive edicts the monarch has set down is to invite open rebellion against the crown and the Church. The Netherlands is my homeland, and I can't bear the thought of war—brothers fighting brothers, father against son, and provinces attacking other provinces. We can't let that happen."

"Matthew, I'm glad you came." Margaret sounded as if she truly meant what she said. "I've read the petition, and seeing all the signatures on this scroll shows me how widespread the discontent is. I will think on what you have said. Surely we can put our heads together and come up with a compromise that will allow me to continue to serve the monarch, yet bend to the concerns of the Dutch people," she said pleasantly.

One of Margaret's advisors interrupted. "Surely,

madame, Your Highness is not afraid of these *gueux*."

"Fredrik," she answered sternly, directing an irritated glare in the rude man's direction. "Only a fool would not be disquieted by the picture painted by these—*beggars,* as you call them. I must listen to them. In fact, I have already written to Philip on a number of occasions asking for an end to the Inquisition and burning of heretics; but I suppose we could make another attempt to help him see the seriousness of the situation here."

The four dignitaries talked for many hours before Margaret agreed to test a relaxation of the edicts against Protestants without waiting for word from Spain. Nassau, Hendrik and Matthew left feeling successful in that they had put a stop to the mounting rebellion—at least for a while longer.

"The regent feels compelled to do as we have asked," Brederode announced in a loud, booming voice to the crowd awaiting his news. "She has instructed the inquisitors to stop their work and has commanded the magistrates to stop enforcing the heresy laws until further notice!"

When the waiting delegates were told the news, a cheer was let out that could be heard high in Margaret's office, where she stood, one solitary woman with the responsibility and fate of an entire country in her hands. It was a lonely position, and she beseeched the Lord for guidance, praying she had made the right decision. Only time could tell. She fell to her knees with her rosary beads entwined in shaking fingers. "Hail Mary, Mother of God . . ."

Running to meet her father and brothers, Johanna

was disappointed to see that Dirk was not with them. He had told her before he left for Brussels that he would come back to Ledenburg only after visiting his parents in Leuven, but she had hoped to see him anyway.

Disguising her letdown with smiles and hugs for the men in her family, she listened attentively as the four excited travelers told of their accomplishments in Brussels. Then, as the weary delegates disbanded to remove the dust of their trip from their bodies and clothing, Johanna ran away from the house, clutching the small parcel her father had handed her upon his arrival at home.

She ran, first to the stream—the stream where she and Dirk had met—then on to her familiar oak tree. Only now she would never think of it as *her* tree again. Now it was *their* tree.

Lowering herself to the ground on the spot where Dirk had taken her young girl's body and turned it into that of a woman, Johanna felt the familiar yearning swell within her.

Spreading her skirt over the grass where their bodies had pressed its greenness flat with the heat of their lovemaking, she tore open the tiny parcel in her hand.

Out fell a brooch on a chain of gold. The Leuven family crest was faultlessly displayed on the front of the gold medal, with inlaid shapes of ivory and ebony-colored onyx surrounded by rich jade. It was the brooch Dirk had always worn, and now he was entrusting it into her care. She was touched beyond understanding by his precious gift and swore to wear it always. Clutching the brooch with one hand, she opened the letter in her lap and began to read.

My dearest Johanna,

When I first saw your eyes flashing sparks of green fire at me from that stream, I knew at that moment I wanted you for my own and that no other could ever take your place in my heart. I send this brooch to remind you of me and my love, and so that I am able to remain next to your heart, no matter how far apart circumstances may take us.

The brooch was destined to be worn by you, and no other. Its jade color will only achieve its full luster when you don it, yet it will remain dull in comparison to your lovely eyes.

I long to be with you, my love, and will hurry to you as soon as it is feasible. I think of you in my arms, and it is this memory that makes our separation bearable.

All my love and devotion,
Dirk

Gripping the brooch and letter to her breast, she lay back on the grass and let herself relive, once again, the time she had spent with Dirk: the first kisses in the icy stream, the stolen moments in the garden, the love-making under the tree and in her room, and the long walks where they had shared their dreams in the quiet of the evening's fading light. In one short week, she had stored up more treasured memories than most people could expect in a lifetime, and she knew it.

Chapter Four

The next months were spent in preparation for the August wedding. Johanna and her mother spent hours penning invitations to be sent out all over the Netherlands and western Germany. There were trips to Brussels to see about housing accommodations near the cathedral for their guests; caterers and musicians had to be contacted; and there were fittings—endless fittings!

The trips to the dressmaker were the most tiring of all for Johanna. Her wedding dress was to be a white ivory brocade, beaded with tiny white pearls; and though lovely, it was unwieldy and uncomfortable. Her slim waist was to be shown off by a deep V-shaped bodice topping a huge skirt gathered over a farthingale—a torturous wooden frame that held her skirt out to a width of three feet on either side of her slender hips. She had argued that she wouldn't wear the ridiculous contraption, no matter what the style dictated. But her protests had fallen on deaf ears; her mother continued her exacting instructions to the seamstress, who sewed for only the most fashionable women in Brussels, including the regent herself.

Johanna stood with the wooden monstrosity around her waist as Madame Felice circled her, pinning and tucking the yards of heavy material. The weight of the gown was so great that Johanna couldn't help wondering if she would be able to walk down the aisle unassisted, and she vowed to herself that her wedding day would be the last time she would ever wear the cruel and ludicrous hindrance to natural motion. She had run and walked unencumbered for eighteen years and saw no reason to allow maturity or her married state to change that. If she were forced to be a lady of fashion, she would simply set her own style. One without farthingales!

During the busy months of wedding preparations, Dirk was only able to visit Ledenburg a few times. His father's health had taken a turn for the worse, and it seemed only a matter of time until his waning strength would give out totally. His one great sadness was that he would not see his grandchildren, a desire which had kept him alive his last months.

With the relaxation of the stern edicts and ordinances of the monarch, the entire country was lulled into a false sense of security. Even Dirk's premonition of violence and rebellion was forgotten as he busied himself with his father's affairs and caring for his parents.

Johanna kept Dirk's many treasured letters in a small wooden casket beside her bed, where they were taken out almost daily to be read and reread. They told her of the household he was preparing for her arrival in Leuven, of his yearning to lie next to her each night, of how he looked forward to awakening every morning with her in his arms; and in July, the letters spoke sadly of his father's death.

Knowing all too well what Countess van Leuven must be going through, Katryn immediately wrote Dirk's mother, Marta, a letter of sympathy, requesting she come and help with the wedding arrangements, since there was just "too much for one person to handle." Katryn told Marta she feared it wouldn't all be finished on time if she didn't have some help. She made it clear she understood how bad the timing was and Marta's probable hesitation, but she said she needed her so desperately that she couldn't possibly take no for an answer.

With the preparations for their trip to Ledenburg made, Dirk saw the color return to his mother's cheeks and the lightness of her step. She was once more a woman of purpose and ambition, thanks to the generous, understanding family into which he was marrying. Traveling to Ledenburg the last time before the wedding, Dirk was filled with new hope and expectations for the future.

As the wedding date drew nearer, Johanna, who had never been one for inactivity, prayed for an end to the activity surrounding her. Pondering her lack of strength and vigor the past three months, she told herself, *You're missing the freedom of the woods and stream. Once the wedding's over you'll feel like yourself again. Besides, you're not the only one who's being affected. Everyone's growing tired of this wedding. But if it's not over soon and I don't get back my appetite and over the queasiness I have every morning, I'm going to waste away to nothing. Or die from lack of sleep! All this has even interfered with my monthly cycle. I don't even remember the last time I had my flow. . . .*

Johanna's hands flew to her mouth, stifling a scream as the realization of her probable pregnancy confronted her. She looked down at her stomach, and her hands dropped to touch it.

With the precious gift growing in her womb taking form in her mind, she wondered what Dirk's reaction would be to her news. Should she tell him before or after the wedding? She was anxious to tell him right away, but decided it would be a wonderful wedding present, so she vowed to keep her secret until they were married—only three more weeks.

But the secret knowledge gave her the strength to face the next weeks with a new determination and vigor that had been missing in recent months. Her appetite returned, and her complexion took on a bloom notable to all who came in contact with her. When she was questioned about her good health, she smiled secretly and said, "Love does wonderful things, doesn't it?"

She and Dirk found it nearly impossible to have any time alone, but she and her future mother-in-law became close friends during the days before the anticipated event, and their relationship put new luster and energy into Marta's eyes, as well.

While the last-minute details of the wedding were being attended to, and as the count of Ledenburg's family, together with Dirk Corlear, now the count of Leuven, and his mother, were readying themselves for their trip to Brussels for the prenuptial festivities, bad news began to trickle in from the west.

There were reports that a small group of Protestants, mostly exiled Calvinist activists who had recently returned from England, had begun smashing and destroying all the statues and paintings in the Roman Catholic churches of West Flanders. These fanatic mobs had caused irreparable damage and destruction.

"Surely this is just a few malcontents acting up," Matthew said to the others in the wedding party as they journeyed toward Brussels. He sounded as if he were trying to convince himself of the unimportance of the happenings in Flanders. "Don't you think when these exiles returned to the Netherlands and found our economy at a new low, they simply needed someone to blame?"

"I hope you're right," Dirk answered, shaking his head sadly. "I understand they have forcibly removed some of their coreligionists from the prisons and are gathering more followers each day. Count Brederode is afraid this is only the beginning and that all the restrictions Margaret lifted will be put back in full force."

Frans spoke suddenly. "Father, I don't think we can take this lightly. There's talk that this 'breaking of the images' will spread throughout the Netherlands. I've been told hundreds of our people are converting to Calvinism each day. They're frightened, and so should they be!"

Matthew shook his head with a worried frown. "If this is the case, I can see no peaceful coexistence between the Catholics and Protestants. I believe in religious toleration, but when corrupted idealism goes against our church, I don't know what to do. Why can't these fools realize we've made progress and that they're destroying the country with their degenerated cause? Their movement will be weakened in the long run. Those of us who have sympathy for their problems will feel obligated to defend our church and to keep law and order. I know Orange is strongly interested in the cause—after all, his brother, Nassau, is a Calvinist and a leader of the *Gueux*—but I know he'll attempt to keep order rather than let our country be destroyed by a few militant hotheads!" When Matthew finished, he rubbed his hands over his weary face in an attempt to wipe away the nightmare he had foreseen.

"Matthew, let's not think of these unpleasant happenings any more today," interjected Katryn. "After all, we're preparing for our only daughter's wedding. This is a joyous occasion, and I don't want it to be marred by politics!"

"Yes, Mother, you're right. We mustn't let these disagreeable events interfere with our enjoyment of the next few days," Matthew conceded apologetically. "When you think of it, Katie, we're gaining another son—one who will make us very proud in the years to come, and one who's going to give us many grandchildren. I have his promise!" he laughed.

Unconsciously, Johanna patted her belly as a small, secret smile played across her lips. "Yes, Papa! We plan to give you lots of grandchildren. You have my word, too!"

Marta van Leuven was delighted with the change of subject and spoke teasingly to Frans. "And when are you going to make your mama and papa happy and produce some heirs to the Ledenburg name?"

Frans's face turned as red as the hair on his head. "It

will be two more years before I'm married, Countess. I am betrothed to a young girl from Luxembourg. She is Anne, the daughter of the count of Hansburg. We'll marry the month of her fifteenth birthday, and then I hope to give my parents as many grandchildren as they want!" Smiling at his mother and father, Frans added an afterthought. "But it will take more than just Johanna and me to bring forth enough progeny to satisfy their greedy wish for heirs! Helst and Hugo are going to have to do their part, too."

The people in the carriage laughed heartily, not only at Frans's remark, but as a welcome release from the tension the talk of rebellion had brought on.

During the rest of the journey to Brussels, the conversation was kept light, as the coming wedding was once again run through verbally to be certain no detail had been overlooked. Nearing the city, Johanna slipped her hand into Dirk's, and she looked questioningly into his worried eyes.

Gazing into the loving green eyes that dimmed the brilliant medallion hanging around her neck, Dirk was filled with an unexpected desire to hold Johanna close to him, never to let her out of his sight. He wanted to protect her from all the unpleasantness he knew was descending upon the Netherlands; and yet, he understood there would be no one unscathed by the difficulties ahead—not even his precious Johanna.

So the troubled young man put his arm around Johanna, and she leaned her head on his strong shoulder. There they remained for the rest of the trip.

The ensuing days were occupied with last-minute fittings for the bride and groom, as well as for the rest of the wedding party. There were mornings spent going over the final arrangements with the caterers and musicians. Afternoons were occupied receiving well-wishers and attending receptions honoring the bridal couple. Dinners and balls filled the evenings, and by the end of the week of flurry and excitement, it was difficult for any of the individuals involved to believe the Netherlands was a country of discontent and uneasiness.

On the morning prior to the long-awaited marriage ceremony, an exhausted Johanna, together with her loyal maid, Hildie, went to the cathedral to make her last confession before she became a wedded woman. Johanna was overcome by the quiet coolness when she stepped into the vast church from the noisy street, already seething in the August heat.

Making the sign of the cross as she knelt, Johanna prayed. She prayed as brides have for countless centuries—for wisdom, for lasting love, for children, for health, and most of all, for a happy and fulfilling marriage.

She was so lost in her entreaties that when the noise of the streets suddenly invaded her quiet sanctuary, she was slow to become aware of the disruption at the entrance of her place of worship.

Perplexed and annoyed by the troublesome intrusion on her solitude, Johanna impatiently turned her head, to be assaulted by a scene of horror and panic.

"You men stand back! You can't come in here!" one of the three priests at the back of the church shouted, as he and his comrades tried to block the entrance with their bodies.

"Sure we can, you Catholic bastard," came a yell from the back of the savage mob which had congregated outside the church doors.

"Just you watch us," another screamed as the horde of crazed men shoved against the wide doors.

"Run, ladies, we can't hold them!" one of the priests yelled desperately. But his words went unheard as the uncontrollable mass of humanity overpowered the priests and forced its way through the doorway. With the only defenders of the church fallen, the hysterical throng rushed into the foyer, crushing the three courageous protectors under their feet as they did.

They were so bent on destruction that none of them noticed the two frightened women at the front of the great chapel as they quietly slipped to the floor. The mob's purpose was to destroy every statue, painting and furnishing in the Catholic churches of the Netherlands, and they were determined to annihilate any sign that represented the Roman Catholic church, no matter how small or inconsequential.

Thus, Johanna and Hildie lay powerless beneath the pews from which they had prayed so earnestly only moments before, watching and listening to the symbols of their cherished religion being overturned and ravaged.

When they seemed to have devastated every visible indication of Johanna's faith, the monomaniacal group began pulling the pews out of the floor while ripping the rich red velvet covering them to shreds with their knives. With her eyes tightly shut and holding her breath, Johanna prayed they would tire of their lewd destruction before they came to the place where she and Hildie lay clutching their rosaries with desperate helplessness.

Suddenly aware of a scurrying motion beside her,

she opened her eyes in time to see Hildie make a dash into the aisle, deliberately drawing the mob's focal point away from the spot where Johanna still lay. She opened her mouth to scream, but no sound would come forth. *Hildie, stop!* she shrilled in her mind, as she helplessly listened to what was happening.

"Look at what I found, boys!" one of the men announced proudly as he grabbed Hildie by the arm and threw her, screaming and struggling, to the ground and flopped on top of her. "I'm gonna have a little treat before we leave here!" he laughed.

Johanna heard the sound of Hildie's clothing being ripped off her fragile body by the man, and the sound ripped through Johanna as though she were no stronger than the fabric of Hildie's dress.

Please, God, send somebody to stop this nightmare. Don't let them hurt my little Hildie.

But no answer came to Johanna's pleading prayers. All she could hear were the raucous shouts of encouragement as the men used Hildie over and over again, until her screams became small animal whimpers, then nothing. Johanna knew Hildie was dead, and she wished for death herself.

"What do we have here?" a coarse voice said very close to her.

Johanna's eyes popped open to see three pairs of men's boots on the floor beside her.

"Looks to me like one of those ladies!"

"Aye, one of them Catholic ladies!" another voice laughed. "The skinny one musta been her maid!"

Johanna peered out from her hiding place to see three viciously amused faces leering down at her, like cats with a defenseless mouse trapped between them.

The man who seemed to be the leader of the threesome spoke. "What're you doing down there, little lady?"

"Yeah!" piped in the emaciated youth standing to the right of the heavy, sweating leader, who wore his shirt open to the waist to expose a huge, hair-covered chest. "Don't seem like no place for a lady to be—on the floor, on her back!"

"Methinks you're right, Jan. You don't suppose she's a whore waitin' for her next customer, do you?" the heavy man laughed.

The other young man, not more than seventeen and appearing even more dirty and unhealthy than the first lad, agreed. "Aye, I heard them priests go without a wench to warm their beds, but I never believed it! Maybe she's the priests' own personal whore!"

Laughing at Johanna's fear as she watched them through frightened, tear-filled eyes, they looked around to see how many others were still in the church. Most of their group had departed after using Hildie, and the three decided they didn't mind sharing their new discovery with the few remaining comrades.

"Hey, fellows, come see what we found!" the older man bellowed to the others.

"Yeah, we found a real Catholic lady, beads and all. And real pretty, at that!"

"We're thinkin' she could be a whore for the priests; and since they got no more use for her, considerin' their recent demise," the leader laughed, "we thought to give her a try!"

"We oughta be gettin' out of here before someone comes," one voice warned.

"Then go on. Me, I always wondered if it was true about Catholic women bein' more passionate than

Protestants." It was a new voice Johanna hadn't heard before, and she automatically looked in the direction of the voice. It was a tall, thin man with a horrible scar covering the entire left side of his face and neck. He had no left ear or any hair on that disfigured side of his head; and when he smiled at his own sick humor he exposed his only six teeth, black and broken with decay. Johanna turned her head away in revulsion as the contents of her stomach rose to her mouth.

"Benjamin goes first, 'cause he found her. Then me and Jan gets a go. Then you're welcome to find out for yourself, Karl," Gustav offered generously. The other men in the group began vying for their turns with the unexpected bonus their work had brought them.

"Well, little lady, come on out and show us what you're made of," coaxed the obese leader of the pack of animals.

"Please," Johanna begged, speaking for the first time. "I'm not a prostitute. I was just here to pray. I'm with child. Please let me go!" she pleaded.

"Just what the Netherlands needs—another Catholic brat! Well, little mother-to-be, how about a few brothers and sisters for your Catholic bastard? Why don't we just plant a few Protestant seeds in your garden and see if they'll grow?"

All the men laughed coarsely as Benjamin pulled the quaking girl to her feet and toward the front of the church, which was littered with the broken crucifix that had hung above the altar only a short time before.

"I'll be missed," Johanna protested as she was dragged, screaming, to the front of the church. "They'll be sending someone for me if I don't return soon. I was due back an hour ago!"

"Good point, little lady." Indicating the front doors to the latecomers, Benjamin said, "You boys guard the entrances and we'll relieve you when it's your turn!

"Thanks, missy. Wouldn't want no interruptions while we show you how a real man feels inside you. It ain't gonna be like one of them prissy Catholic types. You're gonna know you been laid when we get through. Damn shame we didn't find you first, then we could take our time!" he said, shaking his head and licking his lips.

With that, Benjamin threw Johanna to the floor, grabbing the front of her dress as he did, and ripping it down the middle as her weight fell downward, her arms and legs flailing wildly. Johanna screamed, knowing she couldn't let the man do what he was planning.

A huge, grimy paw came down over her mouth, while Jan and Gustav, kneeling on either side of her, grabbed her arms and legs to pin them to the floor with their bodies.

Standing up to open his breeches, Benjamin admired Johanna's quivering body. "Look at her, boys. Just can't wait to have a real man on her. She's so anxious she can't even hold still. Well, missy, you don't have to wait no longer," he slobbered, bringing his entire weight down onto Johanna.

Ramming at her with his lower body, Benjamin put his lips to hers and forced his foul tongue into her mouth, choking off the scream she had started when she felt his vile flesh touch the inside of her thigh.

Bringing her teeth down hard on the intruding tongue, she twisted her body beneath his at the last minute and prevented his penetration.

Benjamin raised his head, cursing in pain. "So, the

little lady likes it rough. So does old Benjamin," he growled, raising a burly hand and slapping Johanna across the face four times, knocking her head from side to side with each blow to her bruised and tearstained face.

"Hey, hold on, Benj. Leave somethin' for the rest of us to look at!" interjected Jan.

"Sure, boys. But if I get bit again, some little whore is gonna pay for it good!"

With Benjamin's mouth descending on hers again, Johanna, in a semiconscious daze, realized there was nothing she could do to defend herself. The only protection from permanent injury she could think of was to lie there, not moving, until they were through.

Holding her arms to her sides and flattening her breasts harshly against his massive, perspiring chest, Benjamin laughed into Johanna's ear, and she barely heard him. "I'm gonna teach you, you high-and-mighty Catholic slut. It ain't polite to bite nobody!"

But before Benjamin could carry out his threat, his intended rape was interrupted by the sound of horses riding over the stone street toward the cathedral. "It's the regent's guard!" one man shouted, frantically making his way to the back entrance. "Let's get out of here!"

"Damn," Benjamin swore, standing to adjust his clothing. With almost no effort, he picked up Johanna and slung her over his broad back. "We ain't finished yet, whore," he threatened, following his companions out the back, just as the authorities burst through the front.

Johanna had a vague memory of being carried through the streets of Brussels draped over Benjamin's shoulder, but her mind had mercifully left her body, giving her the sense of watching what was happening in a dream. She felt no pain, no fear, no regret—nothing.

And when Benjamin finally tossed her to the ground, she had no idea where she was or what was happening to her. Looking up at the heavy man, she felt only slightly apprehensive, and she didn't know what he meant when he finally spoke to her.

"I sure wish I had more time, girlie, but you're slowin' me down, and we gotta move fast," he said, taking an angry kick at Johanna's head, then one at her back.

Laughing at her tortured moans, he dug one last hard kick into the softness of her belly. "This is to make sure you don't go clutterin' up the countryside with another one of them Catholic bastards—not that you're going to live that long."

Suzette Benner was looking forward to washing the family clothing and linens in the river on that hot day in August. The fourteen-year-old girl, strong for her age, worked long hours every day in her parents' inn on the outskirts of Brussels; but she didn't object to the hard labor as long as she was able to slip away once a week to do the laundry and take a bath without interruption. On days like this, when the perspiration was already staining her underarms and rolling off her forehead into her eyes, she practically ran to the river.

Putting her laundry basket down, Suzette plunged into the waist-deep water with all her clothing on. She would wash her own clothes while she still wore them. Then she would bring the linens into the water for their weekly cleaning.

Dipping herself into the water up to her shoulders, Suzette splashed refreshing water on her face and hair, laughing with pleasure as she enjoyed the luxury of her bath. Already she felt better and sighed her contentment.

Lying back in the water to rinse the soap from her hair a few minutes later, she suddenly became aware of someone or something splashing water a few feet upstream. She sat up and glared indignantly in the direction of the sounds. Who dared to intrude on her privacy? This was her own secret place, and no one else had any business here. Besides, the other women all preferred a more popular spot farther downstream where they could meet and gossip.

Then she heard the splashing again, this time accompanied by a whimpering sound that tore at the young girl's heart, melting her anger completely. She stood up and cautiously waded upstream.

Rounding a clump of green shrubs growing out into the water, she gasped in horror. There, on the bank of her peaceful river, was a girl, clutching a dress which had been torn open down the front.

Dabbing pathetically at bloodstains on her legs and lower body, the wounded girl glanced up to stare blankly at Suzette when she heard her.

Seeing that the girl's green eyes were practically swollen shut, Suzette ran to her as quickly as she could move through the water. "You poor thing, what happened to you? How did you get here? Who did this?"

As she looked down into the pathetic, swollen face, already beginning to blacken where it had obviously been struck repeatedly, tears came to Suzette's own eyes. Never had she seen such a tragic beating.

She took the handkerchief from the girl's limp hand and rinsed it in the water. Gently and tenderly, she began to wash away the dried blood caked around her mouth and nose. Blood had even flowed down her face into her ears and hair, matted blond hair that hung wildly down the heartbreaking creature's back and over the front of her shoulders, mercifully shielding a small part of her tortured body from sight.

Although she didn't think the dazed girl had even heard her, Suzette talked while she attempted to clean the deplorable wounds. "Don't you worry now. We'll get you cleaned up, and I'll take you home with me. My mama will make you well." Suzette hurt anew when she realized the girl didn't flinch as her injuries were cleansed—as if she were already dead.

Taking her hands, Suzette gently drew the young woman to her feet and guided her to the spot where the laundry had been left. Carefully removing the soiled dress and underthings from Johanna's listless form, she was further horrified to find more blood and bruises covering the slim body.

Sitting her down on the dress spread over the ground, Suzette wrapped a sheet around her and continued to nurse the evil lesions, marveling at how the girl had managed to survive such brutality.

Unexpectedly, the battered young woman clutched at her belly, letting out a long, agonizing cry of pain. The blood between her legs began to flow more heavily. Then, screaming as if her insides were being ripped out of her by some giant hand, she aborted her baby.

Realizing the girl's attacker had not only hurt the girl herself, but had killed her unborn child in the process,

76

Suzette screamed hysterically at the moaning girl. "Who did this to you? He must pay!" But her fervent look into the tortured green eyes were returned with a vacant stare.

Suzette was brought back to the reality of the situation by the knowledge that she must finish attending to the half-dead girl. The important thing was to treat her wounds, watch over her, and pray to God the injuries to her soul would heal along with those on the surface.

While washing the blood and grime from the blond hair, Suzette found a medallion on a gold chain hanging down the girl's back and caught in her long hair. Disentangling the heavy necklace from the wet hair, Suzette brought it around to the front and gently let it rest between Johanna's uncovered breasts. "What's this?" she asked softly.

Coming to life, Johanna grasped the necklace in both her hands and began to cry as she swayed back and forth in the place where she sat.

"Don't worry, nobody is going to take it from you. We'll leave it right there, and when you want to show it to me, I'll look at it then."

Chapter Five

When Suzette hadn't returned to the inn by the dinner hour, her mother, Mignon, a rotund woman in her early thirties, began to worry. Francois Benner, Suzette's father, was also concerned, but didn't want his wife to fret unduly. So, when he spoke it was with a casualness he didn't feel. "You know girls, Mama. She probably met others her age and they got to talking. The time just got away from them. But I don't want you to worry, *ma chérie,* so we'll go look for her."

"Don't want me to worry? What about you? Confess it, Francois Benner. You are as concerned as I am!"

"Well, perhaps I am a bit," he admitted. "But I'm certain it's needless. She's such a good girl. I know she must have a good reason for staying out so long."

The sky began to darken with the approaching evening as Francois and Mignon walked, hand in hand, to the place where Suzette always did the laundry. With their uneasiness growing, the couple was relieved to hear their daughter's familiar voice calling out to them from the riverbank. "Oh, Papa, Mama, I'm so glad you came. I didn't know what to do!"

They ran in the direction of their daughter's cries, only to be met by Suzette coming toward them. She grabbed their hands and dragged them to the place where Johanna, wrapped in a sheet, lay sleeping.

"I found her on the bank today. Mama, she's been beaten terribly. I don't think she even knows I've been here taking care of her. I cleaned her up and then got her to sleep, but I was afraid to leave her alone. What if whoever did this to her came back? Oh, Mama, it was so terrible. There was blood everywhere, and her clothes were ripped open all the way down the front. I tried to get her to tell me what happened, but all she did was stare at me with those blank eyes. I'm so glad you came. I didn't know what to do. I couldn't leave her. I knew you'd come, though. Did I tell you there was blood everywhere? So much blood. And I think she lost a baby! There was so much blood. Did I mention the blood? But I told her my mama and papa would come find us and make her well. I told her you'd come, Mama," Suzette babbled on, showing the strain she had been under, while her parents hurried to examine Johanna.

Gently, Francois lifted the sleeping girl into his arms and carried her to his home, followed by Suzette and her mother, while the girl continued to relieve the horrors of the day.

"Try to put it from your mind. You have done well today. We are very proud of the way you acted. Now, you must let your papa and mama take care of her."

"Yes, Mama. I knew you'd come. I kept telling her

my mama and papa would come for us. Did I tell you how much blood there was everywhere? Everywhere, Mama!"

Dirk sat with his head in his hands on the steps in front of the once great cathedral. This was to have been his wedding day. Instead, it was the day after his life had ended.

He and Matthew, together with Johanna's brothers, had spent hours frantically searching the streets and alleyways surrounding the church, knocking on doors, investigating uninhabited rooms, all to no avail. It was as if Johanna had never been there.

Remembering the grisly discovery of the afternoon before, Dirk pressed his fists into his eyes, trying to erase the gruesome sight; but the image remained vivid in his mind. He knew he would never be able to forget the way he'd felt when he first saw the mutilated bodies of the three priests and Hildie, their bodies trampled and crushed by insensitive boots bent on destruction.

Poor, poor Hildie. And Johanna! Where could she be? He could envision her being dragged off and tortured by the angry mob, or cornered like a frightened kitten in some dark and dismal alley, or worse still, lying dead and disfigured like Hildie and the priests.

Dirk knew he couldn't give up or let himself think thoughts like the ones he was having. He had to believe she had escaped from the madmen who had broken into the cathedral and that she would find her way back to him. There had to be something he could do! But what?

He sat alone and dispirited for the remainder of the day until Matthew, his own heart breaking, came to take him back to where the wedding party was still being housed.

"Come, son. There is no more we can do here. The authorities are looking for her. All we can do now is wait and pray." Tears were streaming down Matthew's face as he spoke, and at last the two men walked slowly back to their rooms at the inn.

Mignon Benner had finally dozed off in her wooden rocking chair beside the bed where Johanna slept fitfully. After tucking her own brave daughter into bed, the heavy woman had spent the night at Johanna's side. She had kept cold compresses on the girl's face wounds, changing them frequently, hoping to guard against fever. As the sun started to rise, she awakened to find Johanna turning in her sleep and crying out at the pain racking her battered body.

"No, no, please let me go," she screamed desperately, her head thrashing from side to side.

Going to her, Mignon took the girl's hand and patted it gently. "Go back to sleep, little one. You're safe now."

Johanna's lids barely opened, revealing the greenest eyes Mignon had ever seen. To the kind woman, the unseeing eyes seemed like valuable jewels buried in the muck and mire of a terrible cesspool as they stared out of the grotesque, swollen face of varying shades of blue and purple.

"*Emeraude!* You have emeralds for eyes, *ma petite!* Who could have done this to you?" Squeezing the small hand lying limply in her own, she consoled Johanna. "Well, little green eyes, you can sleep now. My Francois will see to it that no one else harms you— ever!"

Soothed by the gentleness in the woman's tone, Johanna closed her eyes and slept once more, this time without nightmares.

Poking his jolly, round head through the bedroom doorway, Francois called out, "How's our patient this morning? Wouldn't surprise me to see her up and around after a night of Mama Benner's special care!" he laughed.

"Shh, you'll wake her," Mignon scolded, prodding her husband out into the hall. "That poor girl isn't nearly over the worst of it yet. To tell the truth, I don't know how she survived this long. She's lost so much blood that she still may not live. You'd better kill another chicken. When she wakes up I want to try to feed her the broth. You know, nothing gets a person back on her feet like a good night's rest and my chicken soup!" she laughed, giving him a gentle shove. "Now, you go on about your business, and let me get back to my patient."

Francois returned his wife's warm smile. "If anyone can make her well, it's you, Mama," he said, planting a loving kiss on Mignon's ruddy cheek. "Has she said anything to tell us where she comes from?"

"No, of course not!" Mignon answered reprovingly. "To tell the truth, I'm not sure I want to know who she belongs to. What if they're the monsters who did this to her? Perhaps a cruel husband? A vicious father? Anyway, her lips are so swollen, I doubt she'll do much talking for quite a while. Now, go on and get me that chicken!" After pushing Francois down the hallway, Mignon returned to her patient.

Seeing that the girl was resting quietly, the woman decided it would be a good time to check on her daughter. The day before had been difficult for Suzette, and as Mignon walked to her room, she decided to give her the morning off from her duties. She felt certain that if her daughter hadn't acted as she had, the mysterious girl she found would have been dead by now. She thought proudly that not many fourteen-year-old girls would have known what to do if they had been in a similar situation. Mignon thanked God once again for her Suzette.

Knocking as she entered Suzette's room, Mignon was surprised to find her daughter up and around.

"Mama, why didn't you wake me?"

"I thought you'd like a chance to sleep in. After all, you had a hard day yesterday, *ma petite.*"

"But there is so much to do. How is she today? I had terrible dreams all night long about what could have happened to her. Is she awake yet? Has she said anything? I want to see her!"

Laughing at Suzette's barrage of questions, Mignon shook her head regretfully. "No, love, she's still sleeping. It may be some time before she'll be able to tell us anything. In the meantime, we'll watch over her while she gains her strength. She's young, and if she's gotten this far, I'm certain she'll heal quickly. I know if we're patient she'll answer all of our questions. But for now, let's give her time to mend. *Oui?*"

"*Oui,* Mama!"

Walking toward the door, Mignon turned back to Suzette. "But since you're awake, why don't you sit with her while I fix breakfast for the guests and put on a chicken to stew for when she wakes up!"

Mignon paused at the door to the bedroom with tears in her eyes. "Daughter, I'm very proud of you. Both your papa and I are. You saved her life, and I know you'll be rewarded for your quick thinking and compassionate care." Pulling her apron hem up to wipe her eyes, she scurried down the back stairs.

Suzette finished dressing and straightening her sparsely decorated room. As she spread the brightly colored blanket over her narrow bed, she thought how fortunate she was to have parents like hers—parents who loved and protected her. The poor girl down the hall must not have had anyone to watch over her. *Well, she does now. We'll take care of her and love her and make up for the terrible things they did to her.*

Tiptoeing into the tiny room where Johanna lay, Suzette was surprised to see that their guest was awake. "Good morning, sleepyhead," she whispered carefully. "Are you feeling any better today? It's good to see you awake. You look so much better than you did yesterday! Can I get you anything?"

Johanna shifted slightly toward the girl standing at her bedside, and Suzette started crying again when she beheld the lost look in the eyes that must have been so beautiful in the past.

Not wanting the girl in the bed to see her tears, Suzette glanced away but continued to talk in the same friendly manner. "Oh, I'm sorry. I wasn't going to ask you any questions. I know it must hurt to even move your lips, much less talk." She clasped Johanna's limp hand and looked at her. "I want you to know you're safe now; and if there's anything you need, we'll get it

84

for you. My mama's the best nurse around here, and you couldn't be in better hands. Why, women bring their children here just to have my mama check them over when they aren't feeling good. She always fixes them right up! As a matter of fact, right now she's downstairs making you some of her chicken broth. If that doesn't make you well, nothing will! Why don't I sit here while you sleep some more. Mama says sleep is the best cure for everything—after her chicken soup, of course!"

Using all the strength she could muster, Johanna squeezed the hand holding hers, and she managed to stretch her distended lips in a slight smile as she looked gratefully at the anxious young girl, so large and yet so gentle. Closing her eyes once more, she went to sleep holding onto Suzette's strong hand. It was there that Mignon found them when she came with the all-healing soup two hours later.

"Mama, she knows I'm here! She tried to smile at me! And she squeezed my hand! She's going to be all right, isn't she?"

"We'll see, *chérie,*" Mignon answered hopefully.

Johanna drifted out of her sleep at the sound of voices in the room, and when she looked up at the two round faces, she could feel their love cascading down on her, causing a slight surge of energy to arise in her lethargic body. She attempted another smile and valiantly tried to sit up.

"See, Mama? She did smile!" Suzette exclaimed, rushing to Johanna's aid. "Let me help you. It's too soon for you to be sitting up alone!" The strong girl carefully lifted Johanna to a sitting position while Mignon put a pillow behind her.

"Would you drink some of Mama Benner's chicken soup, little green eyes?"

When Mignon put her great weight on the edge of the bed, Johanna's weak body rolled helplessly toward the kind woman. Laughing, Mignon ordered, "Suzette, hand me another pillow, will you? She's such a little bit of a thing that I'm apt to sit on her and not even know it!" After straightening Johanna in the bed, she cooed, "Now, let's put some broth in that tiny belly of yours, *ma petite.*"

Slowly and lovingly, Mignon fed Johanna the hot, rejuvenating liquid until the girl would take no more. "One more spoonful?" she coaxed. *"Non?* All right. You've had enough for now. I'll bring you more later. You will sleep again. *Oui?"*

When the mother and daughter started to leave Johanna's room, they saw the fear and panic return to her damaged green eyes. "Mama, she doesn't want us to go! She's afraid to be alone. One of us had better stay until she falls asleep again!"

"You're right, little daughter. You stay with her while your mama tends to her chores." So Mignon left with the half-empty bowl of soup, while Suzette returned to her watch beside the bed, holding the girl with the haunted green eyes.

During the next days, Johanna mended at an unbelievably fast rate. Of course, the bruises, now a yellowish green, were still evident, but the swelling of her face had receded to the point where the Benners could determine how pretty she would be—once the discoloration had disappeared.

Suzette had carefully washed and brushed Johanna's long tresses; and after three days, the girl who had been so close to death was able to get out of bed unassisted. It was still difficult for her to walk, and she took all her meals in her room, but she was definitely on the mend.

Johanna was able to respond to the Benners' love and attention with smiles and a few words, but she still had offered no information about her past or about what had happened to her on that terrible day. The family had ascertained that she was from the southern part of the Netherlands in that she understood French, the main language in the south. And judging from the clothing she'd been wearing when they had found her, she was a lady of noble birth. But until they knew for certain that her *noble* husband or parents weren't responsible for her brutal beating, they didn't want to make any attempts to locate her family.

When the Benners felt certain their guest had recovered enough to talk about what had happened, Suzette and Mignon sat in Johanna's room braiding her long hair into a chignon on the top of her head. As the women worked on Johanna's soft locks, Mignon spoke with undisguised compassion. "We must inform someone where you are and what has happened, little one. We have to know who we should notify. You need to tell us who you are."

Johanna remained silent for a long time. She seemed to be looking within—trying to remember something. Then, grabbing Mignon's hand, she shouted in a desperate high-pitched voice, "I don't *know* who I am! I don't know what happened to me! I can't even remember how I came to be in your home. Oh, Mama Benner, I have no one but you! Can't I stay here with you? I'll work very hard. I'll help Suzette with her chores. I'll cook and do the laundry. Please don't turn me out! I don't know where I would go!"

Mignon, who was crying with Johanna, pulled the tormented girl to her ample bosom. "Now, who said anything about putting you out, little girl? Don't you know you have a home with us for as long as you want? Suzette loves having a sister, and Papa and I would be honored to have another beautiful daughter. It's just that somewhere there are other parents who must be mourning the loss of their own lovely child, with the sparkling emerald-colored eyes. You must try to remember them. But until you do, you can be our daughter."

It was impossible for Mignon Benner to know the truth in her words, but at the very moment she sat consoling the lost and frightened girl, a devastated family of mourners rode past her inn in a large carriage on their way home to Ledenburg, a home that would never be the same now that they had lost their bright and lively Johanna.

The six silent people in the carriage, lost in their own thoughts, had given up hope Johanna could still be alive. After all, it had been several weeks.

Matthew was remembering the little blonde girl he had held on his lap, so lively, so curious, so unique; Katryn was thinking of the free-spirited girl running barefooted in the woods: and Marta was recalling the young woman she had grown to love and was to have called daughter. Johanna's brothers, Helst and Hugo, were remembering, with amusement, their bossy baby sister who tried to mother them and tell them what to do at every turn; and Frans, who had been like another parent to Johanna, was gazing out the side of the coach imagining he could hear her sweet laughter again.

Marta's thoughts were also on her son, Dirk, whom they had left in Brussels, still desperately searching for some clue as to Johanna's whereabouts. He had promised that if nothing turned up by the end of the month, he would give up his search; but his mother knew in her heart he would never fully recover from his loss. She knew that Dirk would keep probing until he had managed to ferret out every wicked soul responsible for his bereavement.

She only hoped that, in an effort to discover those answerable for Johanna's disappearance, he wouldn't follow through on his plan to join the Calvinists who were breaking up the Catholic churches.

But Marta had no way of knowing Dirk was already in peasant's clothing and sitting in a tavern, claiming to be a Calvinist who hated all Catholics—and bragging about the destruction and havoc he had helped to bring on the churches of West Flanders.

"Naw, it wasn't gettin' too hot for me in Flanders. Just thought it was time to be movin' on. I hear Brussels has seen a little action itself in the last few weeks. I understand some of the boys really did a job on that big cathedral in the middle of Brussels. Got 'em a couple of priests in the bargain, they say." Dirk was speaking in the colloquial language of the Dutch. "Yeah, I'm gonna join up with a local group and see if I can't help out some." He laughed, and the men at his table eagerly joined in.

"It's too bad you couldn't have been here when we took that cathedral. The higher-ups were really pissed about them priests, so I guess we'll have to stick to breaking up statues from now on," Gustav chuckled. "But that cathedral sure was somethin'."

"Ah, what do we need with them higher-ups anyway?" growled the heavy man with the yellow teeth. "I don't care what they think. At least we get the job done. All they do is talk. You don't think they really care about us, do you?"

Dirk agreed with the older man and laughed his disgust. "Sure, they got the regent to ease up on the heresy laws some, but you know that's just 'cause they're worried about their own skins and what the king is gonna take away from them. You can be sure they don't care if our kids go to bed at night with empty bellies or if there's no work for us to do!"

Dirk was playing his part perfectly. "Sure, they say they sympathize and want us to have freedom of religion, but I wager Egmont and Hoorne are nowhere to be seen when the goin' gets rough. It's gonna all be up to us in the end."

"This man's right, boys. What do we care if them prissy nobles stand behind us or not? Even the ones that's supposed to be Calvinists. Where were they when we were riskin' our necks in that cathedral?" Jan asked in an indignant tone.

"You boys sound like my kind. Sure would appreciate it if you'd let me tag along with you on your next job. The movement is spreadin' like wildfire. Should be all over the country by the end of the month. And I'd like to do some travelin'."

"Sure thing, young fella," Benjamin answered

90

agreeably. "We can always use good strong men like you in the group."

"Well, tell me, when do we strike next?"

"We can go anytime we want. All we got to do is find a church that ain't too fortified, gather up a few of the boys, and go to it!"

"But we're lyin' low for a few days since Maggie has her boys out in full force after the cathedral," Gustav confided to Dirk.

"Well, I hope it ain't too long, or I might just go out and organize my own little raid. I want to wipe out those damned Catholics, the sooner the better," Dirk said, convincingly vehement. "If the action's not here, I'm thinkin' of headin' north. I hear things are just starting to get hot there."

"Be patient, young fella. You just stick with old Benjamin. He'll show you where the action is. Right, fellas?" The older man laughed secretly, and his two young companions heartily agreed.

"Yeah," Jan said. "You can't never tell what kind of action old Benj will dig up in one of them churches!"

"Go on, Benj, tell him what we found in that cathedral," Gustav coaxed.

The three hoodlums were so anxious to brag about their accomplishments, they didn't notice Dirk's fists clenching and unclenching on the tabletop. Nor did they see the tightening jaw or realize the friendly smile on their new companion's face was gone. "Yeah, tell me! I'm interested to know what you found."

Benjamin grinned and leaned closer to Dirk. "We wasn't plannin' to take nothin' out of the churches, but this was just too good to pass up. You gotta promise not to tell no one!"

"Oh, I promise your words will stop with me," Dirk vowed through gritted teeth.

Looking around to be sure no one else was listening, Benjamin went on eagerly. "First of all, we was just finishin' up, when this little gal comes rushin' into the aisle. She wasn't much, though. Only about ten of the boys got anything off her before she died. But just as we were gettin' ready to leave, we found another one. Only this one wasn't no mousy little maid. She was a lady and the prettiest piece of fluff you ever wanted to set your eyes on—flat on her back under one of them pews and ready to go. I swear, boy, you should have seen her. Little bitty thing with hair so blond it'd knock your eyes out—just lyin' there waitin' for a man to get on top of her!"

Jabbing his elbow into Gustav's side, he continued boasting confidentially. "Most of the others had gone on, 'cept the boys, here, and me—and a few laggards. It sure seemed a shame to let such a find go to waste, her bein' a fine Catholic lady and already on her back, and all. So we decided to show her what a real man felt like inside her!"

"Hey, Benj, tell him about what you said when she told you she was carryin' a Catholic brat in her belly," Jan prodded. "He'll get a kick out of that."

"You mean she was pregnant?" Dirk asked in a low, menacing voice that went unnoticed by the three ruffians.

"Sure was! And old Benj told her we'd plant a few Protestant seeds in her Catholic garden to see if they'd grow!" Jan roared, slapping Benjamin on the back.

"But we couldn't keep her like we wanted to, 'cause she was slowin' us down too much. And to tell the truth, by the time we got her to the edge of town, she was near dead and blithering like an idiot—and she didn't look all that pretty no more. So we dumped her in the river. But I'll tell you, that's one church we ain't gonna forget too soon!"

With a low, tortured groan that sounded as if it had originated in the depths of hell, Dirk flew across the table with his dagger aimed directly at the greasy fat man, who was so stunned he just sat there until the knife was plunged deep into his heart. For an instant, no one at the table moved, as the vicious man's bulging eyes registered the fact of his own death.

Not waiting to see if his attack had hit its mark, Dirk swung his boots off the table in a kick that toppled Gustav, and before the teen could regain his balance, Dirk had grabbed him by the hair and slit his throat from ear to ear.

Seeing his brother's blood spewing all over the floor jolted Jan out of his stupefied state, and he began to run for the door—too late. Before the frightened youth could reach the exit, Dirk, having reached a point beyond insanity, hurled himself across the space between them, knocking the trapped boy to the floor and running his dagger through his chest, all in one swift motion.

Looking up as the tavern operator grabbed him from behind, Dirk turned his head to the other men at the bar. The angry face of the madman they had watched brutally kill three men in less than two minutes was gone. Instead, they saw the tormented countenance of a young man who had been through the agony of perdition, never to be relieved of his suffering. He was crying quietly, the tears coursing openly down his cheeks, and the dumbfounded witnesses knew there would be no more killing this day.

"They raped her and left her to die alone. She was carrying my child and they raped her and killed her. They raped and killed my Johanna. She was all alone."

"Hey, John, let him go. Can't you see he ain't gonna hurt nobody else? Hell, they deserved everything they got."

"Those three were always no good. We all know that. Brussels will be better off without the likes of them."

The proprietor released his iron-tight grip. "Go on, son, before the authorities come to investigate the ruckus. You're already in your own kind of hell, and I ain't gonna be the one to add to your troubles!"

With shoulders drooping and hands dangling lifelessly at his sides, Dirk left the tavern. He had no idea where he was going. He only knew that if he lived to be a hundred years old, he would never love another as he had loved Johanna: Johanna in the stream; Johanna all flustered that first morning at the breakfast table; Johanna under the oak tree, giving him her precious gift of love; Johanna with her head on his shoulder, trusting him to protect her; and Johanna, the mother of his dead baby!

With his arms in the air, as if pleading for mercy, Dirk shouted to God, to anyone who would listen, to no one in particular, "JOH-AAAAAN-NAAAAA!"

Then he wandered, lost and alone, through the streets of Brussels, mourning the loss of his love and his unborn child. When he came to the steps of the cathedral where they were to have been married—a cathedral without a priest to hear his confession—the deserted man cried out his anguish to the stars.

When morning came at last, he knew what he must do. He would join Brederode and Nassau in their fight for independence. They had to take control of the rebellion. It was urgent that they take the struggle out of the hands of animals like Benjamin before the entire Netherlands was destroyed.

Standing up, Dirk allowed himself one last look at the church where Johanna had lost her life. Then, turning his back on his pain, he set out with new resolve to fight King Philip II and his vicious Inquisition.

"Mama, she has to have a name. We can't keep calling her *'little green eyes'* or *'ma petite',*" Suzette implored. "If she's going to be part of our family, we've got to call her by a proper name!"

"*Oui,* child, but perhaps you have a favorite name you would choose for yourself, my little green eyes," Mignon said, smiling into Johanna's upturned face.

"No, Mama. If I am to be your daughter, I would like for you to give me my name," she answered.

"Then I name you *Emeraude* for your emerald eyes. Is that all right with you, sweet thing?"

Smiling happily, Johanna tested the feel and sound of her new name, "Emeraude. Emeraude Benner. Oh, yes, Mama, I like the name very much. Emeraude! Now I'm somebody! I have a name!" she exclaimed delightedly.

Hugging Mignon ardently, she squealed jubilantly, "Thank you, Mama! You'll see, I'll be a good daughter. I'll work so hard and make you very proud of me. I love you all so much!"

The three women were hugging and laughing and

crying when Francois came upon the emotional scene. "What's going on here? Can't I turn my back for a minute without the silly females in this family all acting crazy?" he teased.

"Oh, Papa, I have a name! Mama has given me my own name. I'm your daughter, Emeraude!" Johanna announced, running into the arms of the huge man she had grown to love so dearly.

"Emeraude, huh?" Francois said with a twinkle of his eyes. "Why would she name you that? Could it be because of your long blond hair? No, I don't think it's that. I know! Is it because of your funny face? Not that? Then, I can't imagine why she'd pick that name. Wait a minute, it must be for your eyes! Your great big eyes of . . . blue!" Roaring with laughter, Francois picked up his new daughter and swung her around the room.

"Oh, Papa, you're teasing me," Johanna giggled.

"Of course I am. That's what papas have daughters for—to tease. Otherwise, what good are they? Just stand around all day giggling and chatting," he boomed, putting her down and drawing Suzette and Mignon into his burly embrace.

And so, with the simple change of a name, Johanna Frances van Ledenburg ceased to exist and Emeraude Benner came into being.

Part Two—Emeraude

Chapter Six

Emeraude and Suzette were returning from the river, where they had done the weekly wash, when they spotted an immense dust cloud upstream. Frightened, the girls ran into a clump of the bushes that grew thickly on the banks of the river.

"Is it a storm?" Suzette asked.

"It doesn't look like any storm I've ever seen. Listen!" Emeraude whispered cautiously. "It sounds like footsteps, maybe marching."

"Look!" Suzette gasped as several men on horseback rode out of the rust-colored cloud they were viewing. "It's men on horses!"

"I see that, Suzette! But how many men must it take to make such a cloud or noise? I can actually feel the earth rumbling under me. Can't you feel it?"

"*Oui,* I feel it! Who do you think they are?"

"I don't know, but they seem to be staying in one

place. Do you think it's an army setting up camp? What if the Calvinists have come to destroy our churches again? Oh, Suzette," Emeraude cried urgently, "we must run and tell Papa what we've seen!"

"But what if they see us?" the younger girl asked in a trembling voice.

"They won't notice us. They're at least a mile or two up the river. Quick, grab your basket, and we'll run! But just in case, we'll keep low and stay behind trees and bushes as we go! But I'm afraid we have much more to worry about than being seen from a distance of a mile."

By the time they reached the inn, both were out of breath and found it impossible to speak. The best they could do was frantically point down the road.

"Hold on, little ones," Francois stopped them. "Your old papa needs you to talk slowly. Just take a minute to catch your breath. Then tell me what's got you two silly geese in such an uproar."

"But, Papa!" Suzette pleaded, gulping in huge breaths of air.

"Take your time, girl! Now, what is it?"

Breathing more easily, Emeraude spoke first. "Papa, there are men setting up a camp on the river! Hundreds of men! Maybe thousands! We could see them! Can't you feel the ground moving under your feet at this very moment? How many would it take to make the earth move so far away? Who can they be? What can they be doing there?"

Suzette, still gasping, exclaimed, "Oh, Papa, we were so frightened! I was afraid they could see us, but Emeraude said they couldn't from that far off. Could they, Papa?"

"I doubt it, little girl," Francois answered, his worried gaze turning toward the south. "Now, you two run along inside and put away the laundry. I need to see if I can determine what's happening."

As the girls ran inside with the clothes baskets, Francois walked out to the edge of his property, where he could see what looked like a city of tents taking form in the settling dust. Could it be the Calvinists regrouped? He shook his head, rejecting that thought. The Calvinists never could have gathered so many men into such a large army. Besides, their leaders were too divided and disorganized—and very few of them would be on horseback. That only left one other possibility!

"It must be the Spanish!" he exclaimed under his breath, turning to go inside to tell his wife and guests his horrifying news.

Hurrying toward the inn, he met the entire household, family and guests, coming outside to see for themselves what was happening.

"What does it mean, monsieur?" the high-pitched voice of Madame LeBlanc asked.

Francois shook his head. "Madame, I'm hesitant to say what I'm thinking. But I will tell you that no one I can think of has an army so large—except the king!"

Renée LeBlanc, the maiden lady who lived at the Benners' inn, threw up her hands and screamed. "The Spaniards? Oh, no! What shall we do?"

Emeraude put her arm around the frail, trembling shoulders and said, "Come now, madame, you know what the doctor said about getting excited!"

"But the king's forces!" Madame LeBlanc cried.

"Can't someone quiet her down?" one of the other guests asked impatiently.

101

Glaring at the immense man who stood several inches taller than Francois, who was famous for his own great height, Johanna retorted angrily, "She's old and frightened, monsieur. Try to have a little compassion and understanding!"

"What makes you think it's the Spanish?" a young man in the group asked Francois. "Perhaps it's the regent's troops on maneuvers," he suggested hopefully.

"We can only hope that's who they are," Francois answered, shaking his head doubtfully. "But I've been hearing rumors since January that the monarch was sending the duke of Alva and his soldiers to enforce the Inquisition! The gossip is that he intends to fine and jail even the Catholics who have been known to support the relaxing of the heresy edicts!"

"But surely he knows the regent's troops defeated the Calvinists and ran many of them out of the country last fall," the younger man argued.

"*Oui,* I'm sure he knows. But somehow, I don't think *le duc* will be satisfied until he has established a total military dictatorship, with Philip as the absolute ruler and sovereign over all the Netherlands! They want to replace all our government officials with Spaniards, and they want us to bow down while they march over us, using our agriculture and commerce to support the entire Spanish Empire. *Oui,* I think all of us have great cause to worry—both Protestants and Catholics alike!"

As the troubled group stood huddled together, they noticed horses and riders coming toward the inn from the direction of the camp.

"Oh, Papa, they're coming here!" Suzette wailed. "What do they want with us?"

"Calm yourself, daughter!" Francois ordered sternly. "Go about your regular work. No doubt some of them are just surveying the terrain—or perhaps seeking refreshment!" His own expression falsely gay, he urged the anxious group inside. "Now, on with you! We must all behave as normally as possible. After all, we have nothing to hide. Are we not loyal to the monarch and the Church? Certainly none of us took part in the rebellions of the fall. So, we have nothing to worry about! We will go about our business as usual. *Oui?*"

There was a moment of hesitation while the little gathering of people realized they had no choice but to wait and see what would happen. But the feeling of approaching evil and inescapable destruction hit them all with the violent force of an unleashed electrical storm.

Suzette was in the kitchen helping Mignon with the supper preparations, and Emeraude was in the beer garden wiping tables and straightening benches when the young Spanish officers came into Francois Benner's tavern.

Speaking in halting French, they indicated they wanted drinks brought to them in the garden and walked on through the tavern to the place where Emeraude was working.

Spying her just as she was leaving the shaded garden, one of the handsome lieutenants exclaimed, "What have we here?" in his native tongue.

Another laughed eagerly and said, still speaking in Spanish, "I don't know who she is, but I'd like to spend some time with her!"

Emeraude was frightened, yet fascinated, by the four dashing soldiers who stood blocking her exit. The oldest could not have been more than twenty-five, and she couldn't help but be impressed with the handsome men in the elegant uniforms.

Working in the inn and tavern the past months, she had seen many men traveling through on the way to Germany or France; but most of them had been older, and not the least bit attractive to a girl of nineteen. Never had she seen young gentlemen so spirited and gay as these. All of the men she had served in the tavern were solemn and wore worried frowns on their brows, talking only of politics and trade.

Realizing she was staring, Emeraude made an attempt to brush past the soldiers, and they let her pass only when Francois called for her to come fetch the beer. She ran into the bar, her fair skin having taken on a flush her adopted father hadn't seen on her before.

"Remember, daughter," Francois cautioned. "They're Spanish soldiers and dangerous. They may appear to be charming, but you must be careful. Soldiers of all nationalities, when they are drinking, are often unkind. In fact, I believe I'll serve these particular men myself while you go and help Mama in the kitchen!"

"But, Papa!" she defended. "They weren't rude. I'll serve the drinks, just as I do with all your customers. Besides, the most curious thing has happened. I understand what they're saying! How can I know Spanish, as well as German, French and Dutch?"

Francois sighed. "I don't know. I suppose it is just one more mystery we must solve." Before handing Emeraude the tray, he looked at her seriously, as if weighing the decision. "But, before you take these refreshments to them, you must promise me that you will leave as soon as you serve them. *Oui?*"

"*Oui,* Papa!" she laughed and snatched up the tray to run back into the garden.

"Ah! It is about time, señorita with the *ojos de verde!*"

Emeraude placed the pitcher of beer down on the heavy wooden table, then gave each of the men a stein to drink from.

"*Gracias,* señorita! You have saved our lives with these refreshments—and with one more look into your beautiful *ojos de verde,*" proclaimed one of the more polished officers.

Smiling shyly, Johanna started to leave. But before she could make her departure, a strong arm reached out and pulled her by the waist to the lap of the soldier who seemed to be the leader of the group.

"Don't go, little señorita. Stay and visit with us for just a while," he begged, his flashing eyes looking into her blazing green ones.

Raising her small slipper and stamping it down on his boot of leather, she slipped from the soldier's grasp and declared in perfect Spanish to the surprised Romeo, "Sēnor! If you are a gentleman and an honorable representative of the monarch, you will keep your hands to yourself in the future!"

Marching angrily from the garden, she giggled to herself at the look of astonishment on the four arrogant faces when they realized she spoke Spanish fluently and that she could understand everything they said.

Francois, thinking Emeraude was taking too long to serve the drinks, had already started for the door, only to run headlong into his smiling daughter. "Are you all right, child?"

"Of course, Papa. I'm fine. They just needed to understand the situation. I'm certain they will behave. I must go and tell Suzette about them. You have to admit, Papa, they are a lot more interesting than most of our dreary guests, who only talk about rebellion and religion!"

Watching Emeraude skip cheerfully into the kitchen, Francois shook his head and thought, *Why must I be blessed with daughters? Couldn't we have just as easily found a son by the River Senne? Or at least an ugly daughter? With sons, a man can relax and go fishing. But with daughters, he must be on guard every hour.*

As the evening progressed, the young men stayed on their best behavior, asking Emeraude only the most proper questions each time she served them, and always remembering their manners.

"How is it you speak our language, little girl with the eyes of green?" Reynaldo Moreno, the most handsome and confident of the four, asked.

Innocently flirting with the dark Spaniard, Emeraude laughed. "Oh, I guess I'm just smart!" she said over her shoulder, going inside to tend to her other customers.

"Go ahead and ask her, Reynaldo!" Gilberto prodded impatiently. "I tell you she's asking for it! Did you see the way she looked at you?"

"Gilberto, my young friend, for all your fine background, you still possess the gentility of an ill-born clod! A fine creature like our little green eyes needs to be brought along subtly, not grabbed or forced." Reynaldo spoke knowingly, impressing the less experienced members of his party with his expertise on the subject of romance.

Raul Queiro, who had been quietly watching the cat-and-mouse game Reynaldo had been playing with the lovely blonde girl, was beginning to feel the effects of his beer and spoke out. "I think you've met your match, Reynaldo. I'll wager next month's pay that none of you will get her willingly into your bed this night!"

Reynaldo laughed at the tall younger man. "That's where all of you make the mistake. I am in no hurry. But mark my words, I will have her. If not tonight, then another, but I will have the sẽnorita!" he promised confidently, hiding his villainóus grin just as Emeraude returned.

"Won't you sit down with us? We promise to behave—on our word of honor," Reynaldo crooned in a voice that seemed to caress her.

"But, *mi padre—*" she started, then laughed. "Well, I suppose he won't mind if I stay for a few minutes. But I'm holding you to your promise to be good!" she teased, never sensing the danger she was in as the men on the bench moved over to make room for her beside Reynaldo.

"Tell us, señorita, what does your *padre* call you?" Gilberto asked, trying to imitate Reynaldo's smooth style.

"Me llamo Emeraude," she answered.

"I should have known you would be named for your *ojos de verde,*" Reynaldo murmured intimately into her ear, his warm breath sending chills over her skin.

"Sí, for my green eyes," she said with a blush, suddenly uneasy. Bolting up from the bench, she excused herself. "I must go and tend to my other customers, but I will bring you more beer, and perhaps some cheese from the kitchen."

107

"I swear, I don't see how he does it," chuckled Luis, as he watched Emeraude disappear into the inn.

"All I can say is, we'd better watch and learn from the master!" Gilberto laughed respectfully.

"Or it will be a long cold winter," agreed Luis.

"*Sí,* I hear those winds from the North Sea can get very cold if you are sleeping alone!" Gilberto snickered.

The sound of the raucous laughter in the garden made Francois ill at ease. And even though Emeraude said the soldiers seemed to be holding their liquor well, he had heard drunken laughter on too many occasions not to recognize it this time. He would allow her to take one last round to the inebriated young men, and then he would send her to bed and serve them himself until they were ready to leave.

Just as Emeraude made her final trip to the garden, Francois glanced around to see another Spaniard enter his tavern.

The stranger, wearing the uniform of a soldier with high rank, walked confidently toward Francois. "Allow me to introduce myself. I am Fernando Alvarez de Toledo, the duke of Alva. I will be needing your finest room for the night. While I am having a glass of wine, please have someone ready my accommodations by bringing a tub of hot water so that I may bathe off the dust of my travels, *s'il vous plait.*"

Francois was amazed that the duke possessed such an air of authority when he had only the most basic command of the language. He wondered if anyone were ever brave enough to tell the powerful man no. Knowing the trend wasn't going to start with him, he nodded his head as he whisked out a bottle of his best wine and a fresh glass. "*Oui, Monsieur le duc,*" he said

with a friendly smile, convinced the one way to protect
his family was to keep the infamous Spaniard happy.

Unaware of the distinguished visitor inside the inn,
Emeraude set the fresh ale and cheese on the table and
sat down beside the exciting Reynaldo; and this time
when his leg seemed to accidentally brush hers under
the table, she didn't pull away. The warmth of his flesh
radiated through her clothing, causing her to speak
breathlessly.

"I must say I've enjoyed serving you this evening.
We don't get many young men in here. Mostly, we only
see old businessmen traveling to and from the market
in Brussels. You have all behaved like perfect gentlemen. I'm impressed," she said warmly.

"Impressed enough to dance for us, señorita?"
Reynaldo asked suavely, almost making Emeraude
sigh when she answered.

"But there is no music, and I couldn't dance anyway.
It wouldn't be proper," she giggled, feeling as if she too
had been drinking the amber liquid that filled the
soldiers' steins.

"Oh, but it would make us feel so much less lonely
for our homeland if you favored us with just one
dance," Reynaldo pleaded charmingly, slipping his
arm sensuously around her small waist.

Emeraude was so hypnotized by the soft, smooth
voice and so curious about his statement that she let his
hand stay on her waist where it burned its imprint into
her flesh. "Why would it make you less homesick?"

Nudging Raul with his elbow, Luis whispered, "Will
you look at him operate? He's going to have her

begging him to take her up to her bed."

"Quiet, you fool! She'll hear you," Gilberto warned out of the corner of his mouth, never letting his impressed gaze leave Reynaldo and Emeraude.

Raul was disappointed at the way the girl seemed to be falling into Reynaldo's trap. He had really believed he had detected a spirit in this girl which wouldn't let her become prey to Reynaldo's charms. Finishing off his drink, he noisily stomped his way outside the garden to relieve himself. No one even noticed his departure.

"Hell, man, she's so dazzled by that lucky bastard, she can't hear a damned thing—but him!" snickered Luis quietly. "He's the master!"

"The beautiful women who work in our cantinas always dance for us," Reynaldo answered Emeraude, leaning closer to his quarry, deliberately ruffling her hair with his warm breath. "Lively and exciting dances of romance."

Feeling the heat of his nearness creep through her body and unable to break the spell she was under, Emeraude looked into the Spaniard's dark eyes helplessly. "But I don't know how," she stammered, her voice barely a whisper.

"I will show you, lovely Emeraude. Come," he said, standing and pulling her to her feet to press her mesmerized body against his own muscular torso.

"First, you raise your arms like this," he whispered seductively as his hands glided up her arms, placing them above her head in an unclosed circle. Then slowly he caressed his way back down her arms, over the sides of her rising breasts, where he lingered ever so slightly, then on down to her hips.

110

"It's all in the hips," he instructed silkily, moving her lower body in slow circles against his own desire.

"My God!" Luis exclaimed in an astonished whisper. "He's going to take her right here and now!"

Staring transfixed into eyes of liquid coal, Emeraude continued to move in the sensual dance Reynaldo had shown her. With his face so close to hers; she couldn't resist as he danced her out the back entrance to the garden. And she was oblivious to the fact that his friends followed close behind.

"You dance so well," Reynaldo sneered, disgusted that this one had been no more challenge than any other he had met.

"Gracias," Emeraude uttered in a voice barely audible as her hips continued to rotate suggestively.

Suddenly, his mouth came down on hers, hard and brutal, crushing her tender lips with contempt.

Painful memories of other men and an enormous church cascaded in her thoughts. "Get away from me!" she screamed, striking out at her attacker with her hands and feet. "Let me go!"

"What is going on here?" a stern voice ordered, freezing the three junior officers in grotesque positions of panic.

"I repeat! What is the meaning of this behavior?" the booming voice demanded.

Reynaldo released his hold on Emeraude, allowing her to drop to the ground, and all three soldiers began talking at once in an attempt to explain as they clamored to attention.

"Silence! You men are on report, as of now! Is this how you treat supporters of the sovereign? We are here to punish and destroy *heretics,* not the daughters of

111

loyal Catholics. If I didn't know each of your fathers, I'd have the three of you hung. Now, back to camp with you—before I decide I don't need your fathers' kind thoughts!"

After watching to be sure all three of the men were on their way, the duke of Alva looked down at the petite girl on the ground. She had clutched her knees to her chest and was mumbling pathetically to herself. "No, no, let me go! Don't hurt me again! Please, don't."

The otherwise cold man felt a surge of sympathy for the pitiful creature on the ground and hunkered down beside her. "Señorita, let me help you inside."

The gentle voice of her champion drifted through Emeraude's mindless ramblings, and she was finally quiet.

"Come, little one. I will carry you," Alva said as he picked her up. "I apologize for my men. Please don't judge all Spaniards by their brashness!"

Emeraude slowly opened her eyes to look into the face of her savior. For a brief moment she felt as if she were gazing on the countenance of Satan, but she didn't care. It didn't matter who he was. He had saved her from being raped, and she was grateful, she admitted to herself, her eyes fluttering closed again.

When the duke carried her back into the tavern, he was met by Francois and Mignon, who were coming to tell him his room was ready.

Seeing their daughter in Alva's arms, Mignon and Francois ran frantically to the pair in the doorway. "What has happened to our little girl?" Mignon screamed.

"Forgive me, señora. She will be all right. She is not injured. Fortunately, I arrived in time. Some of my young officers were evidently overcome by drink, as well as by your daughter's beauty, and lost control of their good manners. I promise they will be punished severely for their unforgivable transgressions!"

"Thank God you were there to stop them monsieur. We are in your debt," Francois said gratefully. "Here, let me take her."

"If you will allow me, señor, I will see the little señorita to her bed. Then you may direct me to my own room." Alva's voice left no room for argument.

Mignon directed a confused glance toward her husband, then said, "Certainly, monsieur. Come this way."

Throughout her dreams that night, Emeraude saw a young man with hair the color of golden sand and eyes as blue as the summer sky. And she could hear that he was calling for someone. Listening carefully, she tried to understand what name he was shouting. She knew it was hers, but no matter how she concentrated, she couldn't quite make out what he was saying.

I'm here. Come closer, she called in her dream. But no matter how she tried, she found her voice made no sound. *I must run to him,* she decided. But as she started to run, her legs gave way, and she sank to the ground, her liquid limbs no longer able to support her.

As she melted into the earth, the man disappeared inside a great cathedral rising up from the fog. But long after the mist, the church, and the man were all gone, and nothing but blackness remained, she could still hear his lonely tormented call.

She bolted upright in her rumpled bed. "Don't leave

me, Dirk!" she cried aloud. "I'm here! Please come back!"

"What is it, *chérie?*" cried Mignon, lumbering on bare feet into Emeraude's room, her thick dark hair hanging loose down her back. "There, there, you've had a bad dream. It's no wonder. But see? Everything's all right now! Mama's here!"

"Oh, Mama, it was terrible," the frightened girl sobbed. "I tried to run, but I couldn't move. He was looking for me, but he couldn't find me. I could hear him calling my name, but he didn't hear me. Mama, it was so real!"

As Emeraude continued to weep, Mignon held her close and rocked her as one would a baby. "Who was trying to find you, *chérie?* Do you know what name he was calling out? Was he calling for Emeraude or someone else?" The woman felt certain the dream contained a clue to the girl's identity, and she knew she needed to press the issue.

"I don't know! I couldn't hear what he said." Emeraude closed her eyes for a moment to try to recreate the man's voice. Opening her eyes in frustration, she exclaimed, "I tried so hard to understand him. I just couldn't. But I know it was me he searched for!"

"Who was he, child?" Mignon prodded gently. "Do you know who he was? Did you recognize him?"

"Oh, yes, Mama! I knew him. I loved him and he loved me. I can still see his blue eyes and his lonely, forsaken face."

"Perhaps," Mignon suggested hesitantly. "Perhaps this evening's events have given you the nightmares, and this 'blue eyes' you have dreamed about is someone you have created in your mind to protect you. Our minds can play tricks on us, you know."

"No! He was real. He is real. I know in my heart he exists, and he's out there alone searching for me. I must find him, Mama!"

"*Oui,* you must find him; but for tonight, you must try to go back to sleep and think only good thoughts! Close your eyes, sweet girl; and Mama will sit here beside you until you slumber peacefully." Comforted by the large woman's nearness, Emeraude drifted into a welcome, dreamless sleep.

Chapter Seven

When she awoke with the first rays of light brightly illuminating her small room, Emeraude wondered at how well rested she felt.

She now knew there was a man with blue eyes who loved her and still searched for her; and she realized, at last, that she must seek out her past—at all costs. She could no longer stay hidden in the protective bosom of the Benner family. She had needed these months to heal, but now it was time to leave.

She lay in bed pondering the few clues she had to her previous life. There was the church she had remembered when she was in the garden last night. It had been in her dream, too. So it had to mean something. Only, in the dream, she'd been outside trying to get in. She closed her eyes and concentrated on remembering what the church looked like, and quickly realized it had been a cathedral the size of which could only have been in Brussels.

"So, I have a cathedral in Brussels and a blond-haired blue-eyed man who cares for me, and the fact that I was probably attacked by several men." That part was still very hazy, and she was able to look at it as if she were thinking about a stranger rather than herself. "What else?" she asked, sitting up in her bed and staring out the window.

Well, there was the fact that she spoke four languages. That meant she had an education, which was uncommon for a woman. Then there was the beautiful green-and-black brooch on the gold chain that she kept wrapped in a handkerchief and hidden safely under her mattress. But mostly, she had her dream—which seemed more real than anything. "If I can find the man in my dream, he'll be able to tell me all the answers!"

Strangely refreshed after her distressful night, she bounded out of bed. She felt as if she were returning to life after months of hibernation—months in which she had gathered the strength to unconditionally face her past, as well as the present.

"From now on, I will be the mistress of my own destiny!" she vowed to herself in the mirror. "No more hiding from my past. Whatever it is, and no matter how terrible it might be, I'm going to face it." *And I will find the man with the blue eyes if I have to search for a hundred years.*

When Emeraude ran into the kitchen to begin her daily chores, Mignon and Francois, who had been discussing the events of the evening before, were stunned by what they saw. Instead of the defeated and frightened girl they had expected to find abed this morning, they were bewildered to see a confident young woman of determination. Looking at each other quizzically, Francois and Mignon stood dumbfounded until Emeraude spoke.

"Well, what are you two staring at?"

"After last night . . ." Mignon gasped.

"*Oui!* After last night, we thought . . ." Francois stammered.

"*Oui,*" Emeraude laughed. "I thought so too! But you know what? We were wrong. I found out a great deal about myself last night. I remembered some of what happened on the day you found me; but most important of all, I discovered there is nothing that can destroy my spirit if I don't let it. I survived that day! I survived last night! And I'll survive the future, no matter what it is. I still don't know who I am or where I come from; but somehow last night has given me the courage to seek the answers to the questions I've avoided these past months."

"What do you mean?" Mignon asked uneasily.

"The time has come for me to leave here and go search for my past."

Hearing Emeraude's words as she entered the kitchen, Suzette cried out, "Oh, Emeraude, I don't want to lose you!"

"Don't be a silly goose," Emeraude laughed. "You aren't going to lose me. I promise. You will always be my family, for without you, I wouldn't even be! I'm certain I would have died by the river if you hadn't found me and shared your home and love with me. In a very real sense, you gave me life! I owe my existence to all of you," she said earnestly. Laughing, she added, "Just you try to get rid of me! No matter where my search takes me, I'll keep turning up on your doorstep!"

"Are you sure?" Suzette asked tearfully.

"Oui, little sister, I'm sure," she said, reaching up to wipe away the tears trickling down Suzette's cheeks. "Very sure!"

Taking a self-conscious swipe at the wetness in his own eyes, Francois said, "Well, we had better not stand around here all day! We have a very powerful guest, and he wants his breakfast brought to his room this morning!"

"No, *monsieur le duc* isn't the type of man one tells to come down to the table like the other guests!" Mignon chuckled, shaking her head and returning to her work.

"Let me take it up to him, Mama. I owe him my thanks. I don't think I told him last night how grateful I was for his aid, did I?"

"No, you temporarily forgot your manners last night," teased a relieved Mignon. "You had best make amends immediately. Go on and take him his tray. He's in the front room with the south breeze."

"Can I meet him too, Emeraude? I didn't hear him come in last night. I was out walking."

Emeraude looked lovingly at the younger girl and answered softly, "Perhaps later, sweet one. But for now, this is something I must do alone. I hope you understand."

"Oui," the disappointed girl answered as she watched Emeraude disappear up the stairs with the carefully prepared breakfast.

Lightly tapping on the door to the room where the man who had saved her was sleeping, Emeraude waited. Knocking a second time with slightly more force, she was answered by a muffled, *"Entre."*

Balancing the tray in one hand, she turned the knob to enter the room. There, with sleep still in his eyes and

119

rumpled hair, lay the infamous duke of Alva. How could she have likened his face to that of Satan? He looked like an ordinary man—a fact that surprised her enormously.

"Buenos días, Señor Duque," she announced cheerfully as she set the tray down beside the general's bed. "I trust you slept well."

"It appears I did, young lady. What time is it? I have never overslept in my entire life. It must be the cool night breeze that makes sleeping in the Netherlands such a pleasant experience. You mustn't tell anyone about this," he said seriously. "After all, I have my reputation to uphold!"

"Señor," she answered with equal gravity, "your secret is safe with me. It will be one way in which I can show my appreciation for your assistance last evening. I am truly in your debt!"

"You can be assured, my dear, the guilty scoundrels will be harshly dealt with. Again, let me apologize for their unthinkable behavior," he said, taking a bite of the huge breakfast. "Mmm, this is good, but entirely too much food for me to eat so early in the morning. Won't you share it with me?" he asked charmingly.

"I couldn't!"

"And why not?"

"It would be entirely improper—a girl such as myself sharing a meal with a gentleman of your importance!"

"But you said you are in my debt!" Alva argued. "And I really do need some assistance with this lovely meal, or I must return it unfinished to your dear sweet *madre*. I will dislike hurting her, but what else can I do if I must eat alone?" the elegant man asked with pretended sadness.

Tempted, Emeraude said, "Well, I haven't eaten yet. And I would hate to see Mama's feelings hurt—after she went to so much effort to fix it for you. But you must promise not to tell anyone that I was so disrespectful and lacking in good manners. Is it a promise?" she asked saucily.

"It is a promise, Señorita Esmeralda."

"Esmeralda?" she questioned, sitting down in a straight-backed chair beside the bed.

"Sí. Is not the Spanish word for emerald, *esmeralda?* She smiled shyly. "I suppose it is."

"When your parents called you Emeraude last night as I brought you in from the garden, I knew not why— that is, not until this morning when I saw your lovely green eyes. Do you mind that I prefer to call you Esmeralda?"

"No, I don't mind, señor. You may call me anything you wish," she replied, regarding the interesting man who spoke so kindly. Although not handsome, he intrigued her. In his early sixties, he had serious black eyes and a large aquiline nose. Cut short, his full dark hair showed almost no traces of gray, while his neatly trimmed beard was silvered throughout. Frequent worry had permanently lined his high forehead, and his thick black eyebrows cut strongly across his brow, shadowing his deep-set eyes and making them seem quite small. He wasn't a large man, but she remembered how safe she'd felt when he carried her in his arms.

"Tell me," Alva started. "How is it that you speak Spanish so well?"

"I don't know," she answered truthfully, looking into his probing eyes, an idea taking root in her mind.

121

Could this powerful man who had all the Netherlands quaking with fear be the one who could help her find her past?

"You don't know?" he laughed deeply. "Come now. That is not a statement you can leave hanging. You have me in suspense."

"My past is a complete mystery to me, señor," she explained. "I was found by the river last summer, and the Benners took me in and nursed me back to health. I had been beaten and was nearly dead when Suzette found me, and there's no doubt I wouldn't be sitting here talking to you if they hadn't cared for me."

Alva liked the warm glow that radiated from the beautiful girl when she spoke of those she loved. "You know nothing of your past?" he asked suspiciously.

Not feeling the necessity to share the actual events leading to her loss of memory, Emeraude shook her head. "Nothing."

"Do you mean you don't know if you're married, or if you're Catholic, or if you have a family?" he asked, astonished by the girl's unbelievable story.

"Oh, I know without a doubt I'm a Catholic, and I'm certain I'm not married. I don't know why I know these things. I just do. It's like the Spanish!" she said with a shrug.

"Up until now, I have been content to stay with the Benners and live as their daughter. However, last night I realized I must stop pretending to be who I am not and find out who I really am. But," she said sadly, "I don't know where to begin to find the answers."

Reaching across the breakfast tray, Alva put his long fingers on Emeraude's soft arm. "Come with me, Esmeralda. I will leave no stone unturned until I discover who you are," he urged.

She had only wanted his assistance—but to go with him? "I couldn't," she said, confused by his suggestion.

"You will be my interpreter!" he said propitiously. "As your parents know, my French is not perfect; and it would be to my advantage to have you at my side."

She hesitated. "I suppose I could discuss it with Mama and Papa."

"But what is there to discuss? They are not your true parents," Alva contended.

"They are all the family I have, and I would never do anything they would disapprove of," she said evenly. "I'm certain you can understand that, señor," she said, smilng sweetly, having regained her confidence.

"Very well, talk to them!" he said, finding it difficult to disguise his irritation. "But I warn you, my Esmeralda," he teased. "Once I decide I want something, I'm not accustomed to taking no for an answer."

"I can see that, señor. But perhaps you can see that I am not used to taking orders. So we both may need to make some concessions—should I choose to come with you!" she answered with the same half-teasing tone he had used.

Taking her hand as she extended it to remove the breakfast tray, Alva placed his lips softly on her upturned palm. "I shall await your answer most impatiently, dear lady."

"I won't keep you waiting too long," she laughed, feigning pity. Quickly picking up the tray, she rushed out of the room to leave him to his morning toilette.

Dashing down the back stairs excitedly, she considered how to break the news to the Benners. Of course, she would go with the duke, but it did him good to wait for her answer. She knew she would be beyond harm with the most powerful man in the Netherlands as her protector. There would be no more men who would try to use her for their own lustful purposes.

In the meantime, why shouldn't she use a man to achieve her goals? She would serve as interpreter for the duke of Alva and become his most trusted aide. And in return, he would help her find her past, and the blue-eyed man of her dreams.

"Mama, Papa, Suzette!" she shouted eagerly as she ran into the kitchen. "I have the most extraordinary news! The duke of Alva wants me to work as his interpreter while he travels through the Netherlands!"

"Oh, Emeraude, do you think that is wise?" Mignon asked in a troubled whisper.

"Daughter, remember what I told you about military men. Just because the duke is the commander of an army does not mean he is not still a soldier," Francois warned.

"Papa, I know I was foolish last night. In a way, though, I'm glad it happened. If the disgusting incident in the garden hadn't occurred, I would not have met *le duc,* nor would I have finally faced what I must do. Can't you see that I could easily have gone on living here my entire life? Not knowing where I belong or who I am. Just being content to be your little girl and never wanting to grow up! It would all have been so easy."

"Is the picture you paint so terrible, little one?" Francois asked sadly.

"Oh, no, Papa! Not terrible. Just unreal. In truth, I'm a grown woman, not a little girl. Don't you think it's time I begin to act like one?" she argued convincingly.

"But, Emeraude," Mignon cried. "With the duke of Alva? You've heard all the terrible things they are

124

saying about him."

"Yes, Mama, with the duke of Alva. No matter what they say about him, he is in the position to help me learn the truth about who I am. He has promised he'll leave no stone unturned. Surely you know I cannot continue to hide from the truth in the security of your home. We learned last night that even in this loving environment, no one is totally safe from the evils of the outside world. All we can do is our very best to overcome the hardship and sorrow that surrounds us and hope that in the future there will be a light at the end of the long tunnel. Don't you see, Mama? I have to go and search for that light. And it is your love that has given me the strength to endure whatever lies ahead!"

Suzette was crying pathetically. "Will you come see us, Emeraude?"

"Oh, yes, sweet little sister! Nothing could keep me away. And I will even write you letters! How many letters have you received in your life?" she asked the sobbing girl in an attempt to bring about a smile.

"None. You know I've never received a letter, Emeraude!" Suzette pouted.

"Well, now you will. I'll send you many letters from exciting places you have never seen. Now, aren't you glad I taught you to read? You'll have something to practice on!" she teased encouragingly.

"But I'd rather have you here helping me."

"I know, little one, I know," Emeraude sighed regretfully. "And I would rather be with you, but it can't be. I must go. The time has come!"

"I suppose you must, but we will worry, Emeraude," Francois reminded her. "I fear your decision has put you in grave danger. We will pray for you daily. You have been a good daughter, and you will always have a home with us."

"Oh, Papa, I do love you so much," she exclaimed tearfully, running into Francois's bearlike embrace. "What would I have done without all of you? You're so dear to me, and I will always love you."

Riding through the streets of Brussels, which were crowded with thousands of people straining to catch a glimpse of *le duc,* Emeraude struggled to fight the feeling of dread enveloping her. Her silent countrymen stared out of eyes filled with hate and loathing as the well-guarded carriage moved slowly through the streets. There were no cheers, no waves from the crowd—only frightening, deafening silence.

"Quite a welcome, is it not, *mi cariña?"* Alva asked, looking out from behind the dark curtained windows of the ornate black coach. "It seems the Netherlander is much less demonstrative and emotional than the Spaniard. In Spain, the people would be cheering and throwing flowers at a visiting dignitary."

Second thoughts about what she was doing colliding in her head, Emeraude couldn't look at him. *Can't you see the hate and fear in their eyes? Can't you see how much they despise you?*

Linking his arm with hers and patting her hand, Alva grinned in a way that made Emeraude feel even more uneasy. "Perhaps it is the warmer climate that makes for the hot blood of the Spaniard! Ah! Look ahead! We are coming to our destination. *Sí,* I think I will most definitely enjoy my stay in your country," he laughed with a wicked chuckle, as if he had thought of something terribly humorous.

Seeing the elaborate and enormous palace where Margaret de Parma held court, Emeraude was awed. Not only was she impressed by the immense structure, but she was overcome with the feeling that this was not her first visit to the castle. An idea exploded in her head. Maybe someone in the palace would recognize her! Maybe she would know her identity before the day was out.

Deeply involved in her thoughts about her elusive past, she was able to push her misgivings to the back of her mind. She was too excited about seeking out and solving the mystery of who she was. And by the same token, when she extended her hand to the duke in order to descend from the carriage, she was able to convince herself that the gleam in his dark eyes was only fatherly affection.

The welcome they received in court was slightly more friendly than in the streets, but Emeraude thought a man would have to be an utter ass—or the most conceited being in the world—not to feel the animosity surrounding him here. She knew the duke of Alva was not a fool, and she shuddered inwardly with the realization that he seemed to thrive on being hated and feared!

"Ah, Margaret, you are looking well," Alva exclaimed as the regent scurried across the distance to greet them. Emeraude noticed the duke remained stationary, forcing the powerful Margaret de Parma to come to him—as though he were the one receiving the visitor.

"And you, Fernando!" Margaret said through a strained smile. "You look younger than ever! But tell me, to what do we owe the honor of your visit? We've cleared up our little troubles of the fall. Surely you know I've kept Philip informed."

"Yes, my dear lady. But your brother feels it is time you had a man's assistance in rooting out heresy, once and for all! We don't want any repeat of that unpleasantness, do we?" he asked with an artificial smile. "But allow me to introduce my interpreter," he said suddenly, drawing Emeraude to his side. "Then we will settle in before you and I commence to discuss such mundane matters as how we will run the government of the Netherlands."

Noticing his definite emphasis on the "we," Margaret frowned before turning her attention toward the blonde girl who had been standing, almost hidden, behind Alva.

"Margaret," Fernando said charmingly. "Allow me to present Señorita Esmeralda Verde."

Choking at the sight of the familiar girl everyone thought to be dead, Margaret gasped, "My pleasure."

Then, paying no heed to Emeraude's shy curtsy, she turned a puzzled face to Alva and said seriously, "I must talk to you privately for one moment before you go to your room. It is most urgent! The servants will show your—uh—interpreter to her chamber!" she said nervously, signaling a man to come for Emeraude.

"Adjoining my own, I presume?"

"What?" the agitated regent asked absently. "Oh, of course, if you wish."

"Very well, then we will talk," Fernando conceded. Turning to Emeraude, he said, "You run along, *cara*. I will check on you shortly."

After rushing the servants and Emeraude from the room, Margaret turned back to Alva. "What is the meaning of this? Esmeralda Verde, indeed! Do you know who that young woman is?" she hissed threateningly.

"Why, she is my interpreter," he answered innocently. "And a very good one at that! Do you know that the señorita speaks four languages? Fluently!"

"You must think me a fool!" Margaret shouted, incensed by his assumption. "You know, and I know, that you have no need of an interpreter! That girl has been assumed dead for over six months. Where did you find her?"

"In a quaint little inn on the outskirts of the city, where she was serving beer to weary travelers who stopped there. I'd say I found a buried treasure, wouldn't you?" he asked calmly, enjoying Margaret's frustration and discomfort.

"Serving beer?" she repeated sarcastically. "I don't believe that. She's from a fine family in the south. She would hardly be working as a barmaid in some village inn! The girl you have had the gall to bring here, for God only knows what purpose, is Johanna van Ledenburg, the only daughter of the count of Ledenburg!"

"Are you sure my Esmeralda is your Johanna? She didn't seem to recognize you," he said with a baiting grin.

"Nonsense, I've known her and her family for years. She was with me several different times during the days before her disappearance," the regent scoffed, rejecting his suggestion acidly.

"That may be, my dear, but the poor girl has no memory of her past," Fernando said, his mouth turned down in feigned pity for Emeraude's sad state.

"No memory?" Margaret screeched, forgetting to keep her voice low.

"No memory!" Alva confirmed. "And I prefer to keep it that way until it suits my purposes to inform her of your suspicions as to her identity," he said, with more threat in his smile than any frown could have conveyed. "I wouldn't want to disappoint her if you are wrong."

"But how do you expect me to keep it from her? Surely I'm not the only one at court who will recognize her!" Margaret argued futilely. "Her disappearance caused quite a stir!"

"Then it will be your responsibility to remove those knowledgeable souls from her presence for the time being. Do I make myself clear?" he asked in a polite, even tone. "Now, is there anything else madame wishes to discuss with me before I retire to my chambers for a rest?"

Knowing she was helpless to remove the girl from Alva's evil web of lies, the displaced regent slowly shook her head. "No, Fernando, things will be arranged as you wish." She was defeated. "No one will admit to recognizing her."

"Good! I knew we would work well together, Margaret! Now, while I'm resting, I need for you to gather up your most trusted advisors, and we will meet in two hours to put into effect my plans to completely destroy the heresy that continues to plague the Netherlands!" Then he added, "By the way, you might let it be known that if any of your people feel compelled to repeat your assumptions about the señorita's identity, they will be beheaded within the hour of their betrayal."

Part Three—Esmeralda

Chapter Eight

When Emeraude entered the large meeting hall to assume her duties as Alva's secretary and interpreter, the duke of Alva and Margaret de Parma were in the midst of a heated discussion with the regent's advisors, whom she recognized from dinner the evening before. In no hurry to join the man she had already come to fear and loathe in the few hours she'd been in the palace, she took advantage of the fact that no one had noticed her presence and slipped farther into the shadows to wait.

Her mind heavy with anger at herself for trusting Alva when he had offered to help her find her family, she eyed him resentfully. *When will you learn?* she asked herself, remembering the moment when Fernando had revealed his true purpose for bringing her to the palace. *To men, you're not a person. You're a thing to be used for pleasure.*

A shudder of revulsion shook her small frame as she thought of the feel of his lips on hers when he had come to her room unannounced the afternoon before.

Swallowing back her nausea, she said a prayer of thanks that he'd been unable to follow through with his intentions, claiming he had too much on his mind. But his promise not to "disappoint" her the next time continued to roar in her ears. The next time!

Wrapping her arms across her middle, she gave a silent cry. *Oh, Lord, I can't bear it. Please tell me what to do!*

As if in answer to her plea, the duke of Alva's voice knifed into her thoughts, drawing her attention for the first time to what was being said at the large meeting table.

"According to my investigation of the situation here in the Netherlands, our problems are threefold. First, we must punish the leaders of the opposition for high treason. We must leave no doubt in the minds of others as to the consequences, should they, too, entertain ideas of *lèse-majesté*."

Margaret interrupted. "But many of the leaders of the original compromise have signed my Oath of Allegiance and have been instrumental in helping my army thwart the Calvinist attacks."

Shooting the woman who had broken his chain of thought a quelling glance, Alva continued speaking. "Secondly, we must insure that each town and province is completely dependent upon the central government."

Philip Croy, duke of Aerschot, ventured an opinion. "Is that wise, Your Excellency? Already the provincial governors and town councils resent the government's interference in their administrations. If you continue with your plan, you will be inviting the hostility of even the most loyal Catholics."

"And thirdly," Alva said pointedly, indicating there

was no room for an interchange of ideas in his policy, "we must secure a stable and constant source of income for the support of my government and army! I have begun to compile my roll of the men I know have been directly involved in disputing the king's sovereign power. Good lady, please have one of your pages immediately bring me the petition presented to you last year—the one brought to you by Brederode, Ledenburg, and Nassau."

In her inconspicuous spot in the shadows by the entry, Emeraude tensed. The three names Alva had listed sounded an alert in her brain. Did she know them? Could one of them be her relative?

Laughing bitterly at herself, she shook her head. They were probably just names she'd heard mentioned at dinner the night before. Just the same, it wouldn't hurt to hear what Alva was saying about them. Maybe he would let something slip that would give her an idea of where to start looking for her true identity. Squaring her shoulders, she stepped out of the shadows and cleared her throat.

The people at the table all turned toward the doorway, their startled gazes on Emeraude. "Ah! Here you are," Alva said with a wide smile, as he rose and extended his hand to her. "You're just in time."

To the others in the room, he laughed proudly. "I trust she can write as well as she looks—since there will be many names listed before we are through issuing our warrants!" No one laughed at his crude attempt at levity. Everyone in the room was fully aware that his plans for the future were anything but humorous.

Glancing with contempt at his unappreciative audience, he pulled out the chair for Emeraude. "I plan to found a council which I shall call the Council of Troubles. It will be our duty to hunt down and punish all those people considered responsible for the unpleasantries this country has experienced the last few years. We will have garrisons of soldiers billeted in every town, where they will roust out every Calvinist minister, every nobleman with Protestant leanings, every one of the iconoclasts and rebels who dared to destroy property of the Holy Catholic Church, and every doubter who has had the audacity to question the sovereign's laws in any way!"

"What will I do?" Emeraude asked. "Write the warrants?"

"Oh, no, *mi alma,* there will be scribes to do the routine scribbling. It will be your duty to keep my personal records. I will want to know how many warrants have been issued, and to whom; how many have been carried out, and when; the date of each trial, the punishment pronounced, and the time and place the execution is carried out."

Seeing her shocked expression, he hastily added, "If execution is necessary, of course! I'm certain most of your records will be of prison sentences, fines, and property confiscations," he explained with a sympathetic smile.

"How can this young woman be expected to handle such an enormous responsibility?" the senior scribe asked indignantly. Obviously he thought he should have been given the position as the right hand to the new governor.

"How indeed? I am pleased that you ask," Alva answered. "Señorita Verde is my interpreter and trusted personal secretary. As such, she will be my constant companion. Therefore, since I plan to oversee all of the trials myself, who better to keep my records of verdicts, punishments, and even my private correspondence? Are there any other questions or objections?"

"No, Your Excellency," the humiliated scribe replied.

"Now, if we can dispense with further interruptions, we will begin the first order of the day. Warrants! We will start drawing them up immediately. My plan is that they will all be delivered by my representatives throughout the country on the same day. Of course, until that day—say the ninth of September—no one outside this room will know whose names are on the warrants. But that goes without saying, does it not?" he laughed nefariously.

The duke of Aerschot was first to speak. "But of course!" He smiled ingratiatingly at Alva. "You can trust your confidences to be kept within these walls until you are prepared to release them. With whom do you plan to begin? I suggest we start with the most well known troublemakers, William of Orange and his Calvinist brother, Louis of Nassau!"

"But William is a Catholic and has remained loyal to the government and to the king!" Margaret interjected.

"Dear lady, may I remind you Orange refused to sign your Oath of Unconditional Allegiance?" Aerschot snarled in disgust.

"No, he didn't sign the oath," she admitted softly. "But only because he believes in religious freedom for the Netherlands. Not because he is a traitor. Don't forget, it was Orange who upheld our authority when Brederode attacked Antwerp."

His lip curling with hate for the prince of Orange, Aerschot reminded the regent, "He was stirring up trouble as early as 1561. Have you forgotten his efforts against your very own advisor, Granvelle, when he and Egmont and Hoorne announced they would not attend the Council of State as long as he was in office? Then, even after Granvelle was unjustly removed because Orange didn't care for his 'repressive religious and political policies,' Orange publicly stated that the king didn't have the right to rule over the religious consciences of his subjects. Do you call this a loyal subject, dear lady?"

Taking advantage as Aerschot paused in his wrathful accusations of Orange, Berlaymont, one of Margaret's staunch supporters, spoke out. "But he has always been a champion for the sovereign! The only reason he wants to pursue a moderate policy is to prevent a rebellion."

Glaring at Berlaymont, his look saying he'd deal with the other man at a later time, Aerschot's voice rose to a high-pitched shrill. "You defend Orange? You defend the man who presumed to order the king of Spain to change his edicts against heretics? You defend the traitor who walked out of the Council of State when the monarch refused to lower his standards. This causes me to wonder about your own loyalties, sir!"

Margaret spoke in defense of Berlaymont. "We are defending nor condemning no one, Philip; but before you have the prince of Orange arrested, we do want it known that he supported us last fall when times were most difficult."

"Well, that may be, dear Margaret," Alva said condescendingly. "But I agree with Philip Croy. Orange shall have the honor of receiving the first warrant issued by our Council of Troubles. I told the king four years ago that he should get rid of the man. And the time for action is definitely at hand! I assume there is no further discussion of William of Orange." There was none.

"Good." He turned his satisfied smile on Emeraude. "Esmeralda, you may enter the names of William, prince of Orange, and his brother Louis, prince of Nassau, at the top of your parchment—followed by the names of Lamoraal, the count of Egmont, and Filips van Montmorency, the count of Hoorne," he dictated to her.

Her hand shaking with the sudden realization that she was listing the names of her countrymen whom Alva was planning to destroy, Emeraude picked up the quill and dipped it into the ink.

Obviously helpless to defend her friends, Margaret made one last attempt to stop the madness she could see enveloping them. "Egmont and Hoorne are both Knights of the Golden Fleece! My brother has made it law that they can only be tried by their own order. Besides, they signed the oath!" she protested hopelessly.

Emeraude paused with her pen on the parchment and looked up questioningly.

"No Golden Fleece member is exempt from punishment if he is guilty of stirring up plots against the sovereign. Continue writing, Esmeralda," Alva ordered.

Her posture defeated, the ousted regent sat back and observed the young girl she had known as Johanna van Ledenburg write deftly and quickly the names of people certain to be executed—if they hadn't been wise enough to leave the country already, as she herself planned to do immediately. There was nothing more for her in the Netherlands.

So the day passed, well into the afternoon, and the pages grew in number as the scribes and Emeraude wore out quills and exhausted ink supplies. All four hundred names on Brederode's petition were singled out for arrest—Calvinists and Catholics alike. The list contained the names of commoners, wealthy noblemen, Lutherans, Catholics, and Calvinists. It seemed no one was safe: Hendrik, the count of Brederode; Matthew the count of Ledenburg, and his sons, Frans, Helst and Hugo; Dirk Corlear, the count of Leuven . . . and so went the list, on and on until Emeraude was sure her fingers would be permanently curved in their writing position.

But as the list grew, so did her understanding of what she had to do.

Following dinner in her room, Emeraude massaged her cramped fingers as she intently studied the man with whom she had shared her meal. "Are you really going to arrest all of those men?" she asked in disbelief.

"Oh course I am! Why do you ask?"

"But what if they are all guilty? What will you do with them? Surely the prisons can't hold them all?" she reasoned.

"Have no doubt, my love, they are all guilty. They would not be on my docket if they were not culpable; but don't you worry your pretty head. I'll think of suitable punishments for them."

She felt a dull ache in her heart in reaction to his secret smile. "It sounds as though you've condemned them before you've heard all the facts!" she accused, fighting the tremble in her voice.

"Of course not," Fernando denied, seeming hurt that she would think such a thing. "They will all have trials and will be judged under the due course of the law!"

Wisdom bid Emeraude to hold her tongue before she betrayed her own purpose, so she smiled sweetly, pretending to have lost interest in the subject. "That's good," she yawned, deliberately hiding the anxiety and feelings of helplessness she was experiencing. *My God! I've got to do something. I can't stand by and see my countrymen executed for their beliefs.*

"Here, let me do that, sweet Esmeralda," Fernando said, his words cutting surprisingly into her thoughts. Reaching for her stiff hand, he began to knead the aching digits. "Does it pain you so much?" he sympathized, drawing her fingers to his moist lips. "Did I make you work too hard?"

"No, I'm fine. It's just that I'm tired after such a long day. I didn't sleep well last night."

"I'm so sorry. Well, we must see that you sleep tonight, mustn't we? Let me help you relax," he suggested, reaching for the fastenings on her dress.

Knowing what was coming, Emeraude felt the muscles of her body tighten convulsively, but she managed to hide her fear and disgust behind her smile.

With expert hands, Alva quickly removed her clothing down to her chemise, then carried her to the bed. Laying her on her stomach, he sat beside her exhausted body to rub the tension from her back with vigorous circular motions, pressing and squeezing.

Relaxing in spite of her dread, she didn't even notice when she drifted mercifully to sleep.

Secretly relieved he would not have to run the risk of failure again, Fernando quietly covered her with the sheet and left the room.

When Emeraude awoke the following morning, she felt alone and afraid. *I've got to warn all those people. If only I could talk to Papa. He'd help me think of a way.*

But he's not here, a stern inner voice reminded her. *You can no longer hide behind Emeraude. You are all alone now, with only yourself to depend on. From this moment forward you must be Esmeralda Verde, until you have stopped the duke of Alva once and for all.*

Sitting up suddenly, as if shaking off the last negative and helpless thoughts of the girl she could be no more, she concentrated on devising a scheme to undermine Alva's unprincipled scenario.

I'll become indispensable to him so that I know his every secret. Then I'll find a way to get word to the people he plans to condemn. I may not be able to stop him altogether, but I will definitely put a hole in his evil plot if it takes my last ounce of breath.

A sickening thought occurred to her, and she almost reverted back to being the old Emeraude. *What if he is able to . . . ?*

She took a deep breath and set her expression. "From this moment on, I am Esmeralda Verde, and I will do anything I must do to destroy the duke of Alva!"

Uplifted by her positive plan of action, she vaulted out from under the covers and began her morning toilette, and when Fernando entered her room a few minutes later, he was surprised to find her dressed and ready to begin work.

Cheerfully turning to greet him, she exclaimed, "Good morning, Fernando. I'm so sorry I fell asleep last night," she teased, deliberately putting her plan into action.

"Are you now?" he answered, with mocking sternness. "I'm not certain I can forgive you. I was hurt beyond repair by your rejection," he chided.

"Oh, you must forgive me. Please?" she pouted beguilingly. "I'll be miserable if you don't."

"Only because I possess such a forgiving nature, and because you are such an excellent secretary, I suppose I can be persuaded to hear your appeal," he said, taking her into his arms and kissing her.

Choking back the vile taste that rose in her mouth when he kissed her, she pretended to respond, pulling away as quickly as she could without rousing his suspicions. "Thank you. You are so kind, and I will do my best to be deserving of your kindness," she cooed, exacting the false words from her throat with determination.

The next days were occupied with record keeping and personal correspondence for Alva, with little time for anything else. And much to Esmeralda's relief, when they returned to their chambers each evening, both were so tired that the duke made no further attempts to make her his mistress, leaving her alone in her chamber to write diligently until late at night as she compiled a duplicate list of names to the ones she had written that day.

However, to all outward appearances, Esmeralda Verde was Alva's mistress. She seemed to hang on every word her lover spoke, laughed at all of his tasteless attempts at humor, and agreed with every decision he made. She worked with an energy that shamed the scribes who had thought the position was too great an undertaking for a woman, especially one so young, and no one could fault her for her aptitude for taking care of details to perfection.

By the first of September, not only had Esmeralda written the names of over one thousand accused traitors in the ledger and several missives to King Philip II, but she had learned Alva's most confidential plans—plans known only to himself and his trusted secretary, Esmeralda Verde!

She had discovered that the duke planned to arrest and deport Philip William, the son of William of Orange and a student at the Catholic University of Louvain. This, he had told her, would bring the boy's father out of hiding in Germany. However, when William came to discuss his son's release, he would discover that all of his property and possessions had been confiscated and turned over to the duke of Alva's treasury; and then he would be tried, convicted and executed by the Council of Troubles!

Fernando had also confided that he planned to invite Counts Egmont, Hoorne, Ledenburg, and Leuven, who were all still in the Netherlands, as well as the lesser nobles that rode with Brederode, to meet him at a special conference to reconcile their differences with the crown. "Of course, it will be a farce!" he bragged. "I have no intention of appeasing them. When I get them here, all together, we will go through the motions of reaching an agreement; and then I will have them publicly arrested as an example to all of their would-be followers!"

"What about the other warrants?" Esmeralda inquired, fighting to keep the panic from her voice as she pretended fascination with his great cleverness.

"Yes, the others. They will all be arrested on that

same day. My officers will be awaiting my signal, and as soon as the 'mice' are in my trap here in Brussels, the others will be invited to join them!" he laughed wickedly.

"It sounds very well organized! Will Orange's son be arrested on the same day?" Though her voice was calm and displayed great admiration, Esmeralda's mind was flying frantically to find a way to save the boy who had done nothing to justify his arrest.

"Absolutely! September the ninth will be a day remembered throughout the Netherlands. After that day, no one will dare to speak against the king or his laws. Once that day comes, Protestants and Calvinists will be lining up to convert to Catholicism—or to leave the country," he chuckled perversely.

"Yes," he continued proudly. "After that day, they'll convert—or burn!"

Esmeralda almost lost control of her nonchalant facade and gasped, "Burn?"

"Or hang," Alva chortled. "Then, I may behead a few. That will give everyone something to think about, won't it?"

"I imagine it will," she responded in a low voice, smiling in an attempt to regain the composure that had been lost momentarily.

Knowing she could wait no longer to put the rest of her plan into action, she put down her sewing and went to Alva. "You work too hard. We ought to get away for a while. Do you suppose we could manage a day at the inn with my family? It would be so relaxing. And I miss them terribly. I've written them letters, but it would make my happiness complete if I could spend some time with them. Just a day," she said winsomely.

"I can't get away right now, with all my plans coming together in less than two weeks," he apologized.

"Yes, of course," she said, allowing the disappointment to show obviously on her face and in her trembling voice. "I don't know what I was thinking of to ask."

"There, there, don't be sad. Perhaps we can work something out. Let me think. After all, I don't want my sweet girl to be unhappy, do I?" he consoled, lifting her chin to look into her eyes just as the tears flowed over the edges and trailed heartbreakingly down her delicate cheeks.

"No," she sobbed, allowing herself to be held in his arms while he determined what could be done to return the smile to her face.

"I know!" Fernando shouted excitedly. "You can go alone, with a female companion and my most trusted guards, of course," he offered magnanimously.

Thrilled that he had unknowingly gone along with her plan, Esmeralda hesitated only long enough to be effective. "But my work. I'd feel terrible if you needed me and I were not here."

"Now don't you worry about that. I will miss you terribly, but I'm certain the idiots Margaret used as scribes can do your work for one day. Of course, I will keep my confidential matters for your return," he smiled, wanting her to know she couldn't really be replaced—even for one day.

"Oh, Fernando, thank you," she gushed, throwing her arms around his neck in gratitude. "You are so generous and thoughtful!"

Deciding it would be best to pretend to have second thoughts, she added, "But are you certain it won't inconvenience you too greatly?"

"No, I'll be fine. You go and have a good time. I will take care of things here. Perhaps after we get the arrests started, you and I can go away together for a few days. When I don't have so many matters of such great importance on my mind, I'll really be able to show you how much I appreciate your presence in my life! How does that sound?"

Swallowing back the truth, she said, "Oh, Fernando, it sounds wonderful. But when shall I go to see Mama and Papa? I'm so excited, I don't see how I can wait!" She knew she must go right away if she was going to do any good at all. To wait much longer would be devastating to her plan.

"Well, why should you wait? Why not go tomorrow?" he suggested bigheartedly.

"Tomorrow," she squealed. "Really? But how can I be ready so soon?" she asked, knowing full well that she was already prepared—had been for days!

"That's what servants are for, my dear. Now suppose we get you to bed, since it appears you will have a big day tomorrow!"

Hugging him affectionately one last time before he left her, she whispered gratefully, with more appreciation than he could have understood, "Thank you, Fernando."

Nadine, the old seamstress who had made her new wardrobe for her and had become her only friend in the palace, arrived before the sun was up to help Esmeralda prepare for the day's outing. The old woman was excited about the trip and fussed animatedly as she

147

hurried around the room checking and rechecking the preparations.

"Nadine, it's just for one day," Esmeralda laughed. "We'll be back this evening."

"I know, girl. But it's been a very long time since I had a day in the country air, and I'm looking forward to it!"

"I am, too, and I'm very pleased that you will be accompanying me," she told the woman warmly.

Touched by Esmeralda's sincerity, the old woman turned away to blow her nose, complaining that something must have gotten into her eye.

In her own excitement, Esmeralda was barely able to eat breakfast; and when the carriage drove into the courtyard, she and Nadine were already waiting anxiously to board. The coachmen loaded their bundles—imported cheeses, wines, Ethiopian coffee beans, a basket of fresh fruit, and a bolt of pink lawn for Suzette—and they were on their way shortly after dawn.

When they had been on the road for about an hour, Nadine breathed a loud sigh of relief and suddenly turned to face her young charge. "I'm worried about you, missy."

Surprised, Esmeralda frowned. "Me? Why would you be worried about me?"

"I know it's not my place to speak out. But the truth is, I've become real attached to you, and I've got to tell you, you're in danger. There's many who hate the duke even more than the king."

"Yes, Nadine, I know," Esmeralda answered.

"Just you mind my words. There's talk of another rebellion starting, and this time it won't only be the

Calvinists fighting, I'm afraid. When it starts, anyone who's been close to the duke will be a target for their hatred."

Esmeralda smiled sadly. "I appreciate your concern, dear friend. But I'll be all right."

"That's not the only reason. There are them that are jealous of your place of influence beside him. And they would do anything to remove you from your important position! Some say you're a traitor to the Netherlands, or you wouldn't be helping him achieve his evil deeds. Others say you have him under a spell. They call you the 'green-eyed sorceress.' I've wanted to tell you of the danger you're in, but this is the first chance I've had. Promise me you'll be cautious."

"Green-eyed sorceress?"

Nadine nodded solemnly. "I've told them that kind of talk is foolishness, but . . ."

"Thank you for defending me, Nadine. But from now on you just join them in their hatred of me so they will continue to speak freely in front of you. I will tell you one thing, though. I'm not at the palace by choice, and I would give my life for my country's freedom from tyranny. But you must tell no one! To tell you more would endanger your life. However, I do want you to know how I have longed for a trusted friend at the palace, and I'm so pleased that I have found you." She patted the older woman's hand and returned her gaze to the window, hardly noticing the panorama of late-summer colors which flew by in a blur.

Though Nadine's information was not a surprise to Esmeralda, she was hurt and frightened. The thought of home and the sanctity of Emeraude's old room was almost more than she could bear. She prayed that

Francois and Mignon had not heard the rumors of her rising reputation at court, and that they would be willing to help her try to stop the madness descending evilly upon their country.

But she had no cause to worry, for the Benners showed no signs of reproof as they ran to greet her. They only displayed evidence of love and trust, and Esmeralda scolded herself for thinking it might be otherwise. After introducing Nadine and the guards to her adopted family, she gave her escorts permission to enjoy the comforts of the inn and tavern. Nadine went immediately to inspect the kitchen.

Asking Suzette to go make sure the old woman wasn't getting in Mignon's way, Esmeralda turned to Francois, the expression on her face grave. "I need to talk to you alone, Papa."

Chapter Nine

Holding hands, Francois and Esmeralda walked along the path near the inn. No one would have suspected the pair to be other than a father and daughter enjoying a pleasant reunion, for despite the fact that they deliberately kept their voices low, Esmeralda giggled frequently to confuse any witnesses.

"I knew we should have kept you here with us," Francois said guiltily, glancing around to make certain the guard who was following them at a discreet distance could see his big grin. "You must come home immediately." The urgency in his tone was obvious, in direct contradiction to his jovial facial expression.

"Papa, you know I can't do that!" she insisted. "If I express a desire to leave him, I'll lose all the power I've gained these past few weeks. Right now, he trusts me more than anyone else in the palace. And as long as he does, I have to use that trust to save as many Netherlanders as I can," she argued fervently.

"But, daughter, it's such a risk," Francois groaned unhappily. "If you're discovered, your neck will be on the gallows along with the others!"

"Then I will just have to make sure he doesn't find out my plans!" she reasoned. "I'm hoping you'll be able to help me. I hate to involve you in this, but I don't know where else to turn. You're the only one I can trust. I can't simply stand by and watch our innocent countrymen be executed."

"No, of course we can't just stand by, *chérie*. Since the duke's arrival, people have been very uneasy and are speaking out less, but I'm still aware of travelers who are sympathetic to taking the Netherlands out of the hands of the voracious Spaniards and putting it back under the control of our people. Though what you propose will be very dangerous, I'm certain we can find several who are willing, even eager, to help us," he added confidently, his interest growing.

"Good. I've written brief notes to the people he plans to deceive by inviting them to his conference. If you can find trustworthy messengers to carry the letters, maybe we can stop some of those men from coming to this deceitful meeting. They, in turn, if they take our warning seriously, can get word to the others throughout the country who are slated for arrest on that same day!"

"But from what you tell me, Emeraude, there are thousands of men earmarked for arrest. How will we ever get word to all of them?"

"Oh, Papa," she cried anxiously. "I lie awake nights worrying about those men. I have reason to believe many are already out of the country, and I pray more will follow when my messages get through. It's the best we can do. We just have to hope to save as many as possible. I don't know what else to do!"

152

"It's a good plan, Emeraude."

"You can see why we have no choice, can't you? A country robbed of all its leaders could become a country of slaves to a foreign power. We can't let that happen! We mustn't allow it!" she said emphatically, her fists clenched in determination. "I am prepared to give my life to see that Alva's plans are thwarted!"

Francois agreed, his pride for his adopted daughter overshadowing the fear in his heart. "If only we are in time. What do you want me to do first?"

"After we eat, I'll retire to my room for a rest. I'll quickly put the finishing touches on my letters and put them under the mattress with instructions on where to send each one. As soon as I leave, you must retrieve them! I don't want Mama or Suzette to find them. There's no use in frightening them, is there?" she said with a sad smile.

"What is it, my dear? You seem a million miles away," coaxed Fernando at breakfast several days after Esmeralda had returned to her duties in the castle.

"Oh, nothing, really. I was just thinking about the nice visit I had with my family and how kind it was of you to arrange it," she lied.

"Well, there will be many more, once my conference is over!" he promised. "Now, run along and get dressed so we can go to work. I'm hoping to receive a great many more acceptances today and tomorrow to my generous offers of reconciliation."

"Oh, yes, the invitations," she said, taking care that the interest in her voice was not too evident. "Do you suppose they've all been delivered?"

"I'm certain they have. Already I've had replies from Egmont and Hoorne, gratefully accepting my gesture of rapprochement. Several of the lesser nobles who signed Brederode's foolish petition have also eagerly promised to be present. It will be a grand event!"

"Congratulations. It would appear your plan is destined for success!" Esmeralda sighed, brushing out her hair with vigorous strokes to hide her disappointment.

"Did you have any doubt?" he gloated.

"No, of course not. You have a great talent for achieving your goals, no matter what they may be. You're a very clever and powerful man, Fernando." Her adoring smile did not quite reach her eyes, but Alva didn't notice. He was too pleased with her opinion of his greatness.

But Esmeralda took his knowing smile as evidence of something else. *He knows!* she thought as he left the room without further words. *But how? Were my letters intercepted? Oh, what if I've brought harm to Papa? Did anyone at all receive my warnings?*

Screaming hysterically, Katryn van Ledenburg threw her hands over her face after reading the letter of warning her husband showed her.

"Don't worry, Katryn. We'll go to Germany until things seem safer. I won't go to the meeting," he promised. Catching her in his arms and turning her face to him, he was able to see for the first time the full extent of her horror. "What is it, Katie? I don't understand!"

"That letter!" she shrieked. "Didn't you recognize

154

the handwriting? That warning came from Johanna!"

Matthew choked back his shock. "Don't be foolish, Katryn," he said firmly, his heart breaking anew for his wife's sorrow. "Johanna is dead!"

"She's not dead!" Katryn screamed. "I've never believed she was, and that letter is proof!" She pointed emphatically to the parchment still in Matthew's trembling hand. "That's Johanna's handwriting on that warning!"

"Stop doing this to yourself, this instant!" He shook her, desperate for her to listen to reason. "It only resembles her writing. It's a coincidence! Nothing more! You've got to quit carrying on like this, Katie," he groaned, pulling her against his barrel chest and trying to calm her with soothing strokes. "She's dead, Katie. Let her go. Our Johanna is dead."

But Katryn would not be pacified, and she shook off his embrace. "Matthew, you must believe me! It is Johanna! I know her handwriting like I know my own! No one but Johanna makes her S's and T's like this," she argued, pointing to the squiggles on the paper. "See?"

"But it can't be! Where could she have been all this time? No!" he said unyieldingly, fighting his own tears and the tiny spark of hope his wife's foolishness had ignited. "I refuse to be caught up in your imaginings and wishful thinking! Our girl is dead, Katryn!"

"But, Matthew, don't you see? Whoever wrote that letter is in the palace and knows secrets of the government. Couldn't she be a prisoner there? Perhaps she can't get away but managed to find a way to warn us of the danger—when she's in danger herself!"

"Katryn, please stop this." Matthew's whisper was

an anguished plea for mercy. "It can't be Johanna. If it were, she'd have signed the letter some way! She'd have thought of a way to let us know she was alive."

"My God, Matthew! I tell you, it *is* Johanna! She's not dead, and we must find a way to get to her! If you won't go for her, I'll go alone!" she vowed.

"All right, Katie, we'll think of a way to discover who is responsible for this letter," Matthew conceded, not wanting to add any more fuel to his wife's unreasonable delusions.

"But how? You can't go to Brussels. According to Johanna's letter, it's a trap! You'll be arrested and executed! She says we should go into hiding immediately."

"We can pack our things and leave here tonight. We'll be safe in Germany. But as soon as I get all of you to safety, I'll come back and find out the truth about the warning," Matthew suggested, seeing this as the only way to get his wife to leave.

"Yes, that is the only answer. Oh, pray God that she'll be safe until we can find her!" Katryn cried, smiling through her tears. "She was dead, and now she's alive. We'll see her soon, Matthew! I can scarcely believe it, but I know it with all my heart to be true!"

It hurt Matthew to witness his wife's continued grief, but he was at a loss to know what to do about it. She had never fully recovered after Johanna's disappearance, keeping to herself and only finding occasional comfort in drug-induced sleep. Maybe this bit of false hope would get her through the difficult days to come more easily.

"Yes, that's what we'll do. We'll leave tonight after dark and go to Dusseldorf to join the prince of Orange.

I understand he's gathering forces to fight Alva. With my family safe, I'll be able to concentrate on what to do about saving our property—and Johanna," he told her patiently.

Gently taking the crumpled letter from Katryn's hand, Matthew reread the words one last time, as if memorizing the contents, then tore it to shreds before burning it.

"Why did you do that?" Katryn shouted, frantically trying to put out the tiny flame burning in the silver tray.

"Let it burn, Katie," Matthew bid her. "If this is our Johanna, no other eyes but ours should see that letter. Whoever wrote it would not be safe from discovery should it fall into the wrong hands."

Sadly watching the destruction of the only proof she had of her daughter's existence, Katryn stared at the glow until there was nothing but ashes and a blackened spot where the fragments of paper had been.

Turning their backs on the charred bits of paper, the two walked up the stairs to sadly begin their preparations for evacuating their home, knowing they might never be able to return to its comfort. However, before they could reach the upper level of the house, they heard excited voices in the entryway and turned to discover the source of the disturbance.

"I tell you, I'm Dirk Corlear, the count of Leuven, and I must see Count Ledenburg immediately!"

"Very well, sir, I will announce you," the voice of the frightened servant answered. "Please wait here."

"I have no time for waiting. I'll announce myself!" Dirk bellowed, shaking off the restraining hand on his sleeve and knocking the servant aside.

157

Matthew dashed down the stairs, running full force into a man with dirty hair and a shaggy beard which had been dyed a dark, ugly color. "Dirk, my boy! What is it? What has happened to you? I wouldn't have known you if I hadn't recognized your voice!"

"I've been with Brederode in France—trying to round up an army," Dirk explained hastily. "When I heard Alva had arrived in the Netherlands, I came as soon as I could to see my mother and check on our properties. While I was there I received an invitation from the duke requesting my presence at a reconciliation meeting," he said tiredly.

"The same invitation was delivered here, but . . ."

"Then," Dirk went on, his voice sounding exhausted, "the following day I received another letter from the palace, this one unsigned, warning me that the conference was a cruel joke of Alva's. I was told he has a bizarre plot to arrest and execute all the lords who signed Brederode's petition on that day, as well as Orange, Egmont, Hoorne, and many others."

"We received a similar warning—just today!" Matthew said, the creases between his brows deepening discernibly. "What do you think it means? Do you think the warning is to be trusted?"

"I rode all night to tell you I don't think we can ignore this. I believe you should take your family and leave the country. In the meanwhile, I'll go to Brussels disguised as a peasant and find out the truth. Then I'll come for you. My mother will be here this evening. I'm hoping you'll take her with you and care for her until I can."

"Of course we will." Matthew smiled comfortingly, the concern evident in his blue eyes. "But I hate to see you get so close to the Red Devil—especially if these letters of warning speak the truth."

"I'm inclined to think they do, Matthew," Dirk laughed bitterly. "Reconciliation and cooperation are not ordinarily Alva's ways of operating, I'm afraid. The warnings make more sense to me than his friendly overture!"

"Oh, Dirk! Has Matthew told you the news?" Katryn proclaimed joyfully, bursting into the room where they stood.

"Mother! Now is not the time!" Matthew warned.

"Nonsense," she chided happily. "Dirk! Johanna is alive!"

"Katryn! I told you to be silent until you knew for certain," her husband scolded furiously.

"But I am certain, Matthew!" she argued stubbornly. "The letter, dear! Tell Dirk about the letter!" she demanded proudly.

Knowing he must explain to the stunned young man before his wife could do any more damage, Matthew said, "Katryn is convinced the handwriting on the letter of warning is Johanna's. I told her it's only a coincidence, but she refuses to listen. I'm sorry, my boy! I wouldn't have hurt you like this for the world!"

Silently, Dirk pulled his own letter from his shirt and examined it closely.

Tears gathered in his eyes as he read. Heedless of the wet tracks the tears made down his grimy cheeks, he looked up at the Ledenburgs, his expression helpless. "Why didn't I see it before?" he asked, his voice breaking as he glanced at the warning once more. "How can it be true? They said they killed her!"

Jumping in excitedly, Katryn exclaimed, "No! I

remember you said they left her 'for' dead! Not actually dead. Don't you see? They *thought* she was dead, but by some miracle of Fate, she survived!"

"Why didn't she come to me?" he asked, his words making almost no sound.

"Maybe she tried and couldn't find you? Perhaps she was ashamed and couldn't face you. Possibly she's been a prisoner all this time!" Katryn suggested. "I don't know, Dirk, but I do know that these letters were written by my daughter, and no other!"

Seeing the truth of his wife's discovery in Dirk's tortured demeanor, Matthew suddenly felt as if a weight had been lifted off his shoulders to be replaced by an even greater burden. "I must go to Brussels and find her!"

"No, Matthew!" Dirk said firmly, his posture straightening with determination and new hope. "You must take everyone to Dusseldorf and safety while I go to Brussels, as planned. There's no need for both of us to go. I'll bring Johanna to you as soon as I can!" Turning specifically to Katryn, his voice exceptionally stern, he added, "You must tell no one of these letters or of our suspicions that Johanna is alive! To do so would endanger her. Do you understand, Katryn?"

"Yes, Dirk. We won't mention this to anyone until you're both safely back with us. You're a good boy— like one of my own sons. I know you'll find my baby and bring her home to us." She patted his tearstained cheek and left him and her husband so she could begin packing for her flight from their homeland.

It was a moonless night when the Ledenburgs,

160

together with Marta van Leuven and most of the Ledenburg servants, left under cover of darkness for the safety of Germany.

Riding with the family as far east as Ramillies, Dirk took leave of his loved ones two hours before dawn, sadly watching them until they disappeared into the darkness, knowing he might not see them again. Yet, he was comforted by the knowledge that they would be out of danger; and with the people he loved under the protection of William of Orange in Germany, he knew he would be free to do the things he must do—fight, or even die, for the Netherlands and Johanna.

With the approaching dawn, he found a deserted barn, where he watered and fed his horse before lying down to rest until the shadows of night would once more afford him the cloak of blackness he would need to slip unnoticed into Brussels.

As the ninth of September approached, Esmeralda grew more tense by the hour. She found eating and sleeping impossible, fearing discovery, and not knowing if Francois had been able to deliver any or all of the messages—or if they'd been intercepted.

The morning of Alva's long-anticipated coup de main found her abed with a foul stomach and aching head, certain she would collapse should she try to rise. "Surely you can manage to take some breakfast, Esmeralda," Fernando coaxed, his impatience stinging in his tone.

"I don't think I can eat a thing, Fernando. I'm sorry. I know you're angry with me, but I really am too sick to get out of bed. Please forgive me!" she begged.

"No!" he shouted. "I have no intention of forgiving you. I expect you to be beside me today, and you will be there! Not only do I wish for you to take notes, but I feel that having one of their own countrywomen at my side will convince them of my good faith. I want the arrests to come as a complete surprise, and I expect to have you with me when I deal the final blow to your country's traitors!"

"And I had planned to be there, Fernando. Really I did!" she insisted weakly, the throbbing in her head having reached a clangorous crescendo. "But I don't see how I can manage it."

"Enough of this!" he yelled, his bearded face contorting with anger. "You will stand with me today, sick or not. Willing or not. Do you understand me, Esmeralda? Now, eat something and get yourself dressed!" His smile was hard and cold and sent an involuntary shiver of fear rippling through her.

"But Fernando . . ." Seeing the violence welling in the duke's dark eyes, she stopped midsentence and sat up dizzily on the edge of her bed.

"Either dress yourself, or I will do it for you," he said menacingly. "And I will be very unhappy if I have to use my valuable time to pamper your weakness. Have I made myself clear, Esmeralda?"

"*Sí,* Fernando. You've made yourself perfectly clear. I will dress myself," she whispered, resigned to her fate.

When the duke of Alva finally left her room, desperate thoughts continued to bombard her pounding head in a death-knell rhythm. *He knows what I've done and he's going to arrest me when he takes the others. How did I think I could warn so many people without being discovered? It was inevitable that someone would inform on me.*

In the middle of the storm of negative thoughts, however, her stronger self suddenly took control, and she was able to gather the strength to face whatever would befall her on that day. *If I am to be arrested, at least I can accept my fate with grace. I'll not go to the gallows groveling and whining or begging for his contemptible mercy. After all, if I have been exposed, at least everyone will know I tried to help the Netherlands. No one will call me a traitor anymore. Or the green-eyed sorceress or the Red Devil's whore. They'll know I loved the Netherlands with all my heart and did all I could.*

Entering the room as Esmeralda put the finishing touches to her hair, Alva was pleased to see that she had followed his orders. Of course, he had never doubted that she would. Her intelligence was her best quality—after her unique beauty! "There's my girl! I'm glad to see you are up and around. You even look as if you feel better!"

Attempting to smile, Esmeralda answered with a stilted curtsy. "As always, Fernando, your wish is my command." At this point, she didn't feel the necessity to completely disguise the hatred she felt for him. But he was too pleased with himself to notice the loathing in her scathing tone.

"And don't you forget it!" he laughed, walking toward her to peck her on a cool cheek.

She looked into his narrow black eyes, attempting to catch a glimmer of what she could expect, but all she could see was self-satisfaction—nothing else. "No, I won't forget, Fernando. I never could," she replied meekly, wishing she had the means and the bravery to sink a knife into his black murdering heart!

"Good! Now, let me look at you!" he said warmly, drawing her to her feet. "Yes, you are still the most beautiful woman in all the Netherlands. And you are mine!" Pulling her hard against his length, he kissed her lips with such passion that she felt his manhood hardening against her softer flesh, and she said a prayer of thanks that this would be the last time she would have to yield to his demanding lips. At least, if she were arrested, she would never have to concern herself with the possibility that Fernando would some day be able to function as a man with her. "I hate it when you force me to be stern with you. I much prefer your willing support of my endeavors!"

"Yes, Fernando," she said contritely, with eyes lowered to the floor.

"Now, don't get too docile, *mi alma*. I also like your spirit. I don't want you to be a timid mouse. However, there is a time and place for temperament, and today is not that time. Now, since that is understood and you are feeling better, we will change the subject," he announced with a chuckle as he took her arm to guide her toward the exit from her room.

"There will be a long receiving line," he said as they walked. "Should you feel weak, you may lean on me. In fact, I want you to hold my arm the entire time—so that we present a united image. The new governor and his lady! You will appear interested in everything that is said, but you will offer no comments on anything, other than the weather or the excellence of a certain wine. Mainly, it will be your duty to present a beautiful, and silent, picture to lull our traitorous guests into a false sense of security," he explained malevolently,

164

pleased with the knowledge that his unsuspecting visitors would be in the palace dungeon by nightfall.

Upon their arrival at the palace, the Dutch dignitaries were ushered into a vast ballroom where long oak tables had been placed in one enormous quadrangle, simulating England's famed round table, with no position of dominance or supremacy. No one seemed alarmed by the armed guards who stood posted at the many exits to the meeting place—except Esmeralda.

Standing beside Alva to welcome the trusting nobles to the meeting, she was surprised to discover that less than fifty men had responded to his attractive summons. She had thought the number would have been far greater. Did she dare hope that some of her warnings had actually found their destinations? She knew that the scribes had penned invitations to more than four hundred men of influence—men who wanted peace in their country and would be willing to consider compromise to achieve those gains. Yet, only fifty were present. That could mean only one thing! Her warnings must have gotten through.

She felt a brief sense of guilt for the shameless sense of pride that swept tumultuously over her with the knowledge that she and Francois Benner had possibly been instrumental in saving hundreds of Dutch lives. At least when she was exposed, she would know her own life had not been spent in vain.

Esmeralda was not the only one contemplating the poor turnout, but the duke of Alva was able to disguise his disappointment by using his most friendly and jovial tone with the fifty he had lured into his trap. Besides, the day could not be considered a total loss—not when he had succeeded in duping the counts of Egmont and Hoorne, two of the Netherlands's most esteemed heroes! Each of them would be worth one hundred of the lesser nobles who had signed Brederode's useless petition. It would have been ideal, he thought regretfully, if William of Orange could have seen fit to come. But at least with Egmont and Hoorne out of the way, he would be free to seek out and destroy Orange at his leisure.

Seeing the familiar evil smile cross Fernando's face as he shook hands with Filips van Montmorency, the count of Hoorne, caused Esmeralda to shudder unexpectedly. She prayed he would not notice the gooseflesh that covered her skin; but Alva was so enveloped in the part he was playing in the unfolding drama he had staged that he was almost unaware of her presence.

"Filips, it has been ages since we have seen one another. I trust that when our meeting is concluded, you and I will be able to visit more informally," Alva said charmingly.

"Why, yes, Fernando, I will look forward to it," Hoorne answered hesitantly, for the first time feeling a nagging twinge of suspicion gnawing at his belly. However, he ignored what his instincts were telling him when he spotted Esmeralda for the first time. "And who is this charming creature at your side, Fernando?"

"Forgive me, Filips," Alva apologized warmly, putting a possessive arm around Esmeralda's shoulders. "Allow me to introduce my beautiful interpreter and secretary, Señorita Esmeralda Verde. Esmeralda, *mi querida,* this is an old and dear friend of mine, Filips Montmorency, the count of Hoorne."

"How do you do, Count Hoorne. Fernando has told me so much about you," she responded dutifully as she extended her hand to be kissed by the count.

"Tell me, mademoiselle, have we met before? Yours is a face I could hardly forget," the count said, intently studying her.

Interrupting Hoorne before he could say more, Fernando smiled rigidly. "I think not, Filips. Besides, my Esmeralda is far too clever to fall for that old game. You will have to apply your charms elsewhere. My claim on Señorita Verde's talents is irrevocably established!" The smile on his lips was dwarfed by the hard, cold look of warning in his eyes.

"*Oui,* I see that, Fernando. My compliments to you!" Hoorne chuckled, understanding the full import of Alva's words and forced to admire the older man's stamina and taste in women.

Esmeralda watched Filips Montmorency walk away, cheerfully greeting other comrades as he did so, and she wondered if he had truly recognized her. She wished for a chance to talk to the handsome nobleman alone— out from under the watchful eye of Fernando—but she knew that would never come about.

Brought back to her surroundings by the pressure of Fernando's fingers digging into the flesh of her arm, Esmeralda looked away from the count of Hoorne into the questioning eyes of the count of Egmont, the stadtholder of Flanders and Artois. "I am pleased to meet you, Señorita Verde!" he smiled kindly, as if somehow he understood her plight.

"Count Egmont, the pleasure is mine," she returned warmly.

Egmont, who had been a trusted advisor of the Holy Roman Emperor, Charles V, and had even represented Philip II in his proposal of marriage to the Catholic queen of England, Mary I, squeezed Esmeralda's hand sympathetically before turning back to the duke. "Tell me, Fernando, where did you find this lovely jewel among jewels?"

"That is my little secret," Alva laughed conspiratorially.

"Well, if you should tire of her services, I certainly could use a good secretary myself." Looking back at Esmeralda, Egmont smiled knowingly. "But I doubt there is much chance you would give her up, is there?"

"The probability is highly unlikely, *mi amigo,*" Alva laughed heartily. "But I have some excellent scribes who I would be willing to lend out, should the need arise."

"But none as pretty as Mademoiselle Verde, I presume!"

"You presume correctly, Lamoraal," Alva smiled arrogantly, holding Esmeralda's waist even more tightly.

Taking his leave of the duke and Esmeralda Verde, Egmont wondered if it had been the blonde girl who had sent him the letter of warning which he had considered someone's idea of a joke. When he had first entered the huge hall and spotted her standing beside Alva, he had been certain she was Johanna van Ledenburg; but he knew that was impossible. It was simply a coincidence that Esmeralda Verde looked so much like the count of Ledenburg's dead daughter. Still, if she were Johanna, possibly held against her will, she might have found a way to warn her father's friends of Alva's treachery.

The knowledge that he had stupidly walked into a trap after being cautioned hit Egmont with the effect of a barrage of cannonballs exploding in his head. He had been so intent on finding a nonviolent solution to the problems facing the Netherlands that he had let his common sense be overridden, and he had ignored the mysterious warning. But now, having made his choice of moves on the giant chessboard Alva had laid out, all he could do was wait for the duke's next move—and pray that nothing more than a few pawns were lost. However, seeing the count of Hoorne across the room and knowing the man's value to the Netherlands, Egmont knew the loss would be far greater than mere pawns.

Chapter Ten

The meeting of the lords with the duke of Alva and his advisors lasted through the morning and remained congenial. However, after a lavish luncheon, some of the guests, now feeling overly confident because of the gracious treatment they had received, began to be more forceful in their demands.

They argued against their independent status being undermined; they protested against having occupying forces stationed in their towns; they fought vehemently against the fourteen bishoprics created by papal decree in 1561, giving the church more control than before; and again, religious freedom was the subject of heated discussion.

Alva heard them all, and he appeared to be interested in their concerns and the solutions they offered for the country's pressing problems. Secretly, he was pleased to see that the particular interests of the representatives were divided, realizing that the commercial-business representatives of Holland were not in the least worried about the difficulties of the more agrarian areas like Artois and Hainaut, and vice versa. He knew he would have no problem in carrying out his scheme to insure the total servitude of the Netherlands, once its main leaders were removed from power, and as long as each of the provinces was concerned only with its own dilemmas.

Following the luxurious noonday meal, Alva spoke for the first time. "Gentlemen, I am flattered that you have come here today to discuss and seek solutions to problems that have long plagued us; and I will say that you have been most informative in your speeches. I feel I know each of you a bit better than I did before, and I will immediately write to the king to give him my recommendations concerning your requests.

"We have accomplished a great deal today, and I know this meeting will go down in history. I give each and every one of you my word that you will no longer find it necessary to worry about your authority in your provinces; and you can be certain that you will receive proper credit for your contributions to our conference today, as well as for your past endeavors. Now, let us share our good news with the public, shall we?" he added, smiling broadly as he indicated that they should all follow him to the courtyard, where a large crowd of people was awaiting an announcement.

With Esmeralda still at his side, the duke of Alva took his place on the large outdoor podium, grinning with pretended modesty when a large cheer arose from the mass of humanity packed into the open area. Raising his arms good-naturedly in a pretended attempt to silence the crowd which had obviously been ordered to energetically applaud the new governor, Alva spoke loudly. "Friends, I have good news for you today. As you know, nobles from all over the Netherlands have come together today to voice their concerns for the future of the country. In the past, these men have spoken out against your monarch, King Philip II, on many occasions!"

Count Egmont's gaze swerved nervously around him, quickly spotting the armed guards who were slowly moving toward the cluster of defenseless nobles standing to the left of Alva.

"Today I have tried to give these men a chance to reverse their criticisms of our great king, but still I have heard nothing but vicious slander and maligning reproof of King Philip the Second's policies."

Each of the betrayed nobles now had a soldier standing beside him.

"I am left with no choice but to rid our society of these traitors permanently and to place them under arrest!" Alva announced loudly. "This day, September ninth, the crown hereby places into custody, for high treason, the following offenders . . ."

Unrolling his scroll, with an obvious disregard for the look of shock on the faces of the men who in good faith had walked into his snare, Alva proceeded to read their names.

The crowd was silent, with the exception of a deathly hum of disbelief that rose after each name was proclaimed.

When he finished reading his list, the duke of Alva rerolled it and continued speaking with a look of satisfaction on his face. "Also on this day, I have issued warrants for the arrests of William of Orange; his son Philip William; Louis of Nassau; Hendrik, the count of Brederode; Matthew, the count of Ledenburg, and his sons Frans, Helst, and Hugo; the count of Leuven—"

The listing went on and on, but Esmeralda had quit listening. She recognized many of the names as those of men she had warned and now had reason to hope were safely out of the country—since they hadn't succumbed to Alva's deadly invitation! There was only one final name she was waiting to hear now—the name of the one person she was certain would not escape Fernando's rage. *He must be saving me for last. I wish he would just get it over with!*

Trying to concentrate on the drone of Fernando's voice while he read out nearly seven hundred names, Esmeralda suddenly felt an unbearable physical pain, as if she were being cut to ribbons by thousands of angry swords bent on her annihilation. Unconsciously she stepped back, trying to escape the burning hatred she felt searing through her clothing. But as she did, she was compelled to turn her head to the side to be assaulted full force by the raw animosity and anger of one man's stare.

All the hatred she had believed to be emanating from the crowd was originating from only one man. Not a thousand eyes. Not even a hundred. But only two. Her scalding agony was caused by the icy blue glare of a filthy peasant who had come to hear the duke's message. No one else in the crowd even seemed to be aware of her, but the hate and venom lurking deep in the stranger's frigid gaze wounded Esmeralda more than any physical abuse she had ever suffered at the hand of man.

For though their warmth had been displaced by hatred, and the tears were hidden by rancor and revulsion, she recognized the savage eyes piercing into her very soul as the eyes of the man in her dreams!

Looking straight into the man's scorching, scrutinizing glare, Esmeralda saw him mouth the silent question, "Why?" But she was not permitted to answer, not that she could have, for Fernando reached for her at that very moment and she was forced to return to his side.

She sent a dutiful smile in Alva's direction before turning once more toward the man with the unsettling blue eyes. But he was gone! And the space where he had been was already filled by the shoving crowd—as if he had never been there at all.

Searching the mob for some sign of the vanishing peasant, her thoughts raced wildly, no longer dwelling on or caring when her own arrest would come. *Did I really see him? Who is he? Is he someone I know? Surely there are millions of people with those blue eyes. They couldn't be so uncommon. Yet I've never seen any just like them—except in my dreams. I'm letting my thoughts run away with me. It's my conscience imagining my judge has come to punish me. I won't think about him. There are thousands of men with blue eyes. Besides, he didn't have blond hair!*

Suddenly brought back to the present by Fernando's pounding voice, Esmeralda realized he had completed his lengthy list and no guard had come for her! She listened intently to what he said, still not believing that she was not among those slated for arrest. But what she heard made her heart pound with fear for her countrymen and drove the last shred of self-concern from her mind.

"We will rid our country of heresy at all costs! There will be notices posted for those accused of plotting

174

against the Church. Generous rewards will be given to those who help bring the offenders to justice. There will be money for anyone with knowledge of any under-handed activities on the part of their neighbors or family members. All accusations will be investigated thoroughly!"

Hearing his words and realizing the magnitude of Alva's condemnation, Esmeralda swayed against him, overcome by the viciousness of his scheme to turn brother against brother, neighbor against neighbor, Catholic against Protestant, Netherlander against Netherlander. And she knew that she must endure his tyranny over her personal life, no matter how unbearable, in order that she might fight him at every turn. Since she had not been arrested, she vowed that she would continue to do everything in her power to totally destroy the duke of Alva—even if it meant destroying herself in the process. She swore to herself that he would rue the day he thought to conquer the Dutch people. There would be no price she would be unwilling to pay to see an end put to Fernando de Alvarez!

His posture defeated, Dirk led his horse out of Brussels. How could he have been such a fool? He had been so elated when he'd realized she was alive that he had actually let himself believe she was being held in the palace against her will. The thought never occurred to him that if she were a prisoner it would be impossible for her to send out a warning to her family. And it certainly hadn't entered his mind when he set out to "save" her that she would be living a life of luxury as the mistress of the governor of the Netherlands—and obviously content with her position if what he'd seen on the podium was any indication.

His face twisted with hatred for the woman he'd loved more than life itself. Even after what happened to her in the cathedral, how could she have let them all go on thinking she was dead? Why didn't she come home afterward? Why didn't she come to him? Was she ashamed? Did she think he would blame her for what happened? Didn't she know he would still love her no matter what? But even if she thought he would reject her, how could she have done this to her family and turned to a man like the duke of Alva?

Disillusioned, he shook his head. "Why, Johanna? Why?" he moaned aloud, oblivious to the man and woman passing him, who exchanged puzzled frowns when they realized the young man was talking to himself.

I can't tell her parents what has become of her, he realized. *It will break their hearts. I'll tell them the handwriting on the warnings was not hers and that we must all accept her death once and for all.*

He straightened his shoulders and cast a quick glance back toward the city, then mounted his horse. Turning northward, he vowed to rejoin Nassau's army, which was due to enter the Netherlands from Germany within the next month. From this day forward, he would dedicate his life to ridding the Netherlands of the duke of Alva—and his mistress.

During the weeks that followed, Esmeralda dedicated herself to her mission with consummate single-mindedness and loyalty. She was able to manage frequent trips to the Benner's inn, and Francois had organized an efficient underground network of messengers who could carry one of her warnings anywhere in the Netherlands in a matter of days, frequently making it possible for Alva's proposed victims to vanish before the warrant for arrest could be served. And since no one but Francois knew where the warnings originated, the mysterious guardian angel of the people soon became known to the grateful citizens only as *Ange de Mystère.*

Alva's Council of Troubles, called the Council of Blood by the frightened population, had created a terror all over the country that burst like an exploding barrel of gunpowder. All of Orange's possessions had been confiscated, enriching Alva's treasury greatly; and his son, Philip William, had been arrested and banished to Spain, where he was assumed to be incarcerated but alive. The statesmen arrested in September had been tried by the council on charges of suspected rebellion and heresy; and when all were automatically pronounced guilty, their property was also seized and they were sentenced to death or long prison terms.

It appeared that Alva would carry out his murderous plan with little or no resistance, no matter how diligently Esmeralda and Francois worked to stop him. The few brave souls who openly attempted to fight were arrested and cruelly tortured before being burned at the stake or beheaded in the public squares of the towns. No one was safe. Paid informers came out of every nook and cranny; and if a man had an enemy, it became commonplace to accuse him of heresy, thereby ridding the accuser of a hated rival. Soldiers took advantage of their positions of power, with pillaging and rape becoming the rule. And if the townspeople dared to complain about their treatment, they were immediately put under arrest, given speedy, farcical trials, and executed—often all in the same day. There seemed to be no way to stop him, but Esmeralda and Francois faithfully continued their efforts, despite their discouraging setbacks.

Alva bragged about having executed two thousand heretics in the time he had been governor; and his treasury grew rich with the confiscated properties of three thousand noblemen. It was soon obvious that even if assistance came from outside, none of the downtrodden, terrified provinces of the Netherlands would rise up to give aid in their own defense.

Alva arranged for another mass arrest, and Esmeralda and Francois were able to warn some three thousand people. But still the total arrests amounted to over nine hundred—a heartbreaking loss to the people of the Netherlands, who were being systematically annihilated in Alva's battleless war.

Despite his apparent success, however, Alva was dissatisfied. He was consumed with desire to exert even more control over the ever-tightening yoke around the neck of the country, and he spent hours pacing in Esmeralda's room—using her as his sounding board, still having no idea that she was his enemy.

"I know Orange is planning an uprising," he ranted as he walked back and forth. "He's been traveling all over Germany trying to gain the aid of other princes, and I'm certain he's achieved support by now. We must have these peasants so cowed by the time he attacks that they won't even dare look up to see who has come to save them."

Esmeralda said nothing but continued stitching dainty flowers on a lace handkerchief she was making for Mignon, for she didn't want to interrupt his verbal thinking, since this was a main source of her valuable knowledge.

"Tomorrow we will write a letter to the king telling him not to leave Spain as he originally planned. I think that until his enemies are all dead or in prison, he would be better off in Madrid surrounded by the fops and fools he has at court. Besides, I'm able to work more efficiently without our illustrious monarch looking over my shoulder asking why I did this and when he'll get a memorandum on that. If he were here, it would be necessary to write out an official *consulta* every time I wanted to take a piss!"

Laughing at his own joke, Fernando looked at Esmeralda for approval, and he was not disappointed. She was smiling politely, with the correct amount of chiding embarrassment in her expression.

Realizing how much he depended on her presence, Fernando abruptly changed the subject. "Have I told you, dear sweet Esmeralda, how much I rely on your company? You are the only one in this blasted country I can trust. Without you I would be totally alone in this land of heretics and old women!"

"I'm glad you feel that way, Fernando. You have been good to me, and I appreciate all the things you have done for my family," she answered, effectively hiding her loathing behind a mask of warmth and gratitude.

"I'm the one who is grateful, my love."

"There's nothing to be grateful for, Fernando," she said sweetly. "You know I'm dedicated to your—" *downfall,* she said to herself, but aloud she kept up her false front—"success."

Alva sighed and gave her a kiss on her temple. "If I were only twenty years younger, or if I had less on my mind, I know I could make you happy."

"But you do make me happy," she said, patting his cheek, hiding her constant fear that today would be the day his impotency would suddenly end. She had come to take it for granted, and at this point she wasn't sure she could go through with letting him make love to her.

"*Sí,* you are happy, my loyal and lovely Esmeralda, but I want to make you happier!" He kissed her passionately, and one more time she was able to mask the instinctive cringe she felt every time he touched her.

"Do you really think William of Orange will have the courage to attack your great armies, Fernando?" she asked, forcing the subject away from the line it was taking. Alva was very proud of the forces he had built into the greatest in the world and could go on for hours expounding on their excellence in battle.

"I know he will, but we'll be ready for him," he growled, resuming his pacing. "Fortunately, he is having trouble getting support from those fat German princes. He'll be forced, I'm sure, to rely on the Calvinist iconoclasts who fled to Germany before my arrival; and they will be his undoing. They are untrained and undisciplined, and will be no match for my efficient and well-equipped professional veterans of warfare."

Pausing to glance out the window at the streets below, he laughed and changed the subject. "One good thing has happened. That drunken troublemaker, Brederode, died. Probably drank himself to death! They say he rode all through France trying to find an army, but no one would join him. Serves him right to die penniless and without a home. It will show others who are foolish enough to attempt to ride against my government."

Realizing that his ramblings would tell her nothing more this night, Emeraude put down her sewing and said gently, "Fernando, you work too hard. Are you certain you won't come with me tomorrow to see my family? It would do you good to get away for the day." She always pretended to want him to accompany her on her trips away from the palace in order to avoid his suspicion—and fortunately he always said he couldn't go this time!

"No, my angel, I simply cannot leave; but tell your family that I will see them another time, and give them my best regards," he answered, touched as usual by her concern. "I've arranged for some gifts for you to take along in my place, though!" he announced happily.

"I've told you that gifts aren't necessary. They don't expect them. They appreciate the fact that you let me come so often. That is enough," she insisted.

"And that is why I enjoy sending them, my sweet. It gives me pleasure to do things for the people who saved you for me."

"You are too kind, Fernando," she said with the false smile of appreciation stiff and almost painful on her face.

Word was received in Brussels that Louis of Nassau,

the thirty-year-old younger brother of the prince of Orange, had led an invasion of the northern Netherlands from Germany. At the head of a column of Protestant rebels and exiled lesser nobles, Louis had managed to march unnoticed into Groningen at the northern tip of the country and defeat the Spanish garrison stationed at Heiligerlee. But he was so distraught over the loss of another brother, Adolph, in the battle, that he was not even aware that he had taken the first positive step in freeing the country from Alva's brutal oppression.

"Louis, don't you realize what this means?" Dirk Corlear asked Nassau, attempting to bolster his spirit. "We are back in our homeland! Hopefully, when word spreads of our advance, others will join us to take up arms against that bastard, Alva, and his murdering soldiers," he said earnestly. "Adolph lived a good life, and he died for a cause dear to us all. He was a brave man, and I felt honored to fight beside him. He will be remembered well by many!"

"Dirk, it is kind of you to say that. Thank you," answered the saddened red-haired man with eyes of brown that matched the freckles splattered over his fair skin. "I will be fine. It is only when death hits so close to us that we fully appreciate the value of what we are doing; but I can't help wondering about the cost!"

"We must think of all the poor souls Alva has struck down without warning in his public executions. I'm thankful that so many of our patriots have been able to escape to Germany and France. Otherwise, the grisly count would be far greater!"

"We have a long way to go if we are to fight our way into Brussels, Dirk, but at least we have made a beginning, haven't we? If reinforcements arrive, we will take all of Groningen Province next. Then, when we drive into Friesland, I hope to be joined by our people coming from England by sea. My brother, William, is to make a thrust from the south through Brabant, and another group is coming from the coast of France through Flanders," Louis said, finally able to think about matters other than his brother's death.

"We'll have him trapped from all sides," Dirk said enthusiastically.

"That's the plan, but if the people in the towns don't rise up to support us, I'm afraid we'll not have the strength to take the entire Spanish army," Louis worried aloud. "We're counting on the people. I hope they don't disappoint us!"

"Surely they'll see us as their rescuers and jump at the chance to march beside us against their captors!" Dirk assumed optimistically.

"You would think so, my friend," Louis said doubtfully. "But we shall see. Alva has had time to torture, arrest, horrify, and totally subdue our countrymen. Many may be so afraid of the consequences, should we lose, that they simply do nothing."

"I pray you are wrong, Louis."

"As do I. As do I!" Louis agreed pessimistically. "But enough of this talk. We are here, victorious for the moment, and should rejoice. I know Adolph would be proud if he were with us."

"Yes, he would be pleased with our triumph. If only the armies coming from the other directions do as well!" Dirk added hopefully.

"Dirk," Louis interjected more cheerfully. "How would you like to don your peasant's garb once more?"

Dirk chuckled, pinching his nose to express disgust with the rank odor that accompanied the disguise. "You know how I love to go without a bath for weeks on end, comrade!"

"What I especially like is the way you dress your hair and beard with bootblacking," joked the redhead.

"Yes, we can't forget the hair. Tell me, what do you have in mind? Surely, it isn't that you've come to love the pungent aroma that wafts odorously through the air when I'm in those old clothes!"

"That too!" Louis laughed. "But there is another more serious purpose. Another trip to Brussels."

"But I had planned to stay here and go into battle with you when you make your next tour de force," Dirk stated, obviously disappointed.

"There will be many more battles before we have regained our country, my friend, and many more opportunities for you to endanger your life in combat, as you seem so intent on doing. But for now, I have another even more difficult mission in mind for you."

"Of course, I will do whatever you think is necessary, but is there no other who can do this for you?"

"Of course there are others. None of us is indispensable. But there is no one I trust as I trust you, and certainly no one else with your special talent for blending into the crowd with such ease," Louis complimented with a knowing smile.

"Well, tell me," Dirk conceded. "You've aroused my curiosity sufficiently. What is this great mission?"

"Perhaps you've heard of the green-eyed sorceress who they say has Alva bewitched?"

The muscles tightened in Dirk's jaw. "Yes, I've seen her with him. What about her?"

"They say he values her existence above all others. I hear he would give his life for her—this young mistress with the blond hair and green eyes," Louis said.

"It is said that he discusses all of his unprincipled plans with her and that she knows his every secret," Dirk snarled with loathing.

"Some even believe she's the power behind the man and that he's only doing her evil bidding," Louis laughed. "Although I find that a bit hard to swallow since he's been a son-of-a-bitch all his life, and she could be no more than twenty!"

"So what does Alva's whore have to do with my mission?" Dirk asked disgustedly.

"Since she seems to be Alva's vulnerable point, I want you to steal her from under his nose and bring her to me!" Louis pronounced triumphantly.

"What?" Dirk bellowed incredulously.

"I plan to make him pay dearly for seizing my innocent nephew from the university and shipping him off to Spain, and we will use his weakness for Señorita Esmeralda Verde to force the return of our legal properties to us, as well as seeing that he finances my campaign against him, in payment for Adolph's death."

"But what if she's not so valuable to him after all and he's willing to pay nothing for her release?" Dirk asked, grasping at straws to keep from carrying out Louis's proposal.

"Then we will give her the same treatment he has given our people when he has wanted information they possess. She will tell us everything she knows, and one way or another, she will be of use to us."

Dreading the task he was being asked to carry out,

Dirk knew this would be the most difficult order he would ever be given to execute; but at the same time, he realized he couldn't, in all good conscience, refuse Nassau's request. "When do I leave?"

"As soon as possible. I understand she travels to visit family or friends at an inn outside of Brussels quite frequently. Although her visits are always made in the company of armed guards and a chaperone, Alva is never with her. I'm certain one of these trips would be the best time to seize her," Louis suggested. "To best determine your course of action, though, you will need to go to Brussels and evaluate the situation yourself," he added, never presuming to tell a man of Dirk Corlear's caliber how to carry out a task.

"In that case, I will leave in the morning," Dirk said unenthusiastically.

"I don't understand your hesitation, Dirk. Usually, you're the first one to leap at the chance to go on an adventure of espionage," Louis laughed. "Even when we were children, I remember you sneaking around behind William and Adolph, pretending to be a great spy," he teased his old friend warmly.

Dirk attempted to share the moment of nostalgia with a fond smile, but the best he could muster was a half grin. "I suppose I grew up and the stakes got too high. It's not a game anymore. But don't pay attention to my bad mood. I'll go and be back quickly with your green-eyed whore. Now I had best be getting some rest if I'm to depart at sunup. I won't disturb you when I leave." Knowing this could easily be the last time they met in this world, the two men embraced momentarily, then said good night.

In the months of travel since Dirk Corlear had killed

the three thugs in the tavern in Brussels, he had learned to catch sleep wherever he could. He could sleep sitting up, in alleyways, by day or night, and in marshes where the watery terrain made a dry bed almost impossible to find. Always on the run, he had learned to sleep with one eye open, but at least he had managed to sleep.

However, this night there would be no blessed relief from the obsession that had haunted him for so long. Johanna was everywhere he looked; and each time he allowed himself the luxury of remembering her, Esmeralda Verde would invade his thoughts—laughing wickedly and lying beneath the duke of Alva with her legs spread wide. He thought for the thousandth time how he would have preferred her death to the knowledge of what had become of her.

Finally, realizing that sleep was not to be had, Dirk rose noiselessly, saddled the gray horse that had been his faithful companion since his ordeal had begun, and rode southeast into Germany. He would reenter the Netherlands at Maastricht, sixty miles east of Brussels.

Chapter Eleven

By the time Dirk rode toward Brussels after several days on the road, his appearance was totally changed. His neatly trimmed beard and hair had been dyed with bootblacking and had reacquired the shaggy, unkempt look necessary for his pretended role. His fine clothing had been left in Germany, to be replaced by a woolen tunic, so old and worn that its original blue color and shape were almost impossible to determine. Tied at the waist with a rope of hemp, the baggy knee-length pants of unbleached linen he wore were covered with holes and patches, while his tall, rounded hat was pulled low on his head so that the flat brim hid most of his hair and his blue eyes in its shadow.

Under cover of darkness, he arrived at his destination on the outskirts of the city shortly before sunrise. He sought out a quiet, secluded place off the main road where he and his horse could rest for the day. Hidden safely in a thick cluster of trees and brush, he lay down after eating his meager meal of dried fruit and bread. Although he was finally able to sleep, his dreams were still plagued by visions of Johanna and Alva laughing at him, and his slumber was anything but restful.

As the sun rose higher in the sky, the nearby road grew more busy, but it was midmorning before the noise of wagons and horses loaded with wares to sell in Brussels disturbed him sufficiently to fully awaken him. Dispassionately watching the traffic move slowly past his hiding place, his senses were suddenly brought to full attention by the regal gold-and-red carriage speeding past the other travelers on the road. It was guarded by four Spanish soldiers on horseback, as well as an armed man on the seat beside the coachman and a footman, and as it raced by the screen of trees where he was camped, he caught a fleeting glimpse of blond hair inside the curtained windows of the majestic vehicle.

Dirk didn't need to see her face to know who rode in the governor's carriage, and the intensity of his burning hatred expanded to unfathomable depths he had never imagined.

"I'll kill her," he groaned, slamming his fist repeatedly into the hard bark of the tree which supported his tormented, grief-stricken body.

Forcing himself to regain control over his emotions, he stepped out of his shelter and casually joined the westward travelers, keeping the coach in sight as it pulled to a stop in front of a roadside inn. Stopping his own horse to check his bundles and the animal's feet, he was able to watch as the coachman opened the carriage and two female passengers disembarked.

Seeing Johanna again, even from such a distance, sent an ache through his body that set his emotions soaring uncontrollably, and he knew he had to act immediately. "I'll take her today and get her back to

Louis so I can be done with her, once and for all!" he pledged in a raspy whisper. "To put it off would make this mission all the more unbearable, Fumée," he uttered to the smoke-colored horse that nibbled bits of grass along the side of the road while his master patted his neck absently. With an affectionate slap on the big mount's hip, the man laughed bitterly, "Let's go, fella. It's just you and me!"

Together, the steadfast horse and forsaken man walked toward the inn Johanna had entered moments before. Dirk breathed a relieved sigh when he saw that the guards seemed to be at ease once their cargo had been safely delivered at the front door. Two soldiers set off for the river to water the horses while the others went inside the tavern for refreshments.

Tying Fumée to a nearby tree, Dirk sat down and imitated a weary traveler taking a nap while he studied the situation and planned Johanna's abduction.

As he pondered the least dangerous method of operation, he was surprised to see Johanna and a tall young girl go out the back of the inn, talking gaily to each other—and carrying full laundry baskets.

Dirk gaped, aghast as he realized Johanna's grand clothes had been replaced with an unadorned and loose-fitting dress of fawn-colored woolen stuff gathered at the waist by a white muslin apron. Her beautiful hair was hidden from view by a cap of unbleached linen with a deep flounce that hid much of her face, but he knew it was her.

Curious as to why the governor's mistress would be dressed and working as a common laundress, Dirk stood up and walked to the river to better see what would happen there. He watched as the two young women picked out a reasonably secluded spot, then proceeded to take off their shoes and step into the water up to their uncovered ankles.

Dirk's heart leapt at the unwanted reminder of the first time he had seen Johanna so long ago.

Giggling and splashing one another, the two girls seemed unconcerned with the solitary guard who had followed them from the inn and now stood fifty feet away, out of earshot, but still alert to their every move.

Then, without the least worry about wet clothing, the young women knelt down and washed the dirty articles in their baskets.

Dirk couldn't believe what he was seeing. Could there be some mistake? Could that girl really be Johanna? But before he could question what was happening, there was even more to amaze and confuse him.

When Johanna and the other girl were through with the wash, each of them picked up a heavy basket filled with wet items and placed it on her head for the walk home. Johanna was still so small and fragile-looking, and as far as he knew had never done a day's work in her life, yet she had lifted that weighty basket with ease.

Following the girls from a distance, the soldier seemed uninterested in their activities and took up a new post in the shade while they hung out the washing on a line behind the inn. Only when they were finished with their work and had gone inside did the guard relax his vigil and casually saunter over to a clump of trees to relieve himself.

Having noticed that the unconcerned soldier was about his size, Dirk saw this moment as his opportunity to act. Taking care to stay concealed in the heavy shrubbery surrounding much of the inn, he headed in the same direction as the guard. His months on the run stood him in good stead, and he was able to silently approach the unsuspecting soldier unobserved.

Walking on noiseless feet with the prowess of a lion closing in for the kill, Dirk was behind the unsuspecting man before he could rearrange his clothing. With the speed of an attacking snake, Dirk's arm went around the soldier's unprotected neck, choking the life out of him as his terror-filled eyes bulged and his arms flailed in an attempt to free himself with his last breath. It was over quickly, and with the slightest twinge of regret, Dirk pulled the body deeper into the brush, where he deftly stripped the lifeless corpse of its uniform and weapons.

Running stealthily back to the spot where he had secreted his gray steed, Dirk took no time to catch his breath before he went about skillfully trimming his dyed beard and hair in the style of the dead Spaniard. When the small mirror told him that he had done a fair job, he packed the peasant clothing and promptly donned the downed guard's uniform.

Making a final check of his appearance, he was saddened by the fact that killing had become such a natural part of his existence—he, who as a child would cry when a family cat killed a mouse or bird. He had become a cold-blooded killer with no feeling for the men he cut down, concerned only with the knowledge that they were his enemies.

"Enough of this self-hate, Corlear. You're who and what you are, and there's no going back. You have a job to do, and you'll do it—no matter who is killed in the process!"

Rambling easily into the inn, where he casually ordered a beer, he observed that the four horsemen were enjoying themselves in the beer garden by flirting with a young serving girl, while the driver and footman sat at a table arguing over whose turn it was to pay for the next round. Determining that he had replaced the armed guard who rode up top, Dirk strode back outside after quaffing the remainder of his drink.

The coach stood where it had been left—with the watered horses still harnessed to it. "It's too hot for you horses to be pulling this heavy carriage," he chuckled softly, hurriedly unhitching the harnesses while he pretended to check the animals. Looking around indifferently to reassure himself that his efforts had not been observed, he then walked to the place where the guards' four brown mounts stood tethered.

Strolling toward the uneasy horses, Dirk thanked God that it was the noon hour and hot. Everyone was inside eating or drinking, and there was no one to see him untie three of the saddled mounts so he could take them down to the river and hide them behind a grove of trees. Then, after checking to be certain his own horse was ready for a speedy departure, he went back into the tavern for another beer and a bite to eat. However, he found he had difficulty swallowing, knowing that Johanna was so near and that he would have her in his possession in a matter of minutes—if all went as planned.

By the sounds of benches scraping the wooden floor in the main eating room, Dirk knew the diners were through with their noon fare, and he waited anxiously for his opportunity—which came almost immediately.

The tavern keeper and Johanna came out of the dining room and walked, her arm in his, out the front door. None of the soldiers made a move to follow, all evidently assuming the man lying dead in the bushes would, as usual, be on duty as her personal guard. Fortifying himself with one last swallow of the amber-colored liquid in the stein, Dirk walked out the door behind the man and Johanna.

Obviously they were accustomed to having a guard accompany them on their walks, because neither looked back to see if they were being followed. Debating on attacking the huge man in order to snatch Johanna from his arm, Dirk decided on a different approach, realizing that surprise would be the only way for him to overcome the larger man.

Staying a good distance behind the couple as they ambled toward the river, he quietly took the reins of the one remaining Spanish horse and mounted her just as the unsuspecting people vanished momentarily around a bend in the path.

Taking a deep breath, Dirk bent low over the mare's neck and dug his heels into her sides, deliberately guiding her toward the girl and giant of a man at a full gallop.

When Johanna and Francois heard the fearful sound of the rushing hoofbeats bearing down on them, they instinctively separated to keep from being run over; and just as they split, Dirk rode between them, bending agilely from the saddle to sweep Johanna up into his strong arms and ride away with her draped across his lap.

He held her with one arm gripped tightly around her waist, unconcerned with her screams, as he raced to where his own horse was hidden. With no consideration for her modesty, he hoisted her into the saddle before leaping onto the trusty gray steed behind her. Pulling the Spanish mare behind them, they headed east, not waiting to discover what the guards had done when they found they had no horses and had lost their valuable charge.

"What do you want? Who are you? Let me go!" were the screams of anger and fear the travelers heading west heard as Dirk headed for Germany with his wiggling, kicking human quarry. However, seeing the dreaded Spanish uniform, the frightened witnesses to Johanna's abduction assumed it was another rape of one of their innocent maids, and there was no one who would dare to stand up to a Spanish soldier for fear of dreadful reprisals. Men had been put to death for far less; so everyone who heard the girl's desperate cries for help looked the other way.

In the minutes after Emeraude's sudden abduction, Francois recovered from his shock and ran back to the inn as fast as his legs could carry his large frame, calling for assistance and cursing the guards as he did so. "Damn peacocks stay underfoot the whole time she's here, but where are they when she needs to be protected?"

"What is it?" the soldiers cried, clamoring clumsily to their feet, their reflexes obviously slow from the large amounts of Dutch beer they had consumed.

"You fools! She's been taken right from under your drunken noses. One of your own men rode down on us like a madman and snatched her up from the ground!"

Francois was sputtering and coughing from his exertion, and his face was beet red with anger.

"Well, don't just stand there gaping. Go after them! He has my daughter!" he shouted. "If you don't get her back, you'll hang for certain. I'll see to it personally if Alva doesn't!" he screamed.

The urgency of what the large red-faced man was shouting at them finally penetrated the alcoholic haze the guards found themselves in, and all six went into action simultaneously.

They ran frantically to their horses, giving chase from horseback their ultimate plan. However, when they couldn't locate their mounts, they wasted more precious moments deciding if the horses had been stolen or were just misplaced. "Use the coach," one man finally suggested in heavily slurred Spanish, and they raced to board the waiting vehicle.

The driver yelled out as his whip sailed angrily through the air, signaling the magnificent team of horses to move. And move they did, dragging the helpless driver halfway down the drive before he managed to disentangle himself from the reins. The coach itself remained stationary with its five bewildered military passengers.

Running out of the house screaming, Mignon, Suzette and Nadine began beating the soldiers with brooms and long wooden spoons. "Do something! They're getting away. Why are you standing here doing nothing?" they shrieked at the befuddled soldiers. "Use the horses in the barn!"

Pulling the crazed women away from the soldiers, Francois, who had calmed down enough to think, soothed, "Come, my sweet girls, there is no more we

196

can do. We can only pray she will not be hurt. Whoever he was, he thought of everything. I doubt these fools could catch them now!" Walking into the house with the weeping women, Francois turned to the baffled soldiers one last time.

"You'd better round up your horses. I'm sure they're nearby since the fellow was only riding one of them!" He shook his head in disgust and added with a bitter laugh, "Then you'd better determine how you're going to explain this to your commanding officer!"

Secretly, Francois was glad someone had found a way to get Emeraude out of Alva's grasp; and after thinking it over he was able to comfort himself and the delirious women by saying, "I wouldn't be surprised if Emeraude's abductor was someone from her past. Maybe someone who saw her in Brussels and followed her here. I've felt for a long while that it was just a matter of time before someone recognized her and tried to save her."

"If that's true, Papa, and it was someone who loved her, she'll get in touch with us, don't you think?" Suzette asked tearfully.

"Of course she will. Now, you ladies run along and let me tend to a few things. Nadine, you are welcome to stay with us until we receive word about our daughter," he offered.

Francois walked back outside to check the guards' progress and arrived in time to see them drag the lifeless soldier out of the bushes at the back of the inn. Seeing the dead man stripped of his uniform confirmed Francois's suspicions that it was not a Spaniard who had stolen Emeraude.

The possibility that Emeraude was with a Dutchman eased his mind slightly. Then a terrible thought occurred to him. Many people, thinking she was Alva's mistress, hated her greatly. She could be hung as a traitor by some fool who didn't know who she really was. He decided it was time to disclose the identity of the *Ange de Mystère* by quickly sending the information out through his underground network. Somehow, the daring purloiner who had taken her must be immediately alerted to the fact that he had one of the Netherlands's most valuable treasures, the brave Dutch loyalist who had risked her life and reputation repeatedly for the cause of freedom from Spanish oppression.

As Dirk guided the horses off the road into a wilderness of trees and wet, spongy ground, he could hear their heavy hooves sinking noisily into the sucking mud, and he knew neither of the animals would make it very far carrying extra weight. As soon as he spotted an island of slightly dry ground in the marsh, he leapt from his mount, roughly pulling the girl, who had finally stopped screaming, with him.

"We'll walk from here on," he mumbled, his posture rigid, his eyes straight ahead, not yet daring to look into her tearstained face.

"Where are we going? What do you want with me?" Esmeralda cried, renewing her hoarse screaming at the soldier who had abducted her.

Whirling abruptly around to face her, Dirk grabbed her trembling shoulders and looked into her frightened eyes. "What do I want with you? You're Alva's whore, aren't you? What would any man want with a whore?

What good are you to anyone except for one thing?" he snarled bitterly.

Looking into the intense, hate-saturated eyes, Esmeralda gasped aloud as the familiar eyes, more black than blue in the half-light of the dense woods, glared into her own, which instantly grew wide with new fear and alarm. "You! I recognize you! You're the man in the crowd!" she accused breathlessly.

He laughed sardonically. "Is that the way to greet your long-lost love, my dear?"

"What are you talking about? Who are you?" she hissed threateningly, fighting every instinct to cry.

"If that's the game you want to play, it's fine with me. Only count me out this time around, *Esmeralda Verde!*" he mocked, saying her name as if it left a foul taste in his mouth.

Knowing her life was in danger as never before and that this man hated her with an all-consuming passion, Esmeralda knew she had to escape. The instant he turned his back to check the cinches on the horses, she made her attempt at flight. But she immediately realized her mistake as her feet sank into the spongy mire of mud and slime that covered the ground.

With almost no effort, Dirk reached out and dug his strong fingers into the soft flesh of her unprotected arm. "That wasn't too smart, lady." Without further words he pulled a rope out of the bundle on his horse and adroitly wrapped it around her wrists, quickly looping the other end around his waist. "I know how you must hate being tied to just one man, but no more than I detest the idea of having such as you as a millstone around my waist."

Without warning, he set out with the reins of a horse

199

in each hand, almost causing Esmeralda to lose her balance with the sudden start. Before she had moved three torturous, difficult steps in the clinging ooze, it had claimed her soft slippers, leaving her stockinged feet unprotected.

With the mud caking rapidly on the hem of her skirt, she had to exert more and more effort with each step forward. In his heavy boots, the man seemed undaunted by the inconvenience of the wet, clinging muck. And that irritated Esmeralda more than the mud itself. The fire returned tumultuously to her spirit.

Planting her feet, she refused to take another step. "I'm not walking a bit farther until you tell me what this is all about and who you are!" she announced with determination.

"Have it your way," Dirk said. He continued walking forward, unconcerned that her bound arms stretched out in front of her. When she toppled over into the sludge of the ever-darkening swamp, he continued on another few steps, dragging her disabled body behind him.

"All right, I'll walk," she gasped, dangerously grounded in the ooze between the two horses' hooves. "Just stop long enough for me to get up!"

He halted, not bothering to look back as she clambered to her feet. "I guess you're not as strong as you looked carrying that laundry basket this morning," he mumbled, just loud enough for her to hear.

"You were watching me? How long have you been following me?" she grumbled, struggling to keep from falling again as she followed a few paces behind him. But her questions went unanswered, for he had resumed his indifferent silence.

Tramping through the swamp, Esmeralda used every bit of strength she could muster to stay on her feet rather than have the hateful stranger in a position to say she was weak. She closed her mind to the pain in her calves and the cuts and bruises on her feet, for she had vowed she would not beg or plead with him again! *After all, I've withstood far worse degradation than being dragged through a bit of mud and slime! I survived before. And I'll survive this, too.*

Looking ahead for the first time in what seemed like hours, Esmeralda was surprised to see a glimmer of light in the distance, and she had to suppress a gasp of excitement. They had been in the swamp so long that when she looked at the source of the brightness finding its way through the dense growth that surrounded them, she was blinded for a moment before her eyes began to water in gratitude. If she had to die, let it be in the open—in the sunlight.

Covered as they were from head to toe with wet gray mud from the hellish mire they had walked through, the four mud-caked figures were recognizable as two humans and two animals due only to the number of feet used for walking.

Esmeralda glanced around for some sign of life but was quickly disappointed to find that the grassy clearing beside a stream of rushing water was deserted. "Where are we?"

"Don't you get tired of repeating yourself?" Dirk berated her, his lip curled in an ugly, crooked smile of distaste.

Just keep your mouth shut. I'll get out of this by using my wits. I'll think of something, she assured herself, tightly clamping her lips together on any answer she might have given to his question.

Leading the animals and footsore girl to the edge of the stream, Dirk let the horses drink while he pulled his prisoner into the water with him. Untying her wrists, he ordered her to wash herself.

She didn't have to be told twice to lower herself into the clean knee-deep water. She took off her stockings and apron first, and after rinsing them out, she used them as rags to scrub herself, dress and all.

"What about this?" Dirk asked, snatching the white cap off her head. Long blond hair spilled down her back into the water in a heart-gripping reminder of the past. The muscles in his jaw knotted, and he clenched his fists.

Oblivious to the stranger's stunned gasp of surprise, she snatched the muddy cap from his hand and quickly rinsed it out, too—but not until she had washed the silvery hair that held the man mesmerized.

Then, as suddenly as he had led her into the water, he took her out—long before she was ready to give up the feel of its blessed purity swirling in to cleanse and heal her weary body and soul.

Dirk felt no need to spend more time in the stream's rejuvenating current, and he paid no heed to the protests of the woman he dragged from the water, forcing her to run behind him.

Opening a bundle he took off his horse, he pulled out dry clothing for them both. "Put these on."

Thrilled with the prospect of dry clothes, she forgot for a moment how cruel the man had been and said, "Where shall I change?"

"Where indeed?" he said with a sarcastic grin, his eyebrow raised in sneering surprise at her foolish question.

"You mean I am to have no privacy?" she asked indignantly, the fear in her heart swelling violently. Had she been saved from Fernando, only to be dragged into an even more horrendous situation?

"Of what use is privacy to a harlot?" His bitter laugh cut cruelly into her thoughts, but she managed to hide her feeling from him. Raising her chin defiantly, she returned his angry glare.

"Well, I won't do it! Not with you staring at me with that ugly look on your face," she announced recklessly. With her arms stubbornly akimbo, she challenged him as green sparks of fire from her eyes clashed unyieldingly with the chilling ice blue crystals in his. Despite her apparent courage, she shuddered inwardly. But she would not back down!

"Yes, you will," he told her in an ominous, knowing tone.

"I won't!"

"Then I'll do it for you," he declared matter-of-factly, advancing toward her small, determined person, already shivering with the cold. "I don't need to drag a sick trollop all the way to Groningen. It's bad enough I have to make the trip at all!" he mumbled, reaching for the hem of her skirt.

Steeling himself for seeing her undressed, Dirk took a deep, stabilizing breath and yanked the loose-fitting dress up over her head with one swift motion, leaving her stunned and totally exposed through her thin chemise of white lawn, which adhered revealingly to her body.

Conscious of her visible nakedness beneath the gossamer undergarment, Esmeralda took a step backward, trying to cover herself with her hands as she did. She was suddenly more afraid than she had ever been of the duke of Alva.

With the glorious sun spreading its last rays of the day on the spot where she stood, she was unmindful that dusk had begun to bear down on them. She was too intent on the aching face before her and the deluge of confusing thoughts and emotions flooding mercilessly through her mind.

"Are you going to put these clothes on?" he demanded, the low timbre of his even voice breaking into the pregnant moment of silence.

"Not while you stand there," she yelled stubbornly, finding one last ounce of spunk deep within. "Turn around and I'll do it!"

Afraid that if he touched her one more time he would lose all control, Dirk considered giving in and allowing her to dress with some privacy. After all, where could she go? But he had no intention of making her situation any more pleasant than necessary. He would not be forced to do her bidding—no matter how simple or reasonable her request!

"All right, then. If that's the way you want it!"

He advanced toward her, slowly and menacingly, never taking his eyes from her.

Her first inclination was to run. But of course it was no use. However, she still refused to show her mounting fear and looked insolently into his steel blue eyes with a determination that matched his own—a determination that unnerved him no end, filling him with a desire to choke it out of her.

As he put his hands confidently on the thin material that covered her, his fingers barely touched the pink skin that could be seen shimmering through the opaque, gauzelike chemise; but with that one light contact he became lost in the paralyzing heat of his desire, lost in his own feral need.

Like wildfire, raging and destructive, his restraint, held in check until that moment by only a fragile thread of sanity, was fiercely and totally expunged as the devastating heat from her satiny skin exploded suddenly and violently in every fragment of his being.

Seizing her shoulders in an ironlike grip, Dirk pulled her to him, bringing his mouth brutally down on hers with a savage kiss that sent Esmeralda's senses whirling in a violent turmoil of pain and lust. With arms hanging feebly at her sides, her hands numbing under the pressure of his grasp on her shoulders, she tasted the blood of her own assaulted mouth mingled with the salt of tears.

Aware she wasn't crying, she raised her confused gaze to see tears of anguish and self-hate slide vulnerably down her attacker's bearded cheeks.

"Who are you? Do I know you? Please tell me! I beg of you!" she whispered when he drew his mouth away from hers. She searched his suffering, familiar eyes—the blue eyes of her dreams—but all she could see was hate and agony.

"Perhaps this will remind you!" he groaned, throwing her punishingly to the mossy ground.

In his mad rage, he quickly divested himself of his own clothing and tore the thin covering from her helpless form, flinging it to the side as he crudely mounted her defenseless body. He rode her mercilessly, trying to purge himself of the love and desire he still felt for the wanton woman beneath him. He wanted her to experience the pain and torture he had endured in the months since her disappearance.

"Oh, God, Johanna," he moaned. "Why?"

Part Four — Johanna

Chapter Twelve

Forgetting the mistreatment she had suffered at his hand, Johanna let her arms slide naturally to the position they were yearning to assume, had longed to assume from the first time she had seen him in her dreams. Gently caressing the tense muscles of his strong back, she felt the pain he wanted her to feel and cried out her own anguish to the stranger who was not really a stranger. "Oh, Dirk!"

Hearing his name on her lips, he slammed himself against her in a final, angry attack, emptying his hatred into her. His rage spent, he collapsed on her.

Tears rose in her eyes and ran down her cheeks into damp, matted hair lying wildly scattered over the ground. Crying, she held his face to her breast and stroked the dark hair, still wet from the stream. "I'm sorry I did something to hurt you in the past. I can only tell you I don't know what it was. I only have memories of the last few months of my life."

Dirk rose up on his forearms to examine her face, as if by watching her he could discern the truth. He didn't speak, but studied her intently as she went on.

"I've dreamed of you over and over, and when I saw you—your eyes—I knew it was you who had haunted my dreams. But in my dreams your hair and beard were not dark, and you were gentle, very gentle and loving. Please tell me what I did to cause the gentle, loving man of my dreams to carry such bitterness and anger in his heart. Please tell me who you are. Who I am."

"You're a lying whore named Esmeralda Verde, and I'm on a mission to bring Alva's *puta* back north to be held for ransom," he blurted, abruptly levering himself away from her and standing to dress.

Stunned, she sat up and reached out to touch him. He didn't believe her. "You've got to tell me! Who am I? I'm not Esmeralda Verde! Not Emeraude Benner! Who? I must know who."

"I have to admit you're a better actress than the average, Johanna, but don't waste your time using your whore's ploys on me. That lost-memory pretext won't succeed with me. If you wanted me to believe you, you should have been more careful about calling me by name."

"What name did I call you?" she asked, frantically searching her memory for the name she must have said, furious that both her body and subconscious knew who this man was, but still she couldn't recall his name.

"You'd better get yourself dressed or I might just find another swelling in my breeches that only a whore can assuage," he threatened viciously.

Rising slowly, her body sore and aching from the trek through the swamp as well as the rape she had experienced, she walked over to the rough-woven clothing he had brought out of his bundle for her to wear.

Johanna, she remembered. *He called me Johanna.* She tried the name on her tongue. "Johanna. Johanna? Johanna!" *It feels right, yet it doesn't. Can I have changed so much since I was his Johanna that I'll never be that girl again? He certainly thinks so. He won't believe me. He hates me too much.*

Realizing the negative turn her thoughts were taking, Johanna deliberately concentrated on remembering his name. *Johanna and who? What name did I call out?* But try as she might she could not put a name to the man's face. *Well, what difference does it make?* she asked herself.

But somehow, Johanna knew it made a great deal of difference what this angry man thought of her. And no matter how much he hated her, she had to convince him she had not done the evil things he believed her to be guilty of.

Distraught and feeling defeated, she bent to pick up the shapeless bundle of clothing he had let fall to the ground. It was then she realized he was expecting her to wear a man's shirt and baggy breeches. She shot him a questioning glance.

"They'll be searching for a Spanish officer and a young woman. Needless to say, until we get out of Brabant, you'll wear the disguise of a young boy," he explained impatiently, busying himself with checking the horses.

"I suppose it will be easier to ride that way," she agreed. "But I must wear something underneath, or this material will rub my skin raw."

"Feel free—if you think you can salvage anything," he laughed harshly, pointing to the tattered remnants

211

of Nadine's delicate stitching.

Seeing what he meant, Johanna sighed her resignation and quickly pulled the baggy pants and shirt on over her nakedness. Turning to search for something to protect her cut and bruised feet, she didn't argue when he handed her black buckskin shoes and hose of faded blue.

When she finished dressing, she turned to face him, taunting, "There, are you satis . . ." But the rest of the question froze on her lips, and her gaze focused helplessly on the long knife in his hand.

Without speaking, Dirk grabbed an angry fistful of luxurious blond hair and pulled her up to where her neck and body were stretched to their full extent, her toes barely brushing the ground.

Dangling vulnerably by her hair, she refused to show her fear and met his eyes with a calm she couldn't feel. "Do you really think you can frighten me by threatening to kill me?"

He grinned sadistically, looking ghoulish in the evening light. "Maybe I don't want to kill you—yet. Perhaps I only want to do a little cutting for now. Your beauty was your downfall, Johanna," he said harshly, then released a wretched moan of haunted despair. "And it was mine!"

"Then do it!" she challenged again. "Cut me to shreds. There's nothing you can do to me that will destroy my spirit! Others, far more vicious and imaginative than you and your toy knife, have tried; and they failed. Just as you will fail. The only way you can destroy me is to kill me. But you don't have the courage, do you?" she jeered cruelly, crazily.

Raising the knife up to strike, he looked into shining

green eyes that dared him to go ahead and complete his plan in one swift blow. They stayed frozen that way, each impaled on the other's gaze, neither having the will nor the strength to move, neither knowing what would happen next.

Johanna refused herself the luxury of closing her eyes to await her death, wanting to view life with her last dying breath. Staying alive had been her whole purpose, hadn't it? She had endured shame, hatred, and physical abuse to survive. Was it all to end here in this dark clearing with no one to hear her cries for help, with no one to mourn her death?

Suddenly, the realization that living was no longer important hit her in the chest with a constricting spasm of pain. Looking into the disgust-filled eyes of her murderer, she knew the only important truth was that this man had once loved her and never would again. The knowledge that he existed had kept her strong all the time she didn't know who she was. But the cost of surviving had been too great, for he was unwilling to forgive her for what she could not change. "Go on, please," she pleaded earnestly, no longer able to bear the sight of the unforgiving, tormented face that stared down at her.

In answer to her plea, Dirk's knife whizzed down on Johanna, hacking and chopping at her hair until the ground was baroquely littered with a glittering mat of silvery curls.

Still waiting for the final blow, she kept her eyes on the grim face so intent on destruction—her destruction! But that blow did not come!

Taking one last slash at the hair, he pushed her aside and dropped to the ground to gather up the fallen tresses and bury his face in them, muffling his racking sobs.

Johanna lay on the ground where he had tossed her, slowly becoming aware of what had happened. She felt the scratching material of the shirt where it irritated her clammy skin; she realized the loss of a great weight in the form of her hair; and she knew for certain she was indeed alive! He hadn't killed her!

Running her fingers experimentally through her shorn tresses, she thought jubilantly, *It'll grow back because I'm alive. He couldn't kill me. I'm not dead! I'm alive. My name is Johanna and I'm still alive!*

She waited and watched, afraid to move, afraid her reprieve might only be temporary.

When Dirk finally ended his ritual of mourning, he walked to his horse, where he impersonally stuffed her hewn locks into a burlap game sack. When he returned to the spot where she sat, he couldn't speak. His anguish-filled eyes were absorbed by her face, so conspicuously trusting under the ragged, disheveled hair which stood out from her head in a grim reminder of his temporary madness.

He had no control of his hand as it reached out to gently stroke the place where only minutes before long waves had hung freely. He tried to smooth the butchered hair back from the girl's questioning face, but his hand involuntarily jerked away from the physical contact, as if stung by acid where he touched her.

"Here's something to eat," he said quietly, handing her a hunk of brown bread and a fistful of dried apricots.

Johanna wanted desperately to reach out to the

miserable man and tell him she loved him and that it was all right about her hair, the rape, the cruel words, everything! But she knew she was the reason for his self-torture, and he wouldn't accept comfort from her. Maybe he never would. "Thank you," she answered softly, extending her hand to accept his offering.

Eating her meager meal in silence, Johanna was surprised at the appetite she had built up in the hours since noon, and she ate ravenously. It was another indication to her that she wasn't dead. And as long as she was still breathing, there was hope she would earn his trust and love again!

"When you're through eating, you can take care of your personal needs in those bushes," Dirk said coolly. "I'll turn my back."

"Thank you." She stood up and started across the clearing.

His voice devoid of emotion, he called after her. "Don't do anything stupid like trying to escape—there's no place you could go. When you're through, we'll sleep for a few hours and then leave by the time the moon is up," he explained wearily.

Knowing it was futile to argue or tell him she wouldn't try to run away, Johanna made her way to the clump of green he had designated and quickly dispensed with her personal needs before returning to the clearing to take her place beside him on the blanket he had spread on the ground.

Moments later, she stared into the darkness, acutely aware of the fact that he was only three feet from her. The space between them was rife with electricity, and she wondered if she would be able to sleep after all that had happened that day.

When Dirk roused her out of a sound sleep a few hours later, she was dreaming of a summer of romantic nights when a young man had come to her room often and made sweet, passionate love to her. Turning over in her half-awake state, she was not at all surprised to see that young man looking down at her.

"Hello," she purred, stretching luxuriously. However, consciousness quickly triumphed over her drowsy state of euphoria, and she was brought back to reality with a thud! "What time is it?" she asked angrily, hoping he hadn't noticed her lapse. Besides, she was now uncomfortably aware of the shirt rubbing cruelly against her naked breasts, chafing her tender skin unmercifully and adding considerably to her bad mood.

"Time to go. We have a lot of miles to travel the next few days, and I expect to cover a great many of them tonight." He was readying the horses as he spoke, having replaced the mare's bridle and telltale Spanish saddle with a ragged blanket and halter he had fashioned out of rope.

Seeming to pay no further attention to his prisoner, he took a final survey of the two mud-covered horses and slapped the mare on the rump. "There, no one would suspect you of being such a fine lady," he said affectionately.

"Are you talking about the horse or me?" Johanna ventured sarcastically, brushing the leaves from her loose-fitting clothing.

Looking in her direction, as if seeing her for the first time, Dirk fought the desire to take her in his arms and kiss away the past months. So independent and spirited. In her patched boy's clothing and shaggy, uneven hair, she looked like a young street urchin readying himself for a day of picking pockets in the streets of Brussels.

Hiding the smile that came unbidden to his face, he kept his face averted and his voice cool when he answered. "Both of you, of course!"

"Do I get to make another trip to the bushes before we leave?" she asked contemptuously, feeling daring now that she was rested and knew he wasn't going to kill her.

"Hurry," he replied, admiring her backbone in spite of all that had happened.

Walking toward the brush, she bent to scoop up the torn chemise; and in the privacy of the shrubbery, she fashioned a makeshift protection for her tender breasts by wrapping the torn material around her and tying it securely. Although the peculiar undergarment bound her fullness flat, it was worth it to defend her delicate nipples from the galling roughness of the shirt. When she came out of the privacy shelter, she felt much better able to face a night on horseback. Confidently taking the hat he handed her, she pulled it low on her head, imitating the way he was wearing his, and actually managed a smile when she said, "Let's go!"

However, when he walked closer to her and placed his hands on her waist, her smile faded quickly when she noticed his intense demeanor. She wanted to scream, but no longer out of fear. It was the unbearable excitement his touch brought to her body—even through the thick, ill-fitting clothes.

"We can forget the rope," he coughed nervously, knowing he would be undone if he looked into her jewel-like eyes again.

To steady herself with him so near, Johanna instinctively put her hands on his muscular arms, unmindful of the tightening of the muscles of his jaw when she made that one small, automatic gesture. "I know you don't believe that I can't remember anything, but I really don't know who you are. Can you at least tell me your name?"

Shaking her hands off his arms, he wheeled away from her and bellowed angrily, "Will you stop playing this game! You know I'm Dirk Corlear!"

She frowned. "The count of Leuven?"

"You're giving yourself away again, Johanna! How would you know that, if as you say, you have no memory of the past?" he accused.

"Your name was on a list of nobles who took a petition to Margaret de Parma asking for religious leniency last fall. You were one of the people I sent a warning about Alva's vicious trap. You must have received it. How else would you have known to come to Brussels in disguise?" she pointed out eagerly, seeing this as a chance to convince him she was not a traitor.

However, Dirk refused to be convinced. "You're wasting your time, Johanna! Even if I believed your story about not knowing who you are, I'd find it too great a coincidence that our names simply happened to be on a list you sent random warnings to. No, I think that when you saw our names on Alva's death roll, you couldn't stand by and watch us murdered by your Spanish lover! Even a woman who would let her family think she was dead rather than trust them to love her, no matter what, couldn't do that."

Seeing how foolish she had been to think he would try to understand, Johanna spoke angrily, unleashing her full fury on him. "Frankly, at this point, I don't

218

care what you believe; but it may interest you to know that I sent hundreds of warnings out. And each of my letters told how Alva planned to execute all the men who signed that petition, plus hundreds of others I listed with the hope that the men I warned would get word to them! That day when he dropped the net on those innocent men, I don't suppose you noticed there were less than fifty in his vile snare, did you? In case you can't count, that means there were three hundred and fifty men missing from the meeting, since over four hundred invitations had gone out. No, you were too busy judging me, weren't you? Judging me for crimes you imagined I had committed. Judging me and finding me guilty for surviving, when by all rights I should be dead!"

Unconcerned with the tears streaming down her face, her fists beat wildly at his chest as she bombarded him with her angry words. "That's what you wanted, isn't it? For me to be dead! So you could mourn your poor unsullied love! Well, I'm sorry, I can't oblige you, Count Leuven! I'm very much alive. Not dead, but alive, and I refuse to be ashamed of anything I've been willing to do to stay that way!"

Strangely calmed by the release of her suppressed anger at the cards the fates had dealt her, Johanna straightened her back and lifted her chin to look him squarely in the eye. "I envy you, Dirk Corlear," she said with a tearful smile, her tone scathing with contempt. "It must be wonderful to have never found it necessary to do anything distasteful to stay alive. Never to have had your destiny plucked out of your control at a moment's notice. You are a very fortunate man, indeed!"

When she was through, Johanna turned her back

and walked to the edge of the clearing and stared into the dark forest.

Helplessly paralyzed by her angry tirade, Dirk remembered the soldier he had killed so casually that very morning—for nothing more than the clothing he wore and his horse. Shaking his head, he approached Johanna where she stood.

Placing his hands on her frail shoulders, he drew her to him and rested his chin on the top of her head. They stood that way for a long while, each lost in personal thoughts and sorrow for what was gone and could never be recreated.

Finally, Dirk turned Johanna to face him, lightly lifting her chin with a hand so gentle it might have been opening the petals of a delicate rose. Bending to brush her lips softly with his own, he tasted the salt of her tears on his tongue, and he encircled her in his arms to hold her against his aching breast. He could no longer deny his need to have her in his arms.

Johanna didn't question what was happening or what the next moment would bring. For now, she was satisfied to cling to his strength for as long as he would let her, glorying in his embrace and imagining she could hear the sounds of two broken hearts beginning to heal.

"Johanna, we must leave," he whispered.

"I know, Dirk," she sighed, permitting herself to say his name consciously for the first time. He lifted her into his arms and carried her to the gray horse, where he placed her on the readied mount. Then leaping onto the Spanish mare, he led the way toward safety.

Johanna and Dirk traveled in silence for the

remainder of the night until well after dawn. However, as they rode into the morning traffic moving toward Maastricht, a city only a few miles from the border of Germany, Dirk knew they must stop for food and rest.

Johanna looked so much like a peasant waif in the light of day that he was certain she wouldn't be exposed as a woman, even in the daylight; but if they wanted the horses to survive the entire trip through the German terrain into the northern Netherlands, they needed to stop soon.

Dismounting, they continued into the city on foot beside their weary horses. Still not convinced Johanna was telling the truth, he kept very close watch on her, unsure what she would do if the occasion to escape arose.

Sensing his unease, Johanna couldn't resist goading under her breath, "I could scream for help. I imagine news of my abduction has reached this city by now, don't you?"

"You won't, though," he laughed confidently. "Not if you want to hang onto that life you say you prize so dearly!" he added congenially as he reached over to pull the hat lower on her head in an attempt to hide her eyes and hair more fully.

"Well, you don't need to worry," she admitted. "I have no intention of calling attention to myself. It was only a matter of time until I was discovered as the leak in the duke's security—since I passed on much information that only I was privy to," she confessed.

"Next, you're going to tell me you were waiting for me to come rescue you from your prison of satin and jewels," he grumbled.

Not daring to tell him that he had voiced her repeated dream, she smiled with false sweetness and

221

eyed his patched peasant's garb with a wrinkled nose. "How did you know? You must be my knight in shining armor, the romantic way you dragged me off so gallantly through the swamps," she laughed bitterly, attempting to hide her true feelings—the fact that she didn't care what he wore or where he took her as long as he had come and didn't leave her again. In the light of the bright day, she felt certain that she could make him love her and want her again. But it would take time, and she knew she shouldn't force the issue.

Dirk kept any further comments to himself and veered off the road to where some peddlers had set up a small marketing area to sell their goods without going into the congested marketplace or paying the fee at the tollgate into the city.

"I think we'll purchase some things here before we stop," Dirk informed her pointedly, guiding her in front of him and making it obvious that he intended to ignore her last gibe.

After making purchases of bread, cheese, fruit, and a blanket, they headed off the road to a nearby thicket. Once they were hidden from the road in a shady grove of ancient oak trees, Dirk released his tight grip on Johanna's arm and tossed her a fresh peach.

Biting into the juicy piece of fruit eagerly, not caring about the nectar that dribbled down her chin, she asked, "Are we going to stay here all day?"

Fighting the impulse to wipe her face for her, Dirk answered, "Only long enough to rest and feed the horses. Then we'll be on our way. You've got time to take a nap if you like!"

"What about you? Aren't you tired?" she asked, wiping the sleeve of her shirt across her sticky face.

Amused by her natural gesture, Dirk looked at the

222

ground to hide his smile. "I'll sleep tonight when we get to Germany," he answered, offering her a chunk of cheese speared on his knife.

Johanna took the offered food without hesitating but couldn't blot out the memory the knife brought to her mind. "You really wanted to kill me last night, didn't you?" There was no accusation in her tone, only sorrowful reality.

"Yes," he admitted softly, the one word a tortured groan.

"Do you hate me so much? Is there no love or understanding left in your heart for me?" she appealed openly, knowing she was leaving herself vulnerable to another demonstration of precisely how great his hatred actually was.

But the expected attack didn't come. He remained silent for some time, studying her serious face, still dirty with the dust of the road, as if in her open expression he could find the answers to the questions that haunted him. "I don't know how I feel about you. When I saw you on that podium with Alva, I knew I hated you. I would have killed you right then if I'd had a chance at success. But now I just don't know," he responded honestly. "How did you end up with that bastard, Johanna?" he groaned unexpectedly, punching his balled fist into the soft earth again and again.

"Do you know what happened in the cathedral?" she whispered quietly, looking at the ground around her to hide her trembling lips.

"I know," he said softly. "Is that it, Johanna? Is that why you didn't come back? Were you afraid I would no longer love you?" he asked gently.

"Dirk, I didn't even remember what happened to me for weeks. I simply woke up in a bed in the Benners' inn with no past. They tell me they found me by the river, beaten and nearly dead; but I still have no recollection of it. Mama—Mignon Benner—feared it was my family or an irate husband who had beaten me so brutally, so they were afraid to tell anyone about me until I could tell them what had happened. It was a long time before I fully recovered, though; and by that time, even though I still had no idea what had happened, I felt safe and secure in their home—the only home I could remember. So I begged them to let me be their daughter, and they welcomed me into their family. They named me Emeraude and call me their *fille* to this day. I think of them as my family!"

"This is all very touching," Dirk commented scornfully. "But where does *le duc* come into this warm family picture you have painted?"

"Please try to understand. I was lost and alone. It was as if I were a child again—a little girl with a mother and father to think for me. They fed me, clothed me, held me in their arms when I had nightmares. I would be dead if not for them! They truly gave me my life—a debt I can never repay." She paused, judging the caustic expression on his face and knowing he still didn't believe her, but that she had to keep trying.

"Once my physical wounds had healed, I began to work in the inn, serving in the tavern, helping with the cooking for the boarders, and even doing the laundry with my sister, Suzette." Johanna looked up at Dirk and smiled sheepishly at her reference to the laundry, since he had already seen the evidence of that.

"We were a happy family," she went on. "Except for the fact that we all knew there might be another family searching for me. Papa asked questions all the time,

──── F R E E ────

ZEBRA HOME SUBSCRIPTION SERVICE, INC.

B O O K   C E R T I F I C A T E

YES! Please start my subscription to Zebra Historical Romances and send me my free Zebra Novel along with my first month's Romances. I understand that I may preview these four new Zebra Historical Romances Free for 10 days. If I'm not satisfied with them I may return the four books within 10 days and owe nothing. Otherwise I will pay just $3.50 each; a total of $14.00 (a $15.80 value—I save $1.80). Then each month I will receive the 4 newest titles as soon as they come off the press for the same 10 day Free preview and low price. I may return any shipment and I may cancel this arrangement at any time. There is no minimum number of books to buy and there are no shipping, handling or postage charges. Regardless of what I do, the **FREE** book is mine to keep.

Name _____
 (Please Print)

Address _____ Apt. # _____

City _____ State _____ Zip _____

Telephone (_____) _____

Signature _____
 (if under 18, parent or guardian must sign)

Terms and offer subject to change without notice.

MAIL IN THE COUPON BELOW TODAY

To get your Free ZEBRA HISTORICAL ROMANCE fill out the coupon below and send it in today. As soon as we receive the coupon, we'll send your first month's books to preview Free for 10 days along with your **FREE NOVEL.**

GET FREE FREE GIFT

but no one ever knew where I came from or seemed to recognize me; so I remained Emeraude Benner—until the Spanish troops arrived in Brussels."

Dirk stopped fidgeting with a weed he had picked and lifted his head to watch her face. "Go on," he said suspiciously.

"Soldiers came into the tavern, and after an evening of drinking, they lured me outside. But their plan to molest me was interrupted by their commanding officer, the duke of Alva. What almost happened that night brought the events in the cathedral rushing back into my memory. I still didn't know who I was, but I knew it wasn't my family who'd hurt me. So when the duke offered to help me find my family and suggested that he needed an interpreter, I thought it would be the best way to locate them—and to show the duke my appreciation for saving me from the soldiers."

"His interpreter!" Dirk shouted in disgust. "Is that what they call it in Spanish?"

Ignoring his outburst, Johanna went on, her words coming fast now, as if reliving the past months could purge her of the unhappiness she had endured with the duke of Alva.

"I know it was foolish of me to trust him, and I discovered how truly evil he was almost immediately after my arrival at the palace. But I really believed he wanted to help me when I agreed to go with him!"

"He helped you find your family, all right! He put their names at the top of his vengeance list. Do you know that he has confiscated all your father's properties, as well as those of hundreds of others?"

"They are alive and out of the country, aren't they?"

"Yes, they're alive and safe—for the time being. But

225

do go on. Don't let me spoil this enthralling tale," he grumbled, his lip curling in an ugly smile of disbelief.

With her pain exposed in her moist green eyes, Johanna proceeded to recite the absurd events of the last weeks. She related how once she realized she was a virtual prisoner, as surely as if she'd been put in chains, she had decided to take advantage of her position, disclosing Alva's most confidential secrets to her countrymen. She recalled the hundreds of warnings she had been responsible for sending, and she told him of Francois's part in her conspiracy against Alva and the Spanish army. Then she confessed to the dreams she'd had throughout her ordeal—the dreams of the man with blue eyes who would come and take her away from the hell she was living in.

Dirk stood up and walked to where the horses were tied to move them to a grassier spot. "Some hell!" he laughed derisively. "Did he keep you in the dungeon at night, or what?"

"There are different kinds of hell, Count Corlear," Johanna bristled. "And from the way you've been behaving since you abducted me, I'd say you'd be the first one to know that. I haven't seen any dungeons or chains in your hell," she hissed through clamped teeth, glaring at his back.

His muscles tensing with the truth of her accusation, he turned and stared at her long and hard, his hostile glare threatening. "You'd better get some rest. I'll wake you when it's time to leave."

Johanna took the offered blanket and spread it on the ground. Why had she even bothered to try to explain to him? *He's so devoured by hatred that he'll never understand.*

Chapter Thirteen

The afternoon sun had begun its downward journey when Johanna and Dirk walked their horses back on to the road. Her muscles were stiff from the physical exertion of the past two days, but she was amazed to see how well she felt. "It must be the air outside the confines of those dreadful palace walls," she said aloud as she observed the peddlers walking away from the city, their packs loaded for trips home.

She wondered why there were so few carts on the roads. Most of the tradesmen seemed to be on foot carrying loads much too heavy for them.

As if reading her thoughts, Dirk answered her question. "The roads are in such miserable repair that even with the heavier packs, it's easier to walk than to pull a clumsy cart over the deep ridges. It's a shame too, since these people are forced to pay such great taxes for road maintenance, but you rarely see anything done about the poor conditions."

Walking through the city, Johanna was even more distressed to see the number of people returning from the marketplace with empty sacks. She knew that the peasants who didn't own land had to deliver their harvest to the monasteries or to rich townspeople who owned the fields they worked; but surely they were allowed to keep part of the fruits of their labor to purchase the bare necessities to maintain life.

"Their taxes are so great that by the time they've paid them, they often have nothing left to show for their work," Dirk said in answer to her unspoken question. "Alva wants to raise the taxes even more," he said acridly. "These poor farmers will have nothing to give. I wouldn't be surprised to see bands of them roving the streets of our cities, forced to steal and beg to stay alive," he predicted sadly.

"You did it again!" Johanna exclaimed. "You knew what I was thinking!"

Dirk frowned at her, then shook his head. "It's just a coincidence."

While crossing the Maas River into the province of Limburg, they paused on the St. Servaasbrug Bridge to look out over the water. Built in the thirteenth century, the bridge had been the main entrance from the east to the city of Maastricht for nearly four hundred years. Looking down on the treelined river as it flowed northward from France toward the North Sea, both Johanna and Dirk were struck by their own insignificance in God's master plan.

Forcing himself away from the watery scene below, Dirk prodded Johanna, who looked more like the shabby peasant child every minute, to move on. "No time for daydreaming, *boy!* We've got miles to cover before dark!"

Johanna gave him a pretended look of irritation at

having been called "boy," then took one last look at the enchanting scene below before moving on across the bridge in front of him.

When they could walk side by side once more, she finally spoke again, still treasuring the vision of the river. "I'd like to board one of those barges and float right out to sea!"

He couldn't help smiling, because he shared that same fantasy. "It would be nice—but not very practical. In the middle of a river that floats brazenly through the center of the Netherlands, we'd be easy marks for Alva's troops," he laughed.

"Do you really think it makes any difference? I mean, if we live or die?" she asked, preoccupied and serious.

"I have to think it does," he answered sincerely. "Our lives have to make a difference of some sort—for all the generations that will come to stand on that bridge and wonder at their own place in the scheme of things."

"And do you know your place in the scheme of things?" she asked, wondering about her own reason.

"I hope so. I've made a promise to the Netherlands— I suppose much like a priest makes a vow to the Church. I've vowed to see our land free from the oppression of the Spanish tyrants, no matter what it costs me. I want to be used however our country wishes to use me; and hopefully, this one insignificant man will make a slight impression in the great design."

"At the cost of personal happiness?" she whispered.

"I gave up the prospect of happiness last fall," he said with a disgusted snort. "I suppose it was the price I paid for my calling in life," he laughed unconvincingly. "Enough of this philosophizing and heavy thinking!

We'd best mount up and be on our way!"

Putting her hand timidly on Dirk's arm to stop him, Johanna said, "I also want to make a difference, Dirk. I don't want to be like a speck of dust that's blown hither and yon by the wind. I want to make decisions and help in the fight against anyone who would thwart freedom in the Netherlands. Please believe me, Dirk! It is what I've been trying to do all these months!" she pleaded, not even aware of the single tear that trickled down her face. "That is why I had to make the choices I made."

She could have sworn she saw a glimmer of forgiveness in his distrusting blue eyes, and her heart leapt jubilantly. But as quickly as the light had appeared, it was gone, hidden again behind a mask of doubt and suspicion.

The two horses, having spent several hours resting and eating the rich grass beside the Maas River, were quick to respond when the two people mounted them and dug their heels into the sensitive sides of muscle and animal energy. Riding at a brisk, steady pace, and skirting the towns of Meerssen, Hoensbroek, and Burnssum, they arrived in Germany well before dark.

Loping across the flat marshland of western Germany, Johanna reached up and took off the large-brimmed man's hat she had diligently worn all day. The cool evening breeze whispered gently through her short hair, giving her a sense of freedom she could not remember ever having before. That, and knowing they were reasonably well out of Alva's grasp, brought a glorious sensation to her heart and a smile to her lips. She was really alive!

Spying a small pond nearby and feeling too free to

fear reprisal, she asked, "Are we going to stop soon?"

"Yes, soon." He wondered at the apparent change in her since they had crossed the border into Germany, and he felt an ache in his chest as he was reminded of the beautiful mane of hair stuffed into his game sack—like the pelt of an innocent animal slaughtered for the hunter's glory.

"Do you suppose we can take time to bathe in that pond over there?" she ventured cautiously, watching his jaw for the significant clenching that usually preceded his anger.

But he surprised her by agreeing to the suggestion. "That's a good idea. I imagine these two loyal animals of ours would enjoy some rest, as well as having some of this caked mud washed off their backs."

Without waiting for Dirk to say anything more, Johanna nudged the gray forward with the enthusiasm of a child on the first day of summer, and she rode him directly into the water. Before Dirk and the mare could join her, she had dismounted, thrown the saddle and pack onto dry ground, and was splashing cool water on herself and Fumée. The steady gray horse seemed oblivious to her foolishness as he bent to slurp a long drink of water before she could stir up too much mud from the bottom.

"Don't just stand there staring at us. Get to work," she laughed at Dirk, the gay sound of her laughter sending electric jolts of painful memory through his mind. But he didn't move. He was too lost in recollection.

"Well, if you're not going to wash yourself and that poor horse, I'll do it for you," Johanna threatened, gruffly imitating his stern tone of the day before. She scooped up a hatful of water and daringly threw it on him and the muddy mare.

Brought out of his reverie with the splatter of water in his face, Dirk dropped the reins and advanced purposefully on the giddy girl, who felt too pleased with her aim to be afraid. "So you want a bath, do you?" he asked menacingly, lunging and bringing her down in the water.

They clung to each other for balance as they fell, and he looked into her brilliant green eyes sparkling with mischief, seeing the reflection of his own dissolute hunger mirrored back at him from the deep pools of green.

Suddenly they were in that stream from so long ago, and he couldn't stop himself. His hands slid up her arms to hold her face, and his mouth slanted over hers.

His kiss was surprisingly gentle, and Johanna opened her mouth to him as she wound her arms tightly around him.

His lips on hers, he swept her into his arms and carried her to the mossy bank. With shaking hands he removed her wool shirt and the binding around her full breasts. Groaning aloud as the creamy white mounds were exposed to his ravenous gaze, he cast the wet garments aside and bent to suckle at her.

"Oh, Dirk, my love," she cried without thinking, her head thrashing from side to side as she clutched his head tighter to her breast.

His hands working frantically now, he rose up quickly and removed her pants, then tore off his own. He hesitated, his gaze raking the length of her nude body, and the ache in his heart cried out as strongly as the need in his loins. If he took her now, he might never be able to be free of her.

Lying before him, naked and vulnerable, Johanna knew she should say something to make him stop. He was only using her to slake his desire for a woman—any woman. This didn't mean anything had changed between them. He still thought she was lying. But try as she might, she could not gather the strength to say anything. She had to face the fact that she wanted him as much now as ever.

Lifting her arms to beckon him back into them, she said, "Come love me."

His doubts twisting in his gut, Dirk leaned toward her, his blue eyes clouded with uncertainty as he glided his hand over her flat belly to the downy blond triangle of her femininity. "It doesn't mean I believe you."

Arching her hips instinctively against the pressure, Johanna nodded her head, her tear-filled green gaze never wavering from his sad face. "I know. But for now, it will be enough." She clasped his cheeks between her palms and brought his mouth down to hers. "Now may be all we ever have, Dirk," she said against his lips, still aware of the feel of his resistance. "Right here, right now. Don't let's waste it fighting."

Knowing he was only making his own torture worse, Dirk tossed aside the last traces of his reluctance and rolled into the cradle of her open thighs.

"Oh, yes," she moaned, wrapping her slim legs around his hips and her arms around his neck. *I wish I could hold you like this forever,* she told him silently, knowing that no matter what she had said, now would never be enough.

Kissing her hard on the mouth, Dirk eased himself into the welcoming folds of her body. "Oh, my God," he wailed as the silken warmth enveloped him. He began to move, slowly at first, each thrust a tentative venture into the valley he knew could only bring him more pain than he had already suffered.

But over and over he plunged into her, each time delving closer to the edge of his sanity. Then he was past it all, past the hate, past the unforgiveness, past the memories. There was no turning back. The only thing that mattered was that they were together at that moment. Everything else drifted away on a cloud of mist.

He buried his face in the curve of her neck and shoulder; the muscles of his back tensed, and he cried out as he pumped the full extent of his passion deep into the very core of her.

The muscles of her sex convulsed around him in an erotic spasm of release, milking him of his strength as she lifted her hips up hard to grab and hold him inside her.

Tumbling back to reality, they clung to each other for a long time, the only sounds their ragged breathing, the gentle lapping of the water at the bank of the pond, and the subtle swish of the breeze in the trees.

Finally gathering the power to move, Dirk rolled off Johanna and flopped his forearm up over his eyes. Hating himself all the more for his weakness, he said, "You'd better finish up. We have a way to travel before we reach our destination." With an annoyed grunt, he grabbed up his pants and put them back on.

Watching him walk away from her, Johanna stared after him, knowing now he would never love her again. He had loved the girl she had been, the girl she could never be again—no matter how she tried—and there was no room in his heart for any other.

Thinking to herself as she washed her short hair and clothing before tackling the muddy horse, she decided it was best she knew now that they could never rekindle their destroyed love. Through the day, she had let herself think there might be a possibility he could forget the girl she had been and come to love the woman she had become. But now she knew it would never be.

They finished bathing the horses in silence, both afraid of saying the words that would let the other know how greatly they cared. No matter what words of hatred had been exchanged or terrible, unforgivable trials had been lived, both knew themselves to be chained to each other with a love and devotion that had no chance of survival.

Stepping behind a shelter of shrubbery, Johanna changed into the second set of clothing Dirk had brought for her, choosing the irritation of the material against her skin over the wet improvised undergarment he had taken off her. Bringing the damp bundle of clothing out of her "dressing room," she deftly tied it to the back of her saddle along with Dirk's wet garments, which she had picked up where he had left them.

"I'll need to hang these out when we get where we're going. Don't let me forget," she stated mechanically.

"No, I won't," he responded with equal stiffness. "Are you ready to leave?"

"I believe so. Thank you for stopping. I feel much better now." She spoke steadily, woodenly gazing past his shoulders, afraid that if she looked into his face he would see the love she had for him.

Johanna didn't know how long they traveled, but it

was dark when they arrived at a small farm nestled in the valley of two low hills, and she was very tired.

Leading the horses around the back of the house to the barn, they entered the dark building, which smelled of animals and freshly mown hay. Forgetting her oath of silence, Johanna blurted out a puzzled whisper. "What is this place? Surely, the people who live here don't want strangers wandering into their barn!"

Dirk put the horses in a stall together, and while Johanna helped brush them down he explained. "The people who live here are friends. They've sheltered hundreds of our people who have been driven from the Netherlands by that bastard, Alva."

"Where are they now?" she asked, looking around curiously.

"Oh, they're around. It won't be long before one of them comes rushing out here to see that we have all we need to make our trip to safety. We won't discuss the facts of your escape or disclose your identity to them. No need to put them in more danger than they're already in."

"And just what *is* my identity? Do I have a last name? I've waited all this time for you to tell me, thinking I would make you angry if I kept asking, but you're so secretive, I can't stand it!" she exclaimed, her frustration quivering in her voice.

Shaking his head, Dirk walked toward the back of the barn, trying to escape the haunting thoughts her intense glare brought to mind. "You truly don't know who you are?" he asked, seeming to relent ever so slightly.

"I don't know." She walked up behind him and placed her hand on his arm. However, feeling the muscles tense at her touch, she quickly pulled her hand away. "Does my family know I'm alive? Won't you at least tell me that much?" she pleaded.

Yielding to his intuition—and going against his own good judgment—he answered in a voice that was barely audible. "Yes, they know you're alive. It was your mother who knew first. She recognized your handwriting on the letter of warning you sent to your father, the count of Ledenburg."

"The count of Ledenburg! He's near the top of Alva's list. It can't be! Why is it no one at the palace knew me? I've heard them speak of him many times—and of his sons! No daughter was ever mentioned!"

"No one acknowledged ever seeing you before?" he asked incredulously. "You were a frequent visitor at court before your disappearance. Margaret de Parma even gave a party in our honor before our planned wedding!"

"But she never said a word about knowing who I was! No one did!" Johanna gasped in horror, finally understanding the extent of her betrayal. "Though I remember a strange expression on her face when we were introduced—like shock. But I naturally assumed she was simply surprised to see such a young girl as Alva's interpreter."

"I'm sure she was, especially since she's known you since you were a small child," he bellowed. "Damn her, anyway! So worried about her own self-serving hide that she let us go on thinking you were dead while she stole out of the country before Alva could come up with charges against her too! If only she'd had the courage to inform us, maybe we could have gotten you out of his clutches before it was too late."

Stopping her pacing to look at him intently, she spoke softly, her voice choked with emotion and a last shred of hope. "Is it?" she asked.

"Is it what?" he mumbled, still intent on Margaret de Parma's treachery.

"Is it too late for us?"

Memories of the time spent beside the pond that afternoon exploded in his thoughts, and he abruptly stopped what he was doing and stared at her. His expression filled with contempt and resentment, he regarded her standing before him, vulnerable and trusting. And suddenly he realized that he had started to come back to life after being a walking dead man for so long. Without Johanna, there had been no life, only the torture of endless days piled upon endless nights as he wandered the countryside attempting to make some sense of his existence.

He shook his head sadly and looked at his hands. "Too much has happened to ever go back, Johanna."

Hearing his answer, the tears that had welled in her eyes overflowed, running indiscriminately down her cheeks. She quickly turned her head away from the man who hated her so much, hoping he wouldn't see the demeaning tears. She wiped her face on the tail of her shirt and sniffed, "Where do we sleep? If you don't mind, I'm really quite weary."

Dirk wanted to go to her, touch her, hold her, but he was afraid that if he did, he would never be able to let go. "Johanna," he whispered. "What have they done to you? What have they done to us?"

She turned around and looked into his blue eyes, longing to run into the comfort of his embrace, but fearing his rejection.

238

"What have we here?" a plump, red-faced woman asked upon entering the barn with her husband. "Two more escapees from Alva's dungeon?"

"I tell you, we've had a pack of them through here during the last months—ever since that devil rode in from Spain," her husband interjected congenially.

Spying Johanna peeking out from behind Dirk's larger frame, the woman exclaimed, "Is that madman hanging children now? You poor boy, have you eaten?" she clucked warmly, happy with the prospect of a youngster to fuss over.

"Nein, gutige Frau," Johanna answered in the language the friendly people were using.

"Well, we must do something about that!" Rushing out as suddenly as she had entered, the rosy-cheeked woman arbitrarily ordered Dirk, "Bring that skinny boy to the house in fifteen minutes and I'll have a meal for you that will put a little meat on his bones!"

Trying to protest to the husband, Dirk immediately saw that it was hopeless. The old man held up his hands in relinquishment and shrugged his shoulders, then hurriedly followed his wife out of the barn.

Dirk turned to Johanna, concentrating on hiding his smile, but not quite managing the feat. *"'Nein, gutige Frau'!"* he said, mimicking her with a wag of his head. "What in the hell are we going to do now?"

As she saw the grin behind Dirk's eyes, Johanna's heart skipped a beat and a plan began to take shape in her mind. Maybe refueling their love wasn't as hopeless as he wanted her to believe. After all, if she could make him like her just a little bit more every day, maybe he would gradually fall in love with her again. *That's what I'll do. I'll take it one step at a time. But you are going to love me again, Dirk Corlear,* she vowed silently, giving him a secret grin. "I don't know about you, *gutiger Herr,*" she said aloud. "But I'm going to eat supper. You wouldn't deny that sweet old woman—that generous patriot—the pleasure of fattening up this pitiful, hungry waif, would you?" She laughed triumphantly at the helpless position she had put Dirk in and put on her best underfed expression. It would do him good to worry a little bit.

And Dirk was worried, but he couldn't resist her starving-orphan performance and gave in conditionally. Besides, what harm could come of going, as long as he was there to keep an eye on her? And it was less dangerous to his sanity than being alone in the barn with her any longer than necessary. "I'd have a difficult time denying anyone as funny-looking as you are in those clothes. But you'd better keep your eyes lowered to the floor the entire time you're there. And for God's sake, keep your mouth shut!" he ordered, trying to sound stern and threatening, but failing miserably. "Understood?"

"Ja, Meister," she answered respectfully. "I mean, *ja, Meister,*" she said again in a deeper voice.

Still having doubts, Dirk shook his head and raised his eyebrows accusingly. "Don't you think you've forgotten something?" he asked, indicating the obvious curves under her loose shirt.

She glanced down at her chest. "Oops," she said with an embarrassed laugh. "I'd better do something about that, hadn't I?"

Taking the bundle of damp clothing into an unoccupied stall, she bound her breasts snugly with the wet chemise and then walked into the open, convincingly flat-chested once more. "A bit damp, but a hot meal and some pleasant conversation is worth a little discomfort." With that, she sauntered cockily out the barn door, pleased that she had succeeded in unsettling Dirk Corlear's confidence just a little bit!

They crossed the yard without speaking, but as they stepped onto the porch of the tiny white cottage, Dirk grabbed her arm and jerked her to a halt. "Remember what I said, Johanna!"

"Ja, ja," she returned, her eyes sparkling mischievously, her new freedom giving her courage she hadn't had as long as they were still in the Netherlands.

"Johanna, I'm serious. If Alva were to trace us here, these good people could lose their lives!"

Losing patience with his conversation and mistrust, she wrenched her arm free from his grip. "Will you stop worrying? Whether you believe me or not, I don't want to be exposed any more than you want me to be. And I certainly don't want these kind people to suffer because of me. Now, why don't you relax and enjoy their generous hospitality?"

Then her expression softened. Giving him a cajoling grin, she patted his arm. "All right?"

"Ja, ja!" he laughed in spite of himself, and gave her a gentle shove toward the door to the little house.

Chapter Fourteen

"Axel, our guests are here!" the old woman hollered to her husband—who was standing right beside her.

"*Ja, Mutter,* I see," the old man said with a warm smile, beckoning to Johanna and Dirk. "Come, children. Sit down."

Glancing around shyly, Johanna was enthralled with the tiny house. The entire cottage was one small room, with brightly colored curtains on the windows and a cookstove in the far corner. The wooden floor had been scrubbed to a smooth finish by many hours of hard work, and the sturdy oak table and chairs that dominated the room had the look of years of use. On the south wall, there were two beds covered with fluffy, well-worn down comforters and huge pillows, and the fragrance of freshly baked bread that permeated the room invaded Johanna's nostrils, overwhelming her with a sense of well-being.

"Tell me, what is the lad's name?" the woman asked, speaking to Dirk.

"His name?" Looking frantically at Johanna for

help, he said, "His name is, uh . . ."

"Ich heisse Josef, gutige Frau," Johanna interrupted, keeping her eyes on the polished floor, appearing every bit the self-conscious youth she was impersonating.

"Josef!" the woman cried. "Axel, did you hear that? His name is Josef! Our son, too, is Josef, as was my father!" she clamored excitedly, hobbling to the black stove where the huge soup pot was making delicious-sounding bubbling noises.

If Dirk had been worried that Johanna would talk too much and give away her disguise, it was only because he had not met Klara Böttcher before. Neither he nor Johanna found it necessary to speak at all, for the woman chattered happily during the entire meal, asking questions and continuing to talk before they could be answered.

As they ate the *groentesoep met balletjes,* a filling and savory soup of fresh vegetables, rice, and small, delectable bits of meat, Frau Böttcher told them how she and her husband had left the Netherlands when they had heard rumors of Alva's probable arrival. And Dirk and Johanna learned that the small farm had been left to them by Frau Böttcher's aged father when he died at the age of ninety-eight in a fall from a mule— while going to court a widow on the next farm!

The piping hot bread that came out of the oven brought stories about each of their six children, who were scattered over Germany and the Netherlands, as well as tales of their many grandchildren and great-grandchildren; and during the *rijstpudding* dessert, Dirk and Johanna were blessed with all of Frau Böttcher's gardening tips for growing the best fruits and vegetables, not to mention numerous pointers on slaughtering chickens and swine and making sausage.

Leaving the old couple at the end of a delightful two hours, Johanna hated to go. But her carefree spirit stayed with her even after they left. Walking back to the barn, she laughingly said to Dirk, "Did I say anything I shouldn't have, *mein Meister?*"

"No, you didn't," he conceded, glancing at her out of the corner of his eye. "As a matter of fact, that's the quietest I've ever seen you. You must have been too busy stuffing your mouth. Your disguise was most convincing if anyone were to watch you eat. I don't see where such a small 'lad' put all that food!" he chided amicably.

"Me? What about you? I stopped counting at three bowls of soup. And don't you think eating a whole loaf of bread by yourself was extremely ill-mannered?" she giggled, breaking into a run and leaving him behind.

Dirk thoughtfully watched her for a minute before following her inside. Catching up to her, he said sternly, "Wait a minute! There's a flaw in your disguise!"

Johanna glanced down at herself to see what he meant. "What?"

"I'm sorry to tell you this," he said, shaking his head sadly. "But you definitely don't run like a boy!" He laughed and swatted her lightly on the bottom.

The easy comradeship that had ensued during the short period of time since Klara and Axel Böttcher had rushed into the barn two hours before was suddenly strained.

Johanna looked at Dirk questioningly, and she saw the softening in his expression. Worried that it was but a fleeting thing and that he had, in fact, not changed his feeling for her at all, she answered glibly. "I'll try to work on that. Even worse than having anyone realize I'm a woman would be if they thought I was an unusually effeminate boy. Wouldn't you say?"

Transfixed by her dazzling gaze, Dirk answered, the lightness in his tone not disguising the sadness in his expression. "Yes, it would do my reputation no good at all to be seen with an effeminate lad!"

"Then tomorrow you will have to show me the proper way for a *boy* of my age to run," she stated, walking to where the horses stood munching languidly on the hay Axel Böttcher had placed in the crib for them.

After watching the content animals for a few minutes, Johanna suddenly asked, "Dirk are you certain my parents are nobility?" She was dawdling with a piece of straw she had picked up from the ground.

"Of course I'm certain," he laughed. "What a foolish question! Why would you even ask?"

"It's just that I feel so comfortable in these surroundings and so uneasy in a more elaborate atmosphere. I like the smell of the barn, the sound of the horses eating, the warm feeling I get in the Böttcher's small cottage. I don't even mind these ugly clothes, although I must admit they do itch dreadfully," she laughed. "I feel free for the first time in a long time. It's the way it is when I'm at the Benners'—as if it's where I belong."

Listening to her contemplation, Dirk was reminded of the Johanna he had known the summer before. Johanna who waded in streams, Johanna who preferred bare feet to fashionable slippers, and Johanna who caused her poor mother untold grief with her tomboyish ways and tree climbing.

"Do you have any recollection of the first time I saw you?" he asked with a distant gaze in his eyes.

"No. Will you tell me about it?" she asked, anxious to learn about her past life and love.

Dirk looked into her expectant face, then nervously shifted his eyes. "It was spring—early in April. I was riding to visit your father on political business. I had stopped to rest and water my horse in a stream that runs across your father's property in Brabant. And there you were!" He smiled fondly at the memory. "Right in the middle of the stream with your skirt pulled up around your knees and wading! You were so free and unrestrained, I thought you were a farmer's daughter at first. Though when I shared my assumption with you, you were very indignant!" he laughed.

He went on to tell her the rest of the details of their first meeting. "I'll never forget that day," he sighed longingly, his mind having departed for a more pleasant time in his life. "I loved you the moment I saw you," he admitted, unable to look at her.

"And did I love you the first time I saw you?" She was certain that she had.

"You told me you did—later on," he laughed. "But to tell you the truth, you found me quite irritating that day in the stream!"

Shaking his head to bring himself out of his reverie, Dirk stood up and stretched his long legs. "We'd better sleep now. We'll travel by day while we're in Germany. Then we'll need to ride at night when we go back into the Netherlands." Holding his hand down to offer his assistance, he steeled himself against the agonizing pleasure of her touch.

She put her small hand in his and allowed him to help her up from the straw-littered floor of the barn.

When they were both standing, he made no effort to release her hand from his powerful grip. And she had no desire to pull away. "I wish we were in that stream now. I wouldn't run away again," she whispered, aware that her cheeks were aflame with embarrassment at her audacity and yearning for his kiss.

Unable to give up his hold on the hand that perched so lightly in his own, and powerless to deny his love for her any longer, Dirk brought her into his arms, lightly kissing her blushing cheeks, her temples, her closed eyelids, her forehead, and at last her eager mouth.

With no more hesitation, his hard masculine lips took full possession of hers, making them his own, exploring, cherishing, tasting their softness with his tongue until he left no part of her mouth unconquered.

Taking his lips from hers, he studied her face closely, his own a study in torture and agony. "I want you," he finally moaned, surrendering to the inescapable truth. "God help me, I still want you."

Scooping her into his strong arms, he kissed her again, this time with a feral urgency that was matched by her unleashed passion. He had to have her, no matter what she had done in the past.

He carried her to the back stall, where their blankets were already spread, and lowered her to the ground, his lips never leaving hers. Silently, he removed her rough-hewn clothing in the darkness of the imperfect cubicle.

The unlit space seemed to burgeon into a richly colored display of arcs, bands and streamers for Johanna, and she smiled up at him. Lying before him, her naked body glistening in the half-light of the moon that filtered through the cracks in the wall of the barn, she watched as he lowered himself beside her.

"Oh, Johanna. I've waited for so long," he groaned, his statement a helpless plea.

"I love you, Dirk. Please love me again," she begged, reaching up to pull his mouth to hers.

He parted her lips with urgency, and she was lost in an explosion as her body began to move of its own accord toward his hand, which had gently parted her thighs and was stroking the waiting moistness of her femininity.

Scarcely aware of her own fingers, she unfastened Dirk's clothing while his hands and mouth continued to lovingly demonstrate his worship for her body. And try as she might, she couldn't suppress the gentle moan that rose in her throat when she felt his warm breath soughing across the subtle roundness of her belly. Nor could she stop herself from lifting her hips to meet his mouth, his lips, his tongue as he laved the tender flesh with his kisses.

Then, when Johanna could bear no more of the bittersweet torture his hand and mouth were perpetrating on her vulnerability, he added to her agony. Following the trail his hand had already set afire, he licked and nibbled his way to the origin of her desire to totally make her his slave.

Cupping her buttocks in strong hands, he lifted her upward, his thumbs gently separating the delicate folds of her body to make the tender nub of her passion even more accessible to his hungry kiss. Slowly, deliberately, he brought her to peaks of physical culmination as he took her to new and unexplored heights of rapture with his gentle tugging and tonguing.

When at last Dirk could no longer withstand the tortures of her nearness, and she was mindlessly crying out her blessed agony, he entered her. With her senses honed to unendurable sharpness, she enveloped his hardness in her craving abyss of desire with a primitive frenzy of motion, catapulting the two of them to the zenith of unity.

When Johanna awoke in the morning to the illustrious crow of the rooster, its sound seemed to be announcing not only a new day, but the arrival of new life on earth: the life of Johanna and Dirk, for they were now one entity. Together, they were whole once more, while apart they had been poor imitations of life, existing for no reason other than survival.

Careful not to wake the man beside her, she rolled over and studied his sleeping features. The deep-furrowed creases between his curved brows, which had given his face such a stern appearance, seemed to have been magically washed away during the night, leaving a much younger and less implacable visage before her adoring eyes.

Examining him more closely as he lay sleeping on his back in the straw, Johanna suddenly realized that his eyelashes were blond—dark blond perhaps, but blond nevertheless! She moved closer to scrutinize her discovery and realized that his hair was not the same ebony color it had been the day he abducted her from Francois's inn. It was lighter! And the hair on his exposed chest was not black at all, but a definite gold color!

His hair is dyed! she realized with overwhelming revelation. *I knew it! I knew he was a blond. Why didn't I notice before? Why didn't he tell me when I went on about the man in my dreams?*

Planning what devilish revenge she could take on him, she picked up a piece of straw and held it over his nose, so close that it moved with his breathing.

Make a fool of me, will he? she thought, letting the golden sliver tickle across the tip of his nose.

Again and again he attempted to shoo away the pesky fly that seemed determined to take up residence on his nose; and again and again it was right back to worry him and interrupt his pleasant dreams. Finally, unable to bear the annoying insect any longer, Dirk sat up and sleepily looked around.

"Did you rest well?" Johanna asked, mischief dancing in her green eyes as she lay beside him, propped lazily on one elbow.

"Damned flies," he grumbled drowsily.

"What flies?" she questioned innocently, waving her instrument of torture slowly and tauntingly before his eyes. "I haven't seen any flies."

"You haven't?" he shouted, lunging toward her and toppling her over onto her back. "It was flying around my nose and upper lip, like this," he bellowed, lightly tickling her nose and face with his beard while he kept her hands pinned above her head, leaving her no defense whatsoever.

"Have I told you how much I like dark-haired men?" she giggled against the continued assault of her nose. "Especially dark-haired men with blond eyelashes and blond hair on their chests!" she accused between hiccoughing chuckles.

250

Sitting up, he glanced down at the springy hair curling over his broad chest. "I wondered how long it would take you to notice."

"Well, now I've noticed, and I want to know how long it will take for that awful black to wash off so I can see the real man of my dreams," she cooed softly.

Dirk bent to kiss her lightly before he stood up. "Last time it took a few months to return to its natural color of—green!"

"A few months? Green?" she shrieked. "Well, I'm not going to wait that long. I'm certain Frau Böttcher has some strong lye soap that can lighten your hair again— if it doesn't all fall out first!" she threatened, jumping up to grab a fistful of his darkened hair and give it a spiteful yank.

Dirk seized the hand that was tightly gripping his hair and laughed as he hollered in pain, "Ouch, that hurts! You little devil!' He looked into her bright eyes, scintillating with golden green sparks of playfulness, but he was suddenly saddened when his gaze fell on her butchered head of hair. Running his hand from her wrist gently down her arm to touch her hair, he lamented, "God, I'm so sorry, Johanna."

Reaching up to touch her own hair, as if wondering what he saw there, she realized he was referring to her unusual new hairstyle, and she laughed in sympathy for his obvious sorrow and guilt.

"You mean my new coiffure? Don't be sorry, my love. To tell you the truth, I rather like it. You have no idea how much trouble all that hair is—and so hot in the summer!" Johanna fanned herself with her small hand. "Whew! In fact, I'm thinking of keeping it short permanently. Maybe I'll start a new fashion!"

Smiling sadly into her clear emerald eyes, Dirk knew that Johanna was telling the truth and that the hair really didn't matter to her, but he still promised her, "I swear I'll make it up to you, Johanna."

"Dirk, I give you my word, there's nothing to make up for; and the only promise I want from you is to never let me out of your sight again."

"That may be a bit difficult," he answered with a doubtful smile, avoiding the commitment he knew he could not make. "But I do promise no one will hurt you again—unless they kill me first!" Turning away from her before she could sway him into making promises he couldn't possibly keep, he changed the subject. "Johanna, I've been thinking. Would you like to see your family, at least your mother and father? They're not far from here."

"What are you saying? Of course I want to see them. Where are they? Will it be much out of the way? Why didn't you tell me before? Never mind. That doesn't matter. What if I don't know them when I see them? Oh, Dirk, how soon can we be there and how long will we stay?" she babbled excitedly.

"We can be there today. They're at Dusseldorf, in the palace of William of Orange. It's on the way to my final destination," Dirk answered, looking at the ground.

"You mean *our* final destination, don't you?" she corrected him.

"No, I can't take you where I'm going—not now, Johanna," he answered, the pain showing in his face.

"But I thought . . ."

"You will be safer with your parents in Dusseldorf."

Johanna ran to him, clinging desperately to his rigid back. "Dirk, I don't care about being safe. I only want

252

to be with you. Always!"

"Johanna," he said firmly, gently removing her arms from around his waist. "We're not going to talk about it anymore. It's settled. You're going to stay in Dusseldorf! Now get dressed," he ordered, slipping a loose-fitting shirt over his head.

"But what about your commitment to Louis of Nassau? You promised to bring me back to him! What will you tell him?" she argued uselessly.

"He'll have to find another hostage to use for bargaining. It won't be you!" he answered, determined to stand his ground.

"I know things that can help him. Don't you and Nassau want to question me?" she asked, putting on her own shirt.

"You can tell me, and I'll tell him."

"No, you won't! If I can't go, then I'll keep my secrets and knowledge locked inside me forever!" she wailed dramatically. She angrily shoved first one leg and then the other into the pants she was to wear.

"And confirm everyone's suspicions that you are not interested in our country's survival?" he asked, his voice low and even.

Johanna hesitated only momentarily before the tears came. Tears of frustration—the one weapon Dirk had no defense against. "Dammit, Johanna! Don't cry!" Frustrated himself, he gathered her into his arms.

"But you promised," she stammered between sobs. "How can you protect me if we're miles apart? You said you wouldn't leave me?"

"First of all, I did not promise; and secondly, what good would I be in a battle if I were worrying about your safety?" he reasoned. But his words fell on deaf ears.

"But I could help you fight! And I'd watch out for my own safety. Dirk, I want to help the Netherlands win its freedom, not sit in Germany waiting for word about our victories and defeats—wondering every minute if you're dead or alive. Don't ask that of me, Dirk!"

"Johanna, it's not a fitting life . . ."

"My life hasn't been fitting for a long time, has it? I ride well, and I'm very strong. You saw me lift that heavy basket of wet laundry. Please don't leave me behind in Dusseldorf, in a strange country with strangers!"

"Strangers? They're your family, for God's sake. They love you!"

"To me, they're strangers. The only reason I believe them to be family is because you tell me they are."

Relying on one final surge of resistance, Dirk shouted, "I don't want to hear another word about it. My decision is final!"

And so is mine, Dirk Corlear. I'm going to Groningen with you. The Netherlands is my homeland, too. And no matter what you say, I'm not going to be denied my right to defend her.

Walking away from Dirk with apparent resignation, Johanna began to gather up the things that had been scattered on the floor. "What shall we have to eat?" she asked abjectly. "Would you like bread and jerky or cheese and fruit? I'll pack our gear and saddle the horses while you finish dressing."

"Johanna, I know what you're trying to do, and it won't work!"

"We'd better hurry. I'd like to be there as soon as possible," she answered coolly, ignoring him.

She managed to pack and load the horses in record time, hoping to show Dirk what an asset it would be to have her with him all the time, but he hardly noticed her agile efficiency—which irritated her even more.

Crossing the Rhine into Dusseldorf by ferryboat, Johanna began to dread seeing her natural family. *What if they don't accept me after what's happened? What if they think that I'm a traitor, too? What will I say to them? Will I remember them when I see them? What are they like?*

The closer they drew to the palace of the prince of Orange, the more Johanna was tempted to bolt and run. Sensing her anxiety, although she had hardly talked to him since the scene in the Böttcher's barn, Dirk put his hand over hers where it gripped the rail of the ferry being pulled across the river by cables.

"Johanna, it will be all right," he assured her. "You'll see. They'll be so happy to have you back that nothing else will matter."

"The way nothing else mattered to you, Dirk? You wanted me dead! What if the shame of what happened to me is too much for them? They may think I'm a traitor!"

"They won't, Johanna! The fact that you're alive is all that matters to them. We're coming to the bank. Let's get the horses and be moving on. It's only a few miles to the north."

"But what if they don't want me back? Will you take me with you then?" she asked, almost praying for her family's rejection.

"There's no need to speculate on that. They'll want

255

you no matter what. You can be sure of that!"

I'm not staying with them, Dirk. And you can be sure of that! I've been through too much and seen too many things to be left locked in a palace while someone else decides my fate. A prison is still a prison, no matter if the jailer is my father instead of the duke of Alva. If you won't take me willingly, I'll go alone. But I am going!

Thus, as Johanna planned her escape from the confines of acceptable behavior, they arrived unannounced at the birthplace of William and Louis of Nassau, William now being the prince of Orange.

"You wait here, Johanna. I think it will be best if I prepare your parents before they see you. Your mother's health hasn't been very good since your disappearance, and the shock might be too much for her if we simply walk in on them." Trusting the care of the horses to her, Dirk left her in the stable.

"You've been a good friend, old horse," Johanna told the gray as she stepped around him to unload the gear. "I suppose he'll be leaving tomorrow for Groningen, and he'll take you with him. I shall miss you. I'd feel better if you and I could make our trip together, but I suppose I'll get just as far on your pretty friend here."

Johanna walked over to the Spanish mare who had switched her loyalty to Dirk so easily. "You two need to eat and rest well tonight, because we'll be on the road early in the morning." Nuzzling Johanna's hand, the mare was happy to find a piece of bread, which she greedily gobbled up before searching for more. Giving each horse an apple before pouring grain into a bin for them, Johanna picked up the gear and went out of the stable to wait for Dirk.

Hearing her name called out, Johanna looked up curiously to see two strangers, followed by Dirk, bearing down on her. "Johanna, Johanna, my darling daughter. I knew you were alive. They kept telling me you were dead, but I knew they were wrong. Oh, you poor thing, we've been so concerned." It was the woman speaking, a woman who had similar coloring to Johanna's—the same green eyes and blond hair, although the woman's hair had become dull with streaks of gray.

This must be my mother. Why don't I feel anything? She doesn't seem familiar at all. And the man. He has to be my father, but it's as if I've never seen him before.

Johanna looked desperately at Dirk for assistance. Did they know that she couldn't remember them? What was she supposed to do now?

As the woman warmly embraced her, the man stood back, tears shimmering in his eyes, generously allowing his wife to spend the first emotional moments alone with their daughter.

Uncomfortable with the crying woman clinging to her, Johanna glanced at Dirk again, her eyes now pleading for help. He stepped forward and put his arms around Katryn's shoulders, gently pulling her away from her daughter. "Come, Katryn. Remember, I told you that Johanna has no memory of the past. You have to give her some time."

"But surely you know who *we* are!" Katryn insisted.

"Katie, we promised Dirk we wouldn't put pressure on the poor girl to remember. Is it not enough that she's alive and safely back with us?" Turning to Johanna, the trace of tears in his eyes almost unnoticeable now, he said, "Daughter, I am your papa, Matthew. We are happy we have you with us once more. We've prayed for this moment," he said warmly.

"Thank you, Papa," Johanna said, the words seeming strange on her tongue. "I, too, have prayed for this. And Mama, I do know that you are my mother. Where else could I have gotten my green eyes?" she asked, attempting to ease the strain of the moment.

Smiling at Johanna, Katryn added, "And don't forget your blond hair!" Then she noticed her daughter's shorn locks for the first time and screamed hysterically. "Johanna! What has happened to your hair? They've cut it all off! Your beautiful hair!"

Shifting her gaze quickly to Dirk and feeling his inward cringe, Johanna laughed. "Mama, I'm sorry you don't like it. I felt it would be easier to travel without that mop hanging down my back. Besides, it would have been quite difficult to disguise myself as a boy if I hadn't cut it off."

"And your clothing!" Katryn exclaimed in horror with the full realization of what Johanna was wearing. "Wherever did you find those awful things?"

Johanna smiled sweetly in Dirk's direction, enjoying his discomfort for a change. "Dirk brought them for me!"

Katryn turned to Dirk without warning and cried out angrily, "Dirk Corlear, how could you dress our beautiful daughter in such dreadful rags?"

Dirk was beginning to squirm under Katryn's angry attack, but fortunately Matthew intervened. "Are we going to stand out here all day? What do you say we get our daughter inside and give her a chance to become used to civilization again."

Finally understanding that she would need to let

Johanna come to her, Katryn forced herself to speak in a less excited manner. "Come, dear. We have a room being prepared for you at this very moment. I imagine a bath and clean clothing will be the first thing you will want."

Then Katryn's sense of humor returned, and she chided Johanna warmly, "Although, knowing what a boy you always tried to be, I wouldn't be surprised to hear that you've grown attached to men's clothing!"

Dirk put his arm around Johanna's shoulders to direct her to the main hall and laughed. "You're right about that, Katryn. Maybe you can have some trousers of velvet and silk made for her. She's already admitted to me that she actually likes wearing pants!"

"Oh!" gasped Katryn, her shock leaving her speechless.

Chapter Fifteen

Dressed once more in the rough men's clothing, Johanna rode Mademoiselle into Heiligerlee in the northern Netherlands. She recounted for the hundredth time the events that led up to her departure, and wondered what Dirk and her parents must have thought when they discovered her disappearance. In her note to Katryn and Matthew, she had tried to explain that she had changed too much to wait out the rebellion in the safety of Orange's castle. She told them of her desire to take an active part in the fight, but she was certain they would not understand—especially her mother, who wanted so desperately to make a lady of her.

As she approached Louis of Nassau's camp, she wondered if he would allow her to enlist. Surely, from what Dirk had told her, they needed good men. Perhaps they could use her to care for horses and tack, or as a messenger, or even as a spy! Whatever job she was given, she knew she had to contact Nassau before Dirk arrived—in order to assure herself a position, any position, in Nassau's army.

What did Dirk think when he found my note with Fumée's saddle? I know he was furious. But surely, once he arrives and sees me, he'll be glad to have me beside him. After all, I'll probably make a better soldier than some of those paid mercenaries from France and Germany who fight for whichever side pays the highest wages.

Thinking back to the night she left Dusseldorf, three days earlier, a wave of sadness swept over Johanna as she remembered the emotional farewell to Dirk.

"Johanna, I won't be gone long, and you will be better off here. When I come back, we'll talk about the future," he had promised. "All right?"

"All right," she had answered, taking care to keep her gaze averted to the side rather than chance having him see the truth in her expression. Kissing her at the door to her room, he had stepped back to take one more longing look at her before turning on his heel and leaving for his own room.

Calling after him, Johanna asked, "What time will you leave in the morning? Will you awaken me if I'm still sleeping?" Already she was making plans for her own departure.

"I'll leave before sunup, so I don't want to wake you. We've said our farewells, and I see no point in prolonging them, do you?"

"No, I suppose not," she agreed. "It would only make it harder to let you go now that I've found you again."

"There's a good girl. Now you get some rest. By the way, did I tell you how lovely you look in that dress with your hair all curly?"

"Yes, you did, but you can tell me again," she cried, running down the hallway to embrace him one last time.

"Although I must admit that I rather miss the little fellow I rode in with this afternoon!" he laughed, catching her petite body in his embrace.

"I miss him too, Dirk." She thought of the boy's clothing she had firmly hung onto when her mother had tried to throw it out—or at least give it to the poor.

Brought abruptly out of her remembering by a sharp voice, Johanna jerked her head up to stare into the reddening face of a young man who resembled Matthew van Ledenburg in an unsettling manner. "What in the hell are you doing here?" he demanded.

Startled by the man's booming voice, Johanna lost the confidence she had used to bolster herself during the past three days of traveling alone in the northwest plains of Germany. "I am Josef van der Volk," she stammered in a small voice. "I want to join Louis of Nassau's army and fight for the freedom of the Netherlands."

"Josef of the People, huh?" he repeated. "Where have you been? We thought you were dead! What's the meaning of this deception?"

Johanna's heart began to pound hard in her chest, and her upper lip broke out in sweat. "Deception? What do you mean? Don't you believe me when I say I'm a Netherlander?"

"Oh, you're a Netherlander, all right," he said, advancing toward her, an angry smile on his face. "But you're not Josef!"

Johanna tightened her grip on the mare's reins and looked frantically over her shouder for an escape.

"My name *is* Josef!" she insisted, jerking sharply on the left rein to turn Mademoiselle around.

"Hold on there," he yelled, grabbing the mare's bridle and stopping her. "Where do you think you're going?"

"Uh . . ."

"I don't know what you're up to, but you obviously didn't count on running into your brother, did you?"

"My brother? I don't understand. Who are you?" she questioned him, growing more frightened by the instant.

"You can stop this ridiculous charade, Johanna!" he growled, obviously growing tired of the game. "I'm your brother, Frans, and you know it! Do Mama and Papa know you're alive?" he interrogated her. "Why did you let us go on thinking you were dead all these months? Where have you been?"

Aware that her masquerade was exposed, she answered, resigning herself to the fate of a helpless female of noble birth. "Yes, they know I'm alive," she said forlornly. "But I still want to be part of the fight!"

"You're a woman! Not even a very big woman! It would be all wrong," he sputtered helplessly. "Where in the hell have you been all this time?"

Resigned to the fact that this man was her brother, she told him what had happened to her—and her part in the defense of the Netherlanders Alva had slated for arrest. "So you see, Frans, I cannot go back to being a dependent child! Too much has happened for me to return to the little Johanna you remember. I have no memory of that girl, so for all practical purposes, she really is dead. Can't you see? I'm not her anymore! Besides, I'm more comfortable as Josef than I could

263

ever be bathing in marble tubs filled with scented water or wearing satin gowns and stitching on a piece of meaningless cloth."

Having listened to her entire story in astonishment and silence, Frans could not speak.

"Don't you see, Frans? I shall surely die if you send me back to Dusseldorf to be smothered by all the attention Mama is wanting to lavish on me. Never to ride a horse again, never to step outside the palace walls for fear of abduction, never to be alone to run in the fields again. I couldn't stand it, Frans! I would die of suffocation," she implored.

"It was you who sent all the warnings throughout the country? Do you realize how many people the *Ange de Mystère* is credited with saving? Even more than Alva is credited with murdering! My little Johanna, you are already a great heroine! Isn't that enough?"

"No! It will never be enough until the vicious Spaniards are driven to their knees and have crawled on their bellies out of our country!" she answered emphatically.

"But Johanna, it's crazy! What would you do? You're so small! And what will Dirk say when he arrives and finds you here?"

He's weakening. "That's why you must take me to Nassau at once! Dirk shouldn't be more than a few hours behind me. So I need to already have a purpose with the army when he arrives. Then he won't dare send me away. Besides, there are many things I can do! Carry water to the soldiers in battle, take care of the horses—or cook and do laundry!"

Ignoring the raised eyebrows and doubtful expression on Frans's face when she mentioned doing laundry, she went on listing her abilities. "I could nurse the wounded, or carry messages, or even precede the soldiers into an area and scout out good battle locations. No one would ever suspect a young boy of being a spy!"

"I don't know, Johanna," Frans said slowly.

"Josef," she corrected him, instinctively knowing that he'd never been able to deny her anything.

"Very well, *Josef,* we'll see what Louis says. But understand that any job you take will be near me—so don't let your supposed freedom go to your head," he ordered.

"Oh, I won't, Frans. Thank you!" she squealed, unable to hide her delight.

"First of all, no more of that girlish giggling. Understood?"

Grinning, she nodded her head enthusiastically. "No giggling!"

"Secondly, you must be very cautious. Just because you are in male attire does not mean you will be automatically protected from men's carnal lusts. There are some who prefer young boys to girls, and others who will take a man when there are no women on hand," he warned gravely. "I only speak this way, Johanna, because I want you to be fully aware of the jeopardy you're putting yourself in. You must remember that danger is all around you—not only from the Spaniards. Now, are you certain you want to continue with this foolishness?"

"Quite sure," she said definitely.

"Then let us seek out our commander. I don't mind telling you, he's going to be speechless." Frans put his hand on Johanna's collar and prodded her along the road to where the camp was set up. "He'll have to be informed who you are, but only he and I will know you are the *Ange de Mystère* or Johanna van Ledenburg. To everyone else, you will be Josef van der Volk!"

After Louis heard Johanna's story, it was quickly decided that she would help with the care and feeding of the horses. She would be under the supervision of Fredrik, an old man with poor eyesight and a hearing problem, but a way with horses that could not be surpassed.

"Fredrik will be no threat to you, since he's blind as a bat. And you'll be able to ease some of the burden we put on him. Well, what do you say, Josef?" Louis asked, knowing by the animated expression on the girl's face that she was more than happy with the arrangement.

"I say yes! And you'll see, I'll be the best horse 'boy' you've ever had with your troops!" she promised with enthusiasm.

"I could also use you to help with my correspondence —since you have experience along those lines. However, I don't think we'll be sending you out on a spy mission any time soon," he laughed.

Changing the subject abruptly, Louis said, "Now, are you prepared for some bad news? It's one of the hardships connected with being a soldier—bad news is often more prevalent than good news."

"Yes, I'm prepared," Johanna answered bravely, dreading the worst.

"Alva was so irate at your brazen abduction that on the first of the month he took eighteen of his prisoners

266

out into the marketplace of Brussels and publicly tortured them before burning them at the stake—while forcing the citizens of the city to watch. Most of the men were signers of our petition to Margaret de Parma last spring." Closing his eyes, as if he could blot out the sight of his countrymen meeting such a grisly end, Nassau forced himself to continue. "He has sent out word that he will keep executing prisoners until you're located."

"But can't you use me to bargain with him? Demand the release of his prisoners in exchange for me," she suggested. "Wasn't that your original plan?"

"That was before I knew you were the *Ange de Mystère*. Are you so ready to return to him, little one?" Louis asked sadly.

"I had hoped never to see him again. But if it would save lives, I'd go—for the Netherlands!" she declared.

"Very brave, my dear. But I'm afraid your courage would be wasted if we let you go back now. The minute you were taken from the Benners' inn, word was sent through the underground that the woman stolen was the *Ange de Mystère*. I'm certain the message was dispatched in order to inform the culprits that they were holding one of their own rather than an enemy. No doubt it was meant to protect you from your own countrymen—who had no way of knowing you as anything but a traitor. Unfortunately, I have a suspicion that the truth probably wended its way to Alva's ears also. Should we turn you over to him, for whatever reason, your life would be worth nothing!" Louis explained.

"But what of the men he's going to murder?" she asked, feeling powerless.

"Unless we can gather forces and march into Brussels to open the jails ourselves—which is highly unlikely—there's nothing we can do," he said dejectedly. "Even if we bargained with him, he would betray us and kill them anyway."

"Have you heard anything about the Benners—my stepfamily? I've worried that he would blame them in some way for my disappearance. Do you know if they're all right?"

"No, I've heard nothing, but we'll ask around for information. Now let's see about meeting some of the men before you meet Fredrik!" he said in the soft-spoken manner that Johanna had already come to appreciate.

Having introduced her to several of the officers in his army, Louis laughed while they bantered good-naturedly among themselves. "We must be in pretty bad shape, Louis! Taking in kids to fight with us!" they teased.

"Josef is the son of a dear friend of mine who is unable to fight because of ill health; he has sent his young son to carry the banner for our country. Let it be understood," he said seriously, "this boy is under my protection. Should anything happen to him, I will think of it as a personal attack on me." He smiled, knowing they all comprehended his meaning.

"Now, Josef, finish your food. Then I'll take you to get acquainted with old Fredrik, who will be glad of the help."

Yes, I want to be well settled in by the time Dirk arrives, she thought, glancing toward the south, halfway expecting to see him riding into camp, since he probably hadn't left Dusseldorf more than an hour behind her.

There was no way for Johanna to know that her decision to leave Dusseldorf ahead of Dirk had completely changed his plans—and his fate. When he had found the Spanish mare and gear gone, he knew Johanna had been the one who had taken the horse. His doubts about the truthfulness of her story rose in his thoughts, immediately assuring him that she had returned to Brussels—and to her lover, Alva.

Livid with himself that he'd been duped into believing her story, he had wasted no time in saddling Fumée and riding out, not bothering to pick up the small piece of parchment that had fluttered to the ground when he lifted his saddle.

He retraced their route into Brussels, arriving at the Benners' roadside inn in record time, all the while tortured by the idea that Johanna had returned to Alva. *When I take her this time, I will slit her throat.*

By the third day after her arrival at Louis of Nassau's camp, Johanna had settled into her role as stableboy perfectly. She was quite able when it came to the care of horses, and much to old Fredrik's delight, she didn't talk too much.

"Yes, sir!" the old man rambled loudly as they brushed down the sweating horses that had recently returned from a patrol. "I've had some real poor helpers on this job. Where'd you learn so much about horses?"

"My pa taught me," she answered in a low voice.

"What's that you say?" the old man yelled.

"I said my pa taught me!" she hollered into Fredrik's one ear that had any hearing at all.

But before he could say anything else, a rider came racing into the camp. Jumping off his running mount before it had been brought to a complete stop, the man made an urgent dash into Nassau's tent. It was only moments before Frans came out of the tent calling, "Josef, come quickly."

Throwing the horse brushes she was using to the ground, Johanna ran quickly to the tent Frans had already reentered. She passed the mysterious messenger in the doorway and was taken completely by surprise when she realized she recognized the rider who was leaving. She quickly lowered her head, and breathed a sigh of relief when he paid no heed to the quiet boy who slipped past him.

"Thank you, Karl, for the information. You go and get something to eat and some rest. We'll let you know what we plan to do about this and any message we want you to carry back to Brussels."

As soon as the man had disappeared, Louis spoke. "Jo, we have some very bad news!"

Holding her finger to her lips, Johanna mouthed the words, "Just a minute." Slipping quietly out of the tent and around to the back, she frightened off a dark figure who had been lurking behind the tent, obviously planning to eavesdrop on their conversation. He darted into the bushes as she rounded the corner, but not soon enough to keep Johanna from recognizing the retreating back as that of the messenger who had just departed.

"What in the hell are you doing?" Frans hissed.

"Someone was listening outside the tent. I frightened him off, but I'm certain it was that messenger," she whispered.

"Will you listen to her? She's really going daft," Frans laughed. "I didn't see anyone out here."

"Quiet, Frans. I want to hear what she has to say," Louis said in defense of her actions.

"First of all, you both better refer to me as 'he' and Jo or Josef; and secondly, anything you don't want anyone to know should be said out in the open with no place to conceal spies," she advised in a cautious whisper.

Louis, who had learned to rely on his own intuition, was not one to deny such strong conviction as Johanna was expressing. "Very well, we'll walk as we discuss our news; and then we must decide what we will do."

As the three left the tent, Johanna checked the spot where she knew Karl had been standing and came up with a piece of torn material caught on a thornbush. Nothing more—but if she found a coat or breeches the scrap belonged to, she would have the proof she needed. Holding it up for the other two to see, she said, "What is that man doing here?"

"He brings us information from time to time—for which we pay him well!" Frans answered.

"He's not to be trusted. I've seen him before. He's one of Alva's most regular informers!" she said ominously.

"Are you certain? You could be wrong. We've never had any reason to doubt the information he brings us!" Louis said, his worried voice showing his concern.

"I'm telling you, it's him! I could never forget his evil, grotesque face! How many men do you know with no

271

hair or ear on the left side of their faces? It's him, all right!" She shuddered as she spoke, feeling for some strange reason there was something else she should remember about Karl.

Frans interrupted hastily. "Jo, it's just that horrible burn scar on his face. I imagine he frightens most people when they first see him!"

"But I'm not squeamish about things like that, Frans. This isn't the first or even the second time I've seen your friend Karl. I'm telling you, he works for the duke of Alva!"

"Then that may put a different light on the news he brought," Louis said thoughtfully.

"What is the news?" she asked softly, certain it was bad and dreading hearing it.

"Karl tells us that four days ago Dirk Corlear rode pell-mell into the Benners' inn in an attempt to stop Francois Benner from being arrested for conspiracy against the crown," Louis said.

"Oh, God!" Johanna gasped, choking back the scream that was rising in her throat.

"When they subdued Dirk, they searched his pack and found what appeared to be the hair of Alva's mistress, Esmeralda Verde!"

"Is he dead?" Johanna asked in a low, tortured moan. "What was he doing in Brussels? He was supposed to come here!" Her mind raced madly from thought to thought, her legs became liquid, and she had to stop walking. Certain she was going to be sick, she grabbed her middle and folded in half.

Thinking she was going to faint, Frans caught her around the shoulders and shook her gently. "No, he's not dead. He's alive! But he and Francois Benner have

272

been arrested and are both condemned to die!"

"It can't be," she gasped, embarrassed to feel herself slipping from her masculine role into that of a crying female, but unable to stop.

"Johanna, if you don't get control of yourself, I'm taking you back to Dusseldorf and leaving orders to keep you under lock and key!" Frans threatened. "Do you hear me?"

"Yes, Frans. I hear you. I'm sorry. I'll be all right," she sniffed, straightening her back and lifting her chin with determination. "What are we going to do? I'm the reason they're there. I have to get them out!"

Louis spoke calmly as the three continued their walk. "Of course, I will take men to Brussels and make an attempt to free them—though our chances of success won't be good."

"No! You mustn't be the one to go, Louis!" Johanna's voice was an urgent whisper. "I know how Alva's mind works. He sent Karl to lure *you* into Brussels—using Dirk and Francois as the bait!" she exclaimed.

"Are you certain Karl's the same man you remember?" Louis asked again, still doubtful. "Even if he is, he could be selling information to both sides with no ulterior motive—other than money," Louis suggested.

"Believe me! It's him. And the duke of Alva sent him."

Louis studied her for a long moment, then started walking again. "Suppose I trust your instincts? What would you have me do?"

Strengthened by the knowledge that Louis had not completely discarded the value of what she thought, Johanna went on quickly. "I think we should let it be known that you are sorry Dirk and Francois were captured. However, everyone knows capture is a risk they take when they join the army, and you can't endanger more lives to save only two—not when the success is all but impossible."

Pausing to take a quick breath, she looked from Frans to Louis and continued to speak quietly. "Then, while you stay here and hold the area you control—and keep friend Karl incapacitated—Frans and I, together with one or two trusted riders, will go to Brussels."

"I don't like it," Nassau brooded.

"But you are so well known, and it would be a great coup for Alva to have you in jail or publicly executed—not to mention gold in someone's pockets when you're arrested," Frans mused, having no choice but to agree with Johanna's plan. "In fact, if what Jo says is true, you'd better keep a close watch on Karl. When you announce you're not going, he might attempt to capture you another way. To a man of low scruples, that reward money would look too good to forget about," he warned Louis.

"I hate to risk losing the two of you—when you really have no chance of succeeding."

"It's the only way, Louis. I love them both with all my heart—one as a father and the other as my life! I will die anyway if they're lost and I've done nothing to help them. Don't you see?" she pleaded. "I have to go."

"Yes, I see, lovely Johanna," Louis murmured, looking into her beseeching eyes, his own filled with regret and longing. Yet, being an honorable man, he would do or say nothing to express his feelings as long as his best friend, Dirk Corlear, was alive; and he could do nothing to stop her from trying to save him, the man he loved as a brother and could not go to.

"All right. I'll agree to this rash act of madness, but I don't like it. I'll invite Karl to my tent for beer and conversation. I'm sure the good doctor can come up with a sleeping potion for our friend. We may keep him drugged for two or three days. That should give you time to be well on your way, as well as give me the opportunity to ask Karl some questions."

"And if you don't like his answers?" Frans asked.

"He won't leave this camp alive!" Louis pronounced definitely. "When do you plan to depart?"

"As soon as we can pack our gear and load the horses—assuming that you have Karl snoring in your tent, of course."

"Then it's settled. I will say good-bye and good luck to you now." He chucked Johanna under the chin. "I hate to see old Fredrik lose the best stableboy he's ever had, but I suppose we couldn't have expected to keep such a brave lass mucking up after horses for much longer!" he teased, pulling her hat down over her eyes. "I pray we will meet again—perhaps when my army marches, victorious, into Brussels," he chuckled. But his laugh carried a note of sadness that would haunt Johanna for a long time.

"We'll meet again, Louis," Johanna promised. "Once we retrieve Dirk and Francois, we'll be back to join you in the fight! Thank you for letting me be part of your army."

Before the men could see the tears welling in her eyes, Johanna turned and ran back to the horses, all of her thoughts and energies now focused on Dirk and Francois.

Chapter Sixteen

Johanna and Frans, together with Dolf and Walter, rode unnoticed into Brussels, only to discover the market square jammed with crowds of people. The trip from the north had been relatively uneventful, since all four were excellent riders and they had skirted the small towns where Spanish garrisons were stationed. In their peasant disguises, no one would have taken them for young members of three of the richest families in the Netherlands.

Dolf Kramer, the twenty-six-year-old son of a wealthy businessman in Amsterdam, and his friend, Walter van Altervelde, from the seaport of Brugge in West Flanders, had ridden with Louis of Nassau and Dirk since Louis had organized his army. Signers of the petition to de Parma, both were loyal sons of the Netherlands and were willing to give their lives to the cause. So when they were asked to ride to Brussels with Frans and the *Ange de Mystère,* the two young men had jumped at the opportunity.

"Are you sure a female is up to this sort of gamble?"

queried Dolf when Frans had explained the entire venture to him.

"All I can say, Dolf, is that she rides well, is much stronger than she looks, and has the daring of a man twice her size. Besides, if we tried to leave her behind, I have no doubt that she'd take off on her own!" Then he added regretfully, but proudly, "And knowing my sister as I do, she'd probably get there first and have this task completed before we even had a chance to make our plans!"

Listening to Frans's description of Johanna, Walter was awed by the number of people she had saved and said, "I consider it an honor to ride with such a brave soldier, male or female; and I thank you for inviting me to be part of this mission, Frans. I'm anxious to get started."

"Yes, we need to leave immediately. I understand Alva is hanging more men every day. Pray we arrive in time. We'll leave in the small hours of the morning— once our informative messenger, Karl, has had his fill of Nassau's beer and laudanum!" Frans grinned wickedly.

"I also think it an honor to be part of this venture, Frans." Dolf spoke anxiously, afraid someone might have misunderstood his disquiet. "I was only concerned for your sister's safety, not my own."

Johanna smiled with understanding at the embarrassed man. "We know, Dolf, and I appreciate your thoughtfulness. But believe me, I can take care of myself."

"Then that's settled. We will all go about our regular duties as we inconspicuously pack our gear," Frans ordered in a tone of finality. "It will be just the four of us facing the entire Brussels garrison of the Spanish army. You know the odds are against us. However, if we don't make the attempt to save Corlear and Benner, they will die."

That had been four nights before. And now they were in Brussels, milling in the unusually congested marketplace near the governor's palace—the palace that housed the prison where Dirk and Francois were supposedly incarcerated.

"What do you think it means?" Johanna whispered to Frans as they shoved their way through the throng of people who seemed to be waiting for something to happen.

"I don't know, but I'm going to find out," he answered, walking toward a water vendor. Pulling a coin from his purse for a drink, Frans asked the old man, "Say, what's going on here? I've never seen so many people in the marketplace."

Shaking his head sadly, the wrinkled peddler replied, "More executions! They say the governor plans to rid our country of twenty-two more traitors today. Traitors!" he spat in disgust. "That's what *he* calls 'em. I calls 'em brave patriots. That's what I calls 'em!"

"Old man, you'd better be careful who you say things like that to," Frans warned, looking around to be certain no one had overheard the man. "I would think the Council of Troubles would deal *you* trouble if word reached their ears that you don't approve of their actions," he cautioned, genuinely concerned for the man.

"Council of Troubles, my ass!" the old man hissed vehemently. "Council of *Blood* is more like it! Before that devil is through with his wickedness, the streets of

Brussels will be red with the blood of brave Dutchmen. And we have to watch it happen!" The man's eyes began to tear as he envisioned the events of the past eight days. "Day after day his soldiers bring 'em out of the dungeon where they've been kept—some for months!"

He interrupted his narrative to sell a dipper of water to two young boys. As the youngsters skipped away, he shook his head. "Look at 'em, couldn't be more than eight years old and acting like they've come to a parish fair! Bad enough we're forced to watch—but the children! My God, what's it doing to them? Seeing men murdered right before their eyes!" He was now crying openly.

"Sir," Johanna pleaded, "do you know who's to be executed today?"

Frans glared at his sister, fearing she would give away her disguise. But the peddler had failed to take any note of the young boy through his watery eyes.

"Aye, they do it all proper, they do! Post the names of the condemned on the gates, so everyone can know what's in store for 'em if they do anything but behave like Alva's sheep."

Before the old man could finish speaking, Johanna rushed off to the place where the doomed men's names were listed. "Josef, come back here!" Frans hollered. When his order went unheeded, he turned to Dolf. "Better go after *him,* before we get separated and he gets into trouble!"

His nerves stretched taut, he watched until he saw Dolf catch up to Johanna, then returned his attention to the vendor, who was making another sale.

Finishing with his customer, the old man went on as

279

if there had been no interruption. "Aye, we watch 'em come out of that dark prison every day at noon. Most of 'em have been down there so long that they're blinded by the sunlight and can't even see the crowds of their countrymen waiting to watch 'em die. But they hear 'em! That is, until the screaming starts! Then the crowd gets so quiet, you could hear a pin drop. After that, the only thing you hear are the screams as the whip's applied to the backs of those poor unfortunate men."

Frans trembled as he listened to the man's description of what was happening. Although he was sickened by the picture the old man was painting, he knew he must listen as long as the old fellow was willing to talk—in case there was information they could use.

"Them that reads says they saw Egmont and Hoorne's names on the list four days back. You couldn't recognize 'em, though. All of 'em are in such bad shape! Oh, it's a sad day in the Low Countries when two fine gentlemen like Count Egmont and Count Hoorne are butchered like cattle at the slaughterhouse. Tricked 'em, he did! Got 'em to come to a meeting to talk about their differences. Then he ups and arrests 'em, pretty as you please! Had 'em tried, convicted, and in prison before the day was out! Where will it all end?" he asked no one in particular as he wandered off, disappearing into the crowd.

"Poor old fellow," Walter sighed, staring after the vendor. "Do you think they've been executing men every day? What if we're too late to save Dirk?" he whispered, aghast at the realization.

"There are Jo and Dolf! Let's go," Frans said, hurrying to meet the two who were anxiously rushing toward them. "Well, what's the news?"

"Their names are on the list for the day after tomorrow!" she whispered, relieved that she hadn't found them on any of the earlier postings. "Frans, Egmont and Hoorne were executed on the fifth," she murmured sorrowfully, remembering the two who had come in good faith to meet with Alva.

"I know," Frans said, shaking his head sadly. "The old man told me."

"I sent warnings to both of them. Theirs were among the first I wrote!" she despaired. "Why did they ignore them?"

"Don't think about them now, Jo. You did all you could for them. Their deaths will be a great loss to our country, but now we must concentrate on why we're here!" Frans said gravely.

"I know. I was just startled to see those two particular names on the list. I was there when they were arrested. I talked to both of them that day."

Suddenly the gates to the palace courtyard swung open, and the prisoners were brought out, surrounded by Spanish soldiers. Johanna and Frans watched the pitiful captives walk blindly toward their deaths, all chained together, as if in their emaciated, sightless condition they might actually break and run if they got the chance.

"Frans, it's worse than I thought it would be. I may not be able to watch," she groaned.

"You can watch, and you will," he ordered. "We all will. And while we watch everything that goes on around us, including the executions, we will make our plans!" he growled, enraged at what he was witnessing.

So the four stood, silent, as if hypnotized by the

horror that was unfolding on the platform in the middle of the square. The twenty-two fated men, already reduced to filthy creatures of bleeding skin and bones by the starvation and tortures they had been subjected to in the prison, stood before the crowd blindly staring into the space before them. Some couldn't stand unassisted. Others had almost no clothing covering their scarred and maltreated bodies. And none were recognizable as any human being Johanna had ever seen before.

Looking into the blank, suffering faces, Johanna allowed a low groan to escape from her throat, only to be cut off by the reality of Frans's long fingers digging sternly into the tender flesh of her upper arm. Straightening her spine, she shook off his grasp. "I'm sorry. It won't happen again," she said in disgust at her own weakness.

Just then the soldiers ripped the remaining clothing off the captives, stripping them of the last bit of dignity they had. Each prisoner was dragged to where he was hung by the arms from a huge oak beam. Several seemed to have fainted, so the soldiers threw water in their faces to revive them—insuring that they would feel the full brunt of their punishment.

The whipping began, exactly as it had for nine days! At first, the tortured souls on display made no sounds. They were already accustomed to the beatings they had received in the dungeon. But before the fifth lash was applied, all were crying in agony, begging for the noose.

Johanna watched, biting her own lip until blood ran down her throat and chin. She observed the carnage dry-eyed as hate for the Spanish and their Council of

Blood welled in her breast. She watched as the defenseless men were slowly and torturously put out of their misery by the depraved executioners. Some were burned so that the stench of burning flesh permeated the entire square, causing the unwilling spectators to gag and retch, adding the odor of vomit to the sickening fetidness surrounding them.

Numbed by the horror taking place on the platform, she continued to watch as the prisoners were tortured in every conceivable way, then finally killed. *They'll pay for this. I'll find a way to rid us of these fiends if it takes my last breath!*

Finally, after what seemed like many hours, the last man had died and the soldiers had returned to the castle walls, leaving the stunned witnesses to slowly disperse while the street sweepers and gravediggers came and cleaned up the remains of what were once proud human beings.

Nearing the point of explosion, Johanna clenched her fists in controlled anger and snarled in a voice ugly with the need for vengeance, "Those cowardly bastards! They won't do that to Dirk or Francois. I swear they won't!"

She turned to walk her horse toward the road to the Benners' inn, and the three men followed her silently, each lost in his own thoughts of retaliation.

Walter hadn't been able to watch—he had become sick. Frans and Dolf had watched the savagery through eyes burning and red with stinging tears. Only Johanna's body had not betrayed her, and the small trickle of blood that ran from her mouth was the only outward evidence that she had been touched by the violence they had all witnessed.

So while the three strong men followed behind the small, frail-looking girl they were supposed to protect, they knew it would be her mental strength that would see them through the next days. No longer did anyone question her ability to endure the consequences of what lay ahead. Each man only questioned his own strength—but never again Johanna's.

Walking toward the Benners' inn on the outskirts of town, none of the members of the small group were able to voice the anguish they were feeling. But their silence was finally broken as they approached their resting place, a grassy glade near the river, hidden from the road by a copse of small trees and shrubs.

"I think this will do for our campsite tonight," Johanna said woodenly. "I remember this place from when I lived with the Benners. Very rarely does anyone come by here. Suzette and I used to come here to rest and talk. We can relax and have a bite of supper before dark. Then I'll steal up to the inn to see how Mama and Suzette are faring with Papa gone." Catching the questioning look on Frans's face, she quickly corrected herself. "I mean Mignon and Francois!

"After I've determined the situation there, I'll return to discuss my plan for rescuing Dirk and Francois." She had assumed command of the modest patrol, and there was not one of the physically stronger men who felt qualified or inclined to question the authority of the petite champion of the rebellion.

Taking a loaf of black bread from her pack, Johanna sat down wearily. Leaning back against a tree, she bit off a chunk of bread and chewed silently, letting the men arrange for their own meals.

As the others went about brushing down the horses and setting up a temporary camp, no one spoke to or of Johanna, the strangely competent and controlled boy-girl they were planning to follow into unheard-of dangers. And while they busied themselves, the girl continued to sit and chew on the tough, tasteless bread, while keeping her eyes closed—as if dozing.

However, the turmoil in Johanna's head was not conducive to rest. The bloody, appalling visions projected by her mind on the screen of her closed eyelids were far too vivid to shut out. She could still hear the cries of agony and smell the stench of burning flesh. But still she ate, and still she did not cry! Just as she knew that if she didn't eat she would not have the strength to do what must be done, she was certain that if she gave in to crying, she would never be able to stop.

Johanna was unaware how long she sat that way— leaning on the tree, nibbling on the flavorless bread, and reliving the tortures the men on the scaffold had endured. But when darkness was fully upon them, she rose without speaking and started toward the inn.

Worried about her, Frans stood up to follow, but Johanna turned to him and calmly smiled. "Don't worry, Frans. I'll be cautious, and I know this area very well. I can be in and out of that inn without being seen—one of the rewards of being small, I suppose. You, on the other hand, would be spotted in a minute." Tugging her hat lower on her head, she turned away from her brother and disappeared into the darkness.

"Frans," Dolf said. "I know you said she was strong, but this is beyond strong! It's inhuman. She didn't cry or even look away. What is she? Hasn't she got any feelings?" he asked, still unable to shake the embarrassment he felt at his own reaction.

"Oh, she's human, my friend," Frans answered knowingly. "And she has feelings all bottled up inside that tiny body ready to explode! However, she'll wait until after we have completed our mission before she allows herself the luxury of tears," he said.

"I remember when she was a little girl, not more than seven years old. We had a dog named Cinder—ugly little black dog with a short, funny tail and legs. We all loved that little mutt. But he was especially Johanna's dog. They went everywhere together. He even slept in her bed when she could sneak him past Mama at night." He smiled, remembering the clever ruses the little girl had used to hide the dog in her room.

"Anyway, that old dog was born the same day as Johanna, and she always thought they were meant to be lifelong friends. But that spring old Cinder fell into wandering off in the woods alone—probably had a lady friend he liked to visit!"

Realizing he was rambling, Frans returned to the point of his story. "When he didn't come home for breakfast one morning, the twins, Johanna and I went looking for him. Well, we found him all right—in a wolf trap! Poor little thing had bled so much that it was a wonder he wasn't dead. But he saw Johanna and, as weak as he was, started wagging that stubby little tail of his. With his last bit of strength, he lifted his head and licked her hand—almost as if he had waited for her to come so he could tell her good-bye. Then he died." Frans stopped speaking and sniffed back his tears as he dragged his sleeve across his face. Then he went on.

"Helst and Hugo, who are a year older than Johanna, started wailing and hollering for someone to come help. And all I could think of to do was go find Papa. So I ran home—with the twins right behind me, still crying. No one stopped to take care of Johanna. I guess we just assumed she was going to stay with us."

Tears were openly running down Frans's ruddy cheeks as he told his story. "When we got back with Papa, there she was, putting a little cross of twigs on the small grave she had dug with her bare hands after she had taken her dog out of that trap. She had seen her best friend die a painful and senseless death, and yet she had the self-control and presence of mind to do what had to be done. And she never shed a tear. The boys and I were so upset that all the way home she tried to console us! She was an invincible little girl—even then!"

"She didn't ever cry?" Walter asked incredulously.

"Oh, she cried, but not until she had taken care of all of us and had made Papa promise there would never be another animal trap on Ledenburg property. Then, after eating supper and telling us all good night, she went to her room. That's when the tears came. We heard sobbing all night long. She didn't want anyone with her—not even Mama. So you see, the explosion will come, but I doubt that any of us will see it happen." He finished his narrative in a low voice filled with admiration and emotion.

While the men talked, Johanna stealthily made her way to the back of the inn to an old tree that gave the building cooling shade all summer long. Glancing around for any witnesses and seeing no one, she agilely climbed up the tree, immediately disappearing from view into the thick foliage.

Looking into the window she knew to be Suzette's, she saw no light. *She must not have come up yet. I could go back down and find her. But I'd better wait here if I don't want to be seen.* Then it dawned on her that she hadn't heard any sounds coming from the tavern. *Maybe Mama closed it. Maybe they aren't here at all. But where would they be? Surely they haven't been arrested! I would have heard. Unless it happened since we left Groningen!* She shook her head. *Stop it, Johanna! Think only positive thoughts. They're here! They have to be!*

Brought to attention by the flickering of a candle moving about the room she had been watching, Johanna leaned forward to determine who was in the room. As the figure moved about lighting another candle, Johanna could see more clearly—although the muslin curtains made it difficult. Crawling out on a sturdy branch, she dared to peer through the gap in the window covering to realize that Suzette was indeed in the room—but not alone!

Nadine! What's she doing here? Do I dare show myself while she's in the room?

But before Johanna could decide the answer to her own question, Nadine kissed Suzette and left the room.

"Suzette," Johanna whispered cautiously from her perch in the tree.

Frightened, Suzette looked around to see where the ghostly whisper was coming from. "Who is it? Who's there?"

"It's Emeraude! Don't say anything or you'll give me away. Just blow out the candles as if you're going to sleep and I'll be in. But hurry, little sister. This tree

288

is uncomfortable!"

Recognizing Emeraude's voice, Suzette did as she was told, and Johanna slipped into her room through the open window as soon as the lights had been extinguished.

"Emeraude! What are you doing here?" she whispered, embracing Johanna eagerly. "We were afraid you were dead! Or at least a prisoner somewhere! Thank heavens you've come! The soldiers came and arrested Papa! And no one can help us get him out. We've been so frightened, Emeraude. First you, then Papa! We don't know what to do!" the girl cried.

Speaking scarcely in a whisper, Johanna said, "There, there, little girl. Don't cry. Emeraude is here, and I'm going to go for our papa. But while I do it, I want you to pack a few necessities and take Mama and Nadine away from here by dawn. You can go to the home of Frau and Herr Böttcher in Germany. I've drawn a map. Take a cart and mule, but pack lightly. You will tell them that Josef van der Volk sent you. They will help you get to the palace of the prince of Orange at Dusseldorf. There, you will need to find Matthew van Ledenburg and tell him that Johanna is all right. Count Ledenburg is my father, and he will care for you until I can bring your own papa to you!"

"But Emeraude, I don't understand," the girl whimpered. "You're talking too quickly. I can't remember it all. Won't you come with us? What about Papa?"

"Suzette," she explained, making it a point to speak more slowly. "I've written it all down for you. And I have men with me who are going to help me get Papa out of that miserable prison. But I can't go for him until

I know that you and Mama are safely on your way! Don't you see, once we free him, they will come here looking for him and you could be arrested. You must do as I say and leave before it's light. Have Mama and Nadine carry knives concealed in their skirts. And sweet sister, it would help if you could put on some of Papa's clothing and disguise yourself as a man. Three women alone would be prey to attackers, but two women and a sturdy young man will have a better chance of getting there. Do you understand?"

"I understand, but what if Mama won't leave?" she asked.

"It's up to you to see that she does. You must go!" Johanna said urgently. "It's up to you."

"*Oui,* Emeraude," Suzette promised.

"Now, will you do me a small favor?"

"Of course. Anything! You know that."

"Can you get into my old room tonight?"

"Of course. But why?"

"I had a medallion with a crest on it when you found me. Do you remember it? It's wrapped in a handkerchief under my mattress—as close to the center as I could put it. Can you get it for me?"

"I'll go now," Suzette exclaimed, relieved to be able to do something she was sure of before she embarked on the dangerous journey away from everything that was familiar to her. "Wait right here, Emeraude!"

Knowing how a caged animal must feel, Johanna paced restlessly while she waited for Suzette to return. In a matter of minutes, the girl was back, clasping the small bundle to her breast. "I got it, Emeraude!"

"Thank you, my love. I knew I could count on you! Now, you must promise me that you will take care of

290

Mama and Nadine while I go for Papa!"

"I promise, Emeraude. I'll do exactly as you say. And I'll wear a long knife with my disguise, too. That should scare any highwaymen away!" she laughed, her lighthearted words not disguising the tremble in her voice.

"Now you have the idea!" Johanna encouraged her. "Just think of it as an adventure. I must leave now, Suzette, but I'll find a way to send you a message at Dusseldorf. You take care, for you are very dear to me. You are my only sister. I found three brothers, but no other sisters!"

Embracing Suzette one final time, Johanna took her tiny parcel and went out the window and down the tree, vanishing as suddenly as she had appeared, leaving Suzette to wonder if she had been dreaming.

Lying on her side in the darkness of the clearing where they had made camp, Johanna reviewed the escape scheme she had outlined to the men the night before. As she went over the plan, step by step, she assured herself that they had a favorable chance of succeeding. She was fully aware of the extreme danger they were putting themselves into, and of the fact that the outcome would depend on so many variables. But their main strengths were determination and the element of surprise. No one would expect a small group of men to walk in off the street and take two men out of the prison.

Johanna was so engrossed in her thoughts that when she felt a gentle nudge against her back she jumped, almost allowing a scream to escape from her throat.

Before she could turn around, she was shoved again. This time, the touch was more forceful and accompanied by a soft whinny.

"Fumée! Where have you come from? Oh, Fumée, you are a sight for sore eyes," she laughed, sitting up and hugging the huge smoke-colored animal. "I assumed those beasts had taken you when they took Dirk. How did you escape? Where have you been hiding?" She was standing now, and the horse was rubbing his chin affectionately on the top of her head, before pushing his muzzle against her stomach so she could scratch his ears and neck.

Laughing, she gently admonished the horse, "Hey, I'm glad to see you, too, but you'd better not knock me over with your love. I can't believe you're here. You look so good, and Mademoiselle will be so happy to see you. She hated to leave your sweet company as much as I did. But now the two of you can be together again. And when we find Dirk, all four of us can ride side by side once more!"

She quietly walked the gray over to where the mare was tethered. "Mademoiselle, look who's here. I think he missed us."

Watching the two horses nuzzle each other, Johanna felt some of her own anxiety and tension slipping away. "I know that this is a sign that things will go as we've planned," she told the two animals—certain they both understood what she was saying.

Chapter Seventeen

Johanna watched from a distance as Suzette, dressed in Francois's clothing, led a mule and cart out of the barn before sunup. Shortly before dawn, she saw two heavy female figures, one very tall and one very short, scurry out to the road from the back of the inn to join the waiting cart. As Johanna stood in her hiding place, she prayed fervently, "I beseech thee, dear Lord. Watch over them and keep them safe from harm." Then she whispered into the early morning breeze, "God be with you, my family."

When the three women had finally disappeared into the east, only minutes before the sun began to make its daily presence known, Johanna dashed back to her camp to finish her own preparations.

The men had managed to steal three enlisted-men's uniforms from soldiers found sleeping off a night of heavy drinking, and Dolf and Walter had donned the regimentals before riding the dead Spaniards' horses back to the campsite, looking unquestionably authentic.

"If I didn't know who you were, I'd be scared as hell!" Frans told them. "Now, we need to stow this extra uniform and horse tack under the hay—in case we need it later. Dirk can wear it if he's in any condition to ride. You can take the extra horse behind you, and we'll tie your nags behind the cart Jo is rounding up." He grinned mischievously.

As the two bogus soldiers turned their heads in the direction of Frans's gaze, they found it hard to believe what they were seeing. Fumée had been hitched to a run-down cart that had been loaded with hay and extra clothing for Francois and Dirk. Their horses had been covered with mud, and each carried disguising packs of items to sell in the marketplace: sausages, cheeses, cooking pots, jugs of water, and even two barrels of beer from the tavern. "Well, how do we look?" Johanna asked, her apprehension disguised behind a smile. "Do you think anyone will mistake us for royalty?"

"Where'd you get all that stuff?" Frans asked. "These poor horses will be glad to have our weight on them again—after what you've put them through!"

"Don't worry about the horses. Most of the bulk in the packs is loosely packed hay. The items for sale are only on the outside—for show! And I got this valuable merchandise in the inn!"

"Well, no one will recognize you. That's for certain."

"I thought about adding a couple of chickens to our wares, but I'm afraid they'd be too much trouble—although they would be an effective touch, don't you think?" she asked, feigning a lightheartedness she didn't feel.

"Chickens!" Dolf exploded. "Is she daft?"

Frans chuckled at the look of astonishment on Dolf's face. "Jo, I'm beginning to think you're taking this peddler thing too gravely. After all, we're just disguising ourselves—not starting new careers!"

"In that case, we'll just take one chicken!" She nudged her brother affectionately with her elbow. "By the way," she said more seriously, "since Mademoiselle looks like one of the regular Spanish horses, I thought she could ride behind you in your fine-looking uniforms."

"Too much of a lady for a little mud and a heavy pack?" Walter teased.

"No," Johanna answered, pretending to be insulted by his insinuation. "I simply thought it would be a good idea to have four horses unfettered by bundles—in case we need to leave in a hurry."

"Of course you did!" Frans snickered knowingly.

The release of tension brought on by the brief moments of levity were welcome to the four who would be facing indeterminate peril within the next few hours. "Then we're all ready?" Johanna suddenly said, all frivolity gone from her tone. "Frans and I will lead out with the cart and horses. You two can follow behind us. It would be a good idea to pass us occasionally, and even rest on the roadside some of the way. We'll stay in visual contact, but this will be the last chance we have to talk. Are there any questions?"

No one voiced the misgivings that were nagging at them all.

"No?" she went on. "In that case, since we all know what we must do, let's go." She slapped Fumée on the rump with the flat of her hand, sending the horse out of the campsite.

On the other side of the gentle horse, Frans turned one last time to wish Dolf and Walter the good luck they would be needing. Then the counterfeit peddlers walked toward the road to join the travelers who were journeying into Brussels on this day—like every other day.

So far, the plan had gone like clockwork. Johanna and Frans had arrived in Brussels without mishap, having quickly set up their stall near the palace gates. Deliberately choosing a place the soldiers and condemned prisoners had to pass on their way to the scaffold that stood ominously overshadowing the street, they displayed their wares on a wide quilt-draped board that was propped between two beer kegs. Already they had sold several items to some of the other sellers who had arrived early.

And while Frans and Johanna worked their stand, Dolf and Walter patrolled the area. Jaunty in their pilfered uniforms, they pretended not to be concerned with the glares they received from the citizens in the square.

The tension mounted as the morning hours crept gradually by. Soldiers and carriages entered and left the palace gates, and the crowds grew so dense that Johanna had a hard time telling when Dolf and Walter actually entered the palace compound. Several times she thought she had seen them disappear through the gates, only to have one of them walk casually by her stand a few minutes later and wink in her direction.

This is intolerable. I'm going to lose my mind before it's over. It would have been so much easier if I could

*have gone with them. If only my size wouldn't have
given me away. I know this is the best way, but the
waiting is so hard. If I just knew something. Anything!
All they have to do is walk in there and give the jailer
the orders to release Dirk and Papa for execution
today instead of tomorrow. What's taking so long?
What if something went wrong? What if they're
discovered?*

Johanna was brought out of her tumultuous
thoughts by the sudden hush that descended on the
gathered crowd.

Her gaze swerved to the palace gates in time to see
the duke of Alva in a black-and-silver coach moving
into the throng like a deadly black spider. Afraid of
being recognized by the coachmen, but unable to look
away from the aristocratic conveyance, she was
shocked into action only when the grand rig came so
close to her stall that a horse's tail brushed against her
cheek as the animal swatted at a fly.

She pulled her hat lower on her head only seconds
before the lone passenger in the coach peered out from
behind the curtains that shielded his face from the
curious onlookers.

*It's him! Did he see my face? Did he recognize me?
No, we've come too far to have a fluke like that ruin our
plan.*

Quickly busying herself with straightening her
exhibit of goods, Johanna watched out of the corner of
her eye as the slow-moving carriage progressed around
the square to stop in front of the decorated box that
had been set up so that the dignitaries could view the
horrendous exhibition in comfort.

Frans came rushing back to where Johanna stood

trembling after her near brush with their hated enemy. "Looks like he's going to view the executions himself today!" he growled, disgust and hate seething in his words. "I think we'll be safe, though. With him here, it will make our story even more plausible." Frans shook his head nervously and wiped the sweat from his flushed brow. "He didn't see you, did he? He came awfully close to where you were standing!"

"I'm sure he didn't. I pulled my hat down and was careful that he didn't catch my eye. Anyway, he'd have stopped right then if he thought there was a possibility I was so close I could reach out and touch his carriage. By now, he must have realized how I betrayed him. I imagine there's a price on my head, too—along with you and the others!"

"I wasn't going to tell you, Jo, but he's offering an exorbitant reward for your return—alive! There's also a goodly sum being offered for any information telling of your whereabouts. It's enough money that only our most loyal supporters would not be tempted to try to collect it. You must stay on your guard to be sure no one recognizes you as Esmeralda Verde. Absolutely no one can be trusted!"

The tower clock rang out the noon hour, and Frans smiled fatalistically, quickly taking his station at the end of the cart closest to the gates. "It won't be long now!"

As if taking their cue from Frans's prophetic statement, the giant gates swung open to reveal the day's sacrificial lambs to the waiting mass of people. As the bedraggled prisoners were exposed to those nearest the gates, cries of horror and pity filled the air. But all Johanna could hear was the drumming of her own heartbeat in her ears.

She anxiously searched the blank faces for any signs of recognition as the degraded men were marched or dragged past her stall. But most of them had long since passed the point of humanness, and the only expressions she was able to discern on the tortured faces were expressions of relief. Relief in knowing that soon they would meet their maker, and that they had seen the end of the Spanish dungeon.

There they were! Dirk and Francois! They were at the end of the line and being prodded by guards like the other prisoners. But they weren't chained to the group!

As they came alongside Johanna's cart, Frans, who had wandered toward the gates after the last of the prisoners had been brought out, began hollering and waving his arms angrily. "Stop him! Stop that thief! He has my purse! Someone help me!" he screamed, drawing the crowd's attention momentarily away from the parade of doomed captives.

Dirk and Francois, dazed by the roar of the crowd and gleaming sunlight, were suddenly knocked roughly to the ground by their escorts, who continued walking with their heads high, not permitting themselves the slightest glance downward or to the side.

Johanna immediately responded by shoving the two men with her foot to urge them to crawl under the blanket thrown over the table she had set up to display her wares—and to hide the underside of the wagon. "Hurry," she hissed as they regained enough equilibrium to crawl under the cloth and disappear from view. The entire action had taken place in a matter of seconds, but to Johanna it seemed like hours before she could signal to Frans that the deed was done.

Frans continued to shout expletives into the crowd. Then, still mumbling loud enough for everyone to hear, he came back to the place where Johanna was holding up a cheese trying to entice a customer to step over and purchase it from her.

"How can you be selling cheese when our countrymen are dying on that scaffold?" one indignant woman accused her bitterly.

"People got to eat," Johanna answered churlishly.

The incensed woman wheeled on Frans, who was still mumbling dramatically about his stolen purse, and shouted, "You ought to be ashamed, sir! Allowing this boy to be selling while these executions are being conducted. Have you no respect?"

Turning to Johanna, Frans shouted, "Boy! I told you to stop when the poor devils was brought out!" He grabbed the cheese out of her hand and threatened to beat her with it if she didn't learn to obey orders. Apologizing to the woman, Frans shook his head sadly. "Bought that scrawny boy two years ago. Can't teach him a thing!"

Then he went into another tirade about his missing pouch. But his outpouring fell on unhearing ears, for the woman, satisfied that she had made her point, had rejoined the swarm of spectators thrusting closer to the scaffold, now groaning under the weight of the condemned men and their executioners.

As the attention was drawn away from the cart operated by the red-faced man and grimy boy, no one noticed when the boy slipped under the wagon, leaving the man alone to grumble to himself—in case anyone was listening.

In the shadows under the wagon, a shudder ricocheted through her small frame, leaving her with a horrible sense of foreboding. Forcing herself to shrug it off, she spoke to Dirk and Francois, who were both very still—too still. "Quickly, you must get yourselves under the hay in the wagon. Everyone will be watching the executions, and no one will notice a little rustling in the hay. Can you do it?" she asked, growing steadily more concerned that all of their reserve strength had been used getting under the wagon.

"Emeraude? Is that you?" Francois gasped.

"*Oui,* Papa, it's me," she whispered. "You didn't think I'd let those monsters hurt my sweet Papa, did you?" she said, fighting her tears.

"Mama and Suzette?" he choked.

"Shh. Save your strength for getting onto the wagon. I don't think I can lift you," she teased weakly. "Mama and Suzette are fine! They will be in Germany waiting for us. That's where I'm taking you—to Mama and Suzette in Germany. Now, don't talk anymore. When I go back outside, I'll knock on the cart two times to tell you when it's safe to move. Can you do it, Papa?" she begged urgently.

"*Oui,* Emeraude, I'll do as you say. You're a good girl. You were always such a good girl," he panted, his voice quivering with the effort it took to speak.

"Dirk?" she said quietly. "Dirk, can you get into the wagon?" There was no answer. "Dirk! Can you hear me?" Shaking him, she managed to rouse him only slightly. "Dirk, you must get into the wagon under the hay! Do you understand me?" The panic in her voice must have permeated the haze that shrouded his brain, because he managed to respond.

"Johanna, what are you doing here?" Smiling

301

idiotically, he tried to sit up.

"Dirk, listen to me. It's important!" Speaking slowly and firmly, she repeated her instructions again. "If you don't do as I say, Dirk, we will all be killed! You must gather the strength to do your part. Once you're in the wagon, you can sleep all you want. Do you understand?" she asked again, hysteria mounting in her hushed voice.

But Dirk didn't answer. He couldn't. He had drifted into unconsciousness once more.

Operating on gut reaction, Johanna crawled out from under the cart on the far side near the palace wall, managing to drag the lethargic man with her to the narrow space. Pulling him up by the shoulders, she propped him against the edge of the wagon while she lifted the hay to make room for his inert body.

She managed to get the upper half of his torso on the cart and hidden behind a mound of hay on which the horses were munching nonchalantly. Then, bending her knees so that his buttocks were resting on her seemingly frail shoulder, she straightened her legs, lifting his weight with superhuman strength so that he slid onto the wagon under the dried grasses.

Glancing around to assure herself that her actions had not been noticed, she fluffed the hay over Dirk's inert body and patted the horses before diving under the wagon again.

"Papa?"

"*Oui,* Emeraude?"

"Papa, I got Dirk onto the wagon. Will you still be able to get up there by yourself?"

"I'll get there, *chèrie,*" he wheezed, as the blood in

his mouth grew more difficult to swallow.

"Good, now you wait until I signal. Then move as quickly as you possibly can. *Je t'aime,* Papa," she whispered, kissing him on the cheek before scampering out from beneath the wagon.

"And I love you, daughter," Francois murmured weakly, but she was gone.

"What's taking so long?" Frans snarled out of the corner of his mouth, not looking at Johanna when she reappeared at his side.

"I'll explain later. Dirk's on the wagon, and Papa—I mean Francois—said he can get himself hidden under the hay. He's weak. Has anyone glanced this way?" she asked quietly, her eyes alertly searching the crowd.

"They're too busy watching the horror on the scaffold to be concerned with the likes of us! It's a good plan, Jo. You've done well," he congratulated her.

"Save your felicitations for later, my brother. We're not safe yet," she answered gravely. "Dirk's unconscious and has no idea what's happening to him, and Papa is breathing as if every breath may be his last. I'm worried, Frans. Have you seen Dolf and Walter yet?"

"They're around. They keep moving. But don't worry about them. They're keeping us in their sights!" he reassured her.

"Then I'm going back under the wagon," she whispered, and dove out of sight.

"All right, Papa, it's time to go. Can you do it?"

"*Oui,*" he coughed.

"Don't try to talk. I'll go first and clear the way for you."

Pulling herself out on the back side of the wagon,

again she appeared to be arranging the hay so the horses could reach it. "Now, Papa. Now!" she hissed urgently.

With her heart aching, she watched as Francois Benner dragged his large frame up over the side of the wagon. Putting her hands on his arms, more for moral support than physical, she urged him on. "Come on, Papa. Just a few more feet to go." Looking around as she covered the top of his body with hay, she soothed, "Take a moment to rest, Papa. Then we must keep moving."

Slowly, agonizingly, Francois maneuvered one leg onto the wagon, where he was forced to stay for a moment to catch his breath. Still breathing with great effort, he finally gathered the strength to claw his way across the bed of the cart, pulling his other leg off the ground.

Moving quickly, Johanna hurried to conceal him, then ducked around the horses to rejoin Frans—who was watching the executions in spite of himself. "Don't look, Frans. There's nothing we can do for those poor souls. Watching them suffer will only make things harder."

"I want to watch, Jo," he said through gritted teeth. "I need to see what's happening! I want it ingrained on my soul, never to be forgotten. Do you understand?" he begged, his voice gravelly with unshed tears.

She nodded, her own memories of the past two days exploding horrendously in her mind. "Yes, I understand, Frans. I do understand."

"Josef, lead that horse out! I want to make it home

before dark," Frans ordered loudly. "It's been a good day, and I don't want to tempt highwaymen. I've already had one purse stolen today!" he complained noisily.

Shooting Frans a look that said, "You're over-acting!" Johanna guided the reliable Fumée out of the marketplace—none too soon as far as she was concerned.

The anxious hours following the secreting of Dirk and Francois in the hay wagon had taken their toll on both Frans and Johanna. They had continued to watch the executions until the last man was dead, knowing they could not leave until the street sweepers had removed the evidence of Alva's satanic, ritualistic butchery and the executioners had returned to the palace walls.

Every time a uniformed guard had come past their stall, both brother and sister had held their breath, fearing that Dirk or Francois would make a sound. And when Alva's carriage had passed by again, Johanna had been able to feel the hard, cold glare of the man inside as it rested on her lowered head and shoulders. There was no possible way he could have known he was so close to Esmeralda Verde, but Johanna couldn't help feeling terrified by his immediate proximity.

"Just keep your head down until he passes," Frans directed through unmoving lips, bowing in false respect to the man inside the moving vehicle—and to make certain that Alva did not see his face either.

"I'm shaking all over," she gasped breathlessly as the carriage disappeared from sight. "I'd better sit down a minute," she apologized, collapsing to the ground beside the incriminating cart.

"You rest. We'll be able to leave shortly," Frans consoled. "See? The streets are already starting to empty, and many of the peddlers are leaving—at least the ones who have a long distance to travel today. I'll check the horses' packs and then we'll join them."

But it had been another hour before Dolf and Walter had signaled that it was time for their departure. Frans had continued selling the wares that Johanna had brought along; and by the time they left they were truly justified, since they had run out of merchandise. When they finally merged into the crowd of westward travelers moving slowly through the fortified gateway out of the city, Johanna heaved a cautious sigh of relief.

Brussels had been surrounded by ramparts for protection since the eleventh century, and everyone coming in or out of the city was forced to progress through one of seven guarded tollgates, paying an excessive fee for the privilege of using the roads in any direction. The road they were on had been the main link between towns along Germany's Rhine River and the province of Flanders for a thousand years—since the time when Brussels was nothing more than a fortified castle on a little island in the Senne River, and called Brouc-sella, meaning Settlement of the Marshes. The little community had developed into a market and bartering place where the road and river crossed, bringing increasing numbers of merchants and craftsmen to the area until it had become the large city of the present.

Looking around to determine how close they were to the soldiers manning the gate, Johanna chanced a word of encouragement to the men lying so quietly under the

306

hay. "A few more minutes and we'll be on the road, and you can at least uncover your faces," she whispered softly.

"Keep your head down and your mouth shut, Jo!" Frans warned fractiously.

"Sorry," she apologized just as irritably, the strain of the day evident in her tone, too.

Getting through the portal had proven expensive, since the greedy guards were bent on collecting taxes not only for Alva's treasury, but also for their own pockets. Frans had been forced to pay over half of what they had earned that day in the market. Though he had argued with the guards, not wanting to appear so anxious to put the city behind him that he would draw their closer scrutiny, in the end he had given them all the money they had demanded.

Grumbling after they were out of earshot, he growled, "How the hell do they expect people to live? Do you realize if those guards had known that I had part of our money hidden elsewhere, they'd have taken that, too? Bastards!" he mumbled, walking behind his wagon of human cargo and hay.

"Quit your complaining, brother! We're out of the city and should be in Aalst within three or four hours. But as soon as I spot a shelter of trees, we'll stop and check on our passengers. They were in bad shape when I loaded them in the wagon, and except for an occasional groan, neither of them has made a sound." Johanna's voice was worried. Finally spying a thick clump of birch trees straight ahead, she veered off the road, leading the horses and cart behind her.

"What do you think you're doing?" a soldier barked, riding toward them at great speed.

Certain that their deception had been unearthed, Johanna began to stammer as she turned to justify their reasons for heading off the highway. "W-we were seeking some shade in which to eat our s-su . . . Dolf! What's wrong with you? You scared me to death! Don't you ever do anything like that to me again!"

However, looking up at the grinning soldier smiling down from his spirited mount, she found it hard to stay angry very long. But her ire was spent long before the pounding in her chest had subsided. "I don't think I can take much more," she groaned, giving Dolf an extra glare and continuing her trek through the marshy grasses between the roadway and the grove of birches.

"Quick, let's get them uncovered," she ordered as they reached the safe curtain of green. Without waiting for Frans to respond, she began moving the hay aside, searching for Dirk and Francois. Both were unconscious, and Johanna gasped in horror when she saw their battered faces in the light filtering through the treetops.

Francois was lying in a pool of his own blood, and each breath was a gurgle to stay alive. Their backs and chests were raw from the torture the whip had inflicted on their defenseless flesh; and the bleeding, festered wounds around their ankles and wrists told Johanna firsthand that they must have been chained the entire time they were in the prison. Briefly closing her eyes to erase the grisly pictures from her mind, she said, "Get some water, Frans! Lots of it!"

With the two "soldiers" lounging confidently between their hiding place and the roadway, Johanna and Frans attempted to clean and bandage the senseless men's injuries. Working at a feverish speed, they washed and wrapped their ankles and wrists with strips of material taken from clean clothing they had in their packs. "If we can get these filthy bug-infested rags off and wash their bodies, I think we can protect the wounds from further festering by using this salve and putting clean bandages on them." She had already begun to rip the foul-smelling clothing off Dirk's battered body.

As Frans wiped the blood from around Francois's mouth, Johanna lifted Dirk's head into her lap, where she knelt in the cart beside him. "Here, my love, try to drink this." She gently urged sips of water into his unresponsive mouth, refusing to be daunted when most of the cool liquid ran down his chin to the slowly rising wall of his muscular chest.

"Come on, let's try again," she coaxed. "Just one sip for me. Dirk, you must wake up so I can know you're all right before we go on. Can you hear me, Dirk? Dirk! Wake up!" she urged frantically.

Coughing spasmodically as the water found his throat, Dirk tossed his head from side to side and waved his arms irritably. "What're you trying to do? Drown me?" he mumbled almost unintelligibly.

"Oh, Dirk!" Johanna cried. "Those are the most beautiful words I've ever heard! Here, drink more water!" she insisted.

Too weak to disobey, Dirk did as he was told, managing to down several swallows before he feebly brushed the metal cup away from his cracked lips.

"All right, love, that's enough for now," she said with a thankful smile. "Dirk, do you know who I am? It's me, Johanna! I wouldn't have been able to go on living if those butchers had killed you." She clasped him to

309

her breast with all of her strength.

"Jo, he's asleep again. We'd better be on our way. It's at least 40 miles to Aalst. They'll both be fine now that we've dressed their wounds. And knowing they're with us and out of the clutches of those Spanish bastards will give them strength!" he finished emotionally.

"Let me check on Francois. Then we'll go," she insisted, moving to her stepfather. "Papa, I'm taking you to Mama. You sleep now, and we'll have you safe in her arms soon!" She bent her head to kiss him before she rearranged his blanket of coarse hay.

"Well," she said to Frans. "Why are we just standing here? We've got a long way to travel before dark!" she exclaimed, slapping him on the back and leading the horses toward the road.

Chapter Eighteen

Movement along the rutted road was slow, and by the time they had gone two or three miles, dark clouds began to gather in the west, indicating a storm blowing in from the North Sea—a common occurrence in the central plateau where they were traveling. And by the time they had traveled four miles, the rain had started.

With heads bent low, they trudged into the wind-driven rain, praying the cart wouldn't fall apart or get stuck in the gummy clay of the road. Seeing the rain pummeling down on the hay in the wagon, packing it on the men hidden there, Johanna pushed Fumée and herself harder. The horses and people stumbled and slid helplessly in the mud, finding each forward step more difficult than the one before; but still she drove on, knowing that if they stopped, the wagon would be impossible to get moving again.

"Not much farther now," she repeatedly encouraged the horse, her brother, herself, and the men in the wagon—who she was afraid probably didn't hear her. "We can do it. I know we can! We won't give up after coming all this way. Good horse, Fumée! Tomorrow you can rest! We'll get one of the others to take your place on the cart. Are you all right, Frans? Just keep your head down and hang onto the side of the wagon. Fumée will get us there!" she promised.

Johanna had no idea how many miles or hours she kept the sodden group moving, but no one faltered or attempted to give up, having drawn the necessary strength to endure from their small, determined leader.

Then, just as suddenly as it had begun, the downpour stopped, as though the ferocious wind and rain had been defeated by Johanna's courage and tenacity. "See! The sun is coming out again!" she cried, viewing the golden ball of light in the western sky. "Fumée, you did it! I knew you could! Now, if we can keep going for just a few more miles, we'll have a nice dry stall and some grain for you as a reward for your loyalty. Dirk's going to be so proud of you!" she praised, never thinking to take any credit herself.

Johanna gave the trusty horse another pat on the shoulder and dropped back to check on the men in the wagon. Walking alongside the moving cart, she pulled the wet hay off Dirk and Francois, who both lay shivering in the soggy wagon bed. She reached out to touch Dirk and was startled with the realization that his skin was hot to the touch, instead of cool as she had expected.

"Frans, Dirk has a fever! His head is burning. How much farther to that farmhouse? We've got to get him into some dry clothing."

Checking Francois's forehead, she found his skin cold, and she was slightly relieved. "At least Papa doesn't have a fever. That's a good sign," she said, lifting Dirk's slack hand to hold for the remainder of their journey.

"There it is, up ahead!" Frans shouted, the relief evident in his quivering voice. Running to the front of the cart, he directed the weary horse into the ramshackle barn that smelled of dry earth and animal dung.

Afraid her apprehension would be contagious to the others should she weaken even slightly, Johanna chattered as if nothing were wrong while she quickly removed the wet hay cover from the men in the cart. "I told you we'd get here. Dirk, smell this barn! It's such a wonderful, dry earthy smell. It reminds me of the Böttchers' barn. And I still love it! You must've been right about me being crazy!"

However, pulling Dirk's wet clothing off as she eased him to the straw-littered barn floor, she found it impossible to keep up her gay line of chatter and brave front. His skin was afire with fever. "We've got to get his fever down, Frans. How is Papa?" she asked, quickly dressing Dirk in long flannel pants and a shirt.

"Johanna," Frans started, but choked on his words as he looked into her unanswering gaze. He shook his head. "It's too late."

"Frans, you give up too easily," she spat angrily as she lowered Dirk's head and went to Francois. "Help me get these soggy clothes off him. And for God's sake, let's get him out of this wet hay."

Looking up from where she was now bending over Francois's still body, she shouted at her brother, "Don't just stand there, Frans! Do I have to do everything myself? Help me move him. We must get him dry! He'll be fine once I get him dry. You'll see," she continued, lovingly wiping the dark, wet hair from Francois's expressionless face.

Johanna didn't feel the strong hands on her shoulders, attempting to make her acknowledge the truth. "Johanna, it's too late! He's dead! There's nothing more we can do!"

"Frans, stop it! I don't want to hear you talk that way. He's not dead! He's sleeping. He's very tired and he's sleeping. He's not dead. Do you understand me? He's not dead! I won't let him be dead!" she wailed, her throat contracting as it choked back the unshed tears welling in her broken heart.

"Go ahead and cry, little girl. It's all right. You can cry now!" Frans consoled, tears coursing down his own ruddy cheeks.

"If you won't help me, then I'll do it alone!" Johanna hollered, jumping off the wagon and tugging futilely on Francois's large, unresponsive body.

Realizing that his sister would keep pulling on the dead man until she moved him and had completely spent her remaining strength, Frans hollered for Dolf and Walter, who were just riding up. "It's all right now, Jo. The boys and I will take care of Francois. We'll get him down and dried off. You'd better look after Dirk," he suggested.

Hesitating for a moment, Johanna looked at her brother, then back to Francois. "Be sure you move him carefully. We have to get him comfortable. Poor Papa. Such a good man. He never did a mean thing in his life, and he shouldn't have to endure any more pain. He won't complain, though. Have you heard him moan once? No! And you won't. He never complains. Not Papa!"

314

Guiding her back to Dirk's unconscious form, Frans nodded his head for Dolf and Walter to wrap Francois in a blanket and carry him to the other side of the stable. When they were out of Johanna's hearing, Walter asked Frans, "What about a priest?"

"I'll ask our hosts. Do you boys want to stay in those uniforms tonight?"

"We might as well. In case someone comes snooping around," Dolf answered.

"Then let me go to the house and tell them we're here and what's happened. You fellows did well today. We never could have succeeded without you," Frans praised the two.

Dolf laughed quietly, "I don't mind telling you, we spent some tense moments when we walked, big as you please, through that prison door. I could feel the sweat dripping off me when that heavy door banged shut behind us!"

"I can imagine. We were certainly glad to see you when you came back out!" Frans said, remembering the relief he had felt. "It all really went perfectly. Did anyone give you any trouble when you asked for the two extra prisoners?"

"Not a bit!" Walter bragged. "We walked in there with authority oozing all over the place and told the guard that Alva wanted Corlear and Benner taken care of today instead of tomorrow. He had them brought out immediately, and we walked out with them!"

"Proves a point, doesn't it? People are like cattle. They obey whoever has the biggest voice and most bravado!" Frans mumbled disgustedly. "Well, let me get up to that house and find some hot food and a priest." Frans nodded his head in Johanna's direction.

"Keep an eye on her, will you?"

Frans left the shelter, and Dolf and Walter looked over to where Johanna was holding Dirk's head in her lap and applying cold compresses to his fevered brow. "We'll unload the horses and get them fed?" Walter offered, already unhitching Fumée from the harness he had worn for fourteen hours.

"Thank you, Walter," she said. "It's been a long day. Dirk has a fever and I hate to leave him. Have you eaten supper yet? I think we have a sausage and some apples left. Frans sold everything else," she said with a sad laugh, the strange sound cutting harshly into the macabre atmosphere. "He should be an actor. He really believes in playing his part to the limit. I was afraid he was going to sell the clothing off his back!"

"He would, too, if the price was right!" Dolf joked, hoping to help the girl forget the dead man lying wrapped in the blanket.

"Will you check on Francois for me, Dolf?" she asked, seeming to be reading his thoughts, her red eyes remaining tearless.

"We've taken care of him, Jo," Dolf answered gently. "Frans has gone for a priest."

"A priest? We don't need a priest. I tell you he'll be all right. He only needs to rest. A good night's sleep and he'll be fine." Her voice rose to a high pitch, and she rocked Dirk's upper body as she clutched him to her.

"Jo, Francois is dead. You have to believe it. We can't change what's already happened." Squatting down beside the girl on the floor, Dolf turned her face to meet his. "He died knowing he was loved. You saved him from the horrors and degradation of that Spanish scaffold. He knew you were willing to risk your life for him and that you would take care of his wife and daughter."

"But it was all my fault," she insisted. "It was because of me that he was arrested."

"Are you saying he did the things he did for *you*— and not for the Netherlands? I think maybe you're putting too much importance on your own contributions—and too little on his!" Dolf admonished truthfully.

"Am I?"

"I believe so. My God, girl, the man died a hero. His underground organization is responsible for saving thousands of lives. Mine included!"

"And mine," Walter added.

"And mine," she whispered, thinking how unbearable her months with Alva would have been if Francois had not done what he did. He had given her life purpose. "He was very brave, wasn't he?" she asked, finally acknowledging the fact of his death in her heart.

"Yes, very," Dolf agreed.

Unexpectedly, Dirk began to thrash wildly in Johanna's arms. "He's burning up. We must get his fever down. I saw a water trough outside. Help me get him out of these clothes," she shouted, the emergency driving all thoughts of self-pity from her mind. "Let's get him in that cool water!" she ordered as her hands hurriedly stripped the clothing from Dirk's body again.

Walter and Dolf, already impressed with Johanna's quick and clever thinking, didn't question her instructions, but proceeded to lift Dirk and carry him outside.

"What in the hell are you doing with him?" Frans yelled, running across the yard to where the three stood ready to immerse the naked man. "Are you trying to kill him?"

"She said it will bring his fever down," Dolf replied.

"Put him in the water, Dolf!" Johanna ordered.

With one more quick glance at the cringing Frans, they did as they were told, eliciting a loud groan from the shocked and trembling man in the water. "He's freezing to death, Jo! Look at his teeth chattering. He should be wrapped in blankets to sweat his fever out!"

"Frans, his fever is too high. He's got to be cooled off. Hopefully, the water will do the trick. We can't wait for him to sweat the fever out. Besides, he doesn't even know where he is or who we are!"

Not certain what to do about the torture his sister was inflicting on Dirk, Frans said, "The people in the house sent soup, and they're getting the priest."

"You three go ahead and eat." With her arm under Dirk's shoulder to keep his head from slipping into the water, she groaned, "I think it'll be a while before Dirk will be hungry!"

Dipping the shirt she had taken off him into the water, she made a compress to hold on his face. "There, isn't that better?" she murmured to the man, whose chills were subsiding ever so slightly. "You know I love you, Dirk, and I'll do anything it takes to keep you alive. I never want to hurt you."

"Here, let me hold him awhile," Dolf offered. "You eat something."

"Thank you," she mouthed, aware that she could not keep up her strength without nourishment. Turning Dirk over to Dolf, she watched for a moment as he gently held Dirk in the water, wiping his face frequently with the cool rag.

Reaching for the wooden bowl of steaming soup

Frans extended to her, she smiled her gratitude. "It's all right. I understand about Francois. Where will we bury him, though? I can't bear to think of him not having a proper funeral and burial place."

"They have a family cemetery out back where we can put him, Jo. They've already sent someone to prepare his grave. I wish I had known him. Our country and our family owe him so much," Frans said sincerely.

"Yes, we do."

They were brought back to the immediate situation by loud cursing and the sound of water splashing at the trough. "Let me out of this thing! What the hell are you trying to do, Dolf?"

Running to the water tub where Dolf was struggling with the irate man, Johanna hollered as she put her hand on Dirk's forehead, "It worked! His fever's down. Let's get him dried off and in some more dry clothing," she ordered. Then, as she put her arms around his chest to help lift him out, she added sternly, "I'm warning you, Dirk Corlear, if you don't keep your fever down, you're going back into this tub!"

Dolf and Walter laughed riotously when Frans said, "How can a woman be so hardhearted?"

When they had Dirk dried off and lying on a blanket, Johanna brought him the remainder of the soup. "Can you eat anything, Dirk?"

"I'm not hungry, just thirsty," he answered weakly.

"Well, try a few sips of this," she said, ignoring his refusal and lifting his head to spoon the nourishing liquid into his mouth. "This will make you stronger and better able to fight the infection in your body. Even though your fever is down, you're still too warm to think of yourself as well. So you'd better listen to me," she scolded.

"No more, please. Maybe later!" he appealed to her.

"Just two more bites," she urged. "Then I'll leave you alone and let you go back to sleep," she promised.

In the end, Dirk was able to consume most of the warm broth, then drifted into a peaceful slumber with his head in Johanna's lap. She gently lifted his head to place it on a cushion of clothing and was about to walk away to find herself something dry to put on when he spoke. "Don't leave," he begged in his sleep, reaching out to hold her arm. "Johanna, don't leave me again."

"Oh, my darling, I won't. Never again. I'm right here. You sleep now, and I'll be right beside you," she promised. Kissing his eyes and forehead, she cradled his head until his breathing slowed to an unperturbed and unlabored rise and fall of his chest.

"Will someone bring me some dry clothing?" she whispered. "I don't want to agitate him again."

She paid no heed to where the warm, dry shirt and trousers came from, but she managed to exchange the wet for dry without disturbing the sleeping man further. That done, she stretched out beside him and held his warm body next to hers, falling asleep with a prayer of thanks on her lips.

Dirk improved remarkably during the following days, as the small group of men and horses made their way toward the seacoast. As they trudged across the flat, watery plains of Flanders, drawing nearer to their destination, their spirits began to rise.

Dirk was getting better daily—so much so that he had ridden Fumée for several hours on the third day of their journey. They had been assisted by sympathetic patriots wherever they stopped, and they had been able to avoid any confrontations with the detachments of Spanish soldiers that patrolled the roads. In fact, they all began to allow themselves to believe that their venture was going to be a success.

They were bound for the fishing village of Oostende on the North Sea, about fifteen miles from Walter's home in Brugge. Their plan was to board a fishing vessel that would transport them north to the port of Emden, Germany, only a few miles from Groningen, where Louis of Nassau waited for them before continuing his onslaught of the northern Netherlands.

"Things have gone too smoothly," Johanna said suddenly as they sat resting in a shed behind the Altervelde estate in Brugge. "I'm worried!"

Frans shook his head, unable to believe what he was hearing. "I think you're looking for something to worry about. Everything has gone exactly as you planned it. Tomorrow we'll be in Oostende and should be riding the tides by tomorrow evening. What could go wrong now?"

"I don't know. I only know I feel uneasy tonight! It's the last night of the journey, and perhaps I'm simply looking for something to worry about—as you say! But all of you please stay on guard, if only to humor my feminine excitability!" she implored, laughing at herself.

Having grown accustomed to relying on Johanna's intuition, the men exchanged furtive glances. "Why don't we post a guard tonight, Jo? That should ease your anxiety," Frans offered, nodding his head to Walter and Dolf.

"It might be a good idea to sleep in hidden places, instead of in here," Johanna suggested. "That way, if we're approached unexpectedly, we won't be boxed in."

Walter interrupted. "My family is on guard, and this shed is so far from the main house that I really think you'll see that your fears are unfounded, Jo."

"I'm sure you're right, Walter. I'm sorry I'm such a worrier. Has your father made the arrangements for our escape tomorrow?" she asked, changing the subject.

"We're expected. We'll need to separate to board the ship at different times because the soldiers patrol the wharf. There will be a ship docking to pick us up around midnight. Once we're on board, we can relax." Walter smiled confidently.

"Did he get the fishermen's clothing for us?" Dirk asked.

"We have everything we need. We'll stay in our present disguises until we arrive at a small house in Oostende. There, we'll become fishermen before boarding our boat."

"What about the horses? Are they aware we plan to board horses, as well as men?" Johanna had no intention of leaving Fumée or Mademoiselle behind.

"Yes, Jo, they know," Walter answered impatiently. "We board eight horses and five men. They'll keep the extra three horses as payment for their services. Are you happy now? This was all your plan in the first place. You said they'd expect us to head east, so we would go west. Why all the second-guessing at this late date?"

But before Johanna could answer, Walter's twelve-year-old sister, Kristine, suddenly burst into the shed. "Soldiers!" she gasped, breathless from running. "Spanish soldiers! At the house! Papa is delaying them while I came down to warn you. They said they're making a routine search for some men they have warrants for. One of the names on the list is yours, Walter! You'd better scatter into the woods—and for God's sake, get rid of those uniforms!" she cried in a hoarse whisper, indicating the Spanish uniforms Dolf and Walter had removed.

"Quick, everyone grab something and we'll disappear until they're gone," Walter growled. "I have some childhood hiding places in mind that will be safe."

They scurried out of the shed, working efficiently and quietly, and taking evidence of their presence with them.

They were already hidden in the woods when Johanna remembered the extra soldier's uniform secreted in the hay on the cart. She knew that if the Spaniards found that uniform during their search, Walter's entire family would be in jeopardy. Not taking time to tell the others where she was going, she made a dash for the shed, still quiet except for the occasional shuffle of horses and rats.

Just as she entered the dark building, she heard men's voices, low and commanding. "What's this over here?"

The light of the lantern hit Johanna as she turned to flee into the night. "What have we here?" came the amused, slightly familiar Spanish voice. "Stop, boy! What are you doing here?"

Another man, probably Walter's father, answered, "Just some peddler's boy. I often let them use this shed overnight when they travel between the coast and the east. I didn't know anyone was here tonight. They must've just arrived," he suggested.

"You didn't answer me, boy," came the satiny smooth command of the officer. "What are you doing here?"

"M-me and my papa are on our way to Oostende to get salted herring to sell in Brussels," she stuttered, taking care to keep her head down.

The officer took two strides to where she stood trembling in the doorway. "And where is your papa, boy?" the Spaniard cajoled.

"H-he has a lady friend near here. He's gone to visit her," she answered.

"So! You're here all alone in this dark shed? That's no way to watch over such a young boy, is it, Gilberto?"

"No, Reynaldo, not a good way at all. Something could happen to him out here all alone with no one to protect him," the second soldier agreed with saccharine concern.

Johanna was barely able to control the gasp of horror that rose in her mouth when she recognized the hated names. *Reynaldo and Gilberto! Are the others out there?* she thought frantically, squinting her eyes against the glare of the lantern and trying to determine how many soldiers there were.

"Raul, you and Señor Altervelde finish the search, while we stay here to watch over this young lad until his father comes," Reynaldo commanded, never lifting his gaze from the youth who stood cringing in front of him.

"But—" Raul started.

"Do as I say, my friend," Reynaldo said firmly. "I'm sure his father will be along soon, and we will join you

324

at the main house then," he said in a low voice that was rife with meaning and excitement.

As she heard Walter's father and the other soldier walk away, she chanced a sidelong glance at the remaining men. *Three of them! What chance do I have against three? I should have told the others where I was going.*

"Look at me when I speak to you, boy!" were the words Johanna heard as her face was jerked roughly up to within inches of Reynaldo's face, his penchant for young boys glistening in his lusting eyes.

"Gil, look at this face! If you cleaned him up a bit, he'd be as beautiful as any woman you ever saw. Are you afraid of me, boy?"

"N-no, sir," she stammered, not knowing what she should say.

"You're not? That's too bad. You should be. You see, I find it very exciting to look into eyes wide with terror and alarm—especially a young boy's eyes, such as yours." Reynaldo's syrupy voice sent chills throughout Johanna's quaking body. "Are you still unafraid? Your face tells me that you're very frightened. Is that true?"

"Y-yes. I am. W-what do you w-want with me?" she cried, using every bit of effort to keep her voice in its lowest range.

"Don't you know? Hasn't your papa explained the facts of life to you? That's a shame. Luis, isn't that a shame? His papa should have had a talk with him, shouldn't he? But don't you worry. I'll explain things to you in my little school for innocents!" he laughed, the sound from his mouth ugly and frightening.

Reynaldo took steps toward her, backing her into the darkness of the shed. "You men keep an eye on things out here. I'd enjoy a little privacy for this boy's first lesson in the way of things," he chortled over his shoulder, continuing to approach Johanna's retreating form.

Keeping her eyes on the advancing figure outlined by the lantern, which now hung in the doorway, Johanna backed into the cart with a soft thud. "Where are you going to go now, boy?" Reynaldo laughed cruelly.

Attack! Attack first! It was Esmeralda's strength coming from the core of Johanna's being.

"I can't! I don't know what to do!" she answered out loud, forgetting Reynaldo could hear her.

"I'll show you what to do, boy. First, we get your clothes off!" he answered, his voice betraying an urgency as he stepped closer to reach for her shirt front.

You can't go back to being Emeraude—helpless and afraid. After all you've been through, have you still learned so little that you're willing to give up without a fight? her inner voice goaded harshly.

The soldier was so intent on his pursuit that he did not see the expression on his quarry's face change from fright to wrathful revenge. If he had, perhaps he would not have been so surprised by Johanna's actions.

With the speed of an attacking jungle predator, she flew across the space that separated her from the astonished Reynaldo, her gleaming white teeth bared in a merciless grin of vengeance as she sank her knife into his belly clear up to the hilt.

Instinctively, the man clutched at the blade of the knife, which sliced deep cuts into his palms as she removed it—only to plunge it into his convulsing chest. Using the cart behind her for support, she lifted both of her feet to propel Reynaldo backward and to remove his bleeding weight from her weapon.

As he fell to the ground, she took another slash at him, leaving a diagonal trail of open flesh from the far corner of his forehead, across his eyebrow, the bridge of his nose, and down his cheek to his twitching jawline. "So, you like young boys, do you?" she asked viciously, the ugly grin still fixed on her hate-filled face. "Sorry to disappoint you, señor, but your days of raping and molesting innocents are at an end!"

As the lantern light fell full on Johanna's face for the first time, Reynaldo gasped in horror. With blood spilling from his mouth, face, chest, hands and stomach, his voice was nothing more than a hoarse groan of pain. "I know you," he accused hysterically.

"Oh, do you now?" she chided humorlessly. "I also know you! And you had best say your prayers because as of now, you are no more!"

Johanna took one final swing and severed the pulsating artery in his neck with the knife that had hung, unused, from her belt since she had donned male attire.

Her gaze jerking up from the dead man, she jumped back into the shadows and waited for Reynaldo's partners to come in. *They must have heard us. Why don't they come?*

As if she had conjured them up with her thoughts, suddenly two dark figures appeared in the doorway to the shed, and Johanna backed deeper into the shadows.

Chapter Nineteen

"All right, you bastard. You may as well come out. Your friends can't help you now!"

"Dirk! Dirk, is it you?" Johanna screamed, running out of the shadows into his protective embrace.

Pulling her away from his chest, he looked as if he were surprised that she was real. "Where is he, Johanna? We heard him talking! Did he hurt you?"

"I killed him, Dirk," she whispered, reminding him of a wounded child. "I killed him," she said again, hysteria mounting in her voice.

Running to check the dead man lying on the floor of the shed, Frans confirmed her statement. "She killed him, all right. Looks like several times! He should have known better than to mess with our little Jo, shouldn't he?" There was a note of respect, as well as astonishment, in his statement.

Guiding Johanna to where she could sit down to recover from the shock of her encounter with the soldiers, Dirk hollered out the door, "Get them in here and on the cart quickly before anyone comes back."

Working hastily, the three men loaded the bodies onto the wagon and covered them with hay. "Make sure the blood that pig spurted all over the place is covered up," he called over his shoulder to Dolf, who was already hitching two of the horses to the sturdy wagon.

"I wish I could have seen the look on his face when she came at him with that knife!" Dolf laughed, shaking his head and kicking loose dirt and straw over the blood-drenched area where Reynaldo had died only moments before.

"Now you know what's in store for you, Dirk—if you marry her and don't treat her right," Frans joked.

Dirk knew the men were making their quips as a release from the tension that had built from the moment Kristine had told them about the soldiers to the exploding point when they had realized Johanna had returned to the shelter; but he couldn't help being concerned by the troubled expression on Johanna's blood-spattered face as she continued to stare at the spot on the floor where they had found the dead soldier.

"I'd advise keeping your comments to yourselves until we finish our work here," Dirk said, his tone firm and threatening.

"There was another one." Johanna's voice was small and childlike.

"What is it, Johanna? What did you say?" Dirk asked gently, stooping to put his arm around her shoulders and his ear near her mouth.

"Another one! There were four soldiers. You only put three on the cart. The other one will be back, you know." Her tone was low and lifeless.

Dirk remained silent until Dolf and Walter had

walked outside to watch for the returning soldier. Then he surveyed the shed one last time before turning back to Johanna. "You need to change your clothes before we go. We have to leave right away. Do you want any help?" he asked, handing her fresh garments to put on.

"No, I can do it." She smiled sadly at the anxious concern on his handsome face. Reaching up to push a lock of hair off his worried forehead, she sighed, "Your hair looks like gold in the lantern light. I'm glad it's not black anymore."

He clutched her tightly to his chest.

"Dirk?" she whispered. "Did you know I was carrying a child when those men in the cathedral . . . ?"

"Yes, I knew. I found out later on," he answered compassionately.

"They killed my baby, Dirk," she said, at last giving herself over to her grief and crying. "Poor little baby. He never had a chance!"

"There will be other babies. You'll have lots of beautiful healthy babies," he insisted, fighting his guilt because he knew she believed he meant those babies would be his. But as much as he loved her, and as much as he blamed himself for what had happened to her, he couldn't forget that she had willingly been Alva's mistress.

"We've got to leave," he said hoarsely. Lifting her to her feet, he gave her a lingering kiss on the forehead, then spun away. "Hurry and get dressed."

As he strode to the doorway, his heart ached for the pain Johanna had endured, and he vowed that even if there was no hope of restoring their relationship, protecting her from further harm would be his first concern from that day forward.

Tying the rope that held the sacklike trousers secure around her small waist, Johanna ran and caught up to Dirk. She slipped her slender hand into his and asked, "Can I ride on Fumée with you? Just for tonight?"

Knowing the strength it would take to ride with her in his arms all night, he sucked in a deep breath of resignation and gave her a sad smile. "I wouldn't have it any other way." He gripped her about the middle and swung her onto the large gray horse, then hoisted himself into the saddle behind her.

She reached over to stroke Mademoiselle, who stood beside her, one baleful brown eye watching. "Don't be hurt, girl. It's just that tonight I need someone to lean on."

Johanna was barely aware of the amount of time the journey to Oostende took. She had mounted the horse and leaned back into the security of Dirk's arms wrapped around her lithe form. Feeling safe for the first time in hours, she closed her eyes, attempting to make her mind a blank. But the events of the past two weeks continued to be dredged up by a part of her that refused to forget.

She relived the moments on the edge of the swamp when Dirk had wanted to kill her; the cutting of her hair; the uncomfortable reunion with her parents; the meeting with Louis of Nassau; finding Fumée; seeing Mama, Suzette and Nadine leave for Germany; lifting Dirk into the wagon in Brussels; putting him in the cold water; and the meager funeral service for Francois.

Francois was dead! Somehow, even after seeing his large body lowered into the ground, she could not accept it. His strength had been the source of her own power for all these months. His love. His wisdom.

331

His patience.

She shuddered inwardly when she thought of the bighearted man lying cold and alone in a strange cemetery so far from his home. How would she explain to Mama and Suzette? Would they blame her? Would they know that she would have given her own life if she could have extended his long enough to be with them once more?

Her thoughts shifted to Fernando in his carriage as it had crept past where she was standing, looking like a huge venomous insect crawling through the crowd. She relived the horrifying and ghastly executions they had witnessed. And most of all she recalled the moment she first plunged her knife deep into the flesh of another human being.

"Dirk?" she said after a very long silence. "How did you feel the first time you killed a man?" she asked curiously.

Recalling the men in the tavern who bragged about what they had done to Johanna and her baby, Dirk's jaw clenched tight. Words refused to describe his feeling. "How did I feel?" he asked.

"I mean, did you feel good? Bad? Indifferent? Justified? Guilty? Sorry? Relieved? How did you feel when it was over?" she begged earnestly.

Thinking he understood how she was suffering, Dirk said, "Johanna, you had no choice! The world needs to be rid of filthy vermin like that Spanish blackguard. It was him or you!"

"But how did you feel?" she insisted. "I must know."

"Johanna, I don't know how I felt," he answered impatiently—and with great frustration. "No, that's not true," he winced. "I felt all of those things—good, bad, justified, guilty. I would give anything if I could have spared you this. Why did you go back there, Johanna?"

"I was afraid they'd find the extra uniform we brought for you and blame Walter's family. I thought I had time," she explained defensively. "I was so scared, Dirk. I only knew I couldn't let him touch me."

He tightened his hold on her. "You did nothing wrong. You've got nothing to feel guilty about."

She sat up straight and twisted around to look at him, her expression confused. "That's just it, Dirk! I don't feel guilty. I'm glad he's dead! I killed another human being, and I'm glad! What kind of a monster does that make me? I wanted to stab him over and over. I wanted to cut him for every act of degradation he and others like him have committed against our people. I can't even pray for forgiveness. I've committed a mortal sin, and I feel no need to cleanse my soul!" A low, resentful chuckle escaped from deep in her throat. "The only thing I feel guilty about—is not feeling guilty!"

"You have nothing to feel blameworthy for, Johanna. Nothing at all. You're very courageous. You simply did what had to be done," he defended. "Now, why don't you close your eyes and try to sleep?"

"I don't think I can." But she said nothing else for some time. And when she finally spoke again, it was about the medallion that hung around her neck.

"Tell me about the jade-and-onyx brooch you gave me."

Dirk tensed. "How do you know about that?" he asked suspiciously.

"I was wearing it when Suzette found me. It was

333

hanging down my back, all tangled and hidden in my hair. I guess my attackers didn't notice it or surely they would have stolen it," she explained, her tone still bitter when she referred to the day in the cathedral.

"But how did you know I gave it to you? I thought you couldn't remember before the attack in the cathedral. Or was the brooch in your dreams with my hair and eyes?" he asked with just the barest tinge of sarcasm.

"No," she said with a regretful smile as she realized that even now Dirk didn't wholly believe she was telling the truth. "Frans told me. I had it hidden at the Benners' and retrieved it the night before we came for you. I thought it must be our family crest and asked Frans. That's when he told me that you gave it to me."

Dirk let out the breath he'd been holding as he waited for her explanation. "It was my father's, and his father's before him," he answered emotionally, thinking that the brooch was probably all there was left of his father's estate. "I'm glad you kept it safe. Where is it now?"

"Right here." She pulled the medal from inside her shirt. "Perhaps you should take it back," she ventured softly, her heart breaking at the thought of giving up the one piece of tangible proof that Dirk had loved her once—and the hope that he might again. "After all that has happened, I would understand if you didn't want me to wear it anymore." She started to lift the chain over her head.

Dirk stilled her hands, unable to sever their bond. "Now is not the time to make that decision. For now, you keep it."

Johanna wrapped her fingers around the medallion

and slumped in relief. It had been the hardest thing she'd ever done, to offer to give it back. But he hadn't taken it, and though he'd said they would talk about it later, she took heart from the fact that he wanted her to keep it now. "I'll never take it off again, Dirk," she murmured, closing her eyes. "Unless you ask for it back."

Standing at the rail of the creaking fishing boat as it silently made its way out of the harbor at Oostende, Johanna wondered if she would see her homeland again. She wrinkled her nose in a grimace of distaste as the night breeze drifted over her, heavy with the penetrating odor of years of fishing expeditions. "Do you suppose I'll ever get used to that rancid fish smell?" she asked no one in particular. "You'd think that after staying in the back of that fish salter's place all day, my sense of smell would have become deadened permanently," she laughed, thinking it would be a long time before she'd eat any sort of seafood again—if ever!

"And all this time, you thought people got seasick from the ship's motion on the water," Dirk teased, fighting his own revulsion at the odor permeating the night air. "It was the stink all along!"

"How are the horses?" she wondered, remembering they had all come on board easily enough but had gotten restless as the rocking of the vessel had made their footing unsure.

"They'll be fine. Evidently, this isn't the first time this crew has transported horses. They have them all crosstied in padded stalls so they can't move around and hurt themselves. They'll be fine. I have no doubt.

It's you I'm worrying about. You're looking a bit peaked. Do you feel sick?"

Leaning on him for support, and to hide her embarrassment, Johanna laughed. "Maybe I'll feel better if I lie down. I think there was something wrong with that smoked fish we ate for supper. My stomach feels a little unsettled. I'm sure that after a night's sleep, I'll be better."

Suddenly feeling too nauseated to ignore it any longer, she jerked away from Dirk, staggered to the rail and leaned over to empty the contents of her stomach. Again and again she strained against the barrier to vomit into the churning black water below.

Johanna was unaware of Dirk's presence until he put his hand on her shoulder, attempting to help her to her bunk below deck. "Please go away," she choked, retching uncontrollably. "I don't want you to see me like this."

"Then I won't look at you, but come and let me get you to bed," he laughed sympathetically.

They had taken only a few steps away from the railing when Johanna had to wrest herself from Dirk's grip and run back to the side of the ship. "I'm going to be sick," she explained unnecessarily.

At last, when it finally appeared that her stomach had calmed down enough to get her to bed, Dirk guided her to a hammock in a cabin below. Placing her on the swinging contraption, he pointed to the slop pail he was placing at her side. "I'll be back in a minute. You try to sleep," he said, caressing her clammy cheeks and forehead before leaving her in the dark room, swaying with the motion of the ship.

Johanna didn't know when Dirk had returned, but when she awoke with the first light of day breaking through the funny round windows in the tiny room, she saw that he was sleeping soundly in a hammock nearby. In fact, she was surprised to see that the small area had several of the peculiar beds hanging from the low wooden ceiling, one on top of the other. The man in the bed above hers was moving restlessly, and his weight brought his hammock down close to where she had slept peacefully—once she had stopped vomiting.

Slipping from her own swaying piece of stretched canvas, she realized someone had washed her face and changed her clothes. Seeing Dirk in a nearby bunk, she studied his unshaven face. He'd been so good to her since he'd recovered from his time in the prison. No one could have asked for more gentle or loving care. And he seemed to finally believe her about her memory loss. But she could still hear the skepticism in his voice when he spoke, and she could see it in his eyes when she answered his leading questions, or when he thought she didn't see him watching her.

Her heart bursting with sadness, she looked away. *What I need is a bath,* she told herself, running her hand through the short blond hair that curled in an attractive frame around her small face, despite the fact that it desperately needed washing. *Everything will look better if I'm clean,* she convinced herself as she stumbled out of the cabin in search of a tub, some water and a sliver of soap.

The voyage to Emden took longer than Johanna had expected. However, there had been no recurring seasickness, and she had actually been able to round up a tub of warm water to bathe in. Dirk's behavior had continued to be kind and friendly, and he had treated her with the utmost respect and had never lost patience with her constant need to know about the rebellion.

For instance, she had learned, much to her surprise, that the crew of the *Wilderstand*, who called themselves Sea Beggars, was made up of nobles and gentry with prices on their heads, Calvinists exiled from the Netherlands, and unemployed workmen and fishermen from Flanders and Brabant.

Supposedly dedicated to the overthrow of Alva's tyrannical government, they spent much of their time in the channel between the Atlantic Ocean and the North Sea, where they committed piracy and conducted pillaging raids along the coast on any cities or towns that seemed to support the Spanish monarchy. More than once during the voyage, Johanna and Dirk observed the manifold group of outlaws as they went ashore to loot and plunder a village along the shoreline.

"I don't understand, Dirk. They're robbing and destroying the very people they're supposed to be fighting for," she exclaimed in frustration during an attack on a particularly vulnerable town. "They're nothing more than robbers and thieves! How can they call themselves patriots?"

"It's true. They've proven themselves to be a menace to *all* channel shipping with their blockading activities and piracy. They pay no heed to the flag a ship flies and certainly don't limit their attacks to Spanish ships by any means. But I've been told that Orange feels they can help his cause by cutting off Spain's maritime routes to the Netherlands—*and* by providing prize money to finance his campaign."

Stunned by what she was hearing, Johanna said nothing as she continued to listen with great interest and astonishment.

"Louis says his brother, acting in his capacity as

governor of Holland and Zeeland, is planning to issue these 'Sea Beggars' his letters of marque. That will give them a semilegal status for what they're doing."

"But the prince of Orange is in exile, and all of his properties have been confiscated! By what power can he do that?"

"As far as he and his followers are concerned, he's still a prince of the Empire and has sovereign powers," Dirk explained.

"But I thought he disliked the Calvinists' ways of doing things!" she objected. "Surely he doesn't condone their intolerance. Unless . . . Has he become a Calvinist?!"

"No, but he's no longer a Catholic, either. He's converted to the Lutheran church now. And you're right that he disagrees with many Calvinist principles. But he can hardly ignore their international power when most of the support he's received from Germany and France has been from the Calvinists of those countries!" he said, shaking his head.

"But what about religious freedom?" she protested. "Does he still believe in it for the Netherlands? I think the Calvinists want to be rid of the Catholics as much as Spain wants to destroy the Protestants and Calvinists!"

"He still holds that there is room for all beliefs and religions in our country."

"Well, I hope his followers feel the same way when we rid our land of the Spanish tyrants!" she said, doubting the possibility greatly.

Unfortunately, there was no more time for discussion, since the men were returning to the *Wilderstand* and making ready to sail.

The burden of Johanna's new knowledge weighed heavily on her mind for the remainder of the journey.

But even that was a slight blessing, for slowly she noticed that Dirk treated her more and more like a younger sister or family friend he felt a duty to protect, and less and less like the woman he loved and wanted to spend the rest of his life with.

The last night out, Johanna stared at the ceiling over her bunk. Though she still felt guilty for displacing the ship's captain, she was glad that he had insisted on housing her in his cabin for the duration of the voyage when he had discovered one of Nassau's *men* was a woman. For one thing, it had made it possible for her to bathe in private. But the cabin had also served as a refuge where she'd been able to escape from Dirk's untrusting eyes that continued to watch her as if waiting for her to make a mistake.

As the full realization of the futility of her love for Dirk Corlear had filtered through her wishful thinking, she had been able to concentrate on filling her mind with other things. But now, this last night out before they docked in Emden, she just couldn't shake the feelings of hopelessness she'd experienced since she'd finally admitted to herself that Dirk didn't love her the way she loved him.

"I really thought when we were at the Böttchers' farm that he was starting to love me again," she said aloud to the darkness. *And when he saw I had come to get him out of prison, he was glad to see me. I know he was.* "Of course, it was my fault he was in that prison in the first place," she admitted, her tone filled with self-blame. Her hand rose to clasp the medallion that still hung around her neck. *But why did he tell me to keep the medallion?*

A soft tap at the door interrupted Johanna's mental confusion. Sniffing loudly, she sat up and wiped her hands over her eyes. "Who is it?"

"It's me," Dirk answered softly.

Her hands flew automatically to her hair, and she looked around the moonlit cabin for the brush she'd used after her bath, then down at the oversize shirt the captain had lent her to sleep in. "Just a minute!" she called out, jumping out of bed to go to the door. She cracked open the door slightly and peered out at him. "What do you want?"

Seeing that her cabin was dark and that she was obviously dressed for bed, Dirk apologized. "I'm sorry. I didn't mean to wake you; but we need to talk."

"What about?" she asked, opening the door wide enough to let him enter.

His gaze ran down the length of her petite frame to her bare feet, then up to her face again. Suddenly aware of how appealing she was with her sleep-tossed mop of blond curls and dressed in the long white shirt that hung almost to her knees, Dirk had second thoughts about entering her cabin. "We have plans to make for after we dock in the morning," he said, knowing he should add *But it can wait* rather than entering the cabin he'd avoided for over a week.

"Come in," she said, stepping back from the door.

Unable to muster an excuse for changing his mind about coming in, he breezed past her and set his lantern down on the captain's desk, then turned to survey the room. "Uh . . ." he started, his gaze roving over the room and taking in the rumpled bunk, the bathtub still filled with water, and the scent of warm, freshly washed feminine skin. "I'm sorry I woke you up."

"You said that," she spat, suddenly angry at him. "Besides, I wasn't asleep."

"Oh?" He looked at her face more closely, guilt

knotting in his gut. "Have you been crying?"

Slapping at her face to wipe away the evidence of her self-pity, she curled her lip. "No, I haven't been crying!"

"Yes, you have," he insisted. Forgetting his purpose for staying as far across the cabin from her as possible, he hurried to her. "Why are you crying?"

Presenting her back to him, Johanna rubbed the heels of her hands in her eye sockets. "I was thinking about Mignon and Suzette," she improvised. "How will I tell them about Francois?"

Dirk lifted his hands, intending to console her, but he thought better of touching her and let them drop. It was enough that his nostrils were being assaulted by the smell of her hair. If he allowed himself the slightest physical contact, he wasn't sure he would be able to fight off the desire that was raging through him. "That's what I want to talk to you about," he said, wheeling away from her and crossing back to the safety of the other side of the cabin. "Frans and I have decided it will be best if he and Dolf and Walter go back to Nassau's camp, while you and I go directly to Dusseldorf as soon as we dock."

Resenting having her actions planned for her—despite the fact that they were in line with what she'd been thinking—Johanna wheeled around and glared at Dirk. "Without discussing it with me first?"

"What is there to discuss? It's the only logical plan. I know you want to see the Benners as soon as possible before word reaches them from some other source that Francois is dead, and I need to see about my mother."

Knowing he was right didn't ease the tension mounting inside Johanna. "Are you sure you can bear being alone with me all that time?"

Dirk's blond brows drew together in a frown. "Why would you ask that?"

"Don't look at me like that. You know exactly what I mean. You've avoided being with me ever since this voyage began."

"I don't know what you're talking about. I've been with you the entire time we've been on this ship."

"Oh, you've been with me, but always with someone else nearby to protect you from being alone with me. I have to admit you've been very subtle about it, though. In fact, you were so subtle, it took me a while to notice."

Dirk opened his mouth to protest, then closed it again.

"Why, Dirk? Why have you pretended to be so concerned about me when it's obvious you no longer care for me? What did you and Frans do? Did you draw straws to see who'd be responsible for keeping me 'under control'?"

"You're being ridiculous. My concern for you isn't a pretense. And of course I care for you."

She arched her brows skeptically. Her bottom lip trembled as she choked back the tears threatening to erupt if she said another word. But she couldn't stop herself. She had to hear him admit that he didn't love her anymore. "Then why have you pulled away from me? Why have you stopped loving me?"

"Stop it, dammit!" he yelled. Crossing the cabin, he jerked her to him and shook her. "Remember? You're the one who left me! You're the one who *conveniently* forgot your vows to me. Not the other way around, Johanna—or should I say, *Esmeralda?*"

Chapter Twenty

As though she'd been kicked in the belly, Johanna's eyes widened with horror, the color drained from her face, and she folded in half, her bones turning to liquid.

"Oh, my God, Johanna!" Dirk groaned, catching her before she fell completely. "I didn't mean that. I don't know what made me say it." He lifted her limp body into his arms and carried her to the bunk.

Slightly recovered from her shock, Johanna shook her head and waved her hand back and forth. "There's no need to apologize," she rasped breathlessly. "I understand perfectly. In fact, I don't even know why it came as such a surprise. I think I knew all along that you wouldn't be able to love me again."

"It's not that I don't lo—" He swallowed the remainder of his confession. To say it aloud would leave him even more vulnerable than he already was. Keeping her tight against his chest, he sat down on the bunk and kissed her throbbing temple. "It's just that I can't forget about you and Alva. And even though I believe you when you say you only did what you did because you had no choice, every time I think of you with him, I . . ."

Overwhelmed with compassion for what Dirk was feeling, Johanna brushed back the golden blond lock of hair that had fallen on his forehead. "My poor Dirk. Can you ever forgive me for the torture I've put you through?"

Holding her as he was, Dirk felt the initial stirrings of passion. "You've done nothing to be forgiven for. It's me. I'm the—" No longer able to ignore her warm bottom nestled in the hollow of his lap, or the feel of her sweet breath wafting over the skin of his face and her fingers in his hair, he broke off his sentence.

Crushing her to his chest, his mouth fell hard over hers, as though he meant to extinguish by force the doubts that tore at his mind.

Her own desire bursting into flame, Johanna melted into the heat of his embrace, burrowing her fingers through the thick hair of his temples. It didn't matter that he still couldn't love her anymore. All that mattered was that he wanted her now—and that she wanted him. Opening her lips to him, she surrendered herself to his searing kiss.

With a hungry groan, he stabbed his tongue deep into her mouth, stroking in and out with the same primal rhythm that matched the pulsing ache in the lower part of her body. Desperate to relieve the growing pressure between her thighs, she writhed on the solid ridge of his masculinity that pumped against her bottom.

His hands slid to her front, tearing at the buttons on the nightshirt she wore. His actions frantic, he ripped the shirt open and off her shoulders, exposing her full breasts to his gaze.

Creating a trail of raging fire along her skin with his mouth, he covered her neck with kisses as he lowered her back onto the bed. His fingers molding and shaping her breast, he brought its turgid peak up to his lips.

At the blazing contact, she arched her back and released a helpless cry of passion. Smoothing her hands over his shoulders, she tugged at his shirt, hungry to touch his naked skin.

His breathing ragged, Dirk raised his head and hurriedly tore off her nightshirt, as well as his own clothing. Beyond rationality now, his actions were controlled by instinct of the most basic nature.

Dropping to the deck beside where she sat on the bunk, he bowed his head to kiss her belly. Then he moved his kiss lower.

Johanna threw back her head. "Oh, Dirk," she sobbed as he slowly parted her thighs. She reeled in a maelstrom of ecstasy, helpless to stop herself as his tongue sent her pitching and buffeting into a sea of rapture.

Her head thrashed from side to side as she fought unsuccessfully to catch her breath. When she could bear no more, and when she was insane with the need to feel his strength, hot and solid, inside her, he sat back on the floor, bringing her off the bed to straddle his lap. Lifting his hips high and urgently, he thrust into the slick, boiling interior of her body, at last making his possession complete.

Together, they cried their joy aloud. Hard and straight, he rammed deeper and deeper into the sheath of her body.

Her neck arching back, she tightened her legs around

him and raked her nails hungrily over the sweat-slicked muscles of his back.

Once it began, the crest of their union was quickly achieved, rushing on them with the force of a tidal wave. When it was over, Dirk fell back and Johanna collapsed on him, the spasms of her climax drawing the last of his passion from him.

As their labored breathing slowed to a more normal rate, reality flooded into Johanna's thoughts. It was obvious that Dirk still wanted her physically, even if he didn't want to marry her. And as much as she wanted him and loved him, she was tempted to tell him it didn't matter if he didn't love her anymore, because she had enough love for the both of them. Every instinct in her body cried out for her to tell him the truth about her relationship with Alva. But her own self-respect and sense of pride would not allow her to do it. He wouldn't believe her, and he would only see her words as begging. Besides, hadn't she been willing to be Alva's mistress? No, it would do no good to tell Dirk.

"I think you should leave now," she said bitterly, twisting out of his embrace. She stood up and whisked her nightshirt off the bed.

Confused, Dirk rose from the floor, moving toward her. He reached out to touch her arm.

As if she'd been stung, Johanna jerked out of reach. "You can't have it both ways, Dirk. I won't be your whore. Either you are willing to forget whatever you believe I've done wrong and honor our betrothal vows, or you must release me."

"Are you sure this is what you want?"

Johanna's heart plummeted to the pit of her stomach. Not even a token protest on his part. Well, what had she expected? "That's what I want," she repeated woodenly. "Of course, for the sake of our families, I see no reason we can't remain friends."

Dirk nodded his resignation. "Friends," he repeated forlornly.

"Then we're agreed? We are both released from our commitment to each other?"

Wiping at his eyes, Dirk cleared his throat. "We're agreed."

Her eyes moist, she raised the necklace he'd given her over her head and held it out to him. "I know I said I'd wait until you asked for this back, but I think it's best if you take it now."

Dropping his shirt over his head, Dirk accepted the return of his medallion from her.

The three women from the inn had arrived safely at Dusseldorf and were welcomed into the Ledenburg family with open arms when they identified themselves. Their trip had been an exciting adventure for Suzette, and all of the walking had slimmed her large frame to a slender and very attractive size. Already, Katryn and Dirk's mother, Marta, were busy considering suitable husbands for their young houseguest, and Suzette was glowing in all the attention.

It was into this happy, loving situation that Johanna and Dirk appeared, dirty and weary, with their sad news. When they saw Mignon and Suzette, the trusting anticipation evident on their loving faces, they couldn't find the words to tell them what had happened.

"Mama, Suzette," Johanna sobbed helplessly, running to the dazed pair, who had sensed the truth the instant they had seen her face. "I told you I would save him and I failed. Can you ever forgive me?"

The three clung desperately to each other, and Johanna was finally able to choke out the entire story of Francois's death.

"I tried, Mama," she cried. "I wish it had been me and not Papa. But I promise you I will not abandon the cause he did so much for—not until we've seen every Spanish fiend dead or driven out of the Netherlands! They'll pay for what happened to Francois Benner!" she swore with a vengeance that frightened Mignon.

"Emeraude, my sweet daughter, don't you know that you gave Francois and me untold pleasure the months we called you our own? You have nothing to repay or feel remorseful about. The main thing is, he didn't die alone. He was with you, and now he's with God. And he wouldn't want you to feel that you failed. He would only want you to remember the good times. Can you do that for me, *ma chérie?* For Francois?" Mignon asked gently, using her large hands to wipe at Johanna's tears.

Nodding her head slightly, Johanna said, "I'll take care of you and Suzette now. You will stay here with my family until it's safe for me to take you back to Brabant?"

Hesitating, Mignon answered, "I don't know, Emeraude. Perhaps Suzette and I should make other plans. We can't impose on the generosity of your good family indefinitely."

"Nonsense," Katryn interrupted. "You are Johanna's family, too. So there can be no imposition. Through love, we are all related, and we will stay united. I won't hear of your going elsewhere. Is that understood?" she scolded, tears running freely down her own swollen cheeks. "Besides, Matthew is making arrangements for a home of our own; and with the boys all gone off to fight, we'll need you to help us fill it up!"

During the next three days, both of Johanna's "mothers" tried to convince her that going to war with men was wrong, but she stood firm in her determination to leave again.

"Not only have I sworn to see the destruction of the duke of Alva, but Louis of Nassau has specifically asked that I work as his aide," she argued unwaveringly, chancing a nervous glance out of the corner of her eye to where Dirk sat nursing a brandy and glowering at her—something that had become a habit with him since they'd been met by Nassau's messenger at the docks in Emden.

"What will people think?" Katryn pleaded, still unable to accept the fact that Johanna was fated to be different.

"Mama," Johanna laughed sympathetically. "At this point, there's very little left for them to say. I'm sorry if I'm an embarrassment to you, but I must go!" she stressed.

"I'm afraid I agree with your mother, Emeraude!" Mignon said shyly, still uncertain of her new role in Johanna's life.

Katryn grabbed eagerly at Mignon's support. "You see? Both of us think you should stay here and leave the bloodletting to the men. War is no place for a woman."

The argument raged on for two more days, with Katryn and Mignon, supported by Suzette, Marta and Nadine, presenting her with every conceivable bit of logic and persuasion they could manage.

After a particularly harrowing argument with all five

of her critics, Johanna sneaked out into the garden for refuge. Spying Dirk in the twilight, she started to return to the house. At best their new relationship was uneasy. Then she changed her mind.

Why should I be the one to run back inside? If he wants to avoid me, let him be the one to run away!

Studying him where he lounged back against a tree, his legs crossed at the ankles, his arms across his chest, she tried to ignore the pain that gripped her heart every time she saw him unexpectedly.

"You want to know something really funny?" she asked, determined to sound casual as she approached him with her head held high and a forced smile on her face. "All of this criticism has brought back memories I never expected to have again. Strange little recollections of no importance at all! I know now that this isn't the first time I wanted to do what my brothers were allowed to do—and that my mother hated it! I thought anything they could do, I should be allowed to do, too. Somehow, I could never come up to Mama's expectations of what a daughter should be."

Shifting his lazy stance, Dirk shook his head. "Johanna, you have to change your mind about going back to Nassau's camp. The army is no place for you."

Balling her fists, she propped them on her hips and leaned toward him. "Aren't you forgetting that my 'place' is no longer your concern? Now, for the last time, I'm going to see the Spaniards driven from the Netherlands. And if I don't have your support, I'll do it alone. I've survived before without your protection, and I can do it again!"

Suddenly confronted by the icy stare that met her own angry green eyes, Johanna froze with the realization that she had gone too far. She fell back a step. "I—I mean . . ."

Dirk pushed himself away from the tree and smiled. "I know exactly what you meant, Johanna. And you're right!"

Low and controlled, his words hurt Johanna more than a slap across the face.

"You did survive without me, didn't you. Quite well, in fact! Very well, I'll take you back. But understand this. You will go with me only because I gave my word to Louis. And because I haven't the heart to leave a hellcat with these poor defenseless women, who are guilty of nothing more than loving you."

He walked away from her with slow, relaxed steps. "Be ready to depart at sunup!" he ordered without glancing back at her.

The journey north was strained and rife with physical discomfort. Neither Dirk nor Johanna had forgotten the angry words that had been exchanged the night before their departure; and neither was willing to make the first move to relieve the tension between them. So they made the trip without any but the most necessary exchange of words. And the weather did nothing to lift their spirits. In fact, it added to the strain by fluctuating between a steady drizzling rain and a drenching downpour for the entire three days and two nights on the road.

By the time they rode into Nassau's camp, now located at Jemmingen on the Ems River in northwest Germany, there was no more time to worry about their own personal problems.

"All hell has broken loose" were Frans's words as he rode down the west bank of the rising Ems River to stop them before they could cross over into Groningen as they had planned.

"Alva's forces have taken Heiligerlee and are now in control of Groningen. He's aware that we have Esmeralda Verde in our midst, and he plans to back us into the river if he has to in order to get her back."

Frans's words caused Johanna to glance at Dirk with unsteady apprehension. He was watching her through lowered eyelids that disguised what he was thinking.

"We're making a stand at Jemmingen," Frans stated.

Disconcerted by the sardonic curl to Dirk's mouth as he continued to stare at her, waiting for her to react, Johanna twisted back to face her brother. "Surely Alva won't come into Germany!"

Frans shook his head. "He says he will."

"What are we going to do to stop him?" Johanna asked.

With his harsh gaze still leveled at her, Dirk spoke sarcastically. "Yes, Frans, what are we going to do about the duke of Alva?"

Still unaware of the tension between the two, Frans went on speaking. "We're going to do our damnedest to kill the son of a bitch!"

"I wonder what your sister thinks of that plan." The smile on Dirk's face was anything but pleasant.

Johanna's voice rose indignantly. "And what exactly do you mean by that remark, Dirk Corlear?" She was returning his contemptuous glare with her own angry scowl.

"I thought perhaps after he was so kind to you, it might bother you to think of him dead after all." His face had assumed an artificial facade of thoughtfulness.

Her resentment building to the point of explosion, she managed to maintain an outward calm. She should have known it wouldn't be possible for them to have a friendly relationship despite the fact that they had vowed to no longer be lovers. "No, it doesn't bother me to think of him dead. In fact, it gives me great pleasure to think of him that way! He's a vicious killer, who's responsible for the deaths of thousands of Dutchmen —including Francois Benner, if you will recall." Her last words were delivered with a trembling voice as her self-control began to shatter.

Nevertheless, he continued to goad her heartlessly, the news of Alva's nearness bringing all his suppressed anger to the forefront. "But it's obvious how much he adores you, Esmeralda! He's come all this way to take you home with him. He's actually leading the attack himself. That's what I call a dedicated man." He shook his head and chuckled. "It's amazing what love can do to an otherwise sensible man, isn't it? Of course, now that Louis is your new protector, I don't suppose it matters what happens to your former . . ."

For a few seconds, Johanna stared at him, registering the fact that he thought that she was going to be Louis's mistress. Unable to speak, she turned her horse north toward Jemmingen and the battle—the battle she vowed she would fight from the front lines.

Completely dazed by the exchange, Frans stared after his sister and demanded, "What in the hell is going on here? I thought you two had worked things out!"

"Frans, my friend, I suppose you could say we have. Yes, you could definitely say we have." Dirk's tone had lost the cruel arrogance it had shown moments before, and what was left was a low and lonely whisper.

By the time the three rode into the camp, which was busy with preparations for the battle, Johanna had recovered her composure. She glanced longingly at

354

Dirk, who rode beside her, his posture stiff.

Had there ever been a chance that their love could have been restored? *Maybe once. In the Böttchers' barn,* she remembered nostalgically. *No, even then, he didn't believe me. Perhaps if I had told him the whole truth about my relationship with Alva when he told me that was what he couldn't forget* . . . She shook her head and allowed herself a silent laugh. *He would have only called me a liar again.* Shifting in her saddle, she studied his profile. It was obvious to her that he was just as miserable as she was. Maybe she should try to salvage their love one more time.

Dismounting, she turned to him, vowing this would be the last attempt she would make to mend the break in their relationship. "Dirk," she murmured, reaching out to stop him as he started away.

"I'll tell Louis we've arrived," he mumbled over his shoulder, not looking back at her.

Johanna's lifeless hand fell to her side as she watched him stride away from where she stood, unable to move.

Slowly, she turned to unsaddle her horse, no longer able to stop the tears that had begun to roll down her windburned cheeks. Burying her face in the mare's soft brown mane, she wept, "Oh, Mademoiselle, I really thought he still loved me and that in time I could make him trust me again!"

"Josef! It's good to have you back with us!" the old horsekeeper, Fredrik, shouted as he hurried to greet Johanna. "I've missed your help with the horses."

"*Ja,* Fredrik, it is good to see you, too," she answered, quickly wiping at her face with her sleeve before turning to see the warm welcome on the old man's face.

"Well, are you here to stay this time?" he yelled,

much more loudly than necessary.

"We'll see, Fredrik. If that's what the commander wants me to do, I'll be here," she sniffed, taking one more swipe at her nose.

"You aren't sick, are you, boy? This damp weather's bad for traveling. You'd better take care of yourself," he yelled. "How long since you had a hot meal? Let's get you something to eat," he suggested, putting an arm around her shoulders and guiding her to a fire where an old woman, who looked like a female replica of Fredrik, was standing and stirring a pot of soup.

"You remember my wife, don't you, boy? Wife, let's feed this boy something to get the chill out of his bones. Can't have the best helper I ever had getting sick on us, can we?" he laughed loudly.

Johanna looked at the old couple as they fussed over her, and a warmth spread throughout her body, bringing her sense of humor racing back to her. *At least someone's glad I'm here. So I guess things aren't all bad, are they?*

"Still don't have too much to say, do you, boy?"

"Nein, Fredrik," she answered with a shy, embarrassed-boy smile. "Not much to say."

Johanna had barely finished eating the revitalizing soup when Louis of Nassau and her brother, Frans, came to where she was sitting. She jumped up to greet her commanding officer, anxious to know why he had asked her to come back.

"Don't get up, Josef! Go on and finish your supper. Frans has told me of your brave deeds since we last met. However, when you've had a chance to rest from your journey, I want to hear your version of what happened."

"I'm finished, sire," she said, wiping her hands on the seat of her pants. "We can talk now if you want." The more quickly she got involved, the faster she would be able to put Dirk from her mind.

A few minutes later, when they entered the tent where Louis was organizing his campaign, he turned to Johanna and embraced her warmly. "You are a marvel!" he said exuberantly. "When Frans told me how you planned and carried out your mission, I don't mind telling you I was amazed. Do you realize how few men could have done such a thing?"

Embarrassed by the sudden display of appreciation from the handsome man who continued to hold her slim body against his own muscular one, Johanna drew away from him, turning her head to hide the becoming blush that had crept to her face. "Sire, you flatter me. I only did what had to be done. Nothing more."

"Well, we're grateful to you," he said, thinking how lovely her eyes were. "Now, what can I do to reward such bravery?"

"Sire," she started.

"Louis," he corrected gently.

"I mean Louis—I need no reward. But I thought you called me back because I could be of assistance to our cause."

Louis cleared his throat, feeling only slightly guilty about the real reason he'd requested her return. But he couldn't tell her that he hadn't been able to stop thinking of her since she had left his camp three weeks ago. Not now, anyway.

"Yes, our cause. Of course." He looked down at the scattered papers on his makeshift desk. "I think you can be a great help to our cause. Better than anyone else, you know how Alva thinks. So I hope I can depend on you to anticipate his actions and help me outwit and defeat him."

Disappointed, Johanna made a different request. "I would prefer to fight in the next battle. In the front lines!"

Momentarily surprised, Nassau hesitated before answering. "Johanna, only our most experienced and skilled fighters will be in the front lines. To have an inexperienced soldier, even of your braveness, out in front, would endanger the rest of our army. You wouldn't want that, would you?" he asked, knowing what her answer would be.

"No," she replied meekly. "But I can't just sit around 'anticipating' the duke of Alva's next moves. I will go mad within a week if I'm not allowed to take part in the actual battle. Maybe I could be a runner between battle units, or I could be a water carrier, or a nurse. Anything! But don't make me stay behind the lines. I want to be there."

"Yes, well, I'm certain we can use your talents some way. How familiar are you with ways of warfare?"

Realizing that he was speaking to her as an equal, Johanna had no qualms about disclosing her shortcomings. "Not at all, I'm afraid. But I can learn!" she added eagerly.

"Of course you can, but I'm afraid there's no time. Alva will probably cross into Germany tomorrow. We must be prepared before then!"

"What happened in Groningen?" she asked bluntly. "I thought we were firmly entrenched there!"

"Let me explain what we're up against, my dear. First of all, the Spanish are superior soldiers in every way. They have more and better weapons; greater manpower; unequaled discipline and training; not to mention excellent organization." He stooped to pick up a stick and drew a series of parallel lines in the dirt.

"They are known for their infantry tactic called 'shot and pike.' Have you heard of it? It's nearly impossible to defeat."

Johanna shook her head.

"They've developed a comparatively portable matchlock weapon that can be fired from the shoulder, called the harquebus. In itself, the weapon isn't usually that damaging. But the Spanish make lines of them, twenty-five deep. On command, the front line fires into the midst of the enemy. After firing, that first rank withdraws to the rear to reload while the next line takes its place on the front. They gradually move forward again by successive volleys—until it's their turn to refire. If that's not enough, they have pikemen in the rear to protect the musketeers while they are reloading —ten to every musketeer.

"Then, when the enemy's ranks are broken by the firing power, the Spanish pikemen advance to the front line, shoulder to shoulder, sweeping the opposing field with their long metal-spearheaded poles—the pikes! That's what we faced in Groningen," he finished, the worry obvious on his furrowed brow.

"Can't we do the same thing to them?" Johanna asked.

"That would be nice," he agreed patiently. "Unfortunately, we haven't got the weapons or the men to fire them. We have cannons, but only a few of the handguns."

"But what will we do if Alva uses the same method of attack the next time?"

Louis nodded his head. "He'll use it, all right. Since the Spanish have used the same tactics for thirty years, there's no reason to think they'll change now. Our only course is to beat them with their own predictability.

Consequently, we're moving most of our cannons to their southern flank to surprise them with fire that will rake lengthwise down their lines!"

Johanna studied the diagrams Louis had drawn on the floor of the tent, and she wondered if they had even the slimmest chance at success.

Louis continued to speak. "I want you to stay with me and run messages to our gunners firing the cannons. Will that put you close enough to the battle to satisfy you, little one?"

"Oh, yes! Thank you—," she said, hesitating before calling him by his first name—"Louis!"

"Don't thank me, Johanna. You have your work cut out for you. Now, you had best bed down, since we'll be departing for our new location in a few hours. We'll be leaving only a token number of cannons and pikemen here to confuse the enemy. Once our cannons fire on their flank, our men here will either join us or head north, south, or east—until we can regather."

"What about the camp followers—the women and children?" She had noticed a large number in the camp. "Will they go with us or stay here?"

"Even now, they're already preparing themselves to journey south to wait for us. After all you've been through, I would understand if you would prefer to join them," he suggested tactfully.

Sadness skittered across her features as her original plan to fight alongside Dirk streaked through her mind.

"Oh, no!" she exclaimed. "I want to go with you! I haven't come all this way to wait in the background for the outcome!"

Chapter Twenty-One

"So what do you think of soldiering now, *Josef?*" Dirk asked Johanna as what was left of Louis of Nassau's army trudged south after their disheartening defeat at Jemmingen. "Are you ready to admit battle is no place for a female?"

Johanna directed a withering glance at him, then aimed her gaze forward again. Covered with mud, she was cold and hungry and tired, but she had no intention of admitting how miserable she was. At least she was alive and free, she reminded herself, remembering the hundreds of men who'd been killed or captured by Alva's troops at the battle on the banks of the Ems River two days before.

"War is no place for anyone—male or female," she said, her face twisting as if the words put a bad taste in her mouth. "But if you're asking if I've changed my mind about being here, I haven't. And I never will until the last Spaniard has been driven out of the Netherlands."

Admiring her determination despite his strong

feelings against her being there, Dirk forced a look of unconcern and glanced back at the column of men behind them. They were struggling to move the cannons through the mud caused by a week and a half of rain. Just then, a man slipped in front of the cannon only a few feet behind him.

Dirk's breath slammed against the back of his throat. Not only was it impossible for the soldiers behind the cannon to see the fallen man in front of the unwieldy weapon, but they couldn't let the wheels stop rolling anyway. To do so would mean they might not be able to get them rolling again.

Moving with all the speed he could gather in the debilitating mud, he raced toward the downed man.

Confused by the sudden change in Dirk's face, Johanna spun around to see what had his attention. Immediately understanding the situation, she reacted automatically. Tossing Mademoiselle's reins to the ground, she followed him.

Only seconds ahead of her, Dirk reached the struggling soldier and caught him by the arms to pull him out of the way of the approaching wheels. But the more the frightened man fought to scramble his way out of the cannon's path, the deeper he worked his way into the goo, and the more impossible it was for Dirk to move him.

"Quick!" Johanna shouted at two dumbstruck observers as she wrapped her arms around Dirk's middle and braced herself to add her strength to his. "Hold me around the waist!"

Enveloped in the crush of a man's grip on her rib cage, she tightened her hold on Dirk and glanced nervously at the deadly cannon. It was not more than three feet away from them now. "Pull!" she grunted, concentrating all of her own energy into the tugging.

Under the united strength of the four, the mud gave up the slightest possession of its captive and they all moved a few inches back.

She glimpsed the cannon out of the corner of her eye. It was only two feet away from crushing the man now, and still coming toward them.

"Again," she cried, calling on their united strength for more power. "Pull!"

"Pull . . . Pull . . . Pull . . ." Dirk joined her chant as inch by laborious inch they dragged the man to the side, until only his legs were in danger of being run over.

"Pull . . . Pull . . . Pull . . ." Johanna panted, picking up the pace as she realized the cannon wheel was only a foot away from the man's knees.

With a loud slurp, the mud released its prisoner, sending his rescuers sprawling back into a pile and taking the soldier with them just as the wheels rolled over the spot where he'd been.

Disentangling himself from under the saved man, Dirk rolled to his feet. His face red with exertion and anger, he grabbed Johanna by the arm and yanked her to her feet. "That's it!" he hissed through teeth clamped tight. "I'm taking you back to Dusseldorf in the morning!"

Exhilarated by success, Johanna refused to keep her anger with Dirk under control any longer. Wrenching her arm from his grasp, she balled her fists on her hips and glared at him. "You're not taking me anywhere, Count Leuven!"

"Oh, yes I am!" he snarled in return.

A bitter sneer spread across her face. "What's the matter, Dirk? Can't you stand the fact that you and that man might have been crushed to death by that cannon if it hadn't been for me?" Seeing the flash of light in his eyes, she laughed aloud, her expression enlightened. "That's it, isn't it? You can't bear the idea that I might think you owe me something—like resuming our engagement. Well, don't worry yourself about that, Count Leuven. As far as I'm concerned, any debts or promises between us are canceled. I wouldn't agree to marry you if you were the last man on earth!"

Tears suddenly rose to her throat. Swallowing, she swung around and started to walk away. It was then she realized her outburst had had an audience—and that she had disclosed her identity as a female.

Lifting her chin proudly, she looked each of the open-mouthed witnesses in the eye, daring him to make a comment. Then she brushed past the small group, desperate to make her escape before any of them saw the tears she was trying vainly to hold in.

Angry beyond rational thinking, Dirk started after her.

"Am I to understand that your betrothal is no longer in effect?" asked Louis of Nassau, as he stepped forward and blocked Dirk's path.

"What?!" Dirk yelled, his gaze on Johanna's retreating figure as she made her way toward her horse. Hearing the impatience in his own voice, he relaxed and forced himself to look at his friend. "I'm sorry, Louis. What did you say?"

Louis smiled and turned to observe Johanna, too. "I asked if you have ended your engagement."

Dirk frowned and gave Louis a puzzled look.

"Because if she is no longer committed to you, I plan to tell her how I feel about her," Louis admitted in answer to Dirk's unspoken question.

"You want Johanna?"

"If she'll have me and if the two of you aren't betrothed anymore."

Dirk looked back at the object of their discussion. She had reclaimed her mare and was moving forward with the rest of the soldiers. "Johanna is a Catholic. She couldn't marry a divorced man."

Louis smiled at Dirk's naïveté. "I don't plan to divorce my wife."

Livid at what Louis was proposing for Johanna, Dirk clenched his fists at his sides, fighting the desire to plant one in the middle of the man's grin. "She would never agree to be your mistress."

"Are you so sure, my friend? After all, it's not as if she hasn't had a similar arrangement in the pa—"

Dirk's knuckles met with the skin and bone of Louis's face, sending the surprised prince tumbling backward to land on his buttocks in the mud.

Rubbing his jaw, Louis looked up at Dirk and chuckled. "Am I to take this to mean that you are not relinquishing your claim on Johanna and that I shouldn't discuss my proposition with her?"

Staring in amazement at his lifelong friend, Dirk shook his head in disbelief. This was Johanna's fault, not Louis's. She must have given him a sign that she wouldn't be averse to such a suggestion. Well, she had done enough to shred his life to pieces. She wasn't going to cost him his friendship with Louis, too.

Extending his hand to Nassau, he said, "I'm sorry. I

shouldn't have hit you. Feel free to ask Johanna anything you like. I have no claim on her."

"How dare you pass me on to another man like some doxy you found in the street?" Johanna shrieked as she ripped back the door flap on the small tent Dirk had pitched away from the main camp.

Throwing back his covers, Dirk bolted off the cot he'd been trying, to no avail, to fall asleep on. "Johanna! What are you doing here? I thought you'd be with . . ."

Her eyes bulged and her lower jaw opened and closed several times in succession. "Then it's true!" she finally managed to spit out. "You did tell Louis that he could . . ." Her voice cracked. Never in her life had she felt so betrayed.

Dirk's heart soared with unexplainable joy as the meaning of her presence in his tent soaked into his thoughts. "You told him no?" he said, his tone disbelieving, even though he could see the truth in her anger.

Unable to believe that he could even ask such a question, Johanna felt her blood heat to metal-liquefying temperatures. "Did you really think I would fall into bed with the first man who asked me, Dirk? Well, I have news for you. When—and if—I ever decide to let another man touch me, it will be a man of my own choosing. Do you hear me? Not yours and not my parents'. But mine." Not trusting herself to say much more, she wheeled around and knocked the tent flap aside, stepping outside.

"Johanna . . ." Dirk called after her.

Spinning to face him one last time, she growled. "I don't ever want to hear your voice or look at your face again. As far as I'm concerned, we no longer know each other. And if you ever try to interfere in my life again, I'll—" She couldn't finish the sentence. Taking one last look at the man she still loved despite herself, she broke into a run, determined to put him and his memory out of her thoughts forever.

Walking along the rue des Merciers in LaRochelle, France, Johanna was awed by the unusual houses built over arcades and decorated with grotesque gargoyles in peculiar allegorical shapes.

She had first come to the Atlantic seaport, off the Bay of Biscay in western France, in the early months of the year after three months of riding with Louis of Nassau and his army of rebels; and now they were leaving at last—going back to their homeland!

Her hair, though still shorter than the prevailing style, was no longer cropped in the boyish style of her first days as a soldier, and she now wore a dress instead of pants, but she was oblivious to the flattering glances she received. Her mind was preoccupied, for some reason, by the events that had led her to France.

After they lost the battle at Jemmingen, the time she had spent as an enlisted man in Nassau's army had been hard and discouraging, made worse by the fact that she'd been unable to stop loving Dirk, no matter how she fought it. And of course, it hadn't helped that until recently he'd been with Louis's troops all the time. Always there, watching her every move, never speaking to her. At least now, Louis had sent him to help lead the sea attack on the Netherlands. Maybe she could have some peace at last.

Many of their troops had been captured and severely punished at Alva's hand; others had headed north to join the Sea Beggars plaguing the English Channel. Her brother Frans had been among the latter group. But the contingent she had been with had escaped to the south, where they had joined forces with William of Orange at Dusseldorf.

The combined armies of Orange and Nassau had marched into Brabant in October, where they'd been outmaneuvered by Alva once more. From there they had found it necessary to retreat into France, where they had spent weeks attempting to gain support for their cause from the Huguenots.

Although their campaigns had made Orange more popular than ever with the Calvinists, the weeks since they had left the Netherlands were frustrating and filled with defeats. Alva's government grew more unpopular every day; his troops had become more brutal; and his search for new sources of income to pay for his armies had caused bitter hostility and great impoverishment in the country. Thousands were said to have been executed by the duke of Alva; thousands more were outlawed; and about nine thousand citizens had had some or all of their property confiscated. The time to challenge his rule was long past.

Since they had come to LaRochelle to set up the headquarters for Louis's Dutch and French corsairs that preyed on Spanish shipping, Johanna had acted as the prince's friend and advisor—nothing more. Of course, once it had been learned that she was not a boy, everyone believed that she was his mistress. And she knew it was what Dirk thought. But from the first time Louis had professed his desire for her, Johanna had made it clear that she wanted no emotional entanglements, and he had remained true to his word to never force her.

Sometimes when Johanna saw the longing in Louis's eyes, she would think that she should relent and consummate their relationship; but something always held her back. She just couldn't stop hoping that Dirk might still love her.

Since their arrival in LaRochelle, Louis, Dirk and Johanna had worked diligently to form a coalition against the king of Spain with France, England and the German princes William could count on for support. But again and again their efforts were met with disappointment.

They had hoped Queen Elizabeth of England might be convinced to assist them, since they had been responsible for exposing a plot to send ten thousand of Alva's soldiers to England to help replace her with her Catholic cousin, Mary, queen of Scots. And the thwarted invasion had gained them the queen's sympathy, but she still had her doubts about the costs of sending aid to the Netherlands.

So while England was being convinced it would take another invasion of the Low Countries to rid northern Europe of the power-hungry Spanish, Nassau was working on the French. His close friend, Gaspard II de Coligny, the French Huguenot leader, got himself and Nassau an invitation to the French court of King Charles IX, where he soon gained great influence over the young, mother-dominated king. He and Nassau, together with Johanna and Dirk, had been able to persuade the king to favor a Huguenot plan for intervention against the Spanish in the Netherlands.

They had planned a number of coordinated attacks on the Netherlands for the coming summer. William and Louis were to lead two attacks from Germany with support from sympathetic German princes and Netherlands exiles, while Coligny would spearhead another onslaught from France, and the Sea Beggars would invade from the sea. But things had not gone as planned. Word had come that the Sea Beggars had surprised the Spanish garrison at Brielle, west of Rotterdam, and had taken the port—three full months ahead of the planned attack!

"The fools! They acted too fast and too soon. They may have jeopardized all of our plans!" Louis's fair, freckled skin was flushed with anger as he paced the floor. "William is going to be livid!"

Johanna, who had become quite adept at planning strategy, quickly understood the possibilities of the Sea Beggars' premature move. "If they could repeat the technique they used at Brielle, they could take Flushing."

She was actually thinking out loud, but when Louis realized the importance of what she was suggesting, he ran to her and picked her up to swing her around. "How can anyone so beautiful and so small be so smart?" He lowered her to her feet with a brotherly kiss on her forehead.

His lip curled with loathing at the display of affection, Dirk picked up his glass and quaffed the last of his wine. "It makes sense," he admitted. "If we gained control of the entrance to the Scheldt at Flushing, we would control all of Zeeland!"

Johanna shot a surprised glance in Dirk's direction. He was usually the first one to point out why her suggestions were wrong. Encouraged, she turned back to Louis, who was already examining maps. "You've always intended to support any sea-based attack by invading from France and Germany."

"So why not go ahead and take the Huguenot companies we've mustered in France and strike now?" Dirk asked.

"I will need to send someone I can trust to coordinate the attack on Flushing," Louis mused as he studied the maps spread before him.

Dirk glanced first at Johanna, then back to Louis. "Look no further. You have your man." Though he had no desire to take to the sea, anything would be better than another hour watching Johanna and Louis together—and knowing that he had only himself to blame for the fact that it was Louis of Nassau and not he who spent his nights in her arms. "I'll go."

Louis raised his gaze from the table. "I need you here."

"I'd really like to do this, Louis."

Nassau tilted his head thoughtfully. "There's no one I trust more than I do you. . . ."

Dirk slapped the prince on the back. "Then it's settled. I'll make preparations to leave in the morning. When you arrive in the Netherlands, we'll have Zeeland secured for you." Without another glance in Johanna's direction, he hurried from the room.

Within a week after Louis and Johanna left LaRochelle for the Netherlands, the Sea Beggars, reinforced by English and Huguenot recruits, had run Orange's tricolor flag up in Flushing as Dirk had promised. From that time on, they advanced through Zeeland, seizing towns and plundering churches.

As planned, Louis and Johanna joined Francois de La Noue and other Huguenots on the border of Hainaut; and while La Noue's little company seized Valenciennes, Nassau captured Mons. So, at the same time Alva was losing his grip in Holland and Zeeland, he lost the two towns that controlled the entry into Flanders from France.

Unfortunately, six days after their invasion, Louis received word that Valenciennes was lost to the Spanish once more. "We'll just have to hold out until Coligny comes with his Huguenot army. It shouldn't be too long now, and William will be ready to launch his invasion from Germany any time." He was attempting to lift his own spirits, as well as those of his men.

"Do we have enough men, Louis? To hold out, I mean?" Johanna asked. She was dressed in men's clothing again, although everyone in camp was now aware of her identity.

Looking down into her trusting face, Louis could only shake his head as he held out his arms to her.

Knowing how depressed he was, Johanna went to him willingly.

Enveloping her in his caring embrace, he finally answered her question. "I don't know, Johanna. Neither William nor Gaspard expected to be ready to move before July. And William was planning to enter the Netherlands at Gelderland, not this far south. We'll see, I suppose." He was resting his chin on the top of her head as he caressed her gently.

Her heart was breaking for him as she realized the depth of the dedicated man's despair. If only she could do something for him. Gazing into his sad eyes, she was overwhelmed by her love for him—not the intense, passionate love she still felt for Dirk, but love nonetheless. "Louis, it will be all right. They'll come. You'll see!" There were tears rolling down her slightly tanned cheeks. "We'll hold out until they come."

Unable to tell her how much it meant to him to have her with him, Louis lifted his hands to gently brush away her tears. With her upturned face cradled in his large hands, he spoke in a voice choked with feeling. "I love you, Johanna. I've wanted and needed you for so long. Let me love you," he pleaded.

What are you waiting for, Johanna? He loves you and you love him—in a way. Admit it. Dirk is lost to you forever. He doesn't love you anymore.

Reaching up, Johanna slipped her arms around Louis's neck and drew his mouth down to her own and kissed him. "Yes, Louis, I want you to love me. No more waiting."

"Oh, my love! How I've longed for this moment," he groaned, kissing her again, all the love he had held in check emerging in that one sweet moment when his mouth touched her parted lips.

His heart beating wildly and his fingers trembling, he moved his hands up under the loosely fitting shirt she wore to caress the softness of her back.

Breathing in deeply, she leaned into his embrace and didn't fight when her eyelids fluttered shut. It had been so long since she'd felt loved. So long since she'd felt like a woman.

Her eyes closed, she was attacked by a memory of

sky blue eyes where warm pools of brown had been moments before; and Louis's short, neatly trimmed hair of copper had been replaced by rumpled strands of gold that curled impishly around a face tanned a glorious bronze by the rays of the sun.

Lost now, she raised her head to greet his mouth and called out softly against his lips as her arms snaked around his muscular back. "Dirk, I've waited so long for this moment."

Just as suddenly as it had begun, the vision ended, and Johanna was alone, staring into the dimness at the outline of the man who was walking away from where she stood.

Running after Louis, she cried out for forgiveness. "Oh, Louis. I'm so sorry. I don't know why I said that. I didn't mean it. I want to love you!"

"But you can't, can you, Johanna?" His voice was low and carried a tone of finality in it.

"But I do, Louis! I do love you!" she insisted. "If I could only blot out those words I said," she moaned, pathetically clinging to him.

"You can't blot out the truth, love," he sighed with resignation. "God knows, we've both tried. You've tried to forget him. I know that. And I've tried to forget that you loved him first. I've seen how you start whenever his name is mentioned; and I've seen how you watch him whenever he's present." Louis gently withdrew from her desperate embrace. "I'd better go now."

Hugging herself, Johanna sobbed helplessly. "I would give anything if I could love you the way you want me to, Louis. Can you ever forgive me?"

"There's nothing for me to forgive, love. But I think you should give some thought to forgiving yourself—

and to admitting the truth about how you feel about Dirk."

Long after Louis left her, she stared after him. "Damn you, Dirk Corlear! Damn you!" she screamed at the empty room.

Alva had removed most of his troops from the north to concentrate his effort on the French border, aware—as was Louis—that he could always go north later to take care of the ill-disciplined bands of rebels. However, if Coligny should come with his French army, Spain would lose the Netherlands.

Word was received the next day that William had finally crossed the border from Germany into Gelderland, and that he'd been welcomed warmly by the citizens who had finally had enough of Alva's rule. Then, near the end of the week, Louis was informed that a relief of six thousand Huguenots, under the leadership of Seigneur de Genlis, was marching toward Mons.

With respite at last on the way from the north and the south, the spirit in Nassau's camp lifted decidedly. But the jovial state was short-lived, for the next message that arrived destroyed all hope for success!

It seemed that Alva's troops, assisted by local peasants, had surprised and defeated Genlis's army at the border; and William now felt it would be best to pull back to the Maas River and wait. There would be no relief at Mons!

Louis's face grew haggard; he lost weight; and he finally had to admit that he couldn't hold out much longer. "Johanna, we must get you out of the city. You mustn't be here when Alva takes over."

"I'm staying, Louis. You can't give up! Didn't William write that King Charles of France is bringing an army of fifteen thousand under his own leadership?"

"Johanna, we can't depend on Charles! He vacillates from moment to moment. He listens to his mother, then to Coligny. He doesn't know what he wants to do. He'd like the military glory so he can compete with his younger brother's victories; but he's so unsure of himself that we'll all be long dead before he acts!" His tone was defeated. "I've sent word to William to dispatch someone to come for you."

"Well, I won't go! I wanted to fight with you, and I will die with you if necessary. I refuse to run! Do you hear me, Louis? I'm staying to the end!"

Smiling at her mettle, he kissed her cheek and wrapped his arms around her small, stubborn frame and held her protectively. "Ah, Johanna, if only we had met another time, another place—another life!"

Johanna knew there was nothing more she could say to lift the morose feeling that engulfed Louis, so she stayed quietly in his arms, her cheek resting against the wall of his chest, where she was certain she could hear the sound of his heart breaking.

Then came the final blow! They received word that three thousand Huguenots had been butchered in Paris, on order of Catherine, the mother of King Charles IX, and that Coligny was among those killed. William's news to Louis was the last indication of the hopelessness of their situation at Mons. He had written, "What a stunning blow. My only hope lay with France. Now there will be no French army to relieve you at Mons, and I lack the resources to come to your aid."

"So, that's that," Louis mumbled, his despair too

great to even allow him the release of anger.

"What will you do, Louis? You aren't going to surrender, are you?" Johanna couldn't bear to think of the strong man in the hands of Alva.

"Johanna, we have no choice. William said in his letter that they are sending someone for you. So, as soon as you are safely out of here, we will turn over our arms to the Spanish."

"No, you can't!" she protested fervently.

"It's all over. With the attack of the Huguenots in France, they will have their own civil war to fight. The reason Alva has us besieged here and hasn't completely run us over is that he, too, was expecting the French to come. Now there's nothing to stop him from finishing us off and heading north to take back the cities that are supporting us."

"Then I'm staying!"

"To be hung, or beheaded, or burned at the stake? What purpose would that serve, Johanna?"

"But Louis! I won't be able to live with myself if I desert you now!"

"You won't be deserting me. You'll be living for me. Otherwise, everything I've done will have been for nothing!"

"Will you at least let me stay until the very last? I can hide when the Spanish actually enter the city and leave after they are gone!" she insisted.

"We'll see, Johanna. We'll see."

But there was no need for Louis to make a decision, for no one had come for Johanna before the arrival of Alva's messenger requesting a parley with Louis and his officers.

Having sent back the message that he was ready to talk, Louis went to Johanna. "The time has come,

Johanna. I have made arrangements for you to be secreted in a room at the Church of Saint Agnes. You should be safe there until it's all right to leave the city."

"Louis, is there nothing else we can do?" she begged.

His answer was disconsolate and final. "No, nothing!" Putting his arm around her shoulders, he guided her toward the two soldiers who were to escort her to her hiding place.

As the soldiers walked her out, she stopped and turned to Louis one last time. She wanted to plead with him, but she thought better of it, knowing this was the one thing she could do for him now. "I do love you, Louis. I wish things had been different." And she was gone.

The following day when Alva entered the fortified city, it was a sad and despondent commander who met him. When the first formalities of their meeting had been concluded, Alva asked bluntly, "Where's the woman?"

Nassau was stunned by the question and asked innocently, "What woman?"

"Come now, Nassau. We're both adults here. There's no need and no time for game playing. I want the woman, Esmeralda Verde!"

"She's no longer here. She's in Germany by now," Louis answered unconvincingly.

"I think not! She's here in the city, and we'll find her. You can save us time and trouble, as well as many of your countrymen's lives, if you will lead me to her now. You see, if I send my men to search for her, it will be with the orders to kill every man, woman and child they encounter—until Señorita Verde is returned to my possession. Then, when we have found her, I will give the command to burn this city to the ground.

Am I understood?"

Without waiting for Nassau to answer, the duke proceeded, his voice cold and cruel. "However, should you decide to cooperate, I will consider being lenient with you and the citizens of Mons. Shall we say that the residents of the city will be left unharmed, the city will not be burned, and you will be allowed to leave with the honors of war—all for one very small female?"

God, Johanna! What should I do? I can't hand you over to this butcher no matter how many lives it would save!

As if she'd heard the questions his mind was asking, her calm voice answered him. "There is no need to worry about me, Louis. I would not want to continue to live if innocent people died to save me."

Whirling around to the spot where Alva's gaze was focused, Louis gasped in horror. "Johanna! What are you doing here?"

She smiled. "Surely you knew I would not be so easy to be rid of." Then she graciously extended her hand to Alva with all the composure of a grand lady receiving guests. "Fernando, it has been a long time."

Taking her outstretched hand, Alva kissed it gallantly. "It has been far too long, my dear Esmeralda. You are even lovelier than I remembered."

"And you are looking even more fit than I recall, sire," she responded with an attractive smile. "But surely you haven't gone to all this trouble of seeking me out just to exchange amenities."

"No, that is true. Unfortunately, my dear, I haven't decided what I want to do with you. I have missed your companionship greatly, and it would be such a shame to separate your beautiful head from your delicious body—which I might add is more desirable now than

379

ever. However, you wounded me greatly when you left me without a word; and then there were those annoying messages you sent your Dutch friends while you were my confidante. Tell me, what do you think would be a suitable punishment for your indiscretions?"

As Louis watched the pleasant volley of words between the two seemingly cool opponents—who might have been discussing the weather—he was stunned into total silence.

Johanna smiled as if Alva had presented her with an interesting riddle to solve and walked with her index finger tapping delicately on her pursed lips. "Suitable punishment. Mmm, let me see. It would need to be something befitting your great imagination, wouldn't it? You could always use public torture and hanging. Oh, but that's been done so often. Isn't that what you used on poor Francois Benner and hundreds of others?"

"Yes, that is one of my most efficient and effective methods of extermination. But then, I may choose to administer your chastisement personally—and in private! There is something most satisfying about applying the whip to smooth, unblemished skin. Or I could consider sharing some of your more primitive and earthy talents with my favorite officers."

"Do you really think that would be a punishment, Fernando?" she bluffed, preferring the whip to his last threat. "We could start with those handsome young officers I had the pleasure of meeting the first time I met you. You do owe them something for taking the quarry they had stalked all evening, don't you think?"

"Stop it!" Louis demanded. "Stop talking like that, Johanna! What is wrong with you?"

Coolly studying the distraught man for an instant, Johanna returned her attention to Alva, seeming to have dismissed Louis's questions as unimportant. "What will it be, Fernando? Quick or slow? Public or private?"

"I believe I will think on it. In the meantime, you will be confined."

"Well, since that's settled, are the prince of Nassau and his men free to leave Mons—with the honors of war, of course? I would be quite dismayed if you refused to keep your word on that point." She was still smiling pleasantly.

"Yes," he agreed. "They will have an escort out of Mons, out of Hainaut, and out of the Netherlands."

"Then may I have your permission to bid my friends farewell?" she asked politely.

"Be my guest," he answered, just as cordially.

Turning at last to face Louis, Johanna smiled warmly, refusing to let him see how afraid she was. With tears brimming in her green eyes, she reached for his hand and clamped it between her own two trembling palms. "Thank you for all you've done, my friend. God go with you."

"Johanna, I can't leave you like this," Louis objected hoarsely.

"We have no choice," she assured him. "I owe a debt to the duke of Alva, and it is time I repaid him for the wrongs that have been committed." Patting his arm, she added, "Now, go on. I'm fine."

She watched as the guards came and escorted the unwilling Louis out of sight. Still gazing at the exit, she spoke again, no longer attempting to disguise her sorrow. "Well, Fernando, what happens now?"

Chapter Twenty-Two

By the time Louis reached Dusseldorf, he had paid off his mercenaries and released the Huguenots to fight their own war in France. When his family saw him, it was a stranger they greeted. His usually neat hair and beard were unkempt, and his uniform and person were disheveled and unclean, almost beyond recognition. His depression was such that his friends feared he was dying, but he did manage to relay to his brother, William, what had occurred at Mons. He would talk to no one else—including Johanna's concerned family.

"He'll see me," Dirk declared, storming toward Louis's chambers when, upon his return from Zeeland, he heard about Johanna's capture.

"I'm sorry, Count Leuven, but the prince is indisposed," an elderly manservant announced when Dirk stated his need to see Nassau.

"The hell he is!" Dirk shouted, shoving past the valet and forcing the door open.

"What's going on here, Louis?" he shouted, standing in the doorway as he tried to determine where his friend was in the dark, airless room. Receiving no answer, he stormed across the room and yanked the heavy draperies off the windows. "No wonder you're sick. You need some air and light in here!" He proceeded to throw open the windows before he turned to see Louis sitting forlorn and unshaven in a chair. Dirk raced to the emaciated man's side.

Louis, who'd been so dynamic in the past, looked blankly at the hand that rested on his thin arm.

Unable to speak, Dirk watched as Louis's gaze slowly drifted up to his face. For a moment there was a glimmer of recognition in the red-rimmed, sunken eyes, and then it faded back to the hollow stare that Louis's family had come to know so well in the past days.

Dirk fell to his knees. Holding his friend's skeletal hand, he cried out, "Louis, it's me, Dirk! You've got to shake yourself out of this stupor and tell me about Johanna. They say you handed her over to Alva! That can't be true!"

Louis raised his clenched fist to touch Dirk. "I loved her. But she couldn't love me. She waited all those months for you to come for her, but you never did. You could have saved her when I couldn't. She would have been safe if you hadn't turned your back on her."

Dirk cringed, sick with the realization that Louis was telling the truth. "How did this happen, Louis?" he asked frantically. "How did you allow Alva to take your mistress away from you?"

"My mistress?" the confused man asked. "Johanna wasn't my mistress. She was my friend and my confidante, but never my mistress." He was crying now. "I loved her, Dirk; but she could never forget you."

Grabbing Louis's shoulders, Dirk shook him. "Where? Where has Alva taken her?"

"The word is that he took her back to Brussels for a trial," William of Orange answered as he approached Dirk from behind. "But we're not sure."

Guilt and anger exploding in his thoughts, Dirk bolted to his feet, announcing, "Then I'm going to Brussels!"

"You can't," Orange protested, reaching out to stop Dirk. "You'll be killed."

"Do you think I want to live knowing what I've done to Johanna?"

Johanna clamped her hands over her ears, attempting to block out the sounds of human misery that pervaded the all-encompassing darkness which had been her prison for what seemed like always.

A shivering mass of suffering, she lay on the clammy floor of the cell, oblivious to the sounds of the rats squealing as they fought over the sparse meal of coarse black bread the guard had brought only minutes before. Drawing her knees up to her chest in an attempt to gain some comfort from her own body warmth, she gritted her teeth in a desperate struggle to control their chattering.

She had no idea how long she'd been lying there. Had it been two days, three, since she was able to force herself to eat the foul-smelling swill or moldy bread they brought her once a day? For that matter, was it day or night? Had she been here for days? Weeks? Months? Maybe it had been years! There was no way of knowing. No one had spoken to her since she was first thrown into the tiny cell, and the only light she had seen was the small light that appeared under the door when a tray of food was periodically passed in to her.

In the beginning, she had fought the vermin that shared her cell, by quickly grabbing the disgusting fare and eating it before they could lay claim to it; but as her strength waned, so did her resolve to stay alive. After all, she decided, what was so frightening about death? In fact, she had reached a point where she looked forward to the release it would bring: release from the tortured human cries from nearby cells; release from the rats and mice that scurried over her failing body; release from the incessant itching caused by the insect bites and her own filth; and release from her longing for Dirk. Yes, most of all, freedom from her memories.

So, as Johanna Frances van Ledenburg lay alone and wretched in the dank and squalid cell beneath the palace where she had lived in luxury, she waited longingly for death.

She knew she was where she was because of her own choices. Yet, what would she have changed if at each time a decision had been made she could have magically known the outcome? Would she have chosen to stay with the Benners when Alva offered to help her? Could she have turned her head when she learned what Fernando's plans were for her countrymen? Should she have stayed at Dusseldorf the first time Dirk took her there? What if she had walked away and left Mons at Alva's mercy? No, there were no decisions she could have made differently. She had played the game to the best of her ability, and now she had lost.

Drifting in and out of wakefulness, Johanna found it impossible to keep her thoughts off the past. She had tried counting to a thousand in four different languages; she had played word games with herself—how many words can a person make out of the word rodent? dent, rent, rode, toe, den . . . ; she had even tried to exercise by pacing in the small, confined area.

But now it was time to view her life one last time before death freed her. So she ceased her battle against the memories that had invaded her thoughts every waking and sleeping moment since she had surrendered to Fernando. She relived everything that had ever happened to her, as the events of her life cavalcaded across her mind.

She made an effort to think only of the pleasant memories, and there were many of those—Mama, Papa, her brothers, the Benners, making love to Dirk. Yes, she knew her life had not been a total waste. She had loved and been loved, and perhaps she had even managed to save a few lives. But no matter how she dwelled on her successes, the failures continued to haunt her: failure to return Louis's love; failure to save Francois Benner's life; failure to make her parents happy; failure to regain Dirk's trust; and failure to destroy Fernando Alvarez de Toledo!

Fernando! If she could only find the means to sink a dagger deep into his black heart, she would meet her maker gladly, without any regret for what could have been.

Still able to envision his unctuous grin of pretended kindness and forgiveness, a shudder of revulsion ran through Johanna's slight body. She continued to hear his oily voice as he had pulled her to him once they were alone. "What happens now, you ask? That, my dear Esmeralda, depends on you. What would you like to have happen?" he had asked, looking deep into her hate-filled eyes, his breath ragged with long-forgotten lust. Without waiting for her answer, he had brought his mouth down on hers in a brutal, punishing kiss.

Johanna smiled, remembering how she had used all of her strength to shove him away, managing to free herself from his bruising mouth only an instant before she spewed the contents of her stomach all over the front of him.

"Do you think I want your blood-soaked hands to touch me?" she had screamed hysterically between sobs and further retching. "I prefer death to lying with Satan!" she had gagged.

Having regained his composure, Fernando had spoken with a deadly calm that sent tremors of fear through Johanna's shaking body as she fell weakly to her knees. Instead of showing his anger, he had smiled, evilly patient, as he toweled himself clean. "I'm sorry to hear that, *mi cara*. I had remembered your loveliness with such fondness, and I was hopeful that you remembered our time together with similar tenderness. Ah, but such is life," he sighed, walking away from where she was huddled on the floor.

"Let me see if we can't think of a less terrible chastisement for your betrayal than having me touch you. Surely, in all of my travels, my studies of corporal and capital punishment should afford us the perfect castigation for such a lovely traitor."

He did not look at her as he continued to muse on the quandary of what to do with her. "I had been thinking of a minor punishment, such as branding you with my coat of arms and then resuming our former relationship —with a few minor changes, of course." He laughed at his own foolishness for having trusted her. "That, with an occasional flogging, would keep most women in line. But not my little Esmeralda with the eyes that spit green fire. She prefers death!" he had laughed.

Raising his finger into the air as if a brilliant idea had just struck him, he shouted, "I know! We'll turn to the ancients for the answer to our problem. You know, the Babylonians, Egyptians, Romans, and Persians were particularly adept at punishment. We could boil you in a huge vat of oil. The crowd should enjoy watching as we publicly disrobe your beautiful body and immerse it in the vat. They say that as the oil heats, your blood adjusts to the temperature changes and it takes a long, torturous time for unconsciousness to come."

He paused to give her a chance to absorb his words, then resumed speaking with relish. "Or I could have you impaled on a board of spikes for the crowd to enjoy. Of course, one must be so cautious that the spikes stab only minor areas. Otherwise, the criminal dies too quickly to be of interest to the spectators." He sighed and glanced around the room. "I wonder how the citizens of Brussels would react to a stoning. It would give your death a certain biblical flavor. No, I don't really think so. Stoning is too quick if the crowd is overzealous."

Considering his fingernails thoughtfully, he said, "We must think of something new and unused in the Netherlands. I have it! The perfect solution to our problem!" he shouted excitedly. "The Persians! Now, there's a creative race. Have you heard of their method called the 'boats'? Well, don't feel badly. I doubt anyone in this country has. But it will be something to see. Really a *sweet* way to die! Let me explain it to you, Esmeralda. You will love it!"

Johanna realized his eyes were glazed with lust and his breathing had become more excited with each punishment he had described.

"First of all, your lovely naked body is displayed publicly for flogging. Then you are put in a wooden container they call the boat. That boat is covered with another, leaving openings for your head, hands and feet. Then we feed you, forcibly if necessary, milk and honey. The mixture is spread all over your face, hands and feet, and you are left in the sun, where eventually you are devoured alive by insects and vermin that swarm about and breed within you!"

Looking up at the man who had practically forgotten her presence as he had stared glassy-eyed at the picture he was envisioning, Johanna slowly rose to her feet, wiping her hands on her skirt as she did.

Moving slowly toward the man lost in his own perverted pleasure, she pulled the short dagger from the folds in her skirt and lunged toward him. But her vomiting had left her weak and slow.

Alva grabbed her wrist with a viselike grip, forcing her to drop the knife. "Or perhaps we should use more modern methods," he had gone on, ignoring her attack as he bent to pick up her weapon. Slapping the flat side of the blade against his palm, Fernando had laughed again. "England draws and quarters her traitors. A bit messy, but still effective for discouraging others from turning to a life of crime. Convicted traitors, which qualifies you, my love, are cut down from the gallows while they are still alive. Then, after the executioner extracts the bowels of the offender and burns them before his—or her—eyes, the criminal is beheaded, and his body is cut into quarters."

"What about the rack and the wheel?" she had snarled viciously. "Haven't you forgotten them?"

"No, not at all. They are good for preliminaries—as

are flogging and mutilations. But they really aren't spectacular enough for a lady of your spirited nature. Well, I can see this will require further thought. But tell me what you are thinking, lovely Esmeralda. Do you still prefer death to my loving touch?"

"Yes!" she had screamed. "By God, yes!"

"Very well, I'll see to it that yours is a death not soon forgotten by your countrymen." He had walked to the entrance to the room where they stood and called out, "Lieutenant! Come collect your prisoner. Chains on ankles, wrists and neck! Should she escape, the responsible parties will take her place on the gallows! Is that understood?"

Turning over in an attempt to lie on a part of her back that was not a festering wound, Johanna wondered if she should consider herself fortunate that Alva had left the city. From the very beginning of her captivity, he had told her he would be seeing to every aspect of her punishment personally. He had been true to his word.

She groaned aloud as she recalled the first flogging one of the soldiers had administered under Alva's watchful eye. She had heard it said later that there had been twenty lashes laid on her back that time, but she had mercifully fainted after much fewer. She remembered choking and coughing violently in the dark of the night when one kind soldier had taken pity on her sobs of pain and had drugged her with a mixture of laudanum and brandy.

Now, dying in the lonely cell, Johanna said a silent prayer for the courageous and sympathetic man who had gotten her through those days of torture with his merciful sense-deadening potion, administered secretly only moments before Alva and his whip came to flog her. She had no doubt that she would not have been able to continue to deny Fernando if it had not been for the soldier, Raul. As it was, the endurance she had displayed had amazed the spectators, and soon the men were betting she would hold out one more day.

Finally, Alva had decided on this latest strategy in his war against her will—total isolation! After having her hurled into her tiny cell with orders that no one should have any contact with her until he returned, he had left the city to lead battles in the north.

All the flogging had come to an abrupt stop, and Johanna had temporarily found solace in the lonely cell. However, the blessing was brief. Then came the rats!

"Oh, God, let me die now!" she screamed into the darkness.

So you want to die, do you? a voice inside her head chided. *All your talk of wanting to be a soldier and fight with the men was just that, wasn't it? You should have stayed home and had babies like the weak female you are. You're no fighter!*

"I am a fighter, I am!" Johanna shouted to the walls.

Then why are you lying here wishing to die? Weren't you the one who said that as long as you had an ounce of breath in your lungs, there was still a chance?

"But I tried to fight! I didn't give in to Alva! Should I have let him think I wanted to come back to him? What should I have done?" she whispered to herself.

It's too late to worry about what you should have done. Use your brain! Think about what you can do now. Think, Johanna. Think of a way to fight!

Slowly pulling herself to a sitting position, she cried weakly, "But I've got nothing to fight with. I've got rats, fleas, roaches, this tattered blanket, my teeth, my

391

fingernails, pig slop once a day, and the darkness—the god-awful darkness!"

What else? There must be something else! Think, Johanna! Damn you, fight!

Growing frustrated as she tallied her limited assets, she pounded her fist on the floor. "What's the use?" she hollered. "Nothing! That's what I have—nothing!"

Then lie back down and die.

"But I don't want to die!" she screamed, acknowledging for the first time her desire to live.

Then think! There's got to be something else. What about Fernando? You've outsmarted him before!

"He wants me alive and subservient. Maybe I could use that against him," she mused doubtfully.

Not if you're dead before he returns to the city. What about the soldier who gave you the laudanum? If you can get a message to him, he might . . .

Johanna shook her head dejectedly. "He's already risked too much. I couldn't ask him."

But he helped before.

Johanna was so engrossed in thought as she paced in her cell that she failed to notice the sound of the key slowly turning in the lock, or the sudden silence that came over the furry creatures that shared her prison. She continued to move around the cubicle until she ran, head-on, into someone in the cell with her! The scream of terror that rose in her throat was stifled by the strong hand that clamped over her mouth.

"You must be silent and listen," the masculine intruder hissed in French. "I'm not here to hurt you, but you must follow instructions if you want out of this hellhole. Will you be quiet and listen?" he asked, tentatively removing his callused hand from her mouth.

She nodded, trying to make out the man's features in the total darkness.

"Good." Putting his arms around her waist, he drew her closer to him, bringing his lips to her ear. "From the moment I leave, you must lie silently in a corner of this cell until we come to check on you tomorrow. If no sounds are heard in here, they will send us to check to see if you are dead. They must believe you are! A friend and I are to collect the corpses tomorrow. You must be among them. It's the only way. Do you understand?"

"Who are you?" she gasped, trying to place the voice as she hung onto the strong man for support.

"Just do as I say, and you won't have to spend much more time here." Pulling himself away from her desperate clutch, he added, "Until tomorrow, Johanna!" and he was gone.

Walking to the corner of her cell, Johanna did as she was told. She lay staring at the nothingness of the black room, taking care not to allow any sound of movement to come from her tense body. And when the vermin resumed their nocturnal activities, she ignored them as they crawled and scampered over her still form, all of her thoughts concentrated on the man who represented her salvation.

Who was he? Could it have been Raul? No, I would have recognized his voice. Besides, he spoke in French, not Spanish. Maybe it was a guard Raul bribed. He said "we." He sounded like Dirk, but that's impossible. She shook her head, denying the idea that continued to nag at her thoughts. *Well, whoever he is, he's coming tomorrow. If only I can make it through the next hours. But of course I can! I have to.*

*   *   *

393

After what seemed days rather than hours, Johanna heard the key clanking in the lock on her cell door. Barely breathing, she watched through slitted eyelids as a shadowy figure approached her motionless body in the dark corner. Giving her shoulder a shake, the man turned toward the doorway where another guard stood holding the lantern. "This one's dead!" he said loudly. "Let's get her out of here, and that should be it for this round," he stated callously in a booming voice.

Picking up Johanna's limp form, he carried her out the door and dumped her on top of a cart of dead prisoners. Before she could betray herself and react to the horror by moving or making a sound, the tattered, insect-infested blanket that had been her only covering was tossed over her battered body and face.

"This batch is really rank," the man who had removed her from the cell said casually. She was sure it was Raul, the soldier who had helped her before! "Wonder when the last time was they did a body check here. A couple of these fellows smell like they've been dead for weeks!"

The other guard grunted in agreement, but Johanna could not tell if it was the same man who had come into her cell the night before.

"Well, let's get them out to the trench. The fire's already started. All we have to do is dump them and we can be on our way."

Johanna was certain now that it was Raul's voice she heard speaking so heartlessly and so loudly.

"I've got a sweet little barmaid waiting for me, so this is one job I don't want to prolong. Remind me next time to wear a perfumed cloth over my nose!"

The second guard still did not speak, though he did laugh coarsely at his partner's monologue.

When she thought she could no longer bear the loathsome odor radiating from the decaying cadavers beneath her, she was shocked by the glare of the sunlight illuminating the death wagon. Then she could feel the heat of the inferno the soldier had mentioned burning hungrily in the ditch.

"We're almost there," whispered the familiar French voice of the night before. "Be patient." With his last words, he rolled her off the top of the offensive heap of bodies and began heaving the other bodies into the fiery trench.

As they added the human fuel to the fire, the heat rose to intolerable temperatures, and Johanna saw through the holes in her blanket that everyone had backed a good distance from the flame. Everyone, that is, except the two soldiers who worked quickly and silently to empty the cart of its cargo. Then, with one inconspicuous, swift motion, they swung her back into the cart and pulled it away from the heat.

Walking slowly and purposefully to the stables, they glanced around carefully before removing the half-dead girl and loading her into an empty grain sack, which they left in a dark corner of the feed room.

"All we have to do now is saddle our horses and gather up my gifts for my 'lady love.' Then we leave," Raul whispered to his partner.

"Are you certain we'll be able to pass through the gates with that sack?"

"All the officers take presents to help woo the señoritas. No one will think a thing of it. Besides, she's so tiny that when we put some materials and food in the sack, the whole bundle won't weigh a hundred pounds!"

Raul quickly put the finishing touches on his horse's

gear, then reached for a large piece of magenta silk fabric, a sack of coffee, and a basket of fresh fruit he had secreted in the stall earlier. "Let's get these things in the sack and be on our way. I can't get out of this army any too soon!"

They put the supplies on top of Johanna and tied the bundle on a third horse's back. At last satisfied that they looked like two officers bearing gifts for the ladies, they walked the horses out into the open.

"Looks like you've got enough presents there to gain you many favors, Queiro," one fellow officer laughed as they passed by.

"I'll let you know what the ladies like best, Mendoza," Raul returned jovially. "When's your next leave?"

"Not for another six days!" He shook his head disgustedly.

"Well, I'll think of you when I'm lying in the arms of a lovely señorita."

"I'll just bet you will."

Laughing, Johanna's rescuers strolled casually through the gates, both of them breathing an involuntary sigh of relief as they stepped outside the thick, forbidding walls.

Without speaking, they mounted their horses and led the small packhorse east. "It's not too far from here," the soldier with the French accent said, speaking for the first time.

"Good. She didn't look well." The worried frown on Raul's face etched deep furrows between his heavy black brows.

As they rode, slowly to avoid suspicion, the other man finally asked the Spaniard, "Why are you doing this? Are you in love with her?"

"No. I really don't know her; but I've owed her a debt for a long time." He then told the story of his encounter with a certain Emeraude Benner in a beer garden. "You see, if I had stood my ground against my 'friends,' I could have possibly prevented her from ever meeting Alva. But I was too concerned with what my father would say if I did anything to endanger my commission. So I just walked away, leaving her at their mercy," he explained, the pain of his memory still evident on Raul's dark face.

"What punishment did Alva give them?"

"None! The bastard did nothing but reward them with easy details; he said it was his way of showing his appreciation for introducing him to her," he said with disgust. Then his mouth twisted into a wry smile. "But I have reason to believe they eventually received their just recompense for their treatment of her and other young innocents like her," Raul said with a knowing smile.

"Oh, how's that?"

"We were west of here and they were up to their old tricks. They knew I didn't go for their kinds of pleasure, so I was sent away to give them time to sate their perverted sexual appetites with a young boy. I never saw them again. But I suspect that their final victim got some assistance in ridding your country of them."

"Perhaps they deserted," the other man suggested.

"Perhaps, but I doubt it. Maybe someday I'll find the person or persons responsible for their disappearance and be able to thank them."

"Yes, maybe you will."

Chapter Twenty-Three

"There it is," Dirk announced, pointing to a tailor's shop. "See how it sits off the street? They're waiting for us with new disguises and fresh horses." Glancing over his shoulder to be sure they were not being followed as they rode down the alleyway behind the shop, Dirk led Raul and the horses into a sod-covered shed. Dismounting quickly, he ran to the packhorse and began untying the bundle while Raul bolted the doors to the building.

Flinging the material and food on the floor, Dirk lowered the edges of the sack around the huddled, lethargic girl. "Oh, my God," he groaned, seeing Johanna for the first time in weeks.

Hearing his voice, she lifted her muddled gaze to meet his tear-filled stare. "Am I free?" she asked, keeling over onto the sawdust-covered floor.

Frantically glimpsing around the small area, Dirk dropped to his knees and gathered her limp body into his arms. He sobbed convulsively.

Raul put a consoling hand on his shoulder. "There

will be time for tears later, my friend. But now we must wash her wounds and feed her. Does the tailor's wife know that we have a wounded woman with us? Will she have medical supplies we can use?"

Benumbed by the sight of the pale girl lying unconscious in his arms Dirk nodded. "Yes."

"Well, you'd better go and get her. I don't want to frighten her with my accent."

"You're right. They knew I was being helped by a Spaniard, but knowing it and seeing it are two different things." Slowly, he laid Johanna back in the hay and rose to his feet. Keeping his eyes trained on her unconscious form, he changed clothes, then slipped out of the shed to fetch the woman who had practiced the art of nursing for half a century. "Watch her. I'll be back."

Raul turned back to Johanna and spoke to her as he wiped her forehead with a rag he had dampened in the horse trough. "You'd better live, little one. I don't think that poor fellow can go on without you. I've never seen such a strong love. I don't think he even knows how strong it is. Poor fool." Raul tucked a rough blanket around her, unable to bear the sight of her injuries. "How could Alva do this to you?"

Raul jumped back when he heard Dirk return from the house with the nurse.

Gasping in horror as she pulled the blanket off Johanna's wasted body, the woman immediately took charge. "We'll have to bring a tub of warm water in here. After your friend changes clothes, the two of you can fetch it and fill it with hot water. I've got the water heating on the stove. I started it as soon as I heard you ride in."

Glancing at the two stunned men, who had yet to move, she waved them on. "Go on! You've done your job. Now, let me do mine. We're not going to give up on this little thing quite yet. No, not quite yet," the woman mumbled softly to herself as she carefully examined the inflamed tracks left by the whip on Johanna's back. "Not too deep," she said. "Should clean up pretty well. These bites look bad, though," she murmured, adroitly moving her hands over the girl's thin body, taking particular time to examine for swelling in the groin and armpits.

She looked up from her work as the two men brought the tub into the dim shed a few minutes later. "Get the water quickly! And bring me the strong lye soap near the stove. This child is very sick. And it's not the whip wounds that are worrying me!"

"What else?" Dirk shouted, his voice loud and uncontrolled.

The old woman answered impatiently, "For one thing, the authorities—if you don't keep your voice down!"

"But you said . . ." Dirk uttered, more quietly.

Raul interrupted the distraught man. "Come, my friend. Let us do as the señora directs. There will be time for questions later."

It had been several hours since they first rode into the small shed, and still the old woman continued to hover over Johanna without explaining her diagnosis. Finally, she rose up from the sleeping girl, who had been soaked in the hot water, scrubbed with the strong soap, and wrapped in a soft linen sheet.

"She's fortunate that the lash marks are only superficial and not deep at all," the old woman said, wiping her hand on her apron. "Whoever flogged her must have taken care that the whip did not permanently scar her. For that, we can be thankful," she said with a sympathetic smile. "However, these insect bites are quite another thing. Some are infected, as are the lash wounds; but her condition is so poor that she may not be able to fight the infection, as well as the illness she may have."

"What illness is that?" Raul asked, his outer calm belying his inner turmoil.

"I'm not certain, mind you; but she does have small swellings in the area of her armpits and groin."

"What does that mean?" Dirk rasped.

"It could be the first signs of . . ."

Both men held their breath when she paused before completing her sentence.

". . . black death."

"No!" Dirk cried.

"Are you sure, señora?" Raul asked gravely.

"As I said, I'm not certain, but we must assume that it's true and destroy everything that has touched her. We need to burn that blanket, the grain sack, your clothing, my clothing. Then we'll wash the shed and ourselves with the lye soap and bathe her every few hours. The warm water will help draw out the poison in the infections, and the frequent bathing will hopefully kill any insects that are still on her."

Walking around the shed gathering up straw, clothing, and everything loose, the woman smiled. "If it's a mild case, she could live through this yet. Most people don't realize that the plague doesn't always

401

mean death. We won't give up hope yet, will we?"

Both men shook their heads and began to pick up things that had to be burned.

"When you bathe," she added, "I would suggest shaving off those neatly trimmed beards. Not only do they reveal your Spanish connections, but they are a perfect place for lice to hide!"

Four days passed and Johanna's fever continued to rage, leaving her delirious and prostrate. They had been encouraged when, on the second day, the fever had suddenly dropped; but it had risen again that evening, leaving her confused and disoriented. She recognized neither of the men and seemed unaware that she was out of her cell, though one of them had stayed continuously at her side, taking turns bathing, feeding, and sitting with her through the chills, vomiting, and hallucinating.

Looking at Dirk as he sat holding the sleeping girl's hand, the old woman said, "You look bad, boy. You'd better try to get some sleep or we're going to be nursing you when she's recovered." By now, Adelaide Tailleur was certain the girl was suffering from the plague, and she knew all they could do for her was keep the fever down, keep the wounds clean, and wait—and pray!

Dirk started to answer, but Johanna began to flail her arms violently in an attempt to sit up. "Dirk," she screamed. "Where are you?" Her eyes were searching the dark shed wildly. Then she grabbed her temples between her palms and cried weakly, "Oh, my head, my head. Why don't you come for me, Dirk? I can't go on alone!"

"I'm here, Johanna. I'm here," he soothed, tightening his hold on the thin girl.

"Alva's going to let me die in this cell. If only he would go on and kill me!"

Horrified with the realization that she was still unaware of his presence, Dirk tried to make her see him by directing her gaze toward him.

"It's me, Johanna! See? I came for you. Look at me. You're not in the cell. You're safe now. Alva will never lay his filthy hands on you again. Please listen to me, Johanna," he pleaded to unhearing ears—for she was now giggling uncontrollably. "Johanna, can you hear me?"

Nodding her head as she continued her unreasonable laughter, she snickered, "Of course I hear you! I hear all of you—screaming and crying in your cells. I hear the rats, too," she giggled ridiculously.

"What's wrong with her?" Dirk choked, looking helplessly at Adelaide.

"It's part of the illness, my son. She has no idea what she's saying—or where she is," she explained gently.

"But she's laughing!"

"Giddiness, shivering, delirium, vomiting, headache—it's all evidence of the plague that is consuming her," she answered, shaking her head sadly.

"You're not giving up, are you?" Dirk exploded.

"I've done all I can do, son. She's in God's hands now."

"No! I won't let her die! She can't die! We must do something else." His anguished face broke the woman's heart, and she patted him on the back.

"There, there, she's quiet again. You go on and rest while I bathe her in the cool rags again. They seem to

403

help the fever. She may recover yet." The nurse's tone was not convincing, and Dirk shook his head in determination.

"I can't leave her. I'd better stay here. She might call out for me again," he insisted.

"All right, boy. But at least lean back and try to sleep. You can hold her hand and wake up if she needs you."

When Dirk awakened hours later, Johanna's slender hand was still clutched in his, as if he could keep her alive as long as he held on to her.

Just then, Raul entered the barn with fresh clothing and blankets. "I wonder what my father would think if he knew I've been doing laundry, nursing, and cooking for the last few days." Laughing at the thought, Raul added, "I don't really have to wonder. He'd say he had no son—rather than admit that his male offspring could be reduced to doing 'woman's work'!"

"What would we have done without you, my friend?" Dirk asked with a grateful smile. "You have put yourself in a great deal of danger. I will never be able to repay you."

"No need to think of repayment. I only want out of Alva's army. It's like a disease. The more vile and unfeeling he is, the more his men act like the devils your countrymen have likened them to."

"Is there any news of when he's to return to Brussels?"

"The tailor says that he heard men talking. They say he's retaken most of the rebellious towns in the northeast and is moving toward Holland and Zeeland. His troops are said to be behaving with extraordinary brutality, sacking cities and burning them to the ground after butchering their citizens."

"How many towns are still in the hands of the rebels? Have you heard?" Dirk asked, watching the peacefully sleeping girl beside him.

"Not more than about thirty, according to our kind host's sources."

"What about Amsterdam and Middleburg?" The last Dirk had heard, the two cities felt their commercial interests could best be served by supporting the Spanish, and they had denied entrance to the infamous Sea Beggars.

"Still loyal to Philip."

"It's hard to believe. I was told that on one of Alva's visits to Amsterdam he had a ten-year-old girl drowned in a barrel as punishment for throwing garbage in a canal. How can they ignore something like that?"

Raul shook his head, his expression disbelieving. "Do you want me to sit with her while you clean up?" he offered.

Dirk glanced appreciatively at the handsome man with the olive-colored complexion and dark eyes. "Thank you, but I feel I must be here."

"What good are you going to be to her if you make yourself sick in the meantime?" Raul asked reasonably.

"You're right, of course. I suppose I do need to get up and move about. But I just can't bear to leave her."

Keeping his gentle hold on the limp hand, he rose to sit on his haunches, examining her sleeping face. "Raul! Look at her!" he exclaimed. "She's sweating and the chills have stopped! Get Adelaide! Quick!"

Raul hurried out and was back shortly with the kindly old woman. "Yes," she said after examining Johanna carefully. "The knots in her groin and under her arms seem to be going down. Her skin is much cooler to the touch, and her sleep is more natural, less fitful. God may have taken mercy on us and spared this child after all!"

Once the fever broke, Johanna's recovery was swift, thanks to the competent care of Adelaide Tailleur and her two loyal assistants. By the time the three were ready to leave Brussels two weeks later, Johanna's color and strength had returned remarkably, and no one would have guessed how close to death she had been. The wounds on her back were healing well, and she had even gained back some of the weight she had lost—though she was still too thin.

When she had first realized she was no longer in the dark cell, Johanna found it difficult to understand how she had found her way to the shed behind the tailor's shop. "Don't worry about how we got you here, señorita. We will tell you that story another day. *Oui?*" Raul's French was improving daily, and she was quick to notice.

"Raul, you're speaking French! Very well, too. But you will never pass for a local if you keep using words like 'señorita,'" she teased.

"I beg your pardon, mademoiselle. My error." The Spaniard bowed graciously to the blonde girl sitting propped against hay bales.

Johanna glanced cautiously at Dirk, who stood silently watching them, his expression thoughtful and guarded. Catching her unexpected gaze, his eyes locked to hers for a moment, then shifted away uncomfortably.

She was still puzzled as to why he had come for her. Could it be that he still loved her after all this time? No, she refused to let herself entertain any foolish thoughts like that! She didn't know why he'd risked his life for her, but she was certain it was not for love. Guilt perhaps? A debt to pay? Duty to Louis? A favor to her parents? But not love! Of that she was sure.

Still, she was confused by his behavior since she had regained her senses. She could vaguely remember Dirk's hand holding hers throughout her illness; yet now it was Raul who brought her meals, helped her walk, talked to her. She decided it must have been Raul taking care of her all along, her delirium only making her believe it had been Dirk.

Well, whatever his reason, he's not going to know I still love him.

"And you, Count Leuven," she said, his name trembling slightly on her lips. "What is weighing so heavily on your mind?"

"Yes, Dirk, you've been terribly sober since our patient has recovered," Raul laughed.

Searching Johanna's face for the slightest evidence of the love she had spoken of during her illness—and seeing none—Dirk chuckled at his own foolishness for believing Louis and his rantings. "I was wondering when our 'patient' will be well enough to ride. I'll feel a lot better about things when we get out of Brussels. I'm concerned that we will be discovered. The tailor and his wife have been more than generous. But if we're found here, it would mean death for them—harboring a convicted traitor, a deserter, and an expatriated nobleman."

"You're right, of course," Johanna agreed. "We must leave at once. I'm ready to ride any time you say. Where are we going?"

"You're still too weak to travel," Raul protested.

"Tell him how much stronger I am than I look, Dirk," Johanna suggested pointedly, not bothering to hide her resentment. "Tell him what a survivor I am!"

Ignoring her barb, Dirk directed his words to Raul. "I think we should leave by tomorrow evening. We'll head east on foot during the busiest hour. We'll be less conspicuous that way. We can disguise Johanna as an old woman, and she can ride the donkey if she's unable to walk."

Johanna rose to the undeniable challenge in Dirk's words. "I'll walk, thank you," she quipped irritably.

"What about the horses you arranged for?" Raul asked.

"Friends have secreted them at a small farm outside the city, together with additional food and clothing. However, I do believe we'll go ahead and accept the offer of the donkey." Looking mockingly at Johanna, he added, "Just in case!"

Johanna glared at him, then turned to the handsome Spaniard, smiling sweetly. "Raul, do you suppose you can get me some more of that wonderful broth? I can feel my strength returning with each bite I've eaten."

"Certainly, *cara*. I'll be right back," Raul replied eagerly and dashed out of the shed.

"I see you've added another adoring servant to your collection," Dirk quipped caustically.

"What does that mean?" Johanna's voice rose as she spoke.

"Men just stand in line to wrap themselves around your little finger, don't they, Johanna?" His steel blue eyes hardened as he accused her—of what she was uncertain.

"What's your secret, Johanna? What is it about you that makes men risk their lives and careers for you? Do you promise to love them always? Or is the memory of making love to you what drives them?" His lip curled cruelly as he bombarded her with his vindictive questions.

"For your information, I have no idea why Raul helped me. Maybe he's merely a kind man who expects nothing in return—something you'd know nothing about, I'm certain." Her voice trembled with resentment.

He studied her for a long silent moment, then feigned an interest in the horses.

"Dirk," she stated in an uncertain voice filled with unanswered questions.

"Yes," he answered coldly, directing his gaze back toward her.

Johanna cringed unwillingly under his glowering scowl, her face reddening, and she averted her gaze to the ground. "Nothing important. I was just wondering where you met Raul." She couldn't bring herself to ask the question foremost in her mind. She already knew the answer—Dirk had simply stopped loving her.

"Raul," he growled, the unspoken assumption in his mocking tone and surly grin. "Good man, Raul Queiro. Do you know that he can never return to Spain because of his desertion? The shame would be too much for his wealthy family to bear. He must start all over in a strange country, with no money and no family connections—all for you, Johanna!"

"For me? But why? We don't even know each other!"

"Obviously he's in love with you. Like all the others you've promised to love—Alva, Louis, and . . . who knows how many others!" He turned away from her before he finished speaking, knowing his hurt was too near the surface and easily readable on his face.

Longing to tell the angry man that she had only promised to love one man—but knowing that one man would not believe her—Johanna said, "Raul and I have never discussed love, and I certainly never made any promises to him. Is your opinion of me so low that you can only think the worst of me?" Her voice was quiet and no longer filled with venom. Only her unbearable pain was in evidence now.

Dirk was so uncertain of his own feelings that he was unable to answer her direct question. Ignoring it, he turned and walked toward the doorway. "I'll see what's taking Raul so long," he mumbled at the exit, leaving Johanna alone in the dimness with her anguish.

"Here you are, little lady," Raul announced, looking around the shed as he entered with the fresh bowl of soup. "Where's our grumpy friend?"

"He left," Johanna answered sourly.

"What's the matter with you two? Believe me, this is no way for reunited lovers to behave. You'd never catch a Spaniard acting so foolishly!" He grinned and held a spoonful of soup to her mouth.

"Lovers!" she spat bitterly. "That's one thing we certainly are not! Dirk Corlear can't stand the sight of me, and I loathe him!"

"We must be talking about different men. The man I've known these past weeks loves you more than life itself." He smiled and picked up her hand to pat it affectionately. "The man I'm speaking of loves you so much that he was willing to trust a Spaniard he knew nothing about, just to free you. The man I refer to insisted on endangering himself by coming into your cell in the night—only to be near you for a few moments. I'm talking about the man who stayed by your side continually, hardly sleeping or eating himself, until your fever broke. He doesn't sound like a man with only hate in his heart, does he?"

"He feels a certain sense of duty, I'm sure; but believe me, that's all!"

Raul smiled patiently at Johanna's pouting face. "I don't know what's going on, but he loves you. And you love him. There's no doubt about that!"

"I do not!"

"Oh, I'm sorry. I suppose it was another name that you called out in your sleep when you were Alva's prisoner. And I guess I could have misunderstood when you called for Dirk during the days of your illness. You mustn't forget, little one, I've been here all along to hear the pouring out of your heart!"

Needing time to digest the knowledge Raul had given her about Dirk's dedication to her, Johanna changed the subject abruptly. "Why did you risk everything to help me, Raul?"

"You don't remember me, I'm sure, but I could never forget your face—or the guilt I felt over your fate, Emeraude Benner."

After telling her where they had first met, he explained that when he had seen her again, he had known that this time he had to do something to save her. He told how he had made it known through certain channels that he wanted to defect and bring a woman prisoner with him. That was how he and Dirk had first met. Raul had been told that there was a Netherlander who would do anything to free a certain prisoner; and when they had discovered they were interested in the same captive, they had become natural allies—as well as close friends.

"Dirk thinks you rescued me because you're in love with me," she said in an embarrassed tone. "You aren't, are you?"

"My dear, you are lovely, but I have never thought of you other than as someone I needed to help. Doesn't that tell you how much he loves you, though? He's so consumed by his own love and jealousy that he probably assumes everyone will love you the way he does. Besides, I have another love—one of your countrywomen. She's the other reason I wanted to defect. I met her when our troops first came into your country. I hope to marry her when we are out of danger," he confessed.

"Oh, Raul, I'm so happy for you," she exclaimed, throwing her arms around the tall Spaniard's broad shoulders. "What's her name? Where is she now? Does she know you're coming to her?"

But Johanna's questions went unanswered, for Dirk reentered at that moment to take in the exuberant display of affection. "I hope I'm not interrupting anything too important," he apologized sarcastically. "But I've made the arrangements for our departure tomorrow afternoon. I trust you can both be ready by then." Turning on his heel, he left the two staring after him, their mouths open in silent protest.

Starting after him, Raul said, "I'll get this straightened out."

"Don't bother. He's going to think whatever he wants to think. Nothing you can say will change his mind," she said despairingly as she slid down to the hay-strewn floor and closed her eyes to sleep—for she was suddenly very tired.

Chapter Twenty-Four

When the actual time of their departure arrived, Dirk left Johanna no choice about how she would leave Brussels. With the help of the tailor's wife, she was disguised as an old woman. Her hair was hidden under a white linen scarf topped with a stiffly starched handkerchief which hid her bent head and face from view, and her loose-fitting dress was stuffed with extra blankets and pillows tied in place by a dingy apron that covered all of her dress with the exception of the flowing sleeves and skirt hem. The weight of the excess padding alone was enough to exhaust the still-weak girl, who stood tapping her foot on the ground in a tattoo of irritated rhythms.

"How am I supposed to travel with this mass of padding weighing me down?" she asked, directing her question to Dirk, who stood nearby, adjusting his own peasant attire.

"You'll ride the donkey. No one would expect an old woman to walk all the way to Dusseldorf," he replied, the low timbre of his voice terse and to the point.

"Is that an order, sire?" She baited him deliberately, daring him to turn around and face her.

"Consider it anything you will. Just get on the damned ass!" His voice was tired and sounded bored. Still he would not look at her.

"I think—"

Spinning around, Dirk shot her a silencing glare, the ridge along his strong jaw turning white with the effort of restraint. "Haven't you done enough thinking? Your witless, empty-headed schemes have brought you and others close to death enough times. How many lives will you endanger before you realize you don't have all the answers? Now, shut your mouth and get on that ass before I give you what your doting father should have given you the first time you pulled one of your harebrained stunts." Dirk wheeled from Johanna and resumed his preparations with deliberate concentration.

"You wouldn't spank me, Dirk Corlear," she laughed, planting her feet square on the ground and her fists on her hips.

"One."

"What are you doing?" she shouted, exasperated.

"Two."

"I'm not riding that animal!"

"Three."

"Stop that stupid counting!"

"Four."

"I want to walk."

"Five." Dirk turned to stride lazily and menacingly toward Johanna, who inadvertently backed away from his threatening approach.

"You have no right!" she stammered, continuing

414

her retreat.

"I have every right," he said quietly, reaching out and grabbing the soft fleshy part of her arm and pulling her toward him.

"You wouldn't dare," she gasped incredulously.

With no further words, Dirk plopped himself down on a nearby bale of hay, yanked her across his lap, and walloped her bottom soundly.

Outside the shed, the tailor's wife and Raul stood listening to Johanna's howling. "We must do something," Adelaide begged Raul. "He shouldn't treat that poor girl like that—especially after all she's been through."

Retaining his grip on the nurse's arm, Raul smiled and said firmly, "Let them be. I think they are settling some differences that need to be settled. Haven't you and your husband ever fought?"

"But he's hurting her! Listen to her pitiful cries of pain!"

"The way you've got her padded, she's feeling nothing but indignation and anger," Raul said wisely. Listening for another minute and hearing no further cries from the small building, he whispered, "We can go in now!"

Raul and Adelaide entered the quiet shed cautiously. Seeing the Spaniard, Dirk said calmly, "Are you ready to leave? We're all set, aren't we, Johanna?"

Raul and the old woman followed Dirk's stern gaze to Johanna's sullen figure slumped peevishly on the donkey's back. "Thank you for all you've done for us," Dirk said to the woman, seeming to take no notice of Johanna's angry glare.

"We owe you a great debt, señora—I mean

madame!" Raul said warmly. "Hopefully, some day we can repay you for your many kindnesses."

The old woman reached out to the sulking girl who looked so forlorn. "You take care of yourself, dear; and let us hear from you when you reach safety." She hugged Johanna, who returned her embrace earnestly.

"Thank you for everything. I'll never forget you," she sobbed uncontrollably as she clung to the older woman.

Uncertain how to react to the emotional outburst, the woman looked helplessly at the two men, who appeared to be oblivious to the girl's suffering.

"We'd best be on our way. Thank you again," Dirk said, handing Adelaide a sack of coins to reimburse her for her time and expenses.

"Oh, no!" she said, shaking her head adamantly. "That is not necessary. We do what we do because of love of the Netherlands. Not for pay!" She was flushed with embarrassment.

"Let this be our way of helping the next fortunate fugitives who find their way to the safety of your home. Not payment, but an investment in the future of the Low Countries." Gently closing the woman's gnarled hand over the purse, Dirk smiled and kissed her cheek before leading the donkey out of the shed that had been their home for three weeks.

The two men walked on either side of the little beast of burden, while Johanna rode silently between them. No one spoke as Dirk and Raul plodded slowly toward the edge of the city, keeping their hats pulled low on their heads as they carefully observed the activity on the road for any signs of danger.

Johanna rode stooped over in the posture of an old

woman, her chin resting on the pillow that had been stuffed into her clothing to disguise her young body; and before they had gone too far beyond the gate, the gentle rocking motion of the slow-moving animal had lulled her into a restful sleep.

As they walked alongside the nodding girl, Raul asked Dirk, "How far do you suppose she'd have gotten if she'd tried to walk with us?"

"About as far as the alley entrance to the tailor's shed," Dirk laughed, shaking his head.

"She loves you, you know," Raul commented casually. "And you love her."

"It's too late for us, my friend."

"It's never too late, Dirk."

"I once thought we could have a future together—no matter what had transpired in the past. But too many things have been done and said," he uttered sadly.

The finality of Dirk's tone made Raul aware there was no more he could say to bring the two lovers together—at least not at that moment. But strolling silently along the road, he swore he would think of something, and soon!

"I do love this country of yours," he sighed, inhaling deeply to savor the crisp autumn smells as he beheld the panorama of fall colors displayed in rich reds, oranges, and golds.

Taking in the flat countryside's brightly colored terrain basking in the last sunlight of the day, Dirk concurred with Raul. "I love it, too."

"Once we drive Alva out, things will be different," Raul said, already sounding like a native. "I hear the monarch is thinking of replacing him. Word is that a growing amount of criticism of Alva's administration has reached the court. Responsible and trusted advisors to Philip have reported that the duke is not only greedy, cruel, and corrupt, but that his policies have made Spain and the king repugnant to the people of the Netherlands. They think Alva has brought the latest rebellion on the crown. I believe that if we don't manage to kill him, it's only a matter of time until he's replaced."

Surprised by Raul's information, Dirk asked, "How do you know these things?"

"You forget I have family at court. My father has kept me informed. Actually, he detests Alva and always hated the fact that I was assigned to his army. But he maintains a belief in following one's commander to the death—no matter how odious or vicious his orders may be."

"When this is all over, do you think he'll forgive you for the choice you've made?"

"I don't know. I hope so. But a man must live with himself, so I had to do what I did."

The two walked on in silence, each lost in his own discomfiting meditation. And Johanna continued to doze where she sat on the small donkey's back.

The sun was setting as they drew into a hidden cluster of trees off the main road. Dirk hesitantly touched her petite hand where it rested in her lap. "Wake up, Johanna. We're here."

Raising her head and straightening her slumping back, she opened her eyes drowsily. "Where are we?" she yawned, looking around curiously, at last bringing her sleep-filled gaze to rest on the masculine hand that touched her own.

Hypnotized by the sexuality of the familiar touch,

Johanna let her eyes rove languidly along the sleeve encircling the powerful male arm, over wide shoulders to study the span of curling red-gold hairs that filled the open vee in the white peasant shirt, on to the firmly carved chin and jaw, stopping only momentarily at the slightly parted lips displaying the barest hint of a smile, and finally ending her visual journey in the captivity of intense blue eyes filled with the same longing and pain she felt.

Neither Dirk nor Johanna noticed when Raul slipped unobtrusively away from where they remained enthralled and motionless in the spellbinding moment in time.

Trapped within the perimeter of her magnetic ambience, Dirk was powerless to sever the electrifying current running rampant and unrestrained between them. When he finally gathered the ability to speak, his voice was hoarse and cracked. "Did you have a good rest?"

Johanna searched his face for the suggestion of sarcasm she had grown to expect from him. Seeing none in evidence, she answered huskily, "Yes, I did. Thank you."

Dirk slid his hands to Johanna's waist to assist her to a standing position, and she inadvertently placed her hands on his shoulders for support. Unable to resist the force that was drawing them together, their lips met softly at the same time Johanna's feet touched the ground.

Running her fingers through Dirk's sandy hair, she smiled and kissed him lightly, saying, "Tell me, do you have the feeling that something has come between us?"

He followed the direction of her diverted gaze

indicating the protective padding the tailor's wife had so lovingly and thoroughly stuffed into her dress a few hours before.

Reaching up to the small hands clasped behind his neck, Dirk brought them forward and held them together between his flattened palms, a look of sadness shadowing his face as he kissed her upward-pointing fingertips. "Yes," he whispered and set her hands free.

He turned away, leaving her chilled with the realization of the unintended double meaning to her words. For some reason, her hands remained frozen in a semblance of prayer as he had posed them only seconds before, and Johanna cringed sickeningly with the breaking of the magical spell.

"Well, so much for that," she mumbled under her breath as she untied her apron to allow the blankets and pillows to fall out of her dress, before pulling the concealing scarves from her head. She sighed as her silvery blond hair, shoulder-length now, tumbled free.

Dirk drew a sharp breath as he watched her from the shadows.

Sinking to the ground, she drew her knees up and rested her chin on them. "Oh, God," she prayed, "please give me the strength to stop loving him!" Burying her face against the hardness of her folded knees, she wept silently.

Hoping he had given Dirk and Johanna enough time to reconcile some of their problems, Raul sauntered back to where he fully expected to find them in each other's arms. Grinning as he strolled into the camp, he was taken aback by Dirk, who pounced on him the moment he appeared.

"Where in the hell have you been? We need to let our

people know we've arrived safely, and there was no one to stay with her because you went wandering off not bothering to tell us where you were going!"

Stunned by the attack, the good-natured Spaniard apologized. "I'm sorry, my friend. I was certain you'd appreciate some privacy. Evidently, I judged the situation incorrectly. Please forgive me."

It would be very difficult for anyone to remain mad at Raul for long. Fully aware that he was angry with himself and not Raul, Dirk was ashamed of the way he'd spoken to his friend. "I'm the one who should ask your forgiveness for behaving like such an ass. It must be the tension of these last weeks. I'm sorry."

"The tension, *sí*. That must be it," Raul agreed, knowing that the strain Dirk was under was the worst kind—denying his love and need for the beautiful Johanna. "We'll forget it, amigo. Now, you were saying something about notifying someone of our arrival. I could use some supper! How about you?"

Dirk was back shortly with three saddled horses carrying packs, as well as cheese, bread and a bottle of wine. "Johanna," Raul called out. "Wake up! Dirk's here with food!"

Raising her head, Johanna was thankful the darkness hid her swollen, red eyes. "I wasn't sleeping, Raul. Just resting my eyes for a few minutes," she choked, the evidence of her tears heavy in her tone.

"Well, you had best splash some cold water on your face and come eat—before we leave you nothing but the crusts!" He was offering her an excuse to regather her composure before joining the two of them, and Johanna appreciated her new friend's compassion and understanding more than ever. As she walked toward a nearby stream, Raul hollered after her, "Don't be too long. We have wine, and I'd like to propose a toast."

"I'll hurry," she threw back over her shoulder.

When she did rejoin the men, she was relieved to find that they were discussing the rebellion and nothing personal, but unfortunately, that discussion did not continue.

"Ah, here she is," Raul announced cheerfully. "Now we can have our toast. Here's your wine, *mi cara*," he said, extending a cup of the fragrant red liquid in her direction. She took it without saying anything, but her smile conveyed her thanks to the man who was trying so desperately to bring her together with Dirk again.

Holding his own drink in front of him, Raul spoke blithely as he made his toast. "To life! To all its joys and sorrows!" They all drank, and Raul spoke again, holding his cup up again. "May we look only to the present and the future, and never dwell on the past and what might have been, when we search for our ultimate happiness." Again they drank, and again Raul insisted on proposing another toast.

Glancing slyly from Johanna to Dirk, Raul made his final tribute. "To true love. May we know its rarity and value. May we cherish it above all things if we are fortunate enough to find it just once in our lives—above material things, above pride or self-glory, above past mistakes, above life itself. To true love. May we recognize it when it comes to us."

Raul looked hopefully at the ill-fated couple, peering bashfully at each other, totally unaware of the presence of a third party. Giving them a moment to ponder his words, Raul finally laughed. "I'm hungry. How about you two? Where's that bread and cheese?" he asked, expecting no answer. "Good, here it is. You know, I saw something upstream that I'd like to investigate, so I'll amble up there and eat as I walk along. I hope that's all right with you two. Occasionally, I need some time to myself, and I've had very little of late," he chattered happily, taking time to cut himself a chunk of cheese and tear off a hunk of the bread. Grabbing his wine cup, Raul disappeared before the bemused couple could think to stop him.

Watching Raul dash out of the camp, Johanna chuckled quietly. "Poor Raul, he thinks he's so clever. I've told him it's no use, but he's so in love, he wants the whole world to be in love, too. I'm sorry if his romantic antics have made you uncomfortable," she apologized, standing to leave, surprised at her own control.

"Don't go." The low pleading sound to the request swept over Johanna like the caress of a warm midnight breeze, blessedly echoing in her ears. *Don't go . . . Don't go . . . Don't go . . .*

Afraid she would run into Dirk's arms and be rejected again, Johanna kept her back to him when she spoke, her voice thick with longing. "I thought you would prefer being alone."

Covering the space between them in long, easy strides, Dirk started to put his hands on her shoulders. But he thought better of that and let them drop to his sides. "We wouldn't want to disappoint Raul, would we?"

Johanna continued to face away from the man whose aura could hold her captive without any physical touch. He was so close she could hear his ragged breathing, feel it as it soughed gently across her cheek. She could smell the heady fragrance of the wine

423

he'd been drinking, mingled with his sweet manly scent, which drove her faculties to crazed distraction.

Give me strength, she prayed. *I must walk away. I can't turn around. I have to be strong.*

But even as the thoughts of protest ran wildly through her mind, she turned to face him, the expression on her face uncertain. "No, we don't want to disappoint Raul."

A slight grin formed on Dirk's handsome face—the same grin Johanna now remembered from the first time they met—and he said, "Any minute now, I'm expecting him to jump out of the trees wearing nothing but wings and a smile, and shooting arrows."

Picturing Raul dressed as Cupid, Johanna laughed impishly. "I can see it now! Raul standing naked in the middle of the grove, his wings drooping in defeat, with nowhere to sling his arrows. I suppose after all he's done for us, we owe it to him to stay, don't we?"

The musical sound of her gaiety filled Dirk's empty heart with pure joy. "It's good to hear you laugh again," he said, his voice warm and void of its earlier hostility.

Johanna looked down at her hands playing idly with the rough material of her dress. "And to see you smile," she answered timidly, afraid Dirk would see the blush that had crept to her cheeks.

Placing one gentle finger under the curve of her chin, he tilted her face upward, capturing her gaze with a smoldering look of desire that radiated from deep behind large pools of black, ringed on the very edges by blue that was almost as dark as the shining centers. As he held the lower part of her face resting on his finger, he lazily ran his thumb along the soft indentation

424

below her lips. "I want you," he whispered, his face only inches from her own.

Johanna could not speak as he reached down to catch her hands in his and placed them, one by one, behind his neck. Laying his palms lightly on either side of her face to frame its moonlit perfection, he brought his lips close to hers.

His mouth hovered so near she could feel his warm breath filling her now, although their lips had yet to meet. She didn't trust herself to speak.

"If only you weren't so beautiful," he groaned, continuing to watch her through thick sandy lashes. Suddenly he could wait no longer. Gentleness tossed aside, his mouth descended forcefully onto her responsive lips.

Unable to understand anything but her own hunger, she delved fingers into his hair, grabbing fistfuls of the golden locks which curled carelessly over his ears and collar. Using her grip on his hair, she pulled herself hard against his rangy length.

He plundered her yielding mouth with a tongue that insisted on seeking out and exploring every secret crevice hidden there as his hands slid around her shoulders and down her back to bring her against the rigid wall of his masculine frame.

"I want you, and you want me, don't you?" he accused through lips burning a trail of fiery kisses along her neck from her earlobe to her arched throat.

"Oh, yes, Dirk! Yes!" she sighed, pressing her rotating hips even closer to his body, molding herself to him in a desperate need to feel the hard imprint of his flesh against her own.

"Say it, Johanna. Say you want me," he ordered, his

words a tortured plea.

"Oh, yes, my love. I want you more than life itself," she responded.

"Johanna," he moaned, cupping her buttocks in strong hands and grinding against her. "I've dreamed of this moment for so long."

"Too long," she whispered, her own passion growing frantically. Reaching behind her, she drew his hands to her mouth to kiss their roughened palms and each finger, never letting her own gaze leave his enraptured face. Then, when she could no longer bear not having him touch her, she pressed his hands on the soft mounds of her breasts that strained against the confinement of the bulky dress.

As his flesh came in contact with her erect nipples, hot and hard through the material, a shudder ran through his body, and he groaned aloud. His hands ached from the touch of her, and his nostrils burned with the feminine scent of her. He was left with only one thought.

Wrenching his hands free, he grabbed wads of coarse dress material at her sides and stripped it over her head in one urgent motion, leaving her standing before him in just her chemise, a gossamer veil that did little to hide her nakedness from his hungry gaze.

Sliding the chemise down her arms and over her slim hips and thighs, he kissed every bit of newly exposed flesh as she stood perfectly still, reveling in the adoration of his lips and tongue. At last, when he had lovingly laved her body with his kisses, he stood back to devour her loveliness with his eyes.

Her flesh burned under his avid exploration, as his eyes raked the length of her from head to foot, spending extra time on her full, pink-tipped breasts of alabaster white, and the soft blond triangle at the juncture of her legs.

Reaching out to cup a lush breast in each hand, he moaned worshipfully, "I have never seen anything so lovely."

Johanna entwined her fingers in Dirk's sandy hair and pulled herself up to kiss his mouth, long and lovingly, before she helped him out of his own clothing. When at last they both stood naked, their faces saturated in lust, she dropped to the ground and held up her hand to beckon him to follow her.

Dropping down beside her, Dirk bent his head to take the erect bud of one breast into his mouth, wrapping his tongue around it and sucking until he felt her arching against his mouth, her hips rising helplessly in a desperate search to fill the void that his caresses had created.

When his hand slipped into the blond curls at the portal to her desire, she groaned aloud and lifted her buttocks upward to meet the pressure. She was mercifully lost to passion, and only the moment mattered—only the fact that the emptiness in her soul would soon be relieved.

Dirk filled her mouth with his tongue as his fingers made their presence known to her body. Softly moaning under the artful stroking of his hand between her legs, Johanna suddenly arched her hips and threw back her head. "Love me, Dirk," she gasped as his caresses carried her over the brink of sanity.

Moving quickly, Dirk rolled between her thighs and stabbed into the hot, gripping abyss of her femininity. "Yes," he wailed, unable to hold back his explosion after such a long abstinence.

So full of love and happiness, Johanna clasped Dirk's head to her breast. "Oh, my love, I had given up the hope of ever knowing the joy of being loved by you again. Without you, I've been dead. But now I'm alive."

As if the past had its own identity and had been silent too long, it raised up its ugly head to attack, forcing Dirk to think thoughts he did not want to think, compelling him to say words he did not want to say, and urging him to ask questions he did not want answered. Unable to stop himself, he rolled away from her and stared at the dark sky. "How many have there been, Johanna?"

"How many?" She repeated his question dreamily as she nestled her body to his side and nuzzled her face against his neck, reveling in the feel of his whisker-roughened skin against her lips.

"Yes. How many men have you said those same words to?" he asked, his icy blue glare narrowing as he lolled his head to the side to study her.

A dagger rammed into her belly could not have brought more pain or anguish than Dirk's cruel words. "Oh," she groaned, gripping her middle and turning from the man who seconds before had been making love to her.

"How many, Johanna?" he said again, digging his fingers into her flesh where he held her shoulders from behind.

With the wild mane of hair framing her face and her green eyes glowing yellow in the moonlight, Johanna wrested herself from his grip and leaped to her feet.

She turned on Dirk with the vengeance of a lioness protecting her cub. "How many, you ask?" she shrieked, her face a venomous grin of reprisal. "How should I know? There were too many to count!" she taunted, wanting to hurt him as badly as he had wounded her. "Maybe a hundred, two hundred. A thousand! What difference does it make, Dirk? I wanted them all! And they all wanted me!"

She laughed at the look of astonishment on his face. "Isn't that what you wanted to hear, Count Leuven? Isn't that what you've told yourself to allay your guilt for punishing me for crimes you've decided I committed? But now you have the answer you were seeking. I hope it brings you pleasant dreams and peace of mind!"

Johanna kept her posture erect long enough to stalk angrily away from the clearing—an incredible feat in itself, when what she really wanted to do was crawl into a hole like some dying feline who had been banished from the rest of her pride.

Chapter Twenty-Five

Raul returned to the clearing in the morning to find that his romance-mending endeavors had failed once more, and this time things seemed worse than ever, with no possible solution to be found. In fact, both Dirk and Johanna threatened him, in no uncertain words, with bodily injury—possibly even death—if he interfered in their relationship again. So, not knowing what else to do, he followed their orders and spent the remainder of the journey in silence.

When they finally rode into Dusseldorf, Raul sighed his relief. "This certainly looks good to me," he said, shaking his head. "Traveling with the two of you makes riding with a company of lewd, vicious soldiers look like a pleasure trip."

"I'm sorry, Raul," Johanna apologized. "Perhaps someday you'll understand. I hope you know this has nothing to do with you. You've been a good and loyal friend."

"At least you haven't forgotten how to talk," Raul laughed, bringing a smile to Johanna's melancholy face for the first time.

Before she could respond, her attention was diverted by a group of people rushing toward them, shouting their names. Anxious to lose herself in the protective embrace of her family, Johanna leapt from her mount and ran toward the oncoming party of welcomers. "Mama, Papa, Mignon, Helst, Hugo, Marta!"

When she had hugged them all, she realized that Suzette was missing. Certain she had seen her stepsister in the group coming to greet her, she turned around, her expression puzzled. "Where's Suzette . . . ?" Her mouth fell open in surprise. "Suzette!"

There, safely ensconced in Raul's protective embrace and covering the tall Spaniard's face with kisses, was Suzette.

Stunned, Johanna approached the elated pair, who continued to display their love for each other so obviously. Looking up at the impressive twosome, she smiled in disbelief. "Suzette? It's Suzette you're in love with?" she asked Raul, seeing her answer in his adoring expression. Touching her sister's arm, she laughed, "Why didn't you tell me?"

"I couldn't tell you, Johanna—knowing how you hated the Spanish soldiers. I wanted to tell you they weren't all evil, but I didn't think you'd understand. Not after all that's happened. Please forgive me."

Johanna realized for the first time that Suzette had not only grown up but was really quite beautiful. "Forgive you? For what? My two dearest friends love each other! What could make me more pleased?" she exclaimed, throwing her arms around the handsome, lofty couple.

Linking her arm in Suzette's, she started walking.

431

"When is the wedding to be? I hope I'm not too late to take part in the preparations!"

"Before long, I hope!" Raul suggested. "I've waited for this girl long enough. It can't be soon enough for me!"

Suzette gave Raul a lovingly tolerant look and scolded, "You've been waiting for me, have you? It seems the other way around to me, Monsieur Queiro!" Then she turned to Johanna, the lightness still evident in her more serious tone. "Everything is planned. All I need now is a willing groom and a maid of honor."

The next hours were spent catching up on the events that had occurred during Johanna's imprisonment and illness. Frans, it seemed, was in Holland with William of Orange and his brother, Louis, who had made a remarkable recovery from the depression he had suffered after his defeat at Mons.

"You know Orange was proclaimed governor of Holland and Zeeland last July, don't you?" Matthew asked. "He finally became a Calvinist. He realized they were the driving force behind the revolt and decided it was time to change religions. Though he still vows that he believes in a united Netherlands with room for Catholics and Calvinists alike."

"What's happening in the northern provinces?" Dirk asked.

"Alva took the northeast pretty easily and moved toward Holland and Zeeland, where I don't think he'll find things so simple. He's going to discover well-fortified towns, lakes, rivers, drains, bogs, and a lot of very determined Calvinists. Actually, the citizens have heard of the atrocities committed in the towns that have surrendered, and they seem resolved not to give in to him. If his sea force were better and the Sea Beggars less able, he might do well. But as it is, just fighting the watery land is going to be a battle for the damned Spanish," he expounded enthusiastically. Suddenly remembering Raul, he quickly apologized. "Sorry, son."

"That's all right, Matthew. I know how you must feel, but I hope it will not stand in the way of our friendship."

"It never could. I already think of you as another son."

"I'm glad," Raul choked, touched by the man's confession.

"Well, enough politics! I must know how Suzette and Raul met each other!" Johanna demanded, having held her questions until she could no longer contain herself.

Glancing self-consciously at Raul, Suzette started, "We met the first night he came to the inn. I was outside the garden trying to get a peek at the Spanish officers you were serving, and he discovered me there. We talked and walked—I think it was love at first sight," she said, blushing. "At least for me."

"For me also, *chérie;* but we knew it would displease her father greatly, so we met in secret as often as we could and wrote letters when we were apart!" Raul watched Suzette as he spoke.

"So that's why you never had time to write to me!" Johanna accused Suzette, the grin on her lips broad and happy.

"I'm sorry, Emeraude. I'll do better the next time you leave," she promised.

"You won't have a chance to make up for it now,"

Johanna scolded. "I'm going to end my military career and learn to sew, or cook, or something a little less strenuous than being a soldier."

There was a group sigh of relief as Johanna dropped her announcement on her loving family and friends.

"You mean you're going to stay with us? You're not going to leave again?" her mother asked, afraid to believe the unexpected news.

"That's right, Mama. I'm not even going to put up a fight if you want to find me a suitable husband—that is, if you can find anyone who would want a retired, slightly over marriageable age, and very stubborn female soldier. If you can't, I'll be the maiden aunt to Suzette and Raul's babies; and I suspect there will be lots of them for me to help with—the way these two are looking at each other!"

"But what about you and—" Suzette's question was cut off by the light shake of Raul's head and a warning squeeze on her arm.

"That's all right, Raul. Everyone will know anyway. Dirk and I have decided that in view of the past, it is best to end our betrothal. It's a mutual decision, and we're still friends, so there's no reason why you can't all continue to love us both." She forced a smile, praying no one noticed the slight quaver in her voice. "Now," she said, standing up. "I'm going to have a hot bath. Then I'm going to sink into that soft feather bed and sleep around the clock." Before the stunned group could recover from the shock of her words, she dashed from the room.

After she was gone, they turned to question Dirk, who, they realized now, had been very quiet since their arrival; but he had disappeared, too. "I don't understand," Katryn said, unable to grasp the staggering news.

Mignon put her arm around Johanna's mother. "I'm certain it was only a minor quarrel. You know they still love each other. You can see it in their eyes."

"Yes," Katryn answered thoughtfully. "But so much has happened to test that love. Perhaps it was just too much."

Storming angrily into the barn, Dirk didn't watch where he was walking and tripped over a pitchfork. "Damn! Who the hell left that there?" Bending to retrieve the fallen tool, he bumped his head soundly against the solid post where the implement had been leaning before he had knocked it over. "Son of a bitch!" he uttered noisily, inciting the stabled horses to move restlessly in their stalls.

"Having a difficult time?" the amused voice asked from the shadows. "You should pay attention to what you're doing—it might be a lot less painful." Although she was not laughing outright, it was impossible to disguise the pleasure in her voice.

"What the hell are you doing in here?"

"I beg your pardon!" Johanna replied sarcastically as she stepped into the light. "I didn't realize this barn was your private property. But for your information, they told me Mademoiselle was here, and I wanted to see her. Is that all right with you, my lord?" She turned back to her mare.

"Of course it's all right with me! Why shouldn't it be?" Snatching up his saddle, he walked his big gray horse outside.

"Where are you going?" she asked, following him as far as the doorway.

Slapping the saddle on Fumée's back, he said, "I've decided to go back to the front tonight. Tell your father and brothers that I'll see them in Holland."

Johanna swallowed back her tears. "I'll tell them," she called, staring after him as he led his horse toward the gates.

Her dreams this night were no different than on any other since Dirk had walked away from her two weeks before. She was sleeping in her bed, and suddenly he was there—kissing her lips, holding her to him, calling out her name, telling her he loved her, making her ache for his nearness.

Johanna sighed restlessly in her sleep as the man in her dreams continued to explore the sensitive skin of her neck and shoulder with his warm tongue and lips. It was so real, she could actually feel his breath on her skin.

She knew she had to wake herself up before the dream ended in a nightmare—as it always did. She had to stop it before her dream lover could bring her to a zenith of ecstasy, then throw her aside.

Wake up before the nightmare begins, she tried to tell herself. *I will. In a minute. It's just so good to have his arms around me. Even if it's only a dream. Wake up, Johanna. I don't want to. Wake up, Johanna.*

"Johanna, wake up!" the voice in her head ordered, sounding closer.

"I don't want to. I don't want it to end. Not yet. I want to sleep. Maybe this time it will turn out right. Maybe this time he won't leave me. Maybe, just this

436

once, he'll love me again," she begged earnestly.

"He does love you, Johanna. That's what I've been trying to tell you, but you've got to wake up to listen."

"If only it weren't a dream," she sobbed aloud. "If only you were really here."

"Johanna, you're not dreaming. I'm here, and I love you."

The familiar timbre of Dirk's voice penetrated Johanna's haze as he gripped her shoulders to pull her to a sitting position in her rumpled bed.

She opened her eyes and stared glassy-eyed at him.

"Johanna," he implored. "It's me, Dirk! Are you awake?" he asked, waiting for her to realize he was real.

"Dirk . . ." she said, her eyes fluttering shut again as she tried to reclaim her dream. "I was dreaming that Dirk . . ."

Suddenly, she was wide awake and realized there was a man on the side of her bed in the dark room. "What are you doing here? What do you want?" she screamed, making an attempt to bolt from the man's firm grasp.

"Quiet, you little fool. You'll wake the entire household," he hissed, clamping his hand over her mouth. "Now, I'll repeat myself. It's Dirk. Are you awake enough now to know me?" The pressure on her mouth lifted slightly when she nodded her head. "Are you going to be quiet?" Again she nodded, and he released his hold on her.

"What are you doing here? Get out of my bedroom this minute, or I really will scream!" she threatened, standing in the middle of her bed and pointing toward the door.

Shaking his head in mock regret, he remained sitting on the edge of the mattress and chuckled, "Your temper hasn't improved, I see. I may have to marry you to take you off your parents' hands."

"You may have to what?" she blustered with rage at his audacity.

"Marry you."

"Marry me! I wouldn't marry you if you were the last man on earth, Dirk Corlear. Just who do you think you are, anyway? Sneaking in here in the middle of the night!" she screeched with an ineffective stamp of her foot on the feather comforter.

"I'm the man who loves you and wants to marry you," he confessed, his voice no longer laughing.

Certain he was playing tricks on her, Johanna was silent for only an instant before she attacked. "What's the matter, Dirk?" she chided, stepping off the bed to turn away from him. "Won't anyone else have you? Well, I don't want you either!"

"I said I love you, Johanna," he murmured softly.

"You're too late, because I don't love you!" she retorted, plopping down on the bed with her arms folded stubbornly in front of her.

Dirk stretched his lean body across the space that separated them and laid his hand gently on her arm. "Yes, you do."

As if his touch produced a jolting electric shock, Johanna leapt up and walked away from the bed. "What am I supposed to do, Dirk? Melt in your arms because you touch me? Well, this may come as a shock to you, but I no longer dissolve into a mass of quivering passion at the sight of you!" Her voice faltered with the lie, but her injured pride would not allow her to relent in her resistance to his charms. "So get out of here right now! Or else!"

"Or else what?" he coaxed, walking up behind her

and catching her unexpectedly in his arms.

Johanna hadn't heard his approach and gasped involuntarily as his hands slid around her waist to seductively caress her betraying flesh, which was protected from his advances by only a thin chemise. "Or what?" he whispered, feathering his tongue lazily along the outer rim of her ear.

"Or I'll scream," she murmured unconvincingly, unable to resist leaning back in the charismatic opulence of his embrace. "I'll tell everyone you raped me," she threatened weakly, her thinking growing more confused as she began to give way to her inflamed senses.

"No one will believe you," Dirk breathed into her ear, his tongue continuing to spiral the sensitive tissue in ever smaller circles. "Everyone knows you still love me."

Dirk had loosened his grip on the girl when he felt her relax and was taken totally by surprise when she shook herself from his grip to angrily face him with her hands on her hips.

"Everyone knows what?" she shrieked indignantly.

"Dammit, Johanna, will you shut up?" he begged irritably. "Will you please sit down and listen to me?"

"Why should I?" she asked stubbornly, but she did lower herself into a straight-backed wooden chair. "What could you possibly have to say that I would be interested in hearing?"

"I love you," he said simply.

"Ha! You've said that before. It means nothing to me! Only words!" she laughed derisively.

Knowing he was making a plea for his life, Dirk held back his own sarcastic retort. "I want to marry you, Johanna."

Nodding her head, she laughed delightedly and stood to face the tall man in the dark room lit only by moonlight. "Yes, you've said that before, too! Every time you wanted to get me into bed!" she hissed unforgivingly. "Poor Dirk, are you tired and needing the comfort of a warm body—any body—next to yours? I can hear it now. I'll tell good old Johanna I'll marry her, and she'll be thrilled to relieve my physical needs. Is that what you thought, Dirk? Well, no such good fortune. You'll have to take your sweet lies to some other unsuspecting soul this time. I may be slow to learn a lesson; but once I learn it, it stays learned!"

"Doesn't it mean anything to you that I love you and want to marry you?"

His voice was low and filled with anguish, and Johanna silently chided herself for the compassion she was feeling for him.

"Dammit, Johanna, I love you. I've always loved you! I've tried not to. God knows how I tried to quit loving you, but I can't. I realize now that life without you has no meaning for me. I can't fight it anymore. Please forgive me. Won't you give me another chance to prove it?"

"Very convincing, Dirk," she answered, her cold tone barely disguising the unbidden flutter of her heart. "What now? Am I expected to leap into your arms and tell you how I've waited for you to say those words? Or perhaps I should assure you that it's all right that you continued to judge me for sins you imagined I had committed and for things over which I had no control! Well, as far as I'm concerned, the biggest mistake I ever made was loving you!"

Then, having spent her anger, Johanna let the tears stream quietly down her face, and she thanked God for the darkness. "Now, will you please leave?"

"Not until you've heard me out, Johanna. Will you at least do that for me?"

"All right, if that's the only way to get you out of my life. But I'm warning you, it's too late. Our lot was set in the past and there's nothing we can do about what's already taken place."

"Johanna, I want you . . ."

She shot him a satisfied I-knew-that-was-your-reason-for-being-here look.

". . . for my wife. It's what I've wanted from the first moment I saw you in that stream."

"You certainly have a strange way of showing your love, monsieur!"

Ignoring her interruption, Dirk went on. "When the course of our lives was altered so drastically, certain things began to happen over which I had no control. I didn't know how to cope with them. They obsessed my mind night and day and grew like a huge destructive cancer. I was a fool, Johanna. I know it! I knew it then, I know it now. But I couldn't stop myself." He watched her, seeing no sign of relenting in her stiff posture, silhouetted against the moonlight-filled window.

"Dirk, don't you see? It's too late. The past will always be between us. There's nothing I can do to change it—or to make you forget it. You'll always remember what I was willing to do to stay alive and hate me for it." Johanna was no longer vindictive or sarcastic, only resigned to her fate without the man she loved.

"But I don't want to forget. That's what I'm trying to tell you! It's taken me all these months to realize that what happens in the past is what makes us who and what we are today. Johanna, I loved you when you were an innocent young girl wading in a brook; but I love you more now as a woman—a woman with strength, intelligence, passion, courage—and fire! God, how I love your fire and your spirit! Even when I tried to hate it, I loved that about you the most!"

"Are you saying you've forgiven me for my past errors in judgment and that you've been wrong?" She couldn't believe her ears.

"Yes. But even more, I'm asking for your forgiveness for all the wrongs I've committed. The only thing that matters is now and our lives from this moment on. Our lives together."

"You mean it doesn't matter how many men there were in the past?"

"Yes, my love. The past is just that—the past. All I care about is that I love you and you love me."

Starting to believe what he was saying in spite of herself, Johanna smiled a secret smile, and she asked again, "Are you certain you don't care how many men there have been?"

"I'm certain—as long as there is only one man in your future!"

"I want you to know who they were, Dirk. And why!"

"There's no need, love. Let's put it behind us. I really don't need to know," he insisted, reaching for her in the darkness, slightly fearful of what the knowledge would do to his resolve.

"But I must tell you. It's important to me that there be no secrets between us. I have been in love with only one man in my life, and he's the only man I ever gave myself to. It was always you, Dirk. God must have been watching over me, because the men in the cathedral were interrupted before they could carry out their plan

442

to rape me. Though they beat me terribly, none of them raped me before they dumped me by the road because I was slowing down their escape. And when I would have submitted to the duke of Alva because I had no choice, He intervened again. Fernando was unable to function as a man. Don't you see, Dirk? I wasn't his mistress. There has never been anyone else. No Louis, no Raul, no Alva, no men in the cathedral. No one but you. You are the only man I have ever loved or wanted to have love me. It's always been you, my love—first, last and always!"

"But why did you let me think . . . ?" he stammered.

"Would you have believed me if I'd told you before? Or would you have added lying to the list of crimes you found me guilty of?"

"But in the clearing, you said . . ."

"You were so determined to hurt me by accusing me of the worst, I lashed out by confirming your most terrible thoughts."

Wrapping his arms around her and cradling her head against his hard chest, he rocked her gently. "I'm so sorry, Johanna," he whispered against her hair. "If you'll let me, I'll spend the rest of my life making up for all the time we've lost." He lifted her tear-stained face to ask once more, "Johanna, will you marry me?"

He slipped the green-and-black medallion around her neck.

The brilliance and fire absent from her eyes for so long sparkled, then glittered as she felt the weight of the brooch settle between her breasts. Squeezing it in her hand, she directed her watery gaze to him. "I don't want to rush into anything!" she said with a teasing smile.

Pulling her to him with gentle roughness, he crushed

her against the masculine barricade of muscle and hardened flesh. Holding her firmly in his powerful arms, he kissed her deeply.

"You have about one minute to come up with the correct answer, young lady; and then I'm making the decision for you," he menaced, scooping her into his arms and carrying her toward the bed.

"Well, if you're going to use force," she smiled, "I suppose I have no choice!" Wrapping her arms around Dirk's neck, she planted a series of small kisses on his mouth, nose and eyes, finally giving him the answer he was waiting for.

"Yes, my love! I'll marry you! Yes! Yes! Yes!"

"That's more like it!" he hollered jubilantly, swinging her around.

"Now, will you please leave my room!" she ordered sternly.

"What?" he bellowed, abruptly dropping her in the middle of her bed.

"I wouldn't want anyone to find me in such a compromising position—alone with a man in my room and hardly any clothes on!" she explained. "After all, I have my reputation to think of." Only Dirk could have discerned the devilment twinkling deep in the wide, innocent jewel eyes.

Gathering her to him once more, Dirk laughed as he looked down at Johanna's beaming face. "I can tell life with you is still going to be a challenge, my dear. I hope I'm up to it!"

"Me too," she agreed huskily, drawing his head down until their mouths met, hungrily, passionately, uniting them at last, and for all time.

Author's Note

For the "purists" who demand accurate facts and dates in their historical fiction, I would like to explain that I've taken liberties with the time frame of the duke of Alva's five-year reign in the Netherlands to keep up the fast-paced action necessary in an adventure romance. However, I do want to add that Alva's activities, as I've portrayed them, are to the best of my knowledge and research accurate (with, of course, the exception of the parts my fictional characters played in those events).

The truth is, though Johanna and Dirk and their families are entirely fictional, the duke of Alva (called Alba in some books) was very real and one of the most evil men in early modern history. In the Protestant countries of Europe, his name is still synonymous with words for religious tyranny and inhumanity; and he has never been forgiven for his savage disregard of Dutch tradition and laws, for his vicious policy of violence and terror, or for the atrocities committed by him and his troops while he was governor of the

445

Netherlands. His Council of Troubles, nicknamed the "Council of Blood," is credited with burning at the stake or beheading over *18,000* Netherlanders while he was in office.

The Low Countries did not gain their independence from Spain for many more years. However, they were freed from the yoke of Alva's vicious tyranny in 1573, when he was recalled to Spain by King Philip II, after failing to recapture Zeeland and all of Holland from the Sea Beggars. Never to regain the king's favor, he died in Lisbon in 1582.

<u>FREE</u> Preview Each Month and $ave

Zebra has made arrangements for you to preview 4 brand new HEARTFIRE novels each month…FREE for 10 days. You'll get them as soon as they are published. If you are not delighted with any of them, just return them with no questions asked. But if you decide these are everything we said they are, you'll pay just $3.25 each—a total of $13.00 (a $15.00 value). **That's a $2.00 saving each month off the regular price.** Plus there is NO shipping or handling charge. These are delivered right to your door absolutely free! There is no obligation and there is no minimum number of books to buy.

TO GET YOUR FIRST MONTH'S PREVIEW… Mail the Coupon Below!

Mail to:

 HEARTFIRE Home Subscription Service, Inc.
120 Brighton Road
P.O. Box 5214
Clifton, NJ 07015-5214

YES! I want to subscribe to Zebra's HEARTFIRE Home Subscription Service. Please send me my first month's books to preview free for ten days. I understand that if I am not pleased I may return them and owe nothing, but if I keep them I will pay just $3.25 each; a total of $13.00. That is a savings of $2.00 each month off the cover price. There are no shipping, handling or other hidden charges and there is no minimum number of books I must buy. I can cancel this subscription at any time with no questions asked.

NAME _____

ADDRESS _____ APT. NO. _____

CITY _____ STATE _____ ZIP _____

SIGNATURE   (if under 18, parent or guardian must sign)
Terms and prices are subject to change.   2366